Holiday Stories for Girls

Beverley
Jones

We moved forward, all six of us, in a row towards the big rock...

Holiday Stories for Girls

ILLUSTRATED BY REG GRAY

HAMLYN / LONDON / NEW YORK / SYDNEY / TORONTO

First published 1970
Second Impression 1971
Published by
THE HAMLYN PUBLISHING GROUP LIMITED
London • New York • Sydney • Toronto
for Golden Pleasure Books Limited.
© Copyright Golden Pleasure Books Limited 1970
ISBN 0 601 07450 5
Printed in Czechoslovakia by Tisk, Brno
51010/2

Contents

List of Illustrations

Brenda's Mountain

by Robert Bateman

Its real name was the Kuhlsnaffel, or something like that. We — that is Brenda, Pip and myself — never managed to get the name right, from the moment Frau Schmidt welcomed us at the mountain hotel to the time we said goodbye and took the bus down to the airfield for the journey home.

But it didn't matter. From that time onwards it was Brenda's Mountain to all of us, for a jolly good reason.

It all happened on our last day. We'd had two whole weeks of sunshine, and even *my* climbing was improving. I could feel it in every step I took. No longer was I scared at every patch of scree — the loose stones that could slide away under your feet. I wasn't terrified when there was only a narrow foothold to keep me from tumbling backwards for hundreds of feet.

So on our last day we decided to be ambitious. Perhaps it was silly of us to tackle the Kuhl... whatever-it-was, but we felt terrifically confident, even though the mountain, seen from our bedroom windows, seemed to reach right up into the sky.

'We'd better not tell Frau Schmidt,' said Pip, as she put on her climbing jacket in front of the mirror and whipped a comb through her red hair. 'She'd say it was too risky.'

'We've got tell *someone*,' I said. 'First rule of mountain climbing — remember? Tell somebody where you've gone. Then, if you don't come back, at least they know where to start looking.'

Brenda pursed her lips. 'We could leave a note, couldn't we? Then nobody would know until after we'd gone, but they'd find it if we got into trouble, and send out help for us.'

'We're not going to get into trouble!' retorted Pip, with a fierce shake of her head. 'We're not beginners. We know what we're doing and we have the proper equipment.'

'Mmm.' I said. 'But Brenda's right. Just supposing one of us slipped and broke an ankle?'

We could have wasted the whole day arguing, and Pip saw that. There was an old rule among the three of us, that in all major decisions, two to one carried the voting. Pip shrugged her shoulders. 'All right, then, leave a note if you really think you must.'

We set off for Kuhl... or rather Brenda's Mountain. You'll see why it earned the name, soon enough; I can't get that local name right. Well, as I was saying, we set off from the mountain hotel at about half-past eight. And there was none of that dreary slogging along a road to reach the foothills. Brenda's Mountain started where the back garden ended. We began to climb straight away, up a steep, grassy slope dotted with huge boulders.

The sun beat on our backs. I had the rope, Brenda carried the pitons — the iron spikes for driving into cracks in the rock to make footholds. Pip as usual was chief cook and bottle-washer, which meant she had the sandwiches and the flasks of tea.

We were baking hot by the time we'd gone half a mile. Brenda sat down suddenly, and wiped her forehead. 'Have to knock off for a rest,' she said.

'Me, too,' I agreed.

Pip stumbled up to join us.

We sat in a row on a ledge of rock, and looked down into the valley. The mountain hotel seemed like a doll's house, tucked away between the trees far below us.

'If I had my way I'd live like this, high up on a mountain

slope.' Pip looked dreamily across the sloping grassland.

'Huh!' snorted Brenda. She brushed a strand of dark, curly hair out of her eyes. 'It's all very well in the summer, but just imagine what it's like when winter comes. There'd be a wind cold enough to cut you in half every time you put a foot out of doors. No, this is fine for holidays. I vote we come back another year if we can afford it. But I've no ambition to start building a house up here. I can freeze to death cheaper than that — in our own refrigerator at home.'

'Still. . .' Pip's voice faded away wistfully.

I interrupted the day-dream. 'Let's get on, otherwise we'll never reach the top. I don't want to be caught up there after it gets dark.'

We picked up our loads and climbed another half mile. By then we were past the easy stages. The slope was steeper, and there were more boulders. There were no more sheep tracks to follow, and we began to be watchful about every step.

It was Pip who showed how necessary this was. One moment she was looking back over her shoulder, talking to Brenda; the next she was out of sight from the waist downwards. She'd slipped down a huge crack in the rocks, and we had to haul her out again. Below her there'd been a drop of twenty feet. Brenda wagged a cautionary finger at her.

'Never let me hear you grumble again because you've got broad hips!' she grinned. 'If you'd been a beanpole like me you'd have shot down there and we'd still have been picking up the pieces.'

Brenda took over the lead. Presently she halted. 'I think it would be better if we roped up,' she said. 'It's getting much steeper from now on.'

Pip rubbed her hands together. 'Real climbing!' she

I swung outwards from the rock wall, hanging on with my fingertips...

gloated. 'Look, up there ahead of us! It goes on for hundreds and hundreds of feet.'

We roped up in our usual order, Brenda leading, Pip in the middle, and myself at the end. With a name like Charlotte it was only natural that I should have been picked as Tail-End Charlie in all our expeditions, I suppose. I liked it. It meant I never had to do any trail-blazing. I could never make up my mind which was the best route to take when there was a choice straight ahead of me.

Brenda hauled herself up a ten foot wall of rock, jamming her climbing boots expertly into the narrow crevices scarred by the boots of thousands of other climbers in the past. The Kuhl... there I go again... Brenda's Mountain wasn't one of the really big ones, but it was popular with tourists. It was supposed to be fairly difficult, but good training.

Pip followed. The wind whipped her hair out behind her as she climbed. Her short, plump legs wriggled up the rock face as if holding on by magnets. I watched from below, wishing I could move upwards with the same ease and confidence as my two friends.

I made a false move straight away. I'd gone up only three steps when my left foot slipped in a narrow hold, and I swung outwards from the rock wall, hanging on with my finger tips while I recovered my foothold. There was no drag on the rope, so there was nothing to attract Pip's attention, but all the same I had a feeling she knew, and was purposely taking no notice.

That made me hopping mad. It's as bad having your mistakes carefully ignored as it is having them laughed at. Red-faced, hot, with my teeth clenched, I almost *walked* up the rest of the way to the ledge where Brenda and Pip were waiting for me.

'All right?' asked Brenda. 'Then on we go. You see that

rock chimney straight ahead? I don't like it much, so I suggest we go to the left of it.'

That started another argument. 'There's a clear climb up the centre,' said Pip. 'All we have to do is reach the next ledge, and then there's a simple route to the top. Why, I can see every foothold from here.'

I tried to see what she meant, but with the best will in the world I couldn't. I sided with Brenda again.

And that made Pip hopping mad. For sheer blistering temper, a red-headed Welsh girl is hard to beat. Colour came up in Pip's cheeks in a wild burst. She looked at each of us in turn, and for an awful moment I thought she was going to start a fight, here on the ledge with a drop of hundreds of feet below.

'Why d'you always side with Brenda?' she stormed at me. 'Why does it always have to be me who's the odd one out?'

Brenda grinned at her. 'Maybe because you're usually in the wrong? Cool off, Pip. Half-way up a steep mountain is no place to pick a fight!'

With an effort, Pip stifled her temper, but she sulked throughout the next bit of the climb, which was a pity, for the view across the valley was marvellous. When I reached a spot with firm hand and footholds I dared to look over my shoulder — not down, because that can easily make you giddy, but across at the enormous mountains in the distance.

'Look across the valley!' I shouted to the others. 'Isn't that Mont Blanc?'

But there was no answer from Brenda. She was on the ledge, staring upwards at a sheer wall of rock.

Pip and I scrambled up beside her. 'There!' said Pip smugly, 'I told you so. Unless we've all grown wings, we'll have to go down again and do it *my* way.'

'We could use pitons,' said Brenda doubtfully.

'Pitons?' Pip laughed. 'We'd need half a ton of them. D'you realise how high that is?' She pointed up at the ridge which capped the granite wall. 'Hey, there are two people up there already. Two men.'

'Then they must have been up there all night,' I said. 'There wasn't anyone climbing in front of us.'

Pip was still staring at them. 'They're going at a snail's pace. At that rate we'll be at the summit before them.'

Then I spotted something extraordinary. 'They're not using a rope!' I shouted. 'Either they're brilliant climbers or raving lunatics.'

A shower of small boulders came crashing down from the ridge. Brenda ducked against the shelter of the rock wall, and grabbed Pip, dragging her away from the brink of the ledge just as a rock the size of a cricket ball landed only a foot from where she'd been standing. She looked at me.

'There's your answer!' she said uneasily. 'They're raving lunatics. I don't feel much like going up behind them.'

Pip laughed a little wildly. 'At least we won't have to climb to the summit. They'll chuck it down to us!'

'Don't you think we ought to warn them?' I put in. 'Seriously, this is no mountain for beginners without a rope.'

Pip sighed. 'Oh, *no!* Do we have to? Think of it — this is our last day. We don't want to spend it nursing a couple of frightened beginners down to the valley.'

Brenda looked up again. 'Somebody will have to,' she said grimly. 'Look! They're stuck!'

She was right. One of the men had reached the end of the ridge, and was grappling in a ham-handed way with the next vertical climb. I saw his hands move across the rock and back again, searching for a hold. His companion was squatting behind him on a tiny ledge, staring upwards at a smooth thirty feet of rock which would be difficult with pitons and a rope, but which was impossible without either.

'Don't panic!' said Pip. 'They'll see it's hopeless, and come back.'

Brenda moved out from shelter. 'I'm going up,' she said firmly. 'If we pay no attention and one of them falls, it'll be a nasty thing to have on our consciences.'

'Oh, all right!' Pip burst out irritably. She took her place behind Brenda, and waited impatiently until our leader had reached a point twenty feet up-at which the rope could be belayed tightly round a strong outcrop of rock.

Then she went straight up on the rope, walking the rock wall almost horizontally, hauling herself up by her hands.

It was a stupid thing to do. In climbing, a rope is there for safety, not for stunts. Brenda faced her angrily when she reached the halting point. 'Don't do that again when you're climbing with me!' she said, white-faced and angry. 'You're as big a fool as those two.'

'Oh, phooey!' muttered Pip. 'I'm bored with this whole climb. We've come up the hardest way, and now those fools are going to ruin the whole day for us. If we'd gone up my way we'd have been at the summit by now.'

'If you'd stop arguing and watch what I'm doing you'd see we've moved across and we're on your blessed chimney after all!' said Brenda. She took a deep breath. 'You were quite right, and I was wrong. I'm sorry.'

Pip's ruffled feathers seemed to smooth down. 'I should jolly well think so. Right — now let's get up to those fools and find them an easy way down. Then we can go on to the top.'

But the 'fools' had vanished!

We stared up at the point where the rock rose above the ridge, but there was no sign of them. It was as if the rock had opened and swallowed them.

'Oh, crumbs!' gasped Pip. 'D'you think they've fallen?'

'Let's hope not.' My voice was almost a whisper. I was so terrified of what might have happened that it took all my courage to say, 'Come on, we'd better get up there quickly!'

It was the fastest and most nerve-racking climb in my life. Mountaineering is something you should do slowly if you want to be safe. Hurried searching for hand and footholds is a sure way of finding trouble. You don't test each hold thoroughly before trusting your weight on it, and you're inclined to move from one hold to the next too rapidly, leaving yourself with both a hand and a foot in the air at the same time.

We arrived at the ridge breathless and shaken. Pip was white as a sheet; twice she'd nearly slipped, and only Brenda's stout belay above her had prevented her from dropping back a sickening distance to the ledge.

Brenda didn't wait once we were all safe on the ridge. She began moving along it, on all fours, heading for the end where the two men had disappeared.

When she reached it she halted at the new rock face. She stood in exactly the position the man had been in, flat against the rock. But her hands weren't groping for holds. She was staring to her right.

'There's a hole — a kind of cleft!' she muttered. She inched her body round the rock, then ducked her head and disappeared.

Her voice boomed back at us. 'I'm in a kind of cavern. Careful as you come round — some of the footholds are loose.'

It was a good job she warned us. The first narrow ledge on which I tried a foothold crumbled away the moment I touched it. Perspiration was running down my face when I grabbed Pip's outstretched hand and with much difficulty managed to clamber into the dark, narrow entrance of the cleft.

Brenda was already ten yards inside. It was no more than two feet wide, and so deep in the rock that we had to move in semi-darkness, though high overhead there was a strip of vivid blue sky.

The climb was steep, but with the walls so close, there were handholds on either side. The cleft turned, and to our relief there was daylight ahead.

Brenda burst out into the sunshine, and threw herself down on a patch of rough grass.

'Can you see them?' I called.

She looked all round her, then shook her head. By that time Pip and I had joined her. Pip shaded her eyes and stared further up the mountain. 'It's not much use searching for them if we don't know which way they've gone,' she said. 'I vote we have lunch. I'm famished.' She sat down and opened up the packets of sandwiches. Then she brought out her pocket radio and tuned it until she found a music programme.

It was a pleasant spot. Below us was what now looked like a sheer drop right into the valley, though of course the mountainside was really not vertical at all, otherwise we'd never have been able to climb it. The mountain hotel was no longer visible, but we could see the village church, looking so small that it was as if one could pick it up and put it in a pocket.

The music stopped, and a news bulletin began. Pip reached over to switch off the radio, but Brenda signalled to her to wait. She was concentrating hard on understanding what was being said. Her French was better than Pip's or mine, but it was still an effort to follow anything as complicated as a news bulletin.

'Oh, come off it!' said Pip. 'Let's find some more music.'

'Sssh!' said Brenda, holding up her hand. 'Wait a minute.

This is interesting. Have you heard of the Calipur diamonds?'

I hadn't, but Pip's head nodded. 'What about them?'

'They've been stolen. Somebody pinched them after a ball in Paris. They're supposed to be worth hundreds of thousands of pounds.' She stopped, and listened again. 'Crumbs, some thieves have a cheek!'

'Why, what happened?'

Brenda laughed. 'The police think the thieves got into the house by landing a helicopter in the garden, and then got away in it again afterwards.'

Pip made a face. 'I'd be furious if somebody stole *my* diamonds!'

I chuckled. 'D'you mean that glass necklace you wear at parties? The one that looks like spare parts from a chandelier.'

Pip glared at me. 'It's *supposed* to be real,' she said doubtfully. 'Anyway, fill your face with another sandwich, and stop being rude.'

We were so hungry that our lunch was finished in ten minutes. Brenda stood up again, and stretched herself. 'I don't want to be a bore, but I'm still worried about those people. We'd better get after them.'

I rubbed my aching legs. '*Must* we? By now they're either safe at the top or flat as pancakes at the bottom.'

Brenda suddenly looked very responsible. 'I think we must,' she said quietly. 'Don't you, really?'

She was right, of course, only neither Pip nor I felt much like pressing the point. It was so pleasant sitting on the grass with a view across the valley that it would have been easy to push the thought of the other climbers right out of our minds.

We stood up, and packed our belongings. Then Brenda began walking up an easy slope towards the next rock face.

It was then that we saw the two men again. They were

a hundred feet above us, edging their way along a narrow ledge which rose gradually to the top of the rock face.

'They're in ordinary suits!' said Pip. 'Ordinary street shoes, too. They must be crazy!'

'D'you think we should give them a warning shout?' I asked.

'No!' replied Brenda quickly. 'It might give them a shock, and without ropes they wouldn't stand a chance if one of them slipped. We'll have to go up there after them.'

The climb wasn't difficult, but it took a long time, and the two men had disappeared long before we reached the top. Ahead of us was a broad strip of level grassland before the final breathtaking rise to the summit of the mountain.

And in the middle of the grassland the two men were wandering round in circles, bending forward towards the ground.

'There,' said Pip firmly. 'I told you they were crazy.'

I stared at them. 'It seems to me they're looking for something.'

Pip's eyes flickered in my direction. 'Now what on earth would they be looking for up here, thousands of feet up a mountain?' Her voice was scornful. 'Haddocks' eyes, maybe — like the old man in the story?'

'I just thought... Oh, I don't know.' I stared at them again. 'Perhaps one of them dropped something. A pair of glasses, or his watch, or something like that.'

And it was at that moment they found what they were looking for! One of the men waved to the other, who dashed towards him. They lifted up a big metal box by the handles at each end, and staggered with it towards a flat rock, on which they put it down. One of them appeared to be fiddling with the lock, then seized the lid and rattled it up and down.

'Get out of sight!' hissed Brenda.

We hid behind a boulder. 'What's the matter?' asked Pip.

'Look, Pip,' said Brenda patiently, 'two men don't climb a mountain in town clothes and try to smash the lock on a box they've found on the grass without making me suspicious.'

'Who d'you think they are, then?'

'How in the world should I know? There's only one thing I feel certain about — that they're up to no good.'

The two men were now lifting the box and slamming it down with terrific force on the rock. But after a few moments they stopped. One of them wiped his forehead. Then there seemed to be an argument, for both men waved their hands wildly, and made gestures towards the box. Finally one began walking briskly towards us.

'Oh, crumbs!' muttered Pip. 'D'you think they've spotted us?'

'No, you booby!' Brenda pushed Pip's head down, so that her mop of ginger hair wouldn't be visible. 'I think he's decided to go down the mountain for a rope, so they can take the whole box down with them. They want something from inside it, but they haven't got a key and the lock's too strong for them to break it.'

The other man was now following, slowly and reluctantly. He went about ten paces, then looked back over his shoulder. He ran back to the box, lifted it off the rock, and pushed it out of sight in the grass. Then he hurried to catch up with his companion.

'What d'you think...?' Pip began, but Brenda clapped a hand over her mouth. There was a brief gurgle of protest, then silence.

The two men arrived together. Luckily they had begun arguing again, otherwise I don't see how they could have missed seeing us. The vivid tartan seat of Pip's slacks stuck up above the level of the grass, and my green climbing jacket must have been visible round the boulder even though I tried to squeeze myself tighter and tighter into a tiny cleft where it would be hidden.

They passed within ten feet of us, and then began to climb down the way they had come.

Pip promptly jumped to her feet, but Brenda reached up, grabbed her by the waist, and hauled her into cover again. 'Don't be stupid!' she whispered. 'Wait a minute before you start jumping about. Supposing they come back again?'

Pip breathed heavily and crossly, but said nothing. Brenda still hung on to her tightly, however, until a full minute had gone by. Then she stood up, and went cautiously to the edge.

She turned, and nodded her head. 'It's all right,' she said quietly. 'They're twenty feet down, and going fast. Come on. Race you to the rock!'

Brenda might be the best climber, and Pip the most daring, but this was where I came into my own. I sprinted past them, and reached the place where the box was hidden when they were still puffing and blowing twenty yards behind me.

The box looked much bigger at close range. It was about eighteen inches long, a foot wide, and a foot deep. It was painted black, but some of the paint had been chipped off by the two men in trying to burst the lock. Brenda and Pip took hold of the handles, and lifted it up on to the rock.

'Look!' I said. 'There's a crest on the side.'

Not only was there a crest, I discovered, but also a label on which was engraved in block capitals, 'LADY JOCELYN MARGETTS'.

I pointed it out to Brenda, whose eyes opened wide. 'But that's the owner of the Calipur diamonds! I'm sure that was the name they said on the radio.'

'Then d'you think...?' I gestured towards the box.

'There's a lot more in that box than just the Calipur diamonds,' said Pip. 'It weighs an awful lot. My arms are aching. I expect there's all her other jewels and other things besides.' She took the handle of the box again, and strained at it. 'Feel the weight for yourself. No wonder they've gone down for ropes.'

'I see it all now,' said Brenda suddenly. 'At least, I think I do. The helicopter flew over the French frontier. The police will be searching for the jewels *inside* France, and at all the Customs posts along the borders and at the seaports. Nobody would suspect that the jewels were already outside the country. And what safer place to drop them than on a grassy ledge half way up a mountain? Those two men must be the accomplices.'

'That's all very well,' I said. 'But what can we do about it? We can't stay here and fight them. Two men against three girls is the kind of battle that can have only one ending.'

Brenda frowned thoughtfully. 'Time,' she murmured. 'That's the biggest problem. Look, if I stay here, and hide the box, can you two get down the mountain quickly and bring up the police?'

I nodded.

'You won't be able to get down before they do, so the main thing you've got to avoid is bumping into them when they're starting back with the rope.'

I looked at her uneasily. 'What happens if they arrive back here before we can catch up with them with the police?'

'That'll be my worry. Pip, you've got a big torch in your pack, haven't you? Leave me that, and any food you can spare.'

'*Spare?*' Pip burst out. 'You can have the lot. I could no more eat than fly. What about you, Charlotte?'

'I'm too excited to eat.' I looked at Brenda again. 'You

will be careful, won't you? I don't care for the idea of you getting kidnapped, or bashed over the head.'

'I'll keep out of sight. The torch will help if it gets dark and I have to signal to the rescue party.'

We shook hands. It was rather a serious and solemn moment. I'd been able to see the faces of the two men as they passed us. I didn't much fancy the idea of Brenda meeting them on her own. 'Look,' I said at the last moment, 'you're a better climber than I am. You go down with Pip, and I'll wait here.'

She shook her head. 'I can throw rocks harder and straight on the target,' she laughed. 'Go on, both of you — don't waste time.'

We hurried to the edge of the rock face, and began the descent. When we were half-way down I spotted the two men, working their way along the ridge beyond the narrow cleft. 'Let's go round another way,' I said. 'We might be able to get down first.'

Pip studied the outline of the mountainside, sizing up the chances. 'I don't think there is another way,' she replied. 'At least, not one that would be any quicker. Anyway, we don't want to get in front of them particularly, do we? By the time we've found the village policeman and he's sent a message for more men from the town, they'll have started back up the mountain with their rope.'

'I suppose you're right. Only what worries me is that we've got to stay a long way behind them on this route, otherwise we may be seen.'

Pip shrugged her shoulders. 'I don't think...' Then she paused. 'Look, there *is* another way, after all! D'you see that big boulder over there on the left? Surely there's an easy way down just beyond it?'

It certainly looked as though she was right. In place of

the rock chimney and the ridge, we should have a steep slope of scree — a bit dangerous, but much faster.

'Come on!' I said. 'Let's chance it. I'd like to make sure of being down first if we can. Then we can be sure those men can't reach Brenda before the police catch up with them.'

We scrambled our way across to the big boulder, and then started down the scree slope beyond it. At first it was easy. The stones were well embedded, and most of them held firm when we used them as footholds.

The first warning of trouble came as a yell from Pip, who was ahead of me. Clutching wildly for support, she slithered down ten feet in a cloud of dust and rubble, and I barely had time to make a belay round an untrustworthy looking rock to hold her.

I looked at the rock. Already it was beginning to shift. 'Have you got a foothold?' I shouted anxiously. 'Get your weight off the rope as quick as you can!'

Pip's scared face looked up at me. Her fingers were gripping a rock shelf no more than half an inch wide, and her feet were waving below her, hunting for anything that would hold firm.

The rock on which the rope was belayed made a sudden grating noise. If it fell, I realised, it would go straight down on top of her.

'I'm loosing the belay!' I yelled, and did so just in time. The rock settled back into place. I inched myself downwards, with my feet dislodging cascades of small stones which tumbled past Pip and then vanished over what seemed to be a sheer cliff face somewhere below us.

'I c...can't hold on much longer!' Pip gasped.

By now I was nearly level with her, two yards to her left. 'Keep hanging on,' I whispered. Then I moved further to the left, trying to reach a new belaying rock that stuck out of the slope like a giant thumb. It looked firm enough to hold the weight of an army, if only I could reach it before Pip's aching fingers loosed their hold. If she dropped now, she'd go over the edge, and the strain on the rope would take me down with her.

Perspiration was streaming into my eyes. I wiped it away hurriedly on my sleeve, and then shifted my foothold again. It brought me close enough to the boulder to fling a loop of rope round it.

As a belay, it wasn't up to much. It depended entirely on the degree of friction between the rock and single loop of rope, but there was no time to do anything more.

'Right!' I shouted. 'Let go, and fend yourself off.'

Pip released her handholds with a gasp of relief. Her body dropped five feet like a sack of coal, then swung to the left on the end of the rope. For a horrible moment she hung over what seemed like a bottomless chasm, and then her feet landed safely on a broad ledge of granite.

From my position it was easy to scramble down to join her.

'Thanks!' she said briefly, then, 'Huh! So much for short cuts. That's wasted twenty minutes. Why do I always have to think of bright ideas?'

'Never mind. It looks easy from now on.'

It was, thank goodness. There was no more serious climbing — only the simple kind of rock scrambling that's easy even for beginners. Soon we were on the grassy slopes again, and as we headed down towards the back garden of the mountain hotel we could see the two men only a quarter of a mile in front of us, on a route which would lead them into another part of the village.

Pip was running now, but my long legs made it possible for me to keep up with her at a brisk walk.

We didn't go into the hotel, but rushed down the main street to the police station.

'Who's going to do the talking?' I asked.

'You'd better,' gasped Pip. 'Your French is better than mine — and I've got no breath left, anyway!'

I ran up the steps and pushed the door open. The village policeman gaped at me as I stammered out the story. Then he picked up the old-fashioned telephone and wound the handle round and round. He talked into it rapidly for a few moments, then turned back to me. 'They will come,' he said. 'In five minutes they will be here. Four policemen who are all expert climbers. They will meet you at the hotel.'

It was much more efficient than I had expected. We were barely at the hotel door when a car drew up. The police jumped out, waving to us. They carried ropes, pitons, and packs on their backs.

I led the way. I was desperately tired now, but the sun was dropping down towards the horizon, and I knew that within an hour it would be dark. The thought of Brenda up there on the mountain with nothing except a torch and stones to defend herself against two criminals made me set a fast pace. One of the policemen walked with me, another fell into step beside Pip.

I went over the story again, slowly, gasping for breath as we reached the steeper slopes. There was no sign of the two men. That meant they'd had a very quick turn-round in the village and were already far ahead, or that they were taking a different route.

'*Is* there a different route?' I asked the policeman.

He smiled. 'There are four,' he said slowly in English. 'One is much easier, but the start of it is a long way from here. Another is like this, fairly difficult. The fourth is only for madmen. It is over the scree.' He shuddered.

So did I. 'We know it well, that's the way we came down.'

He looked at me with amazement. 'Then you are lucky not to have reached the village far sooner — flying through the air! That scree is the worst for many miles around.'

We were now at the foot of the rock chimney. Roped together we went up it, but our pace was slowed up by the bad light. The sun was almost gone, and heavy couds were moving across the sky. Twice I fumbled a handhold and only the rope kept me out of trouble.

Then, somewhere high above us, I saw a flash of light.

'It's Brenda,' I said.

The policeman looked at me. 'Don't forget those two men may also have torches.'

I thought of Brenda, scrambling among the rocks in the twilight to avoid being caught by two men desperate to find out where she'd hidden the box. It wasn't a pleasant thought.

We reached the ridge, and moved along it to the narrow cleft. My arms and legs were now aching so much that I began to wonder if I'd be able to complete the climb. Pip was tottering along immediately behind me, her face set, her teeth clenched, fighting exhaustion with nothing but will-power. I could tell that the same thoughts were running through her mind as through my own.

Then we were on the last section of the climb.

And from above came another flash of a torch, and a crash of a rock being thrown. There was a yell in a deep male voice, then the sound of running feet.

I urged myself upwards, keeping on the heels of the police-man.

And then, sooner than I had expected, we were over the lip of the slope, looking across the broad strip of grassland.

It was almost dark.

There was not a sign of life, nor a sound. I heard Pip

say, 'Where have . . . ?' but one of the policemen must have silenced her.

We moved forward, all six of us, in a row, towards, the big rock where the box had been.

Still there was no sound.

And then, beyond it, I saw a shadowy figure. For a moment I couldn't tell whether it was Brenda or one of the men, but then I spotted the glint of a white silk scarf that Brenda wore round her neck.

I couldn't keep quiet any longer. 'Brenda!' I shouted. 'It's all right! We're here.'

The torch flashed on.

Behind me, I heard a burst of laughter from Pip. It was an almost hysterical sound of relief. For the torch was shining on the two men, who stood side by side with their hands above their heads.

'What has she done?' said the policeman beside me, puzzled. 'Has she bluffed them by pretending she's got a gun?'

But then I saw blood running down the face of one of the men. And in Brenda's hand was a stone, ready for throwing. Behind her on the rock was a pile of them — a small arsenal of ammunition ready for what might have been a long battle.

There was no doubt about it — Brenda was deadly accurate with a stone. Accurate enough to terrify two tough criminals!

And the rest of it? Well, it was simple after that. Lady Jocelyn Margetts got her Calipur diamonds back safe and sound, and the insurance company paid for our climbing holidays for the next five years.

Every time we go climbing, we spend at least one day of the holiday going back to the spot where Brenda fought and won.

And for that reason we know it as Brenda's Mountain. We've never learned to spell Kuhlsnaffel the proper way!

Holiday Rivals

by James Stagg

The slim figure stood poised momentarily at the edge of the high diving board and then gracefully cut through the air in a somersault to open out and knife into the water clean, swift and straight.

Mary joined in the terrific applause enthusiastically, and turned to David Shawfield, sitting next to her. 'She really is wonderful, isn't she?' she said.

David smiled. 'She'll win the diving as easily as she did the short-distance swimming races,' he answered. 'You were rather lucky to have her put in your chalet, Mary. You might have had some dull, uninteresting girl foisted on you. As it is, you're rooming with the most popular girl in Golden Sands Holiday Camp.'

Golden Sands was a luxury holiday camp on the north coast of Devon. To it, for their fortnight's holiday, had come Mary Brandon and her father and mother. Dark-haired Mary, lively, average at most things but with a pleasant personality, had a chalet next to that of her parents. She knew she would have to share it with another girl, but it was not until two days after the fortnight began that her room-mate appeared.

Slim and golden-haired, Mary admired June Allday from the first moment she had been introduced to her as her room-mate. And June, with her vivid personality and her easy approach to people, soon had the whole camp at her feet.

'It really is remarkable,' Mary went on, as the applause died away. 'June arrived two days after everybody else, and already everybody knows and likes her.'

Two more competitors made their dives, but there was

no doubt that June was well ahead of the six finalists and the final points awarded by the judges gave her an almost easy victory.

When she had received her prizes and changed, she joined Mary and David at the side of the pool to watch a water-polo match.

'That was a wonderful performance, June,' David said.

'Yes,' said Mary. 'You were terrific, June.'

June smiled as if she were pleased with the praise, but said nothing.

They watched the water-polo for a few minutes, then Mary spoke: 'This five-day treasure hunt sounds exciting, doesn't it?'

'Tell me about it,' said June, with a slight, characteristic toss of her fair head. 'I've heard about it, but haven't had time to get any details.'

'Well, it lasts for five days — or rather mornings. There are five clues to be found on each day between nine o'clock and noon.' Mary explained. 'They're hidden in the country-side round the camp. The time you take in finding the clues counts, and if you don't find all the clues on one morning, you start where you left off on the next. There will be wonderful prizes for both the winners.'

'Winners?' queried June.

'Oh, yes. I forgot. Two people team up to search for the clues.'

'It sounds like a lot of fun,' said David, and went on: 'Another thing you forgot, Mary, is that there is a checker at every other clue — hidden so you can't find him until you've discovered the clue. That's so nobody can do any cheating, like missing clues three and four and going straight on to clue five — if you are lucky enough to stumble on it.'

'Any idea what this wonderful prize is?' asked June.

'No, they really are keeping it a secret. But I'm told that the last prize was one of those new baby cars,' said Mary.

'Good gracious,' exclaimed June, 'that's for me! I think I shall enjoy this treasure hunt.'

Mary saw a tall, grey-haired man waving to her from the other side of the pool. 'Uh-uh,' she said. 'Daddy wants me for something. See you later, June. See you at the dance competition tonight, David?'

'In full rig,' he grinned.

When Mary got back to the chalet to change for dinner she found June already there and nearly ready to leave.

'Oh, Mary,' she said, 'I've got to fly. David has asked me to join him and his mother and father at the dance tonight.'

Mary felt a twinge of disappointment. Before June had arrived David had hinted that he would like to take her. But the disappointment quickly faded.

'It looks like being a wonderful night,' she said.

'I suppose everybody and anybody who thinks they can dance at all will be entering for the competition.' June spoke in a slightly superior tone.

'Why, of course,' Mary replied, a little surprised at the tone of June's voice. 'That's the fun of the thing.'

'Oh!' June's voice was flat, and she already seemed to have lost interest in the converastion. By now her hand was on the door handle, her wrap was over her arm, and she was ready to leave.

* * *

'Well, I must go now and collect David,' she said. 'See you, later Mary.'

''Bye,' answered Mary.

June went off in the soft light of the summer evening,

leaving the door of the chalet open behind her. Mary smiled, and closed it, and told herself that June was just forgetful about little things like that. Then she looked round the room and smiled again, ruefully this time. 'But she might be a little more tidy,' Mary said aloud. 'Everything all over the place. Just look at it.' She shook her head slowly.

Mary bathed and changed, and then kicked off her slippers and went to fetch her dance shoes from the small shoe cupboard. As usual, after June had been to it, the shoes were in a heap. With a feeling of annoyance, Mary began to hunt through the pile for the high-heeled silver shoes that would add the finishing touch to her ensemble. But they weren't there!

Frantically she searched through the two small rooms of the chalet, but still the silver shoes remained lost.

And then she found them at the bottom of the wardrobe — not her shoes but June's. Silver they were, and the same size as her own. But the thin, delicate strap on one was broken, making it impossible to wear.

For a moment Mary couldn't believe the obvious answer that sprang to her mind. June's flowing gown had hidden her feet, and although Mary had silently admired the dance frock she had been wearing, she had not paid particular attention to June's feet.

Mary's lips set in a firm line. This was too much. June Allday might well be the life and soul of the party; she might be brilliant at most things, but to calmly walk off to a dance in another girl's shoes, when it was obvious that she had but the one pair with her, without saying so much as a word...

'Of all the cool cheek!' Mary exploded, and two small red spots made their appearance on her cheeks. Furiously she sorted out the lightest pair of shoes she had — old red sandals — and put them on. It was no good trying to get her silver dance shoes back. By now June would be sitting with David and his family — her mother and father might be there too — having dinner. And one just couldn't go to the crowded open-air café and say to the most popular girl there, *Thanks, June, but I'll have my shoes back now.*

Or could one?

A voice from outside brought her out of her frowning reverie. 'Mary, how long are you going to be? Mother and I are going over.'

'Coming, Daddy.'

At the outdoor café the Brandons' table was next to the Shawfields', and as Mr Brandon held the chair for her mother. Mary saw David wave. Almost before she was seated, however, June came across.

'Mary,' she said, 'the shoes are as comfortable as if they were my own. Thank you for being such a pet.'

Mary's jaw dropped slightly, and before she could reply June, with a polite word to Mr and Mrs Brandon, had returned to the Shawfields' table.

'Shoes?' queried Mrs Brandon. And Mary had to tell the story. When she had finished, her father, to her dismay, laughed loud and long.

'It's no laughing matter, Daddy,' said Mary.

'I know,' replied her father, still laughing, 'but you've got to give the young woman full marks for cool cheek. Anyway,' he said, 'what about this dance competition?' He bowed with exaggeration. 'Will you accept me as your partner, ma'am? Your mother's turned me down.'

Mary in turn pretended to curtsy. 'Providing you promise not to tread all over my feet. I shall be delighted, sir,' she simpered.

'Your servant, ma'am,' said her father grandly, as he led her to join the other dancers on the floor.

*   *   *

She couldn't remember when she had enjoyed herself so much. Her father danced well and he took Mary through all the preliminary competition dances faultlessly. Gradually the numbers were reduced, until there were but half-a-dozen couples left on the floor. Mary and her father and David and June were among them.

Up to now Mary had looked on the whole thing as good fun, but suddenly, now that she and her father had got so near to winning, it became important to her to at least beat June.

A couple dancing near them suddenly left the floor at a signal from the judges, and Mary found that there were but two couples left dancing — herself and her father, and David and June.

She felt no tiredness, only a glowing confidence. To have got this far was an achievement in itself; to win would be wonderful. She felt a slight loss of rhythm, and quickly pushed everything from her mind to concentrate on dancing.

They circled the floor again, and out of the corner of her eye Mary could see that they were right opposite the judges who were seated round a large table.

Then it happened. Just as she took the weight on her left foot to turn she felt her ankle-strap break. As she brought her foot round, her sandal skidded across the floor towards the judges, and Mary stumbled heavily.

*   *   *

For a second or two Mary felt that the end of the world had come. All her hopes of beating June had suddenly, at the snap of a strap, melted into thin air.

Then she saw the funny side. Spectators and judges joined in her laughter, adding their applause for Mary's sporting acceptance of the accident.

It was at breakfast the following morning that David came to the Brandons' table to ask Mary if she would partner him in the treasure hunt. 'Why, of course, David, I should be happy to,' she replied.

'Thanks, Mary, that's grand. See you in half an hour at the start. They're handing out the first clue then.'

Back at the chalet, where she changed into suitable slacks to cope with any climbing or clambering they might have to do in search of clues, Mary found June preparing to leave. The question of the shoes 'borrowed' by June had not been raised by either of them, and the only coolness that existed was on June's part.

David was waiting for Mary at the start of the treasure hunt just inside the beautiful wrought iron gates of Golden Sands Park.

Sealed envelopes were handed to all the competitors, and when Mary peered over David's shoulder after he had opened theirs, she saw that the clue leading them to the first clue proper of the hunt was written in some sort of code. After a few minutes David nudged Mary. 'I've got it, Mary,' he said excitedly. 'Come on!'

Out on the narrow road, sunk between green banks covered with summer wild flowers, David said: 'It was fairly easy to decipher. We've got to get to Raikes Farm. I've a rough idea where it is.'

They found the first two clues, reporting to the checker at Clue Number Two, having found him hidden at the bottom of a haystack, and moved on quickly to start the search for Clue Number Three.

'We shall find Clue Number Three in a fifteen square-yard

area, twelve paces on the north side of the signpost at the crossroads on Gorse Common, says Clue Number Three,' David said. 'What luck, Mary! I know a short cut to Gorse Common from here.'

However, they were more than a little suprised when, upon arriving at the signpost at the crossroads on Gorse Common, they found June and Henry Tissolme already there, searching among the huge clumps of gorse for the third clue.

'Your short cut can't have been as short as you thought, David,' said Mary.

'I can't understand it,' David answered, a puzzled frown creasing his forehead. 'That short cut we took is a real short cut. It saves nearly two miles.'

June looked up from where she was probing a gorse bush in the hope of finding the hidden clue, and saw them. Her face hardened slightly, but she put on a thin smile for David.

David counted the steps from the north side of the signpost and then paced out fifteen yards. 'Here we are, Mary,' he said, 'Clue Number Three is in this area. And a pretty chance we have of finding it amongst all these prickly gorse bushes,' he added ruefully.

'Come on,' said Mary briskly. 'We've found the others all right. We'll find this one easily too. You take that half, and I'll have a go at this. The other two,' she went on, 'seem to have miscounted their paces or something. They're in an entirely different area. Anyway, that's their affair.'

They separated and Mary scanned her part of the little area for likely hiding-places. She had been searching for about five minutes when she suddenly saw right at the very base of a thick gorse bush a newly dug hole, similar to that scraped out by a rabbit. She scrambled underneath the prickly branches of the bush, and after many scratches reached the burrowing. She carefully put her hand down the hole.

And there it was — a small white card — Clue Number Three.

In her excitement she shouted out as she scrambled out from underneath the bush: 'Quick, David, I've got it!'

David came running from the area he had been searching — and June came running too. Before Mary could pass the card to David, however, June was beside her.

'Let me see that!' she cried, snatching the card from Mary's hand.

She read it quickly before either of the other two could act, and then ran off, calling: 'Come on, Henry, I've found Clue Number Three!'

She held the card tightly in her hand until Henry joined her, and then the two of them ran off, June just dropping the card to the ground as they went.

The two angry spots made their appearance on Mary's cheeks again, and she ran to where June had dropped the clue.

'That's sheer selfishness, bad sportsmanship and bad manners,' she fumed. 'That girl thinks of nobody but herself.'

'Oh, I don't know,' David said, half-heartedly. 'Excitement and all that, you know...'

'Excitement, my foot!' snapped Mary. 'Anyway, let's see what the clue says. It's silly to waste time.'

'Easy,' said David, when they had both scanned it.

He ran off to the spot where Mary had found the clue and replaced it.

At Clue Number Four they discovered the checker and reported to him, and then made off for the next one. 'Well done,' the checker had told them, 'you're second so far. Keep it up.'

'We can't be far behind,' Mary said, 'and this is the last clue this morning, and we've heaps of time before midday.'

They reached the area in which Clue Number Five was

'Let me see that!' she cried, snatching the card from Mary's hand.

hidden, but there was no sign of June and Henry. 'I wonder if we've gained on them?' Mary said breathlessly as they searched round the disused wellhouse of a tumbledown, unoccupied cottage.

'We may have,' answered David, reaching up to feel between the roof support and the tiles. Suddenly his face lit up. 'I've got it! By a stroke of luck I've put my hand right on it.'

He pulled out the card from its hiding-place, and they peered at it expectantly. After a few seconds their faces clouded. Mary said: 'But this is only half the clue. Look, the card has been cut just at the vital place. It's useless.'

They stood looking at the card for a few more moments, and then Mary said again: 'Put it back, David. It's no good, we'll have to report it when we get back to camp.'

They trudged out on to the road again, and made their way back. They had not been walking long before David said, looking at his watch: 'It's twelve o'clock. Shouldn't think anyone else will have reached Clue Number Five yet — only us and the people who cut the clue.'

'David,' said Mary slowly, 'perhaps it hasn't been cut. Perhaps it's a deliberate move on the part of the organisers. You know — a sort of trick clue.'

'By jove,' exclaimed David, 'perhaps you're right! Maybe we had better wait a bit.'

As he finished speaking June's voice hailed them from behind. 'Hello, you two,' she called as if she had done nothing unusual that morning. 'We didn't manage to get to Clue Number Five. Did you have any luck?'

'Oh, sort of,' Mary answered shortly.

The four of them walked towards the chalets, and Mary marvelled at June's many-sided character. There she was, talking and laughing as if nothing had happened.

Perhaps David is right, Mary said to herself. *Perhaps June gets so excited that she just doesn't think. There are people like that.*

They went into the chalet, and June said: 'Do you mind if I take the shower first, Mary — I'm so weary it isn't true.' She put her handbag on the dressing-table.

Mary sank into an armchair, and said: 'No, go ahead. I can rest my weary limbs for a bit.'

She heard the water splash from the little room that housed the shower, and got up to get her frock from the wardrobe. She passed the dressing-table and, as she brought up her hand to open the wardrobe door, she knocked June's handbag on to the floor.

The bag burst open, spilling its contents over the floor.

Mary stooped to gather the bag and its contents, but her hand froze, hovering above a small rectangular piece of cardboard.

Mary peered more closely at it, and caught her breath. It was the missing half of Clue Number Five!

For a moment Mary couldn't believe her eyes. She had fought against the idea of June and Henry cutting the clue card in half to gain time for themselves, but they were the only ones ahead of them in the Treasure Hunt. Yet June herself had said that they had not yet got to Clue Number Five.

There was a sadness in Mary's heart as she collected the contents of purse and handbag and returned them to the dressing-table.

For a few moments she sat on the edge of the bed, holding the piece of Clue Number Five in her hand. Should she go to the organisers and tell them what she had found? she asked herself. Perhaps that was what she ought to do but, after all, Mary told herself, she and David were the only ones who had suffered from this piece of cheating, and the damage could be repaired quite easily before anyone else knew about it.

On the other hand, June's grabbing of every chance — sharp practice they called it in business — was getting a bit too much. Perhaps it would be better for everybody's sake to go to the organisers. It would stop any further trouble...

Lost in her thoughts Mary didn't hear June enter the room, and jumped when June, very red in the face, snapped: 'So now we've descended to prying in people's handbags. Give that back to me at once.'

Mary looked down at the piece of card in her hand and then up at June, calmly and without heat. 'It's no good, June. Bluster won't help you. I think this had better go to the organisers.'

The heightened colour drained from June's face. She was beaten, and she knew it. Suddenly the hardness left her face. Her voice was hoarse when she spoke.

'Mary, you can't do that. Please, please don't do that. We didn't mean it to happen this way. It was to be a joke on you and David. I was going to cut the clue in half, and hide both pieces in the roof of the well-house, close together.

'We had it all planned — we were going to hide and tell you at the last minute if you hadn't found them. But you came along before we'd finished, and I panicked and ran off out sight with one of the pieces still in my hand. I was going to go back this evening, paste the two pieces together again, and replace the clue.'

'But you said you hadn't managed to find the clue, June!'

June shrugged her shoulders helplessly, and Mary felt her determination softening. After all, it would be most unpleasant all round if, as June protested it had, a prank had misfired.

'All right, June,' she said suddenly, 'I'll tell you what. You and I will go back and replace the card — now. I'll borrow Daddy's car. I've got some glue somewhere. We'll stick the two halves of the clue on a piece of paper — and no one need be any the wiser.'

June's face showed a momentary relief, and then clouded again. 'Oh, Mary, thank you,' she said, 'but could you possibly do it for me — you see I'm partnering David in the tennis tournament later on this aftenoon.'

'June, who do you think you are? I'm playing in the tournament this afternoon, too. Why should you get out of this, when in the very first place it's your fault? Either you come with me now — or I go to the organisers!' Mary had never felt so angry in all her life.

June pressed her lips together. 'Oh, all right,' she said, 'but it's awfully awkward. It'll mean missing lunch.'

It was easier than Mary had imagined to replace the clue properly and, having taken a note of the clue, as she was entitled to, they returned to the camp, and Mary reported to the checker at the camp — as the clue had instructed. The checker accepted her story of being unavoidably held up and unable to report sooner.

The next two days passed without much incident. The four of them traced Clues Eleven to Twenty, still keeping their advantage over the rest of the competitors. But each evening, when they looked at the notice board where the progress of the hunt was posted, Mary and David were puzzled over the time advantage that June and Henry gained slightly each day.

'I can't understand it,' said David. 'From what you told me about the cutting of Clue Five by June, they weren't all that amount ahead then. And I know the country better than either June or Henry, and the short cuts we've taken should have given us quite a good lead. Yet here we are — still behind.'

'Well, there it is,' Mary said resignedly. 'They have to report to the checkers — there's no way of dodging them. Perhaps they've been lucky and come across the clues quickly, when we have had to search for them a bit longer.'

'I suppose that must be it.'

*　*　*

Mary and David found four of the last five clues on the final day easily, but as they read Clue Twenty-Four, David said: 'Whew, this last one's a corker! You know Gull Island — that low, rocky mass about half a mile off the coast? Well, the final clue is there. How we get there is up to us. Come on, let's get down to the beach quickly and see if we can find a boat anywhere.'

Ten minutes' brisk walking took them to the sand dunes that spread out from the base of the cliffs — the nearest point on the mainland to the island — and they threaded their way between the small sand hillocks towards the sea, still a good half mile away. As they rounded the largest sand dune, they saw some wheel tracks that had come from another direction.

'Somebody's going to get stuck in this soft stuff', said Mary as they walked on. 'Looks like a car.'

'Who'd want to bring a car down here?' asked David.

They walked on and, suddenly, as they followed the tracks round another dune, they came upon the car.

Stuck fast, it was up to its axles in the sand. And standing helplessly by it, gazing at it in exasperation, were June and Henry.

'So that's how you've managed to increase your time advantage, is it?' cried Mary. 'Just another rule broken in Miss June Allday's march to fame and success.'

'I told you we'd get stuck in the sand,' grumbled Henry to June, 'but you would insist.'

'Come on, David,' said Mary, and she began to walk past the stranded pair.

June caught her arm pleadingly, as she went by.

'Please, Mary. We've only used it today. Just this once,' she said, 'and we haven't gained anything by it.'

'Only today,' sneered Henry, and the implication in his voice was enough for Mary to see that June was not telling the truth.

David, however, had apparently not heard the remark.

'That's true enough, Mary,' he said. 'It looks as if they've lost all the time they might have gained. Let's not make any unpleasantness — I mean, don't let's say anything to anybody.'

Mary looked squarely at June, then said quietly, 'No, June knows that this is the last straw, don't you, June?'

June turned away, and her shoulders shook with sobbing.

David turned furiously to Mary. 'Can't you stop being so blooming self-righteous?' he said angrily.

Mary appeared not to hear, but she was affected by June's sobs. *After all,* said a little voice in her mind, *we are on holiday. Is it all that important?*

She scraped the toe of her shoe through the sand. 'Oh, all right,' she said. 'It's just a silly treasure hunt, after all.'

June's sobbing ceased at once, and Mary noticed as she turned round that there were no tears on her face. Her eyes were shining, but Mary felt that it was with triumph that June's eyes were bright, and not with tears, as she had pretended.

The four of them, leaving the stranded car to be pulled out later by a breakdown lorry from the village garage, walked on through the dunes to the sea. There was a strained silence, which David did his best to ease without a great deal of success.

'We'll pool resources to find a boat and get to the island,' he said breezily, 'and then, once we're on the island, it's every man for himself.'

Luck seemed to be with them, for as they left the sand dunes for the beach proper with its firm, hard sand washed by the tides of centuries, Mary spied two children playing by a boat that was drawn up just out of reach of high tide.

The four of them ran over. David asked the boy, a sturdy little lad of about eight: 'Do you know whose boat this is, and do you think they would lend it to us to get to Gull Island?'

'It's my boat,' answered the little lad, 'but Daddy won't let me take it out. Not until I'm bigger, he says. He takes us out. But I expect it would be all right for you to have it for a little while. But only,' he added, quickly spotting an advantage to be gained, 'if you take Sheila and me with you.'

'Will it hold all of us?' Mary queried, taking in the size of the dinghy and then looking at the rollers coming in from the Atlantic.

'Of course it will,' said June impatiently. 'It's a lovely calm day, and on this part of the coast the sea is as gentle as a lamb.'

'I don't know,' David sounded a little doubtful. 'There are some big black clouds coming up.'

'Oh, come on,' June cried, more impatient than ever. 'We can all swim, anyway, and even if anything happened I could easily bring one of the children in. I've got life-saving certificates galore.'

'Come on then, kids,' said David to the two children, and as they pushed the boat into the sea and lifted the children in, he said to the little boy: 'What's your name, then?'

'Alexander,' said the lad, 'but mostly I get called Pops —
'cos I'm a little fat, you see,' he added seriously.

'Okay, Pops,' said David, 'away we go for a life on the
ocean wave.'

He and Henry took an oar each, and it was not long
before they were beaching the boat on the only small patch
of sand Gull Island boasted — just enough to pull the boat
out of the water.

Clue Twenty-Four took them to the north part of the little
island, and the four of them began searching frantically for
the final clue — a password which both members of each
team had to repeat to the checker back at the camp.

None of them noticed that while they searched, and while
Pops and Sheila played among the rocks, the heavy clouds
had come up.

Then a gust of wind blew sharply across the little island.
It was followed by another, and then another, until it seemed
as if an October gale had broken in midsummer. Within a
matter of minutes spray was splashing over the island from
one end to the other.

And in the midst of it all, David came to Mary and said:
'Pastrycook.'

She looked at him blankly, her attention caught by the
change in the weather.

'It's the password, silly,' said David.

'Look down there, David,' Mary said, pointing to the angry
waves. 'We must hurry back before we are trapped.'

'By golly, it has come up rough,' said David. 'Come on.'

Mary suddenly remembered Alexander, commonly called
Pops, and Sheila. She ran to where she had seen them playing
last, and found them huddled in the partial shelter of a small
dip. Pops with his arms protectively round his small sister.

'Look down there, David,' Mary said, pointing to the angry waves.

Mary smiled reassuringly. 'Come on, you two,' she said, 'it's time we got back to the mainland.' She lifted Sheila into her arms and, with Pops trotting by her side, went back to the boat. She found the other three already there.

A wave crashed on to the small sand patch and flung the boat near the rocks. Mary drew back. 'David, I think, after all, it would be safer to stay on the island until this blows over.'

'I'm not staying here any longer than I can help,' said June, her voice a little shrill. 'If this keeps up the waves will be washing over the island — and we'll be in a nice mess. Come on. Let's get into the boat and make for the shore.'

David said doubtfully: 'Perhaps June's right, Mary. It would be better to get to the mainland now, before the storm gets any worse.'

Just then there was a vivid flash of lightning, followed almost immediately by a crash of thunder.

'All right,' replied Mary, 'if you think it will be better...'

With difficulty they scrambled into the boat. David remained on shore last to launch it, jumping in himself just before the ebb wash of a wave drew the small craft away from the island.

The boat seemed to stand on its end as a big roller caught it, and he and Henry — pale and nervous — dipped their oars gallantly to take them to safety.

A larger wave than the rest suddenly caught the boat broadside on and tipped it almost on its side. June's eyes dilated with fear. In a panic, the wind blowing her fair hair wildly about her face, she half stood up. A second wave came crashing in and, before any of them knew what had happened, they were all struggling in the water.

Through a film of water Mary saw that Pops had been flung right in front of David, who, after getting rid of most of the water he had swallowed, grabbed the little lad and struck solidly for the shore.

Little Sheila was in the water close to June. For a moment it looked as if her pitiful, outstretched hands were going to be grasped by June, to draw her to safety. But with a surge of horror Mary saw June push the helpless child aside and strike out, panic-stricken, for the shore. Mary's heart almost stopped beating as she saw Sheila slowly disappear beneath a white-capped wave!

Frantically she struck out for the spot at which Sheila had disappeared, took a deep breath, and pushed herself beneath the water. She drove herself downwards with steady thrusts and, just as her lungs seemed about to burst, her hand brushed something solid in the liquid darkness.

She grabbed it and struck upwards. As she broke the surface she took deep, thankful draughts of air into her lungs, and pulled the little bundle above the water at the same time. It *was* Sheila. Keeping the child's head above water — no mean feat in such a sea — Mary struck out for the shore.

It was slow, exhausting work, and it seemed to Mary that she would never reach the shore. Occasionally, as a wave thrust them both towards the sky, she had a blurred vision of a hundred small faces peering anxiously seawards from the beach. Then there would be nothing but a mass of water in front of her.

Suddenly, when she could go no farther, she felt Sheila being taken from her hold and saw the face of David close by.

'Can you manage, Mary?' David shouted breathlessly.

Mary nodded weakly. Now that her burden had been taken from her she felt more able to swim the short distance that remained.

As her feet touched the sand she began to stumble through the water to the beach. She thought she heard a sound that drowned the pounding sea and the roar of the wind, the sound of cheering. Then a mist came down over her eyes...

Mary woke up in a comfortable room in Golden Sands Mansion to find her father, mother, David and Henry sitting by her bed.

Her father smiled at her and, his voice a little husky, said: 'Hello, my dear. We're all rather proud of you.'

'Is Sheila..?'

'The little girl is no worse for her ducking, thanks to you. Young — what do you call him — Pops is fine, too.'

Mary lay back more relaxed on her pillow. Her father went on: 'Word got round very quickly, when the storm blew up, that four people were on Gull Island — little Sheila and Pops were too small to be seen, apparently, by whoever first spotted you out there. I think most of us arrived just as the boat was tipped over.'

His face became serious, and he went on: 'And most of us saw what happened immediately after that. Miss June Allday and her parents have already left Golden Sands.'

David broke in: 'Mary, you were great. Really great. I'm sorry I was so bad-tempered with you.'

Mr Brandon patted David's shoulder. 'You didn't do so badly yourself, young man.'

Henry, who had been sitting silently and awkwardly, said: 'I'm more sorry than I can say for my part — you know — cheating in the Treasure Hunt. I went to the Chief Checker and told him. You were great, Mary.'

There was a movement from the door, and Mr Brandon went to it at a signal from someone who poked his head through.

In a few minutes he came back with a huge bouquet in his arms, and an impressive looking card in his hand. 'They seem to like you, my dear,' he said to Mary, his eyes rather bright, as he handed her the bouquet and the card. 'They've awarded you and David first prize in the Treasure Hunt and... well, see for yourself.'

Mary looked at the card attached to the flowers. It read: *To a very brave girl, from all of us at Golden Sands.*

David, who was peering over her shoulder at the card, said a little shamefacedly: 'I was right, Mary, when I said earlier, "If you're really good at things you can't help showing it — can you?"'

Mine of Mystery

by J. A. Storrie

It was getting on towards evening when Gina Carson came hurrying down the crooked country lane, as fast as she could, with a suitcase in her hand. In her other hand she carried a torn piece of paper with a roughly drawn map on it. Gina kept glancing at it and looking about her at the high hedges on either side of the lane.

She had been invited by her friend, Jane Watson, to spend the summer holidays with Jane in her uncle's caravan which was parked near Hedgecombe, her uncle's farm. Jane had written to Gina, giving her directions on how to get to the caravan and had even drawn a map. It was this same map that was puzzling Gina at the moment. She sighed and put down her suitcase.

Dusk was falling fast and Gina was getting a little worried. Then she caught sight of a small stile leading into a field.

'Well,' she shrugged, and picked up her case, 'I only hope this is the right way.'

After about five minutes, Gina began to doubt that it was. The field was ploughed which made walking difficult, and Gina stopped by a big thorn bush.

Suddenly, a crouching figure stepped around the side of the bush, and bumped into her. She could not help giving a scream. The figure straightened up and peered through the dusk at her. A man's voice said:

'Oh, pardon me, young lady. My fault entirely. I didn't see you there.'

Feeling somewhat reassured by a human voice, Gina's heart stopped its wild hammering and she looked closely at the man. He was older than she had thought at first. His shoulders were slightly stooped and he was dressed in an ancient cloak, draped loosely around his shoulders, baggy trousers and a shapeless felt hat. In one hand he carried a small geologist's hammer.

'Excuse me, do you live here?' Gina asked.

'Yes. I live over there on Dunhill's farm, just beyond Hedgecombe,' he said, waving his hammer vaguely behind him.

'Hedgecombe!' Gina exclaimed. 'Then you must know the caravan near there.' 'Caravan?' the man seemed doubtful. 'Caravan?' he repeated again. 'Oh, yes, there is a caravan there, now that I come to think of it, near the old hill quarry.'

'Well, could you show me where it is, please?' asked Gina.

'Yes, by all means. I suppose we'd better introduce ourselves first. My name is Professor Hackett. I'm a geologist.'

Gina introduced herself and the Professor bowed and shook her hand. Then he took her arm and they started off for the caravan.

In a few minutes they came to a gate leading into another field, and in the background Gina saw the square shape of a lighted window with the big dark bulk of a hill behind it, topped by a tall chimney.

That must be the quarry the Professor was talking about, she thought.

'There's your caravan, Miss Carson,' the Professor said, pointing with his hammer.

'Thank you very much!' Gina said. 'It was very kind of you to show me the way.'

'Not at all. Goodnight,' he said abruptly, and stumped off into the darkness.

'What a nice old man,' Gina muttered as she made her way through the gate towards the caravan.

Gina broke into a run as she approached the caravan. She panted up the few steps, the door opened under her push and she almost fell over the threshold.

'Jane!' she cried. 'I'm here! I've had...'

Then the words died on her lips. A boy was kneeling down before a desk at the side of the caravan. His rugged, startled face was turned towards her, but his hands were busy amongst some loose papers in the drawer of the writing desk. For a moment they stared at each other, both equally surprised and neither of them saying a word.

Seconds dragged by. Then from the top of the desk, a small clock gave a whirr and struck nine tinkling notes. At the same moment footsteps sounded from the other side of the caravan, beyond the green door. The spell was broken.

In a flash, the boy closed the drawer and stood upright, just as the door on the other side opened and Jane, small and dark-haired, entered, talking as she came.

'No, Roy, she's not there. She must... *Gina!* There you are! Where did you spring from? I'd just about given up hope. I thought my note must have gone astray. You must be fagged out. Couldn't you find us? You had my map, didn't you? She looks tired, doesn't she, Roy? Here, sit down.

'I'm so glad to see you, Gina. I thought you must have lost your way and I went over to Hedgecombe, thinking you might have turned up there. I left Roy to look after things while I was gone. Oh, have you met Roy, by the way?'

'No,' Gina said slowly. 'We didn't have time. I'm afraid we both surprised each other,' she added, and smiled inwardly as she saw Roy look quickly away.

'Well, I can fix that in four words,' Jane smiled. 'Gina Watson. Roy Vickers. Roy, would you mind putting on the kettle while I set the table and talk to Gina.'

Roy busied himself at the stove.

'Roy lives just over beyond the quarries,' Jane explained. 'His father used to be manager of the quarries, but he's been sick for a long time and they've been closed down. No one works there any more. Roy lives so near he's always dropping in to see us.'

And then for the first time, Jane noticed her friend's silence.

'You're very quiet, Gina,' she said. 'Is anything wrong?'

Gina forced a smile.

'No, of course not, silly,' she said. 'But I was never any good at map reading, especially your maps. But I met a funny old man near the lane, Professor Hackett, and he showed me the way.'

'Oh, yes. The Professor,' Jane said. 'He's a dear. He lives over at Dunhill's Farm where Roy works. He's quite a fanatic at geology. He's always messing around the quarries. Ah, here's the tea.'

Roy stood beside Gina's chair and poured out her tea while she listened with one ear to Jane's innocent chatter.

As Roy sat down to his tea, Gina spoke directly to him.

'I'm sorry to hear about your father,' she said.

'Thanks,' Roy said. 'I work over on Dunhill's Farm and manage to make enough money to keep us going, but it's a bit of a struggle sometimes to make ends meet.'

'And is there any chance of reopening the quarries?' Gina asked.

Roy looked at her sharply.

'No,' he said shortly. 'None at all.'

After they had finished tea and washed the dishes they sat down. After about half an hour Roy stood up.

'Well, I'd better be getting along,' he said, avoiding Gina's eyes. 'I'll see you tomorrow. Goodnight, Jane.' He paused. 'Goodnight, Gina,' he said, and turned on his heel and left.

'Well, I think we'd better get to bed early tonight,' Jane said. 'You've had a hard day. You take the top bunk and I'll take the bottom one.'

Within a few minutes the caravan was in darkness and Gina lay down, but not to sleep.

Her restless thoughts would not give her peace. Why was Roy prying into Jane's desk? And what did he expect to find?

Gina lay on her back, feeling that sleep would never come. She felt vaguely uncomfortable without knowing why. There seemed to be something close in the air.

Perhaps it's the change of atmosphere, she reflected.

And then her hand touched something sticky on the sheet. Wondering what it was, she held it up to the moonlight coming through the window above her head. Her hand was black and smeared. Gina smiled in the darkness.

Dear, scatter-brained Jane, she thought. *It looks as if she's dropped the sheets in the mud. But I don't remember noticing they were black when I got into bed. On second thoughts, it looks more like soot than mud.*

Gina sat up in bed and then gasped aloud. The bed clothes were covered with the black substance and some of it was on the front of her pyjama jacket.

And then she sat bolt upright. Smoke was coming from outside, drifting in through the window. She could see it clearly in the moonlight. Gina looked out of the window. What she saw made her catch her breath in amazement. The smoke was coming from the chimney of the quarry! Sinister against the moon, the tall chimney belched out a cloud of black smoke that drifted towards the caravan. Someone was working in the old quarry!

For a moment Gina stared fascinated at the smoke pouring from the stack. She wondered what was going on inside that hill beneath the chimney. There was only one way to find out.

Gina clambered down from the bunk and shook Jane by the shoulder. Jane groaned and sat up.

'Gina, whatever's the matter?' she asked, sleepily. 'Is the place on fire or something?'

'It's all right,' Gina assured her friend.

Swiftly she explained what she had seen, and soon Jane was wide awake, listening to every word. When Gina had finished talking the two girls went over to the door and looked out at the chimney, smoking away into the night sky.

'It looks awfully creepy, doesn't it?' Jane said, as she stared at the chimney.

'I vote we go and investigate,' Gina suggested.

In a few minutes both girls were dressed and creeping towards a small rise in front of the chimney. They scrambled up the stony side of the incline and halted.

Below them in the bright moonlight stood a big two-ton truck. In the background lay the hill with the smoking chimney on top of it. Underneath the chimney and near the top of the hill was a large black opening.

From this gap two thick, parallel pulley cables led down through the air to the ground near the truck. The pulley lines carried small open cars loaded to the brim with soil. The cars halted one by one over the back of the truck and released their load. Then they made a circuit and travelled back on the other parallel pulley to vanish inside the opening.

The two girls stood staring at this activity.

'I thought you said the quarry was closed down,' Gina said.

'So I did,' Jane hissed in return. 'And it is. I mean, it should be. I can't understand...'

Then Gina suddenly pulled Jane down to the ground by one arm.

'Shh — not so loud,' she said quickly. 'Look over there!'

Following Gina's pointing finger, Jane saw the red glow of a cigarette.

'There's someone there,' Gina gasped. 'It must be the driver.'

'He hasn't got long to wait,' Jane pointed out. 'There's only one left to unload.'

The last car stopped over the truck and, with a sudden rumble, the bottom swung open and its load dropped into the back of the truck.

The machinery stopped and the last car went on for a few yards and then halted, close to the ground. The girls saw the driver climb into the cab of his truck and drive off along the tough track.

Gina clutched Jane's arm.

'Now's our chance, Jane,' she breathed. 'Before that car starts moving again. They'll have to take it back into the hill to hide it. We've just time to climb inside and ride right into the quarry.'

Jane's mouth fell open.

'You're not scared, are you?' asked Gina.

'Yes,' Jane said briefly, but as Gina started down the slope towards the car, Jane followed in her wake.

At the bottom of the hill they paused. The cable here came very near the ground and the last car was on a level with their heads. Gina grabbed the top of the car and scrambling on the side, she managed to drag herself over the top. As she fell untidily on the rusty floor, the car jerked, the cable above her head ground in its pulley, and the car began to move.

'Jane, hurry!' Gina called.

She grabbed Jane around the shoulders and heaved. As the car began to climb smoothly upwards on its cable, the two girls fell together in a heap on the steel floor.

Gina said: 'We'd better keep our heads down in case someone is watching.'

The friends knelt on the hard steel floor.

Jane looked up over the side. The car, climbing higher all the time, was only a few yards away from the mouth of the open cave at the top of the hill.

'Keep your head down,' Jane warned. 'We're going in.'

'Jane! Are you there?'

Then, without warning of any kind, the floor beneath them gave way... Gina fell into a pile of soft earth and rolled sideways. Jane fell almost on top of her and the two girls, gasping and spluttering, rolled sideways down a slope to land with a thump on hard ground.

Gina sat up dazedly and looked about her. As her eyes became used to the darkness she saw the outline of Jane's form.

'What happened?' Jane asked.

'The floor dropped from under us,' Gina told her. 'I should have guessed.'

The girls stood up and over their heads Gina saw the black shape of their car, along with several others. They were standing at the bottom of a huge hill of soil in a chamber hollowed out of the solid rock. Gina felt along the rough wall with one hand and as she did so, she found a small passage leading off to the right.

'There's a passage here,' she whispered to Jane. 'If only we'd brought a torch.'

She heard a rustle beside her and Jane pressed into her hand a cold, metal torch. Gina gave a little gasp of surprise.

'Well, you were in such a hurry, I knew you'd never think of it,' Jane whispered.

Gina switched on the torch and by its light they groped their way forward.

Gina heard a sound and switched if off. She saw someone coming down the tunnel towards them.

'Down, Jane — quickly!' Gina whispered frantically.

A torch beam swung towards them as they both crouched down against the wall, their hearts beating fast. It passed over their heads and in the light they saw the stern, set face of the person holding the torch — Roy Vickers! Then he had passed by and they were watching the bobbing light going off down the tunnel.

'What does it mean?' whispered Jane. 'Why is Roy working the mine, if it's supposed to be closed down?'

Gina shook her head wonderingly.

'And if the mine's run out, what can he hope to find?' she asked. 'Let's have a look where he came from.'

They walked out into a large cavern with an enormous stove just to their right.

'Roy *was* working here,' breathed Gina, excitedly. 'See — these ashes inside the oven door are still warm and smoking. Roy must be digging up something from the quarry and carrying it away secretly.'

'But he can't be doing anything wrong if his father owns the mine,' Jane argued.

'Well, if it isn't wrong, why hasn't he said anything about it?' Gina asked. 'My goodness, it's twelve o'clock. We'd better be getting back.'

The two friends retraced their steps through the tunnel and found a flight of steps cut in the rock, leading downwards. In a few minutes, they were standing in the moonlight close to the hill, with their caravan only a few hundred yards away.

They made their way across the grass towards the caravan.

I'll have to have a wash before I can get into bed, Gina was thinking when a gasp from Jane made her look up quickly.

Jane had stopped suddenly and was staring at the caravan.

'Gina!' she cried. 'The caravan door is open! Someone's inside!'

*   *   *

The two girls stared at each other for a moment and then Gina squared her shoulders and marched forward.

She pushed open the swinging door and Jane, at the bottom of the steps, saw her friend stop and stare into the interior of the caravan. Jane pushed up behind Gina and peered over her shoulder. Her eyes widened in astonishment.

Professor Hackett was in the caravan, humming quietly under his breath. He was sitting with his back to them, holding a cup of tea in one hand while in the other he held a thick wad of papers close up to his spectacles. A big-bowled pipe poked out from his mouth. He looked perfectly at home.

Jane knocked loudly on the caravan door. Professor Hackett tilted back his head and blew a large cloud of smoke at the ceiling. Furious, Jane banged her knuckles on the hard wood again.

The Professor put down his cup, swung round and glared at them.

'Well, well, well!' he said testily. 'I said, "come in", didn't I?'

The two girls came in meekly and closed the door.

'What's the trouble?' the Professor asked.

'Well, er,' Jane began.

'Speak up, don't be bashful,' the Professor prompted her. 'What do you want? My home is yours,' he added, with an expansive wave round the caravan.

Jane saw her chance.

'Well, that's just the point,' she said, quickly. 'Your home *is* ours.'

The smile went from the Professor's face, as if someone had wiped it off with a cloth.

'I beg your pardon,' he said stiffly.

'This is *our* caravan,' Jane said meekly, and heard Gina beside her say doubtfully under her breath: 'I think.'

Professor Hackett looked about the room slowly and carefully and then a great light seemed to break in on him.

'My dear young ladies,' he said, 'of course it is. Of course it is. But what am I doing here? I thought this was my caravan. I do apologise most sincerely. I had no idea.'

Professor Hackett looked so forlorn at his own absent-mindedness that Jane's heart was touched.

'That's quite all right, Professor,' she smiled. 'There's no harm done. Caravans *are* very much alike, I know. It could have happened to anyone, really.'

'Yes, but it always seems to happen to me,' the Professor mumbled. 'I can't understand it. Perhaps I was sleep-walking,' he said suddenly, looking at them. 'Yes, that's it. How interesting. I must make a note of that.'

He opened his notebook and immediately dropped it on the floor. He bent down to pick it up and then sat on the couch, with his eyes fixed on Jane's shoe.

'Let me have your left shoe,' he said.

Jane looked surprised, but she unbuckled her shoe and handed it to Professor Hackett. The Professor turned it over and looked earnestly at the sole, humming to himself as he did so.

'Good,' he said aloud.

He put the muddy shoe into his coat pocket, shoved his pipe in his mouth and bowed to the two girls.

'Thank you very much, young ladies,' he said. 'It was very nice of you to have me at your place, but I'm afraid I must go now.'

'Let me have your left shoe,' he said.

Then he was gone. Gina burst out laughing and Jane joined in.

'I don't know about you,' Jane said firmly, 'but I think we ought to go to bed. Throw your messed-up sheets and pyjamas in the laundry basket and take these clean ones.'

The two girls climbed into their bunks and were asleep as soon as their heads touched the pillows.

Next morning, the girls awoke late and their first job after breakfast was to wash the sheets and Gina's pyjamas which had been soiled by the smoke. They set up their wash tub outside the caravan.

They had talked over the events of the previous night, but they were still as much in the dark as ever. Then, as Gina looked up from her washing, she saw Roy coming across the fields towards them. As he drew nearer, they could see that his pleasant face was sombre and he greeted them quietly. Then there was an awkward silence.

Jane finally broke the long silence.

'How's your father?' she asked.

'Hes' much better, thanks,' Roy replied and then abruptly he continued. 'You know this land belongs to us?'

'Yes,' said Jane wonderingly.

Roy looked down at the ground as he spcke.

'Well, I'm afraid I'll have to ask you to leave as soon as you can — tomorrow, if possible.'

'Tomorrow!' Gina cried.

'But why?' asked Jane. 'Have we annoyed your father in some way?'

Roy's face flushed.

'It isn't my father's idea,' he said uncomfortably. 'He doesn't know about it. *I'm* asking you to leave as soon as you can.'

'But why, Roy?' asked Jane softly.

He groped in his pocket and brought out a thin piece of pink ribbon which he handed to Jane.

'This might help to explain matters more fully, without more words of mine,' he said. 'Good morning. I'll be round tomorrow to see if you've gone. I hope I shan't see you again. Goodbye!' He swung round and strode off, his head bowed.

Jane stared at the ribbon in her hand.

'It's my hair ribbon,' she said sadly. 'I must have lost it in the quarry last night. Roy found it and guessed that we had seen him. He *must* be doing something illegal in the quarry or why would he want us out of the way?'

'Never mind him now,' interrupted Gina impatiently. 'Just take a look at this.'

She gave Jane a torn piece of notepaper. Jane read the pencilled words on it: •

Make it earlier tonight. Come to the tunnel on the east side of the quarry at about ten. Harper.

'Gina, where did you get this?'

'It fell out of Roy's pocket, just now,' Gina explained. 'When he fished out your hair ribbon.'

'Harper. I remember that name,' Jane said slowly, frowning. 'Of course. Roy told me once that Bill Harper was the foreman who used to run the quarry.'

'There you are!' exclaimed Gina. 'He's in league with this foreman. Anyway, this is our only chance to find out once and for all what this mystery's about.' She consulted the note. 'Ten o'clock at the tunnel on the east side of the quarry. That must be the tunnel we used last night. Let's get this washing hung out to dry and have dinner. Then we'll sleep until about nine.'

At half-past nine, the girls were crouched outside some bushes near the tunnel leading into the quarry. The minutes dragged by and then Gina grabbed Jane's arm.

'Here he is,' she hissed. 'Now we are getting somewhere!'

Roy was coming around the side of the hill towards them. They watched as he stopped and looked towards their caravan which was dark and lightless in the background. Then, apparently satisfied, he stooped, pulled aside some bushes from the tunnel mouth, and disappeared. Gina waited some seconds and then she rose.

'Now's our chance,' she whispered.

The two girls crept to the tunnel mouth and entered. It was pitch dark.

'Switch the torch on,' urged Jane.

But before Gina could obey, a large sack was suddenly thrown over her head. She heard Jane cry out beside her and then rough hands picked her up and carried her away through the darkness!

* * *

Gina kicked and struggled as she felt herself borne along the tunnel. Then, abruptly, with a bump that jarred her from head to heels, she was set down on the hard ground. The sack was whipped from around her head and shoulders and she blinked in the strong electric light in the cavern. Jane was standing beside her, her hair ruffled.

Several grimy men, dressed in singlets and trousers, were working nearby and moving in and out of the tunnels that branched off from the main cavern. A big, burly, unshaven man, clad in rough, mud-caked trousers and a sweaty shirt, stood in front of her.

'So you're the kids who've been giving us all the trouble,' he said. 'Lucky we were lying in wait for your boy friend here, or we shouldn't have caught you until it was too late.'

He moved aside and behind him Gina saw Roy, bound

hand and foot, propped up against the rock wall in a corner.

The big man turned to two of his men and said: 'Tie these two up. And make the knots good and strong.'

After the two men had carried out his order he spoke again.

'All right! Take them all into the storeroom in Tunnel Five,' he commanded. 'And then come straight back here. We've got to make a big drive tonight and get well away before we release these brats and they raise the alarm. We can't keep on after tonight, so this load will be our last.'

Gina, Jane and Roy were lifted and carried down a lighted, winding tunnel. Their captors finally stopped at a ramshackle door set in the rock wall. The girls were carried inside and laid down in pitch darkness by the side of the wall. Roy was brought in after them, and then the door closed, leaving them in utter darkness.

'Roy, I am sorry,' said Jane's voice from the blackness. 'We saw you last night here in the tunnel, and we thought you were involved with the gang and working on something illegal. We thought you'd told us to move from the caravan because you were afraid of being found out.'

Roy heaved a sigh.

'Don't apologise, please, Jane,' he said. 'It breaks my heart to think how we were at cross purposes all the time. I've known for months that someone has been secretly working the quarry and I've been searching everywhere for clues. Even your caravan, I'm afraid, Jane, but I've never been able to catch them till now.'

'Don't feel too badly about it, Roy,' Jane begged.

'Yes, but we've lost our only chance now to catch the gang.' Roy's voice was intense. 'This stuff, whatever it is that they're mining from the quarry, rightly belongs to Dad, as the owner. After tonight, they'll be out of the country with their loot and never come back again. They'll take us away to a lonely place and set us free, but by that time it will be too late.'

A melancholy silence fell on the trio.

'It's so dark in here,' Gina said finally. 'If only we had a match.'

From the darkness, a vague, hesitant voice said:

'A match? Yes, yes, I think I have some here. Now where are they?'

Jane started up, bewildered, and then she laughed shakily.

'Oh, Roy. You and your imitations. That was just like Professor Hackett.'

'But I didn't...' Roy began.

His voice was cut short by the scratching of a match. The light showed Professor Hackett's mild, owl-like face blinking in the light.

Roy, Jane and Gina stared at his reflected face in utter amazement.

He put the flame to a stub of candle which he brought from somewhere, and Gina voiced the question that was uppermost in all their minds.

'Professor! How did you get in here?'

'Why, though the tunnel, my dear,' Professor Hackett said. 'These old quarries are honeycombed with tunnels, and there's one leading from just behind your head to the outside of the quarry. I'm always prowling around here, and I've discovered quite a lot of them. But what's all this about being tied up?'

The Professor pulled out a knife and quickly cut the ropes. They stood up, stretching their cramped limbs.

'Now listen carefully, Professor,' Roy said. He began to explain to the Professor what had happened.

The Professor pulled out a knife and quickly cut the ropes.

When Roy had finished speaking, the Professor asked: 'And this gang of yours, are they still inside the quarry?'

'Yes,' Roy told him. 'They're making a final bid tonight to get the last of the loot out of the quarry and away in trucks.'

'I see,' Professor Hackett said keenly. 'And our plan is to stop them.'

'That's quite right,' Roy said.

'Well, there are too many men for us to tackle alone, and I'm not very strong,' the Professor said.

'I know that,' Roy said patiently. 'I thought one of us would have to go through the tunnel and bring back the men from the farms round about to help us. But the gang will be finishing their work here very shortly and we have to find some way of delaying them.'

The Professor's eyes gleamed in the candlelight. 'I have an idea!'

He began to feel along the wall with one hand. Suddenly he gave a grunt.

'Ah! Just as I thought. Here it is,' he said. 'The smoke abatement control. Just the thing. You see,' he explained, 'if I give this dial here a slight turn, the smoke coming from that big chimney outside does not flow away, but rises sluggishly. If I give it another turn — so — the smoke does not rise at all, but remains stuck in the chimney and flows back into the quarry — a kind of reverse gear,' he added, with a chuckle of amusement.

'But what good will that do us?' asked Gina. 'Besides filling the tunnels with smoke. Oh, I see,' she said slowly.

'Yes, exactly,' said Professor Hackett. 'Besides filling the tunnels with smoke, it will also fill the eyes of the workers with smoke. Nothing harmful, of course, but just enough to make them rush for the open air with streaming eyes. Now, I think I had better lead the way through the tunnel.'

Within a few minutes, led by the Professor, the girls and Roy were out in the open air. The Professor pointed up at the chimney.

'See,' he said. 'No smoke.'

The Professor was right. Only a thin thread of smoke was coming from the smoke stack. The rest of it was trapped below the hill. Roy set off at a run for the farms and quickly returned with a dozen men, armed with stout cudgels and ropes. He stationed them at the various entrances to the quarry. As the members of the gang cane staggering out, coughing and spluttering into the open air, they were easily rounded up.

Professor Hackett stood smiling as the gang were put into one of the trucks which they had thought were going to be loaded up with the spoils from the quarry.

Roy scratched a puzzled head.

'I still can't make out what they were mining for,' he said.

'Oh, that's easy,' the Professor said, airily. 'Pitchblende.'

'Pitchblende!' gasped Roy.

'But that's very valuable, isn't it?' Gina put in.

'*Most* valuable!' the Professor told them. He settled his spectacles on his nose. 'You see, uranium is extracted from pitchblende. It is a kind of native oxide of uranium found in pitch-like masses and, apparently, also in your mine. The Government will be very interested in this discovery. If I were you, young man, I should register this valuable property at once, before anyone else gets wind of it and tries to take it away from you.'

'But how did you know about it, Professor?' asked Jane.

'Your left shoe, my dear,' smiled Professor Hackett. 'It contains samples of pitchblende ore with gravel from the quarry. I conducted various tests on it and made the discovery. Unfortunately, I burnt the shoe to a crisp,' he said sadly. 'But I'll replace it, never fear.'

'Oh, Roy, how wonderful!' breathed Jane. 'Now your father can get back to work and start up the quarry again.'

Roy smiled at her and the Professor smiled at everybody.

'Good!' he said. 'Now, if you would care to accompany me to my caravan, I will make you all a cup of tea!'

And he led the way across the fields while the friends linked arms and followed him, laughing as the Professor, even more absent-minded than usual, headed like a homing pigeon straight for the door of their own caravan!

Clare and the Arab Princess

by Arthur Catherall

'Now, can you think of anything I have forgotten, Miss Clare?'
Monsieur Blanc asked. 'I have reserved the sleeping compartment for you. When you reach Marseilles tomorrow, breakfast
will be waiting, and I have reserved a cabin for you aboard
the ship which will take you to Algiers.'

'You make me feel like the daughter of a millionaire,'
Clare Elliot chuckled. 'And if I don't enjoy my three weeks'
yachting along the North African coast it won't be... Oh,
sorry,' and she stood aside while the porter helped a girl
into the sleeping coach and pushed a bright yellow leather
suitcase in after her.

'You must get in now,' Monsieur Blanc advised. 'The
train will be off in a moment. Have a good holiday.'

A few moments later, the famous Blue Train began to
move slowly out on its all-night journey to the south of France.

One man had already hurried out of the station. He had
followed the girl with the yellow suitcase and now he went
to a telegraph office. The message he addressed to Hassan,
19 Rue Pont, Marseilles, contained only nine words: *Girl
carries yellow suitcase. Has berth in sleeper seven.*

Clare Elliot was also in sleeper seven, and she had just
begun reading a gay Parisian magazine when the door of
the compartment opened and the girl with the yellow suitcase
peered in.

'Excuse me, please,' she said. 'May I come in for a moment?
I am frightened, very frightened, and I wondered...'

She stopped, her eyes brimming with tears. She looked so
pathetic and helpless that Clare could not resist her appeal.

'Come in and close the door,' she said. 'I suppose you are going away for the first time... and that's made you feel a bit blue.'

The girl shook her head. 'I am not going away,' she whispered, 'I am going home. That is why I am so frightened. You see, I am not French. I am the daughter of the Caid... the ruler of the Kabyles.'

The girl went on quickly: 'We live in the Atlas Mountains of Algeria. I am Mamoona, next ruler of the Kabyles when my father dies.'

'Delighted to meet you,' Clare said, holding out her hand. 'I'm Clare Elliot, and I'm going to Algiers for a yachting trip.'

'You go to Algiers?' Mamoona stared for a moment, then in a rush asked: 'May I please travel with you? If I am with you perhaps they won't dare do it.'

'Do it? Do what?' Clare asked.

'I have been in Paris for three years at school,' Mamoona explained, bringing out a sheet of paper, 'and this morning I received a letter. If you can read this you will understand why I am frightened.'

Clare smoothed out the paper and began to read. It was in Arabic but she read it easily for she had lived in North Africa nearly all her life. Translated, it read:

Mamoona, your father is seriously ill. Come home at once, but tell no one. Leave the school secretly. Your cousin, Abd El Shuad, plans to kidnap you. He means to marry you, so that when your father dies he will become Caid of the Kabyles. Tell no one who you are. Love, Suki.

'Suki? Who is she?' Clare asked.

'She was my nurse,' Mamoona explained. 'She would die for me. So when she writes a letter like that I know there is great danger. I am so terribly afraid.'

'You stay with me,' Clare said firmly. 'If anybody tries to kidnap you there'll be trouble. But they won't try, they daren't.'

'You do not know our people,' Mamoona said quietly. 'We are not ordinary Arabs. The Kabyles are descended from sea-rovers who came from Scandinavia hundreds of years ago. That is why I am fair-skinned and have blue eyes.'

Clare looked closely at Mamoona.

'Yes,' she agreed wonderingly. 'You certainly don't look like my idea of an Arab. We could almost pass as sisters.'

'I wish I was your sister,' Mamoona said soberly. 'In the Atlas Mountains the men are fierce and warlike, but the women must behave like sheep, always doing as they are told. That is why, if my cousin did kidnap me, I would have to marry him.'

'Oh, bosh!' Clair said impulsively. 'Now listen. You are going to travel with me, and you've got to make up your mind that this bullying cousin of yours is not going to do anything to you.'

'But he is a very powerful man. Because my father is ill he will try to make me marry him. He would not dare attempt such a thing if my father were well and strong.'

'You can stop worrying,' Clare said. 'Take your hat and coat off. We'll have a sandwich and I'll tell you what we'll do.'

While they were enjoying their supper, Hassan was reading the telegram in Marseilles.

He then scribbled a message to be cabled to an address in Algeria: *Will arrive at sunset with Mamoona. All goes well.*

When this was done Hassan went out to a little dockside cafe and signalled to a man seated at a corner table. When the man came out Hassan said quietly: 'I've had word from Paris. Mamoona is on the Blue Train. She left Paris today.'

'How will you know her?' asked the hired man quietly.

'She is carrying a yellow suitcase. Anyway, you have the launch ready. I'll bring her along about nine o'clock. I've cabled Abd El Shuad that we'll reach the Algerian coast about sunset, so make sure your engines are all right. You know what El Shuad is like if anything goes wrong.'

'Nothing will go wrong,' the hawk-faced Hassan was assured.

Hassan nodded and went back to the Rue Pont. He was smiling, for everything was going well.

Aboard the Blue Train, Clare learned a lot about the Kabyles and somehow persuaded poor, frightened Mamoona that nothing could happen to her.

The train lulled them to sleep and all went well until they were within forty minutes of Marseilles. Mamoona went to wash and Clare lay back on the bunk and closed her eyes — then it happened.

There was a sudden, grinding crash. Clare tried to sit up, but the coach was tottering, brakes squealed wildly as the train left the rails.

For several minutes she lay in a heap against the bunk wall, then she slowly began to climb back from unconsciousness.

She was aware of the cries of men from a nearby village who were already swarming over the coaches to locate trapped passengers.

Then a man called to her and a moment later was clambering into the compartment.

He helped her climb out, then pushed out her bag and the yellow case belonging to Mamoona.

'There was only one passenger in this compartment,' the villager said, 'so both bags belong to her.'

In the washplace Mamoona was huddled in a corner, dazed and frightened. The door was jammed and it was some time

There was a sudden, grinding crash!

before she recovered herself enough to start shouting for help.

Clare, meanwhile, had been taken across to the nearby village. A doctor washed the slight cut on her forehead, then she was given a warm drink into which had been slipped a couple of soothing tablets.

Cars were now beginning to arrive, and into one of these Clare was carefully lifted.

The man was ordered to take his passenger to Marseilles at the exact moment that Mamoona was being helped from the wrecked coach.

Clare might have begun to think about Mamoona but for the sleeping tablets and soon she drifted off into a lovely doze.

As the car drew up outside St. Charles Station in Marseilles, a railway official opened the door and asked: 'You have friends here, mam'selle?'

'Friends?' Clare murmured sleepily.

From what seemed to be a great distance, she heard a soft voice say: 'Ah, M'sieur, I will take charge of her. I have a car here in which I shall take her to her friends. I came to meet the train.'

It was the hawk-faced Hassan. He had spotted the yellow suitcase and was sure this was Mamoona, daughter of the Caid. 'I'll bring my car across,' he said.

Clare was lifted gently into Hassan's car and for half an hour they drove at a furious speed along the coast road, then braked to a stop near a lonely fishing village.

The driver carried the two suitcases down to a launch. Hassan carried Clare.

'Now,' he said, turning to the other man. 'Get us moving as quickly as you can. I won't feel safe until we are out of sight of land. Abd El Shuad is playing for high stakes and if I don't deliver this girl to him by midnight, my head won't be safe.'

The mooring lines were cast off. There was a sudden boil of white water at the stern of the launch and she began to nose her way out into deep water.

Gradually the speed was increased until she was leaving a long, foaming line of white behind her, while her bows were pointing across the blue sea to Algeria, four hundred miles away.

Algeria and the mountains of the Kabyles, the snow-capped Atlas peaks where Abd El Shuad had his home.

* * *

Clare remembered nothing of the dash across the Mediterranean and woke only when she was being carried ashore at a lonely spot on the coast of Algeria. The night was like ink and the only sounds she could hear were the braking of waves on the shore.

For a few moments she lay quiet, trying to remember what had happened; but when Hassan began to put her into a car she woke properly, for the driver had switched on his headlamps and they lit up a signpost a dozen yards away on which was the notice: *Alger 70 Kms.*

'Algiers... seventy kilometres!' Clare muttered, disbelief in her voice. *It couldn't be true.*

Turning to the hawk-faced Hassan she asked sharply: 'Who are you? What am I doing here?'

'You'll learn very soon,' Hassan said, pushing her into the back of his powerful car which moved off quickly.

Clare laid a hand on the door, but did not turn the handle.

The driver was already in top gear and the needle of the speedometer swung steadily round to 95 kilometres an hour.

Clare suddenly caught sight of a yellow case on Hassan's knees. Mamoona's case!

As she stared at the case she began to remember what had happened. The train crash... Mamoona had not been in the compartment when that had happened.

Suppose, just suppose, the men detailed to kidnap the Princess had made a mistake. She was not unlike Mamoona. Her heart began to thump wildly at the thought.

The car screeched through a tiny village and she had a glimpse of dark-faced men in Arab dress gathered about a small, candlelit coffee house.

Soon they were out of the level plain and climbing into dark, forbidding hills.

A few minutes after midnight the car turned off the road, bumped for miles along a rough track and finally squealed to a stop in the courtyard of a big house.

As Clare stepped stiffly from the car there was a patter of feet and a moment later she was being hugged by the biggest woman she had ever seen.

Half laughing, half crying, the woman whispered: 'Oh, ma cherie, Mamoona, so they did kidnap you. I've been praying you'd be able to keep out of their way, and...'

Clare struggled to free herself and said fiercely: 'Look, I'm not Mamoona and...' She stopped, the words frozen on her lips.

In the light of the car headlamps she had a glimpse of a tall, powerfully-built Arab, with flashing eyes and a cruel face. Clare knew without being told that this was Abd El Shuad, Mamoona's cousin. The man who had arranged the kidnapping... The man who intended to marry Mamoona.

Clare was frightened, but whatever happened she meant to tell this man who she really was. She opened her mouth, but a moment later the big woman, whom she guessed was Suki, Mamoona's old nurse, clasped a hand across her lips and whispered: 'Shhh! Don't speak!'

'But I must,' Clare managed to splutter. 'If I don't. . .'

'If you do,' came an agonised whisper, 'you'll be dead before morning. Lean against me. I'll get you into the house, where we can talk.'

Clare obeyed and Suki called across to Abd El Shuad: 'She is very tired and not feeling well, O Highness. I shall take her to her room.'

'Tired!' El Shuad snapped, and tugged at his short black beard for a moment before adding: 'Very well. I shall see her at sunrise. You can tell her the great future I have arranged for her.'

There was a note of mockery in his voice as he went on, 'Goodnight, my cousin. Rest, for at sunrise the leaders of our people will be waiting to welcome their new Caid. . . and his wife.'

Suki led her gently but firmly through the white archways round the house and into the dark interior.

Once in the room she released Clare and said quickly: 'Ma cherie, before you say all the angry things you want to say, listen to me. I don't know who you are, or how you came here. They think you are my little lamb, Mamoona. One thing I want to tell you. If you wish to live, don't tell Abd El Shuad who you really are.'

'But I must,' Clare insisted angrily. 'I can't stay here. My friends will be anxious about me. . .'

She stopped. Suki was shaking her head solemnly as she said, 'If Abd El Shuad finds out he's got the wrong girl, you'll never leave these hills alive. Never!'

Before Clare could think of anything to say to that, there was a knock on the door and two veiled women came in carrying a pile of richly-embroidered ceremonial clothes.

'Abd El Shuad commands you to inspect the wedding attire, O Most High Mamoona. The needlewomen await your commands if everything is not as you wish.' The woman bowed low, then followed her companion out of the room.

'He thinks you are Mamoona,' Suki said quietly.

'But he'll realise his mistake the moment he sees me,' Clare said, suddenly beginning to smile. 'I hadn't thought of that.'

Suki frowned and shook her head. 'He has not seen Mamoona for over three years. However, if you will put your trust in me and be brave, everything can turn out well.'

'I can't do it,' Clare protested.

'It is that, or death,' Suki assured her. Then she knelt before Clare and pleaded, 'Do it for me and for my dear Princess Mamoona! It will only be for a few hours. I'll send for some food, and then I'll steal out of the house and get word to the French in Algiers.

'They'll have soldiers here every quickly and everything will be all right. Promise you will do it! Your life, and mine, depend on it.'

The big, brown eyes were fixed on Clare, imploring her to help.

Clare felt as if she was in the middle of the worst kind of nightmare possible. Her heart was hammering and there was a lump in her throat as she finally nodded agreement. Suki gave her a rib-crushing hug.

'Allah will bless you for this,' she said, and there were tears in her eyes. 'If I can get the French soldiers here, then El Shuad will be put in prison and you'll be safe and my lamb Mamoona will be out of danger.'

Suki clapped her hands, a signal which was answered at once by an old man. At Suki's order he brought food and the moment he had gone, Suki jerked down a long curtain cord. She tied it securely to a heavy couch, then threw the free end through the window.

For a woman of her size she was extraordinarily nimble and

strong. Before getting through the window to lower herself to the ground outside, Suki assured Clare. 'I'll be back before sunrise, so don't worry. I'll be here when El Shuad sends for you, and there won't be any wedding.'

She waved a hand, then slithered out of sight.

Clare ate some of the food, then lay down on the couch in the alcove. She had no intention of sleeping, but lay waiting for the return of Suki.

Somewhere in the big house weird music was being played; there was the clash of cymbals, and the sound of weird pipes and drums.

Slowly the gold rim on the hills grew into dawn, with the sun sending the shadows flying. Suki had not returned and it was morning.

Clare started when someone knocked on the door. It was the old man again, and behind him were two maidens bearing food.

When the trays had been set down and the old man was about to leave, he said: 'Your handmaidens will come in a few minutes to prepare you for the wedding, O Most High Mamoona, and my master, Abd El Shuad, commands you not to be longer than fifteen minutes from now.'

He bowed and turned to go. Clare watched him, too petrified to move.

As the old man was leaving the room Clare found her tongue.

'Listen,' she said sharply, 'I do not want any handmaidens to help me. Send Suki here at once.'

The old man looked startled and stood for a moment, gently stroking his chin.

'That cannot be, O Most High Mamoona,' he said slowly. 'Know you this, last night she was caught by a guard, trying to steal away from the house. She meant to desert you, so my master has cast her into a cell beneath the house.'

Clare's knees felt as if they were going to give way under her.

Suki a prisoner — captured before she got away!

'You will be ready in fifteen minutes, O Most High Mamoona,' the old man said gently and turning, left the room.

For a minute Clare remained absolutely still. Her knees were trembling and she felt cold from head to foot.

Clare turned towards the door as someone knocked gently. At her command to come in, the door opened and two Arab women entered.

'Abd El Shuad and the chiefs of your tribe await you, O Most High Mamoona,' one of the women said. 'The hour has come for your wedding.'

Clare merely nodded. As if in a trance, she allowed the two women to help her into the ceremonial dress, then obediently went before them into the corridor.

The moment she left the room there was a terrific clashing of gongs, which grew louder and louder as she approached the great room where the ceremony was to take place.

Clare was scared, but determined. No matter how domineering Abd El Shuad might be, she intended to defy him.

Suddenly the brazen clanging of the gongs died away. She had reached an archway shrouded by lovely curtains. These were thrown back and Clare could look into a great room, thronged with bearded, fierce-eyed tribesmen, all clad in their best robes for the occasion.

At the far end of the room was Abd El Shuad, and with him a holy man to perform the ceremony.

The sound of Clare's slippered feet as she walked across the room seemed quite loud, so still was everyone. In the centre of the room she stopped.Facing the semi-circle of men she waited a moment, then said: 'I greet you, O chiefs of my people.'

Abd El Shuad turned to the holy man, who removed a covering from a cushion, revealing a wonderful jewel.

It was a star, glittering with precious stones. Mamoona had told Clare about it. It was like the crown to an English king. The Star of Islam was worn by the Caid and, while he or she wore it, everyone in the tribe must bow and faithfully obey the Caid's commands.

'Thy father is very ill and will soon die, O daughter of the Caid,' the holy man said gently, fastening the jewelled star just below Clare's throat. 'So, in his wisdom, he has said thou art to be leader, ruling in his place.' Having said that, the old man knelt and touched the ground at Clare's feet.

In the tense silence which followed Abd El Shuad said loudly: 'And now, having had the wedding feast, Mamoona and I shall marry.'

With a mighty effort Clare controlled her trembling voice and, turning to El Shuad, said coldly: 'When I marry, cousin, I shall choose my husband — and I shall choose the day. I am not ready to marry.'

Clare went on hurriedly: 'I am your Princess. I wear the Star,' and she touched the jewelled star with her right hand. 'Am I to be obeyed, or is this Star a worthless thing?'

For a moment there was a breathless silence, then Abd El Shuad made a great effort. He dropped his hand away from his dagger, and, drawing a deep breath, said loudly: 'I am thy cousin, Mamoona, and therefore I say, for thy father's sake, marry me — I order it so.'

In a ringing voice she replied: 'I refuse to marry anyone until the women of this tribe have more freedom. They are like slaves.'

The rest of her words were drowned in angry jeers from the chiefs. They were on their feet now, shouting and booing.

Clare's eyes flashed with anger.

When the uproar had died down a little she said bitterly: 'How brave you all are — fifty chiefs against one girl! Shall I tear off the Star and throw it at Abd El Shuad's feet?' And, as if she meant to carry out the threat, she tore the lovely jewelled Star from her dress and lifted it to crash it to the ground.

The effect was immediate. There was a loud gasp of horror, then silence.

Clare fastened the Star on her dress again, then looked defiantly at Abd El Shuad.

'Cousin,' she said coldly, 'I am the new Caid and if there are any commands to be given... then I will give them.'

Turning to the assembled chiefs she said: 'Go now, I am tired. I shall think quietly and will speak to you all again tomorrow... in the market place. Go, and Allah be with you.'

A command from one who wore the Star of the Caid was not to be disobeyed and the men began to file from the room, murmuring to one another at this unbelievable thing. They had never known a girl of their people to behave in that way before.

Clare was halfway back to her room when Abd El Shuad caught up with her.

'Well?' she said coldly. 'What do you want, cousin?'

'I merely want to show you something,' he said and there was a smile on his dark face now. 'Come with me for a moment.'

They went down a passage and some steps, along another darker passage; more steps, all leading down, and finally they came into a small chamber.

Bending down Abd El Shuad lifted a square of wood from the floor, revealing the mouth of a well.

'That well is thirty metres deep,' he said soberly. 'Once it held water. Now... who knows... snakes, rats, all manner of things.

'I am going to give you half an hour of quietness, during which time you will change your mind about marrying me. If you refuse at the end of that half hour's grace... you go down that well and stay there until you are ready to obey me!'

'You wouldn't dare!'

'Cousin,' Abd El Shuad said coldly, 'I would dare more than that. I am only marrying you because I want the French to believe that I became Caid by legal means.'

Clare did not reply. She was staring with horrified eyes into the black depths of the well.

Allowing the wooden cover to fall with a sudden bang over the mouth of the well, Abd El Shuad turned and walked up the steps and Clare hastened after him.

Showing her into her room again, Abd El Shuad paused at the door.

'I will give you half an hour from now to think over what you will do. You can make your choice.'

He walked out, closed the door and shot the three bolts one after the other. Clare sat down and looked round. There was no other door in the room and only one window. There was a guard squatting against the wall outside. Escape that way was hopeless.

She got up and paced round the room like a caged tigress. She was trapped...

At the end of half an hour there was a rap on the door.

Immediately following that rat-tat-tat on the door came the harsh voice of Abd El Shuad. 'Have you made up your mind, my dear cousin?'

'Yes.' Clare's wits, which had been frozen, now started to work again. In a very subdued voice she asked: 'Will you give me another minute or so?'

'I thought you'd come to your senses,' Abd El Shuad chuckled. 'All right. You can have five minutes.'

When Clare heard the sound of his footsteps die away she darted across the room towards the window.

She then lowered the end of a long curtain-cord through the window, but made no effort to escape. Instead she hurried back and slithered under the bed.

Several minutes passed, then again came the knock on the door, followed by the clatter of bolts being withdrawn. Clare held her breath as she heard the door open.

'Now, my cousin, everything is...' Abd El Shuad stopped. His sharp eyes had seen the cord going over the window ledge.

With a yell of rage he hurried to the window and peered out.

Almost gibbering with fury, he turned and rushed out of the room, yelling like a maniac: 'Out! Out! Everyone out! Mamoona has escaped. She's got away through the window!'

For several minutes there was pandemonium in the big white house as servants hurried out into the courtyard, to be sent this way and that in order to cut off her escape.

In five minutes the house was deserted and Clare crept from her hiding place. 'I've got to find Suki,' Clare decided. 'She'll know what to do. It's my only chance.'

She stole quietly along the corridor, but as she was passing a door a black arm clutched at her. Clare gave a little squeal of dismay.

'Missie... Missie... Please, I only want to help.'

Clare's uplifted hands dropped slowly to her sides. This was no brawny Arab, but a slender boy who pleaded: 'I am Ali... my mother is Suki. Won't you help her, please? She is in a dark room below,' and Ali pointed downwards.

'Take me to her,' Clare urged. 'Quickly! We've got to get her out.'

Ali led her down a long corridor. They went through a doorway and almost at once were face to face with the jailer.

'Take me to see Suki,' Clare ordered.

The jailer gave her a starled look and an apologetic bow, then muttered: 'O Highness, my master has ordered me...'

'I am giving the orders now,' Clare snapped with authority.

The jailer winced, and his face went a sickly grey: 'I will lead Your Highness to the cell,' he said in a trembling voice.

A big key clanked in a lock and a moment later they were in a corridor, along each wall of which were the cells.

Almost as soon as they stepped into the corridor, the voice of Suki was heard demanding: 'Well, you trashy key-jingler, have you come to set me free?'

'Silence,' the jailer roared. 'I have brought you a visitor — the Most High Mamoona.'

'Yes, and she commands you to release Suki,' Clare said arrogantly. 'Open the cell door at once.'

The jailer gulped. 'O Most High Mamoona,' he quavered, 'my master...'

'Do you dare disobey me?' Clare snapped and, taking a step forward, she held out her hands. 'Give the keys to me.'

Clare took the keys from the nerveless fingers of the jailer and, a moment later, the rusty old lock had been turned.

She whispered to Suki, then asked the jailer: 'How can we get out of here without Abd El Shuad knowing?'

The jailer thought for a moment, then frowned. 'No one ever comes down here,' he said slowly, 'it would be best to stay here until sundown.'

They made themselves comfortable and every hour Suki's son crept up to see what was happening in the big house.

After what seemed hours, Ali was sent up again to see if it was night, and when he came back his eyes were big and frightened.

Without thinking what the effect would be on the jailer, young Ali said: 'They have got the real Mamoona. A party of horsemen caught her on the road. She was in a car and she admitted she was Mamoona, telling them of a train accident in France.'

'You are not the real daughter of the Caïd!'

The Arab, who had been Suki's jailer, spoke in a voice harsh with anger: 'You say that my master has caught the real Mamoona? Then who are you?' He pointed an accusing finger at Clare.

'You are not the real daughter of the Caid. I shall tell Abd El Shuad.' He turned on his heel and began to race up the stone steps which led to the house above.

Clare raced after him. The jailer was three steps from the top door when Clare made a lunge upward and caught his ankle.

The jailer was tripped neatly as his feet were jerked from beneath him.

He did not topple far, for Suki had been following Clare and she caught the man, whipping him down to the bottom and through the doorway so quickly it was like magic.

'What shall we do now?' Clare asked.

'There's only one thing to do,' Suki replied. 'We'll go down to the village. I'm going to proclaim you daughter of the Caid and you are going to lead a revolt.'

'But I don't see how that can help Mamoona... or get me out of this mess,' Clare protested.

'Leave it to me,' Suki said. 'Come on. We're getting out of here now.'

The jailer was locked in a cell, then the trio. Clare, Suki, and her son Ali, went quietly up the stone steps. Ali peeped out and gave the word when everything was clear and they slipped across the courtyard and into the stony field beyond.

When they arrived at a village Suki left Clare in a dark alley and went away. She was soon back again.

There was no chance of getting out of the village, except by force, for Abd El Shuad's guards were barring the way.

'Go to the little market square,' Suki said, 'and I'll bring the women. Think of something convincing to say to them...'

Five long minutes went by and then, like ghosts, dark shadows began to slide quietly into the square.

Very soon the little square was packed. Then Suki came, carrying a lantern.

'I've told them you are the real Mamoona,' she whispered, 'and that if they'll follow you and refuse to come back to the village until Abd El Shuad surrenders, you'll make things better for them when you are Caid.'

'But I can't do anything for them,' Clare protested.

'No, but Mamoona will,' Suki insisted.

Climbing on to a low wall, Clare stood there while Suki turned up the lantern.

Then, to Clare's amazement, every woman present went down on her knees and touched her forehead to the dust.

'That means they accept you,' Suki whispered, 'and they'll follow you anywhere. Tell them that we're going to the fort on the hill.'

Feeling less and less sure of what was going to happen, Clare did as Suki suggested. At once there was a chorus of approval and the women formed up into a solid mass, with a space in the middle for Clare and Suki.

Then, beginning to chant a queer wailing dirge, they moved off towards the hills.

Fifty minutes later, fires were being lit in an old fort.

'You'd better lie down and sleep,' Suki said to Clare. 'I've made a place for you. My son has gone to try and get word to the French police and, if we can hold out for a day or so, everything will be all right.'

Clare went to a spot near a fire and lay watching the Kabyle women moving quietly about. Some were acting as sentries; others were collecting brushwood for the fires.

She finally dropped off to sleep. When she awoke, with Suki shaking her gently by the shoulder, the sun was up.

'They're coming,' Suki said, and she could not keep the excitement and fear from her voice.

Clare jumped up and, going to the crumbling wall of the fort, looked down the hill. About a quarter of a mile away a band of men was climbing nearer and she thought she recognised the tall figure of Abd El Shuad at the head.

He stopped when he was some thirty yards away and in a sneering voice said: 'You had better surrender at once, or you will all be punished severely.'

Clare knew that every Kabyle woman was looking at her and, bracing herself, she answered: 'Send this false Mamoona here, my cousin. You shall never be Caid. I mean to rule and see that my sisters here are better treated in the future.'

There was a buzz of delighted whispering from the Kabyle women, but it died away when Abd El Shuad gave a great jeering laugh.

'I shall marry the real Mamoona, who is in my house at this moment, just as soon as I have taken the Star of Islam from you,' he shouted. '. . . And that won't be long. I've got a powerful friend working for me now — the sun. You'll soon be thirsty.'

'We have a stream of pure water,' Clare called back, 'that won't dry up for a long time.'

'Go and look at your water,' was the scornful retort as he turned back to his men.

Someone did, and a minute later Suki was at Clare's elbow whispering anxiously: 'They've put something into the stream higher up the hill. It's undrinkable.'

Heavy-hearted, Clare turned away. The sun continued to blaze down and the rocks of which the old fort was made became too hot to touch.

Noon came and went. Clare grew more and more desperate. Several babies were crying and the Kabyle women never stopped staring at her. They were all depending on her to do something to save them.

By the afternoon Clare could stand it no longer.

'I'm going to speak to Abd El Shuad,' she said quietly.

Suki nodded and Clare went to the end of the old fort and called down to Abd El Shuad. He came up to within a dozen yards, a guard of armed men a few yards behind him.

'I'll hand over the Star of Islam,' Clare announced, 'if you will promise not to...'

Abd El Shuad interrupted her with a scornful laugh.

'Go back and grow thirstier,' he taunted.

'Did you know that I had sent a messenger down to Algiers, to inform the Governor that I had been kidnapped?' she demanded. 'The soldiers ought to be here by sunset or, at least, by sunrise tomorrow.'

To her surprise, Abd El Shuad turned and stalked down the hill. He reached his men and a minute later they all began to climb up the hill, Abd El Shuad urging them on from the rear.

Clare gasped and turned to Suki. 'Tell them they have got to stop the men,' she said, pointing to the Kabyle women.

Suki turned and began to speak rapidly to the Kabyle women, but her only answers were forlorn headshakes. Thirst had already knocked the fight out of them.

A couple of minutes later the first men were scrambling into the fort.

Clare was hustled across to meet Abd El Shuad, while the Kabyle women started to walk back down the hill towards their mud houses.

Abd El Shuad snatched the Star of Islam from Clare, his face a grinning mask of triumph.

'Now the French dogs can come as soon as they like,' he jeered. 'They won't find you, little spitfire.'

'You can do what you like,' Clare said, 'but you won't be able to get away from the message I sent.'

Abd El Shuad's eyes narrowed. 'I don't believe you've sent any message.'

'Then try to find Suki's son, Ali,' Clare snapped.

Taken to Abd El Shuad's home, she waited while a search was made for Ali. At the end of an hour he still had not been found.

Abd El Shuad stalked into Clare's room, livid with fury. 'I'll give you one chance to save yourself,' he snarled. 'You must promise, when the French come, not to tell them that I kidnapped you.'

'Will you promise not to force Mamoona to marry you?' Clare asked, and shrank back from his infuriated yell.

'You can agree to my command, or die!' Abd El Shuad was in no mood for arguing.

There was no other way out. Reluctantly, Clare whispered: 'All right. I swear that if you release me I will not tell the French that you kidnapped me.'

Not until mid-way through the following morning was she allowed to leave the room, and then it was to meet a lieutenant of the French Foreign Legion.

'I have arrested Abd El Shuad,' the lieutenant said, saluting her, 'and he will return with us to Algiers for trial. Kidnapping is a serious crime...'

'Did my messenger say I had been kidnapped?' Clare said, feigning surprise at the message given by Ali.

'Will you bring Abd El Shuad here?' she asked. 'I gave him a promise and I would like him to know I have not broken it.'

The sullen Arab was brought into the room.

'They think you kidnapped me,' Clare said, smiling, 'but that is something we need not worry about at all.'

'What did I tell you!' Abd El Shuad snarled, holding out his manacled hands.

The lieutenant of the Foreign Legion was mystified. 'Well,' he said slowly, 'if you say he did not kidnap you, then I suppose I'd better release him.'

'Wait,' Clare said. 'I'd like you to see something in the cells. Will you come with me?'

Clare took the French lieutenant down into the gloomy cells and showed him what three of them contained. They were stacked high with machine-guns, cases of ammunition and automatic rifles.

'I saw them when I came down here to rescue my friend Suki,' she explained.

The Legion lieutenant smiled broadly. 'We have had our suspicions of Abd El Shuad for some time... but could never find any proof. I think he will get more than a taste of French cells for this. Yes — more than a taste.'

Abd El Shuad and his chiefs were taken away, but before Clare left she spent a happy hour with Mamoona and Suki.

'Soon, when you have another holiday,' Mamoona insisted, 'you must return to us in the Atlas Mountains.'

'I'd love a holiday here,' Clare agreed, 'as long as I don't come next time disguised as the daughter of the Caid. I prefer to be plain Clare Elliot. I'll write to you and next year, all being well, I'll return.'

She climbed happily into the waiting car and a few moments later began the journey to Algiers and her delayed holiday.

Unwelcome Guests

by Clare Robinson

The little local train came to a creaking halt, and two girls in the end carriage jumped to their feet.

'Hurry up, Barbie!' Jill shouted. 'We're here. Help me with this case and these boxes.'

Jill pulled heavy cases and boxes off the luggage rack and almost threw them down. Then she opened the carriage door and leapt out on to the platform, dragging two of the cases with her.

Her tall, dark-haired friend, Barbara, followed calmly, lifting out the remainder of their luggage and stacking it neatly on the platform.

'I don't know how you can be so calm,' Jill said admiringly. 'Oh, help! I've forgotten my handbag.' She dived back into the carriage and retrieved the bag. The guard blew his whistle just as Jill leapt out of the carriage for the second time.

'Trust me to get in a panic,' Jill gasped. 'I'm worn out already.' She surveyed the pile of boxes and cases around them. 'I only hope,' she added, 'that Uncle got my letter.'

'So do I', Barbie said. 'I can't imagine lugging this lot four miles!'

The girls grinned at each other, but their smiles faded as they turned to survey the platform. There was only one other person on the tiny station platform, and that was a man weeding an immaculately kept flower-bed with the name of the village, 'Floxton', picked out in white stones across its middle.

The two girls walked up to him.

'Excuse me,' said Jill brightly, 'but has Mr Holmes arrived yet?'

'Mr Holmes? Mr Holmes?' said the man, straightening up and scratching his head, 'Oh-ah! The new hostel chappie! No, haven't seen him around this station since he arrived. It must have been two weeks ago now.'

'Oh, dear!' Jill said. 'I just knew this would happen. Uncle Ted couldn't have got my letter. Are there any taxis in the village?'

'No, but a friend of mine will run you up to the hostel — if that's where you want to go.'

'Yes, we do. Can you tell us where we can get in touch with your friend?'

'You can phone him from the call box just outside the station gate,' the man replied.

'Thank you,' Jill said. 'Can you give me the number?'

'Here it is, but you'd do better to stay in the village tonight, at Mrs Pargeter's, and go up there in the morning,' he called after them. 'The hostel isn't a very comfortable place for young girls like you.'

Jill refused to be put off, and phoned up the porter's friend. When he arrived, they piled the boxes and cases into his car under the close scrutiny and disapproval of the porter, and set off for Highridge Hostel — where Jill's Uncle Ted had recently been installed as the new warden.

On their way through the village, Barbie stared out of the car's windows at the small village, with its four shops, a post office, and triangular patch of village green surrounded by square white cottages.

'It's such a pretty village,' she said. 'I can't understand why the hostel isn't busy all the year round.'

'Yes, it does seem odd,' Jill replied. 'But Uncle Ted has high hopes for the future. And with the three of us working hard, it'll be cleaned up and ready for business in no time.'

Barbie groaned. 'I *had* hoped this was going to be a really restful holiday.'

'A change is as good as a rest, they say,' Jill retorted, 'and it will certainly be that! Running up and down ladders, making curtains, splashing on paint. Wonderful! You'll go back full of renewed vigour.'

Jill sounded cheerful, but she was beginning to feel a little nervous about the task that lay ahead. When her uncle had written and told her about his new charge, a dilapidated hostel in the heart of the country, it had seemed a wonderful idea to rush down and help him get it ready. Now she was not so sure... Even the porter's friend looked disapproving when they had asked for Highridge Hostel.

The car chugged its way slowly up a steep, winding lane, turned sharply into a drive, and pulled up outside the door of a large cottage. The driver helped them out with their luggage, grunted: 'Thank you,' for his tip, slammed the door of his car, and drove off as if he hadn't a moment to lose.

'Wait there, Barbie,' Jill said. 'I'll go and find Uncle.' She hurried off round the back of the cottage while Barbie inspected her new surroundings.

'Could be worse,' she murmured to herself, 'but it certainly doesn't live up to the rest of the village.'

The cottage was a pleasant square shape, with dormer windows and a thatched roof, but everything about it, and its garden, had a neglected look.

Tattered curtains hung at the windows, kettles, bottles and weeds littered the garden; a broken sign saying: 'Hostellers this way' creaked eerily in the breeze. Barbie shivered as she looked around.

Just as Jill came running from the back of the cottage shouting, 'I can't find him,' a tall figure hurried up the path towards them. Jill rushed up to him and hugged him, then babbled excitedly:

'Gosh, am I glad to see you, Uncle! I thought I had dragged Barbie — oh, this is my friend Barbie — down here on a wild uncle chase, or something. Why weren't you at the station? Didn't you get my letter?'

'No, I haven't heard from anyone since I've been here. I think my letters must be going astray somehow. Never mind, you're here, and I'm very pleased to see both of you. Come inside and make yourselves at home. I'll go and make some tea.'

Jill's uncle led the way into the front room of the cottage, which was littered with tools and packing-cases. Then he went to bring in their luggage.

'Whatever have you got here, Jill?' he asked, staggering under the weight of assorted boxes.

'It's a gift from Mummy — paint and curtains and stuff. Barbie and I have come to help you give the place a real spring clean'.

'Well, that makes me feel a lot happier,' said Jill's uncle. 'I've had no luck getting help locally. They all say there's too much to be done on the farms at the moment. The builder said he didn't think he could fit me in before next year!' He frowned puzzledly. 'They don't seem a very friendly bunch around here. Never mind, we'll do without them.'

Uncle Ted took them upstairs and showed them their room. Then, while Barbie unpacked, Jill hurried off to the village to get some nails for Uncle Ted.

The bell on the door of the ironmonger's clanged and jangled as Jill stepped inside. A young freckle-faced boy stepped forward to serve her.

'Yes, miss?' he asked.

'A pound of nails, please.'

'What size do you need-do you know what they're for?'

'Oh! Well, they're for Mr Holmes, at the hostel. He bought some here last week.'

'I remember. So you're at the hostel, are you?' the boy said. 'Well, I wish you luck, but I'm afraid Mr Holmes will have a hard time making a success of it.'

'Why do you say that?' Jill asked quickly, but at that moment the bell jangled and another customer came into the shop.

'Can't tell you now,' the boy said in a low voice. 'Come back tomorrow. Good morning, Mrs Pargeter,' he greeted the new customer as Jill walked out of the shop with her parcel.

Jill hurried back to the hostel, very puzzled at the attitude of the boy who had served her. She was determined to go back to the shop the very next day and find out what he was going to tell her. There seemed to be an atmosphere whenever the hostel was mentioned in the village, and the people all seemed to be suspicious. She could not pin it down, but things were definitely not all as they should be between the village and the hostel. She decided not to say anything about it to her uncle, or to Barbie, until she had something to go on.

Everyone was asleep early at the hostel that night, to be ready for hard work the next day. At six o'clock Jill was already up and dressed in jeans and an old jumper. She shook Barbie awake and then hurried out to the barn to begin mixing distemper. But on her way there she stopped dead in her tracks. Written on the side wall of the house, in foot-high red letters, was: 'GET OUT, HOSTELLERS!'

Jill stepped forward to touch the paint. It was still wet. A determined look came over Jill's face; she had been right in her surmise on her way back from the village shop the night before. A lot of people in the village were against the

On her way past the hostel she stopped dead in her tracks!

hostel, and she was going to do her best to find out why!

She decided to tell Barbie and her uncle, but before going indoors Jill searched about for some clue to the author of the notice.

'H'mm,' she muttered. 'Now what clues do they find in detective films — bits of cloth, strands of hair, tyre marks...'

With her fair head bent low, Jill examined the soft earth by the side of the cottage. She was so intent on her search that she did not notice the approach of her friend. Barbie was dressed, like Jill, in jeans and a jumper, but looked far less dishevelled, with her short, dark hair neatly brushed.

'What on earth are you doing, Jill?' Barbie asked. 'You look like a bloodhound!'

'That's just what I'm trying to be. Look what somebody did during the night.' Jill pointed to the notice.

'What a rotten thing to do!' Barbie said. 'Any idea who did it?'

'No, but I'm going to find out!' Jill said.

Barbie looked at the big red letters on the cottage wall, then she turned to Jill.

'Well, let's start looking for clues,' she said.

After a minute's close inspection of a flower-bed, she straightened up.

'I think I've got something, Jill. Do tyre marks count?'

'Of course they count!' Jill replied. 'What sort of tyres?'

'Bicycle tyres — across that soft bit of mud by the rain barrel.'

Jill rushed across to examine the mud. She tested it carefully. 'Fresh today — maybe two or three hours old! Well, none of us has a bike, so it must have been a stranger — *the* stranger, in fact. What do we do now, I wonder?'

'Well,' said Barbie, 'now we know how the stranger got here, we ought to find out what he did his painting with!'

'Marvellous, Barbie. You're a born detective!' Jill rushed off to the barn where she had stowed away her paints and distemper the previous evening.

She reappeared holding a red, dripping paint-can. 'What a cheek! He even used my paint to write his notice then he walked off with my brush.'

'Well, there's a clue at any rate,' said Barbie consolingly. 'Find the paint brush and you have the villain!'

'We might even be able to do that,' said Jill mysteriously. 'I'll put my friend in the village on the look-out.'

Jill told Barbie about the boy in the ironmonger's shop. 'He promised to tell me something interesting about the hostel today. Come on, let's both go down and talk to him!'

The two girls went indoors for their coats and then set off immediately for the village. But as Jill pushed open the door of the ironmonger's shop, her face fell. It was full of people; the boy would never get a chance to speak to them.

She was just discussing with Barbie whether they should come back later when the boy came to their end of the counter. He grinned at Jill and said: 'Excuse me, but I think you left this yesterday,' slipping a catalogue across the counter.

Jill started to say it wasn't hers, then changed her mind, picked up the catalogue and hustled Barbie out of the door.

Outside the shop, Jill quickly unfolded the catalogue, then she shook it. 'That's funny,' she said. 'I thought he was trying to give me a message.'

'Perhaps there's something written on it,' said Barbie.

The two girls peered at the catalogue. It was brightly-coloured and showed a picture of some tents and caravans grouped on a cliff. Across the top was written: 'Come to Paxton Holiday Camp,' and underneath it said: 'The ideal holiday spot for campers and hikers, with a private beach, electric light and running water.'

'If that's meant to be a clue, I don't think much of it,' said Jill, tucking the catalogue in her pocket. 'Paxton is about fifteen miles from here. It couldn't possibly affect the hostel.'

'He grinned when he gave it to you,' Barbie said. 'Perhaps it was his idea of a joke.'

'Well, it's not a very funny one. If that's all he had to say, I shan't bother to go back. Let's go to the post office, Barbie, and see if there are any letters.'

Jill and Barbie hurried down the short row of little shops beside the green and went into the post office. A hatchet-faced woman, with dark hair drawn severely back into a bun, glared at them through the metal grille.

'Yes?' she snapped.

Jill stepped forward. 'I wonder if there are any letters for Highridge Hostel,' she said politely. 'I wrote from London over a week ago, and my letter still hasn't arrived yet.'

'Perhaps you forgot to post it,' the woman said acidly, reaching down a bundle of dusty letters from a shelf and flicking through them. She banged the bundle of letters on the counter, then put them back on the shelf and said: 'Nothing here!'

'That's very odd,' said Jill persistently. 'My mother's letter has not arrived either.'

The postmistress scowled. 'Ask George the postman, if you like. He sorts all the letters first.' She turned her back on the girls and pulled open a filing drawer. Jill and Barbie shrugged at each other and walked out of the shop.

Outside, a man in a postman's uniform was leaning his bicycle against the wall. 'That will be George,' Jill said. 'I *will* ask him.' She walked over and cleared her throat. 'Excuse me, but have any letters arrived for Highridge Hostel recently?'

'That broken-down old place,' said George. 'Shouldn't think they've ever been sent a letter! Be a good idea if them hostel people gave it up — just a waste of money as it is.'

'It's soon going to look very different,' said Jill. 'My uncle is the new warden.'

The postman flushed and held out a paint-stained hand. 'Pleased to meet you, I'm sure.'

Jill shook hands and glanced at the stains. They were red. 'Are you a painter, too?' she said, smiling innocently.

'Oh, that,' said the postman. 'Been helping the postmistress with a bit of renovating. Must be getting along now. Goodbye to you both.' He hurried into the shop. Jill was already striding across the green.

'What's up?' said Barbie, trotting at her heels. 'There's no law against other people using red paint. It doesn't prove he painted the notice.'

'No, but he has got a bicycle, and there was something else I noticed... the postmistress had my letter all the time! It was in that bundle. I know, because I dropped a big ink blot on the back of the envelope, and I saw it as she went through them!'

'Phew!' whistled Barbie. 'Things are getting complicated. We'd better go back and see what your uncle has to say.'

They walked thoughtfully back towards the cottage, turning over the 'clues' in their minds.

'I suppose we are rather jumping to conclusions,' said Barbie, less and less sure of herself.

'I don't know,' said Jill. 'After all, there's the bicycle tyre mark, and the paint stain. The one thing we don't understand and can't explain is why anyone should bother to do all this.'

When they reached the cottage they didn't have time to tell Uncle Ted their news. He met them at the gate, looking very harassed and worried.

'This must be my unlucky day,' he said dejectedly.

'What's the matter, Uncle?' said Jill.

'The carpenter who said he would come today hasn't turned up,' he said.

Jill looked thoughtful.

'I know what you mean, Uncle Ted,' she replied. 'It all seems to mount up. So many things going wrong. It can hardly be coincidence.'

Uncle Ted nodded glumly. 'That isn't the worst of it, by a long chalk,' he said. 'Farmer Kent, next door, has fenced off the right of way we used to have across his meadows. He said he didn't want any silly hostellers tramping across his land.'

Jill's eyes blazed, but when she spoke her voice was controlled and determined.

'That's the real clue, Barbie,' she said. 'They don't want us here. But it's more than ordinary hostility towards outsiders. Country people don't usually object to holiday-makers — at most they may grumble a bit. But it's beginning to add up!' Turning to her uncle, Jill added: 'We'll soon discover who is at the bottom of all this, don't you worry, Uncle Ted.'

'And so, you see, the postmistress must be at the bottom of it!' Jill explained triumphantly, as she came to the end of an explanation of the clues she and Barbie had found that day. 'She keeps your letters, sends the postman to write horrid notices, and makes Farmer Kent unfriendly to you.'

Uncle Ted shook his head. 'I'm not so sure it's quite as simple as that, Jill. There's a lot more to this than we know. Why, for instance...'

'Yes!' chipped in Barbie enthusiastically. 'Detectives always look for the motive first. Once you know that, you can be sure who did it.'

'The motive's the most difficult thing of all. I can't see why anyone should want to get rid of Uncle,' said Jill. 'And if hostellers come here in large numbers, the shops are bound to benefit. Why, this village might even become a resort!'

'Talking of resorts, Jill,' said Barbie, 'show your Uncle what the boy at the ironmonger's gave you.'

Jill fished in the pocket of her dress and pulled out the brightly-coloured catalogue, very much crumpled by now, advertising Paxton Holiday Camp.

Uncle Ted examined it carefully and read every line, from the description of camping facilities, wonderful views and sea-bathing, to details of weekly charges for caravan hire — payable to John Dawson, Esq., c/o Poste Restante, Post Office, Floxton.

When he had finished he looked up excitedly. 'Do you realise, Jill, that this is the most important clue of all?'

'Oh, dear!' said Jill. 'We thought it was just a joke.'

'But don't you see, at last we have found a motive! The postmistress has some connection with the holiday camp; therefore she doesn't want the hostel to be a success. If only we could find out what that connection was.'

'Quick, Uncle!' Jill whispered. 'I can hear someone creeping up the drive. Perhaps it's the stranger with the paint-brush coming back to write some more notices!'

'You two go out of the front door and try to catch him that way. I'll go round by the back door,' said Uncle Ted.

The three separated and Jill edged open the front door of the cottage inch by inch. Barbie, following close behind, stifled a giggle. 'I can't see anyone,' she whispered.

Jill pointed across the yard. In the half-light of evening they could see a dark shape leaning a bicycle against the wall of the barn.

'Come on,' Jill whispered. 'Let's go.'

But Uncle Ted got there before them. He jumped out of the shadows and gripped the stranger firmly by the arm.

'W-w-what's this?' said the stranger in a startled voice.

'That's just what we'd like to know,' said Uncle Ted severely. 'You'd better explain what you're doing creeping around here.'

Uncle Ted pulled the stranger into the light. Jill and Barbie gasped in horror. It was the boy from the ironmonger's shop.

'Uncle,' said Jill, 'this is the boy who gave me the catalogue. I think there must be some mistake.'

'That's right,' said the boy, 'my name is Jim Trent and I just came to see if I could help.'

'Really?' said Uncle Ted suspiciously. 'Well, you'd better come inside then.'

Once inside, Uncle Ted began to look less severe. 'I'm sorry I jumped on you,' he said to Jim Trent. 'But we thought you'd come to write another threatening notice.'

Jill quickly told Jim about the notice and the red paint on the postman's hands. 'So we're on the look-out for my missing paint-brush,' she ended up.

'From what you've told me, it all points to Mrs Steel, the postmistress,' said Jim. 'She was the one who dropped that catalogue in my shop. I knew she'd been spreading unpleasant gossip about your Uncle here, so that's why I gave it to you. I thought it might explain why she was doing it.'

'It certainly does, Jim,' said Uncle Ted. 'Thanks for the tip. Jill had better cycle over to the holiday camp tomorrow and try to find out exactly what connection it has with Mrs Steel.'

'Well, I have to pass Mrs Steel's garden on my way home,' said Jim. 'Would it be any help if I just glanced in her tool shed? She might have the paint-brush...'

'Good idea!' said Jill impulsively, before her uncle had

time to voice his disapproval. 'See you in a minute!' she called, picking up her coat and hurrying Jim and Barbie out of the cottage.

A few minutes later, they were hurrying down towards the village. Jim left his bike in the narrow lane that ran behind the post office.

Mrs Steel's tool shed was built on to the fence bordering the lane, but the entrance to it was only from her garden.

'Wait here, and whistle if you hear anyone coming,' Jill whispered fiercely to Jim and Barbie. 'I'd recognise my paint-brush anywhere, even if it has had the paint cleaned off it.'

Jim stationed himself close to the fence, and Barbie watched the front, while Jill carefully pushed open the garden gate, slipped inside, then unbolted the door of the tool shed.

Jim shifted uneasily from foot to foot and watched the back window of the post office while Barbie looked down the lane. Suddenly Jim stiffened. Someone had opened the door from the post office into the back room and had switched on the light. They might come through into the garden at any moment!

'Whee-oo! Whee-oo!' Jim whistled, hoping it sounded like an owl to everyone else but Jill.

The door of the shed opened, Jill slipped out, bolted it and joined Jim and Barbie in the lane, just as a shaft of light cut across the garden from the back door. They stood there, too petrified to move, as a tall, gaunt figure — obviously Mrs Steel — stepped out into the garden, looked round suspiciously, then went back inside again.

They all breathed a deep sigh of relief when they heard the back door being sharply bolted.

'Phew!' breathed Jill. 'That was a close one. Let's move away from here. It was so dark in the shed, I didn't have a chance to find the brush.'

Jim collected his bicycle and they said goodbye, after thanking Jim for his help.

As Jill and Barbie were walking past the front of the post office on their way home, the door clicked open.

'Look out! Here comes trouble!' Barbie whispered.

Jill turned round quickly to find Mrs Steel coming out of the door with a spiteful grin on her face. 'I thought I saw you come into the village,' she said with sugary sweetness. 'Would you mind taking this telegram back to your uncle? It has just arrived and it looks rather important. Now you can't say I don't deliver your mail promptly,' she added, wagging a finger playfully. 'Goodnight to you!'

Jill turned the yellow envelope over in her hands. She dreaded taking it back to her uncle.

It was quite dark by the time Jill and Barbie got back to the hostel. They walked into the kitchen, Jill clutching the telegram nervously.

'Well, have you found the paint-brush?' asked Uncle Ted.

'No, but I was given *this* by the postmistress,' Jill said, handing over the yellow envelope. 'She looked so pleased about it, I'm afraid it must be bad news.'

Uncle Ted tore open the envelope and read the message out loud: 'ARRIVING TWO P. M. FRIDAY—TURNER.' — Suffering cats! That's all I needed!' he said, sinking into a chair.

'Why, Mr Holmes?' Barbie asked. 'Who is Turner?'

'He is the Director of this group of hostels. He'll be coming down to see how I'm getting on. It couldn't be at a worse moment. No wonder the postmistress looked so pleased! Turner will probably decide to close the hostel if he notices the bad feeling in the village.'

'He can't do that!' Jill protested. 'It wouldn't be fair. Any rate, we've got a day and a half before he's due to arrive.

We've just got to try and get this mystery sorted out by then.'

'Don't forget, Jill, I want you to cycle over to Paxton Holiday Camp for me in the morning. You can use my bicycle. We'll all have to make an early start tomorrow. We'd better get to bed right now.'

At seven o'clock the next morning, Jill was already halfway to Paxton. As she pedalled furiously down the lanes, the loveliness of the countryside almost made her forget the troubles and unpleasantness she had left behind.

'They're relying on me to sort this out,' she thought. 'I mustn't let them down!'

Barbie and Uncle Ted had been left hard at work distempering the inside of the cottage, starting in the hall, to make a good impression. 'It's the first impressions that count,' Uncle Ted had joked, trying to be cheerful.

Jill glanced at her watch, as she freewheeled down a short hill. 'Must be nearly there by now,' she thought. 'That looks like it, on the side of the next hill.'

She pushed hard on the pedals and looked warily ahead. 'I'm in "Injun" country now. Got to keep my eyes skinned.'

However, apart from a farm labourer driving a tractor, there didn't seem to be anyone about. Jill leant her bike against the fence surrounding the camp site. Now she had actually got there, she wasn't quite sure what she had to do. In the clear light of morning, the camp didn't look such an exciting place as the catalogue made it out to be.

A row of rather shabby caravans straggled up the hill, and from where Jill was standing there was certainly no 'sea view'.

'H'mm,' murmured Jill, watching a girl running down the hill with two large buckets, 'and I suppose that's the running water!'

The girl was hurrying towards her and Jill could see that she was tall and thin, about sixteen years old, with the same sort of severe expression on her face as that worn constantly by Mrs Steel, the postmistress. In fact, there was a definite likeness. 'I wonder...' murmured Jill to herself.

'Good morning!' Jill called out cheerfully.

'Oh! Oh!' The girl started and turned towards Jill. 'I didn't notice you standing there.'

'I wonder if you could help me,' Jill asked pleasantly.

'I'm looking for Mrs Steel. Do you know where I could find her?'

The girl looked at Jill suspiciously. 'My mother doesn't come here very often. But you can always find her at Floxton Post Office. She's postmistress there, you know.'

'Oh-oh, yes,' said Jill. 'Thank you. I'll try there.'

Feeling that she had found out all that the girl was likely to tell her, Jill started on her journey back to Highridge Hostel. Now, at last, she could understand why Mrs Steel did not want the hostel to be a success. She feared it would affect the holiday camp and her daughter's job there.

The journey back seemed to be much shorter. It wasn't long before Jill was once more leaning her bike against the wall of the cottage and rushing inside to tell her uncle and Barbie what she had found out.

She picked her way carefully over a pile of distemper buckets, dust sheets, rags and brushes and found the others still hard at work. They both 'downed' brushes and sat on the trestle-table while Jill told them her news.

'You were lucky to find that out,' said Uncle Ted. 'It explains a lot. I'm more worried for the moment about the state the cottage is in. Farmer Kent was so unpleasant about the footpath yesterday, I don't like to ask him a favour. But without ladders now we're absolutely sunk.' He pointed to the cracked and dirty ceiling of the hall. 'We won't even be able to give a good *first* impression.'

'I'll go over to Mr Kent's farm and see if he'll lend me some ladders,' said Jill, striding purposefully out of the back door.

'Good girl,' said Barbie. 'Don't be long. There's plenty to do here when you come back!'

When Jill knocked at the farm-house door, a rosy-faced woman answered it.

'Sorry, Farmer Kent isn't here just now. Can I help you?'

Jill explained her mission and the woman shook her head.

'I'm afraid I can't help you, my dear. But if you go down to the long meadow you'll find Farmer Kent there, helping with the marquees. He's organising tomorrow's village fête. I'm sure he'll lend you the ladders,' she added with a smile.

'Must be a record,' murmured Jill to herself, as she walked down to the meadows. 'That's the second friendly person I've met in this village!'

In the long meadow, everything was bustle and confusion. Red and white striped marquees were being put up. Long trailers were manoeuvring into position. The sound of men shouting, mallets hammering and engines roaring, filled the air.

Jill hurried across the meadow towards a small knot of people. She had no difficulty in picking out Farmer Kent. He was barking out orders in a gruff tone to the group around him.

Jill waited until the group had dispersed to their various jobs, then she walked up to Farmer Kent.

'Excuse me, sir,' she said. 'But I'm from Highridge Hostel and we urgently need some ladders. Do you think you could possibly lend us some?'

'What?' roared Farmer Kent, turning on her. 'Certainly not! Can't you see we need 'em? Now run along with you!'

'B-b-but, sir,' Jill stammered, 'it's very important —'

'Sorry, quite impossible,' said Farmer Kent sternly, and turned to talk to another helper.

Jill walked away dejectedly. There was nothing more she could do. She threaded her way slowly through the marquees and their tangled guy-ropes. She was just about to climb the stile and start on the path back to the hostel, when her attention was attracted by a rustling behind the hedge.

Jill peered through the branches, and saw the postman in his uniform, bent double. He was pushing what looked like a petrol can into a ditch under the hedge. Then he began to cover it up with branches and clumps of grass.

'That's very strange,' Jill murmured. 'Now I wonder what he's up to?'

Jill walked slowly back to the hostel, a puzzled frown on her face. Some instinct told her that this business of the postman and the petrol was vitally important. He was planning something that must be forestalled, or it would prove the final blow to their hopes of establishing the hostel. 'The more I think about it, the less I like it,' Jill murmured to herself. 'He's been up to no good ever since we came here, but just why would he be hiding a can of petrol?'

She stopped near the back-yard of the hostel, and leaned against a low wall, to think. The only other use for petrol, apart from running a car, or cleaning things, was... to burn things. Of course!

Jill gasped. That seemed the inevitable conclusion. The man was planning to burn something — but what? Surely not the hostel — why hide the petrol up near the long meadow?

Jill's mind was racing furiously. The long meadow. That was where the marquee was being erected. The only thing to burn up there was the marquee itself. But surely, if the postman planned to burn the marquee he must be mad. That wouldn't harm her uncle and his plans for the hostel. Suddenly, the truth dawned on her. Of course, the plot was to burn the marquee, and pin the blame on to her uncle and herself. This was to be the final blow — with the whole village roused in anger against them and a serious criminal act blamed on to them, they would be lucky to escape being charged with arson, and the hostel scheme would be finally doomed.

Jill turned round and began to race back to the long meadow again. At any moment now the marquee might go up in flames, and the farmer and the rest of the hands would remember that she had been there only a few minutes previously, asking for the loan of ladders. They would all see this as merely a pretence to cover her real motives. Unless she could expose the plot, and maybe even catch the postman red-handed, nobody would ever believe she was not guilty.

'I only hope I'm in time,' she thought, as she sped down the path. She cut across one corner of the field so that she wouldn't be seen entering the long meadow. This way she could slip behind the big marquee without being seen.

Jill looked about her. There was no one in sight. She glanced at her watch. It was fifteen minutes past one. Everyone must have gone home to lunch. She'd never have time to run back to the farm to fetch help.

She edged her way cautiously round the big marquee, then she stiffened. She could hear voices. One of them was certainly Farmer Kent. His gruff voice was unmistakable. Jill was just about to rush in and plead for his help when she recognised the voice of the second speaker. It was Mrs Steel, the postmistress and the hostel's enemy.

'I shall have to be clever about this,' Jill thought. 'If Mrs Steel has a chance to warn the postman, we'll never catch him red-handed. Farmer Kent will just think it's me being spiteful and nasty.'

Jill cleared her throat nervously and hurried into the marquee.

'Please come quickly, Mr Kent!' she said. 'One of your bulls is loose! He's just behind the small marquee. If you go round to the left now you'll head him off.'

The farmer muttered his thanks and hurriedly left the tent. Just as Mrs Steel went to follow him, Jill placed herself in front of the doorway and said: 'I'm afraid I've got some very sad news.'

'Oh?' The postmistress looked interested. 'About the hostel?'

'Yes. It looks as if my uncle will have to leave.'

Mrs Steel's eyes glinted with triumph. But suddenly the expression in them altered. Outside could be heard the noise of a scuffle, then Farmer Kent returned, gripping the postman tightly by his collar.

'Do you know what this scoundrel was about to do?' said Farmer Kent, shaking the postman like a puppy. 'He was about to set the marquee on fire! He had already soaked the canvas in petrol. I was only just in time to stop him. What have you got to say for yourself, fellow?'

'Nothing, sir,' said the postman sullenly. 'She made me do it.'

'She? Who is she?' Farmer Kent demanded.

'Mrs Steel, sir. She said we could blame it on the hostel people.'

'Oh, she did, did she?' Farmer Kent swung round angrily to face Mrs Steel, but the postmistress had already used the opportunity to slip out of the tent. 'Never mind, we'll sort that matter out later. Young miss, I'll see you up at the hostel later.'

Later that afternoon, Farmer Kent knocked at the hostel's front door and asked to speak to the warden.

'You two young ladies had better stay and hear what I have to say,' he said to Jill and Barbie. 'This is by way of being an apology to you from the whole village. I'm afraid we allowed ourselves to be led astray by Mrs Steel's spiteful tongue. She was always making up some story about Mr Holmes here, and I'm afraid that a lot of the time we believed her. I thought she really had the good of the village at heart when she said that hostellers would ruin the place. She even persuaded me to fence off that footpath,' said Farmer Kent shamefacedly. 'I still can't understand what made her do it.'

'I think it was because of her daughter,' said Jill.

'I'd almost forgotten about her. She doesn't come to the village very much.'

'Well, she works at Paxton Holiday Camp. I think Mrs Steel was frightened that a successful hostel would take business away from the camp.'

'Which is not true, of course,' Uncle Ted added, 'as hostels are for people without cars and tents. They're for quite a different sort of person, in fact.'

A clock struck six in the distance. 'Well, at this rate,' said Uncle Ted, looking about him at the mess of buckets and half-painted walls, 'it looks as if Mrs Steel is going to be successful.'

'What does that mean?' asked Farmer Kent.

Uncle Ted explained about the impending visit of the director of the hostels. 'With all this trouble, we haven't made much progress with the re-decorating.'

'Don't you worry,' said Farmer Kent. 'I'll get the boys here to help you.'

Within half an hour, six farm labourers were hard at work with the others re-decorating the hostel. Distemper was applied vigorously, the front flowerbeds were dug, broken windows repaired, cupboards mended, curtains hung.

At ten o'clock Uncle Ted sent Jill and Barbie to bed, but the men worked on. When the girls got up next morning the cottage looked entirely different.

Even though the work was not half-finished, the cottage had lost its dilapidated and rundown look. The front rooms looked clean and bright, with their yellow distempered walls, the windows shone, and the front door had been painted red.

The villagers did even more than their share to make amends. When the director eventually came down to make his tour of inspection, they crowded around the gates of the hostel and waved and cheered.

With this flattering reception and the trim look of the newly-decorated hostel, the director was duly impressed.

'You've really put the place on its feet,' he said, beaming at the two girls and Uncle Ted. 'And what's almost more important, you seem to have created a really good impression and secured the friendship of the local inhabitants. I shall make a special mention of this in my report.'

The two girls grinned happily, and Jill winked at Uncle Ted. The trouble at Highridge was over at last!

The Fiesta Intrigue

by Neil Rogers

The dark-skinned Spaniard behind the iron grille of the little bank gave Sheila Johnson a slightly suspicious look.

'I'm sorry, señorita,' he said coldly. 'I cannot change this cheque.' Sheila stared in surprise and shot a quick side glance at her companion, Lita.

'But why not?' she demanded. The clerk tapped the travellers' cheque which he had just pushed back under the grille. 'It has not been stamped by your bank at home. It is against the law for me to change it.'

Lita fumbled in her handbag and pulled out her own travellers' cheques. Both girls scanned them anxiously. Lita's cheques had not been stamped either.

They stared dolefully at each other as the truth of their plight came home to them. This was awful! They had arrived in Puerto, a little town on the Mediterranean the previous day, to spend a wonderful holiday celebrating Sheila's passing of her advanced Spanish exams. Lita Palmer her friend, was a South American girl and naturally spoke Spanish fluently. Together they had planned to have a holiday in Spain and to perfect Sheila's Spanish ready for her final honours exam in the autumn. Now here they were miles from home in a strange land and almost penniless.

'Well, it's a good thing our hotel bill was paid before we left England,' said Lita. 'But surely,' she pleaded, turning to the bank clerk, 'surely something can be done?'

'Not by me,' said the clerk, rather curtly. 'You must telegraph, or return your cheques. There have been too many attempts to evade the regulations.'

The girls left the little white building and went out into the blazing sunshine.

'I suppose he thinks we're acting for some crooks or something,' said Sheila indignantly.

Lita shrugged with typical Latin resignation.

'Who knows what he thinks?' she sniffed. 'But it would take ages to do what he suggests. What can we do in the meantime?'

They looked around the little Spanish square. It didn't look quite as cheerful now, Sheila thought. The gay colours of the women's dresses didn't seem to glow with the same brightness. The narrow, winding streets, lined with their quaint medieval houses and shady trees didn't seem quite so charming and inviting.

'I've got a few pesetas left,' said Sheila. 'Let's have a cool drink while we think this over. I've never been so hot in my life!'

They walked across the cobbled square to a little cafe. It had the name 'Mario' above the doorway. Outside, in the forecourt, were tables shaded by gay, coloured umbrellas. Only one table was occupied, and the man who sat at it was fast asleep.

'There aren't many people around, are there?' remarked Sheila.

'It's siesta time,' laughed Lita. 'Only us mad ones are out in the midday sun.'

'You can say that again,' replied Sheila, but she didn't really feel like joking.

'I say,' Sheila said, as they sat down, 'I read in a magazine about two girls getting jobs abroad as waitresses to learn the language. We both speak Spanish, so why don't we get jobs? It could be fun, and what better way to improve my Spanish?'

'We can try,' replied Lita brightly. 'It can't be so difficult!'

Just then a fat, genial Spaniard came out from the shop and

waddled across to their table. He wore a dazzling multi-coloured shirt as if to match the umbrellas.

'What can I get you, señoritas?' he asked in a deep booming voice.

'Two lime drinks, please,' replied Lita in Spanish.

His eyebrows shot up in surprise at her perfect accent. He smiled and waddled back into the cafe.

'Perhaps that's Mario,' whispered Sheila. 'He seems friendly. Let's ask him. He may need help, you never know!'

'All right. But it doesn't look very hopeful,' said Lita, nodding at the empty tables.

When Mario came back with their drinks, Lita said: 'We were wondering if you need extra staff during the next few weeks.'

Mario looked from one girl to the other in surprise.

'But you are tourists, señoritas! Why do you want jobs? You should be basking in the sun, not working — you are on holiday, no?'

'It's a case of necessity,' replied Lita, and explained their situation.

Mario nodded sympathetically.

'You see,' Lita concluded, 'we must get a job if we are going to continue our holiday.'

Mario nodded. 'I do not see how I can help you, señoritas,' he said.

'As you see, I have only a small café. I do not need staff. My wife and I can do all there is to be done.'

Sheila looked glumly at Lita. Lita shrugged. There was a moment of silence.

'I have an idea,' Mario said, his face creasing in a smile.

'Maybe I *can* help. In this town you have not that much chance.' He flicked his pudgy fingers together. 'But in the next town it should be different. My friend has a café and he will help, maybe! I will go and telephone him. You can but try!'

'Oh, good! Where is it?' cried the girls.

'In Soller de Mar. It is not far from here by bus. But you should not dress quite so much like — er — English tourists. Your Spanish is very good. If you dressed more like Spanish girls...'

'Oh, thank you so very much,' Lita said. 'You are a real amigo!'

Mario beamed with pleasure. 'For two such charming ladies in distress it is a privilege,' he said. 'Now, you get the bus in the square. It goes in about an hour. The café is in a little street called Rambla del Centro. It belongs to Antonio Delfores. Just say that Mario sent you. I will telephone him right away.'

'About these dresses,' said Sheila, as they hurried back to the hotel. 'We have no money to buy any. I have just about enough for the bus fare.'

'Let's take stock,' said Lita, as they ran up the steps of the hotel.

Once in their room, Sheila opened the wardrobe and took out a red and gold dress. Lita nodded approvingly.

'Yes. All we really need are shawls.'

'I'll ask the maids to lend us a couple,' said Sheila, hurrying to the door.

Half an hour later, two 'Spanish' girls hurried out of the hotel.

As they rounded the corner of the winding little street that led to the main square, they saw an ancient bus with Soller on the indicator board.

'Come on, Lita,' cried Sheila, 'hurry or we'll miss it.'

'And remember, speak nothing but Spanish from now on,' said Lita, as they broke into a run.

They clambered aboard the bus and twenty minutes later it bumped its way across a crowded square and pulled up with a violent jolt opposite the church. The driver called: 'Soller!'

The girls stepped down. Everything in the world seemed to be going on. The little houses and stalls were gay with flags and garlands. Everything was gay and festive!

'There must be the fiesta tonight,' said Lita.

'That's wonderful,' said Sheila, forgetting everything else for the moment.

'Let's find Rambla del Centro and see if we get a job, before we think about the fiesta,' laughed Lita.

'Come on then!' Sheila replied. In her excitement she spoke English. She realised her mistake immediately, and she saw a sallow-faced Spaniard give them a strange glance. He hesitated and was about to speak, but suddenly he hurried away, almost knocking over a stall that was loaded with fruit. The stall-holder yelled threats after him and shook his fist.

'I'm sorry, Lita,' Sheila whispered.

'Don't worry,' replied Lita, 'but stick to Spanish.'

'Can you tell me the way to the Rambla del Centro?' Lita said to the stall-holder.

The man shook his head. 'There is no street of that name in this town, señorita.'

'Are you sure?' asked Lita.

'Of course I am sure,' said the stall-holder, indignantly. 'I have lived here all my life. There is no such street.'

'That's odd,' muttered Sheila.

'Perhaps he's just unco-operative because we didn't want to buy anything,' said Lita.

She walked on a few paces, and asked again. This time she spoke to a señora.

But the lady only shook her head, then the light dawned suddenly.

'Ah, but yes — that is in Soller de Mar,' she said.

Now Lita looked blank. 'But this is Soller de Mar,' she said.

The lady shook her head again. 'Soller,' she corrected.

Lita groaned. 'I might have guessed,' she said to Sheila. 'We are in the wrong town. And I don't suppose there's another bus for hours!'

'Now what do we do?' asked Sheila, looking at Lita in dismay.

'Let's find out when the next bus leaves,' replied Lita, 'and how we get to Soller de Mar.'

'Do they have policemen in towns like this?' asked Sheila, looking around her at the medieval houses, cobbled streets, and busy square.

'I expect so, anyway we can ask someone,' replied Lita.

Suddenly from behind them came a voice: 'Can I help you, señoritas?'

They turned round to see the sallow-faced Spaniard who had given them the strange look when they arrived in Soller. Sheila didn't like the look of his eyes, they seemed to stare right through her, and she felt a cold shiver go down her spine.

'What is the matter, señoritas?' he repeated. 'You look lost! I am Corus Mentez. Can I help?'

Lita was the first one to pull herself together: 'Thank you. We wanted to know when the next bus leaves.'

Sheila noticed a curious expression flash across his face and he came closer. 'It does not leave until after the fiesta!' he whispered. 'So you will stay until it is over?'

Sheila gasped. She didn't know if his last few words were meant as a question, but they sounded like a threat.

'Yes, I suppose we will have to, but . . .' Lita's reply was cut short.

'Good, then it will be time!' he said sharply, and walked away into one of the narrow side streets between two tall white houses with balconies.

'Well, what do you make of that?' asked Sheila, when he

had disappeared. 'That was the strangest answer to a question. What could he mean?'

'I don't know,' replied Lita. 'It's a complete mystery to me.'

'It now looks as if we are stuck here until after the fiesta, so we'd better make the most of it,' said Sheila, dismissing the incident from her mind.

'Yes, I suppose so. After all, we are on holiday, aren't we?' replied Lita, brightening up. 'How much money have you got left?'

'About sixty pesetas.'

'Well, I don't know about you, but I think we should get something to eat, I'm hungry.'

'I don't know what we can get for sixty pesetas, I'm sure,' said Sheila, 'but let's try that little café over there.' She pointed to a café on the corner of the main square.

They walked across and took seats at one of the tables.

'It's a bad thing when you have to look at the prices rather than the food, isn't it?' said Sheila, as she studied the menu.

They ordered tortillas and drinks, then settled down to wait for the fiesta to start.

As the sun began to sink behind the hills and the dying rays made the white houses look crimson, lights began to come on in the windows of the houses. Sheila felt that the town was changing into a fairyland. The lights shining through the wrought-iron grilles across the windows made strange patterns on the cobbled square. People began to appear on the balconies that were gay with flowers.

Lita touched Sheila's arm. 'Look,' she said.

Sheila saw that several men in typical Spanish dress had built a huge bonfire in the square and were lighting it.

'The fiesta will be starting soon,' remarked Sheila, as they heard music in the background. The women were bringing out all kinds of food and putting it on long trestle tables. The bells of the ancient church began to chime and the torches, set at intervals around the square, were lit. They glittered in the velvety darkness, and people came jostling and laughing along the streets leading to the square.

Suddenly the thrilling rhythm of guitars and castanets momentarily stopped the gossip and chatter going on around the two girls.

Into the centre of the square leapt the figure of a young Spanish girl in a long red and white dress with a black lace shawl.

She stood still for a moment in the flickering firelight and then, as the guitars struck a note, she began to dance, slowly at first, the castanets at her fingertips echoing her every movement. As the rhythm of the guitars increased into tempo, she began to whirl round and round the square.

Sheila and Lita sat enthralled by this sight of real Spanish splendour.

There were cries of 'Olé!' from every side, as the people began to get caught up in the festive spirit. Soon nearly everyone was dancing to the thrilling rhythms.

'Come on, we'd better move,' Lita whispered to Sheila, 'before we get dragged into the dancing as well, and I, for one, can't dance that way.'

'Let's go round to the tables and see if we can get something to eat,' Sheila replied. 'I don't know about you, but I'm still starving.'

As if in reply, Lita got up and began to walk round the square to the heavily laden tables.

They were offered as much food as they could eat, and soon they retired to a seat under some trees in the shadows, so they could watch the celebrations without being conspicuous.

'I'm glad we didn't get asked to dance,' Sheila giggled, 'because I'd feel rather silly trying to waltz to this music.'

'Yes, I agree...,' Lita broke off. 'Don't look now, but that man who calls himself Corus Mentez — you know, the one we asked about the bus — has spotted us. He's coming over.'

The sallow-faced Spaniard stopped in front of them and bowed.

'I hope the señoritas are enjoying themselves,' he said, with a flicker of a smile on his lips.

'We are,' replied Sheila in Spanish. 'Thank you very much!'

'Good!' He smiled broadly, showing his white teeth. 'But remember to watch for the signal... then it will be time.'

He bowed again and walked away towards the dancers.

'What did he mean by that?' Lita asked, when he was out of earshot.

'I've no idea,' replied Sheila. 'Perhaps he realises we're not Spanish and is playing a joke.'

Lita didn't reply for a few seconds, and Sheila looked at her in surprise. 'What's the matter?' she asked.

'Well, do you remember he said "then it will be time" when we asked him about the bus?'

'Yes, I remember! I remarked on it,' Sheila said, laughing at Lita's seriousness.

'Look!' cried Lita, clutching Sheila's arm. 'He's going into that big house on the right of the square.'

'What's strange about that?' replied Sheila, looking across at the man.

He stepped on to the top step, turned and looked in their direction, then hurried inside. 'I don't know what you're getting so worked up about,' Sheila continued. 'You're making too much of this — I still think he's playing a joke on us!'

'Well,' said Lita slowly, 'I don't think it's as simple as that.'

'What do you mean?' said Sheila, puzzled.

'I think he's got us muddled up with somebody else!'

'That could happen to anybody,' laughed Sheila.

'If he was expecting someone, why didn't he say? Probably because it's a secret. And that's not all — there must be a meeting or something, or why would he ask us to watch for the signal? You can be sure that something funny's going on here tonight, and we're in the middle of it.'

Sheila gasped. Lita was deadly serious.

'You don't really think...' she began.

'I do — and what's more, I think we'd better keep our eyes open for the signal — whatever it's going to be!'

Sheila sat silent for a moment, her mind in a whirl. Could Lita be right? Had they become involved in a mystery? It certainly looked like it.

'Well, we can only sit tight and wait,' she whispered to Lita.

Half an hour later, nothing had happened, and Sheila began to think Lita had been mistaken when, from the roof of the building they had seen Corus Mentez enter, she saw a torch being waved slowly backwards and forwards.

'That must be the signal,' cried Sheila. 'What do we do?'

'I don't know,' replied Lita. 'Let's wait and see if anything happens.'

They watched the house, and Sheila saw three men enter, and a few minutes later two more climbed the steps and disappeared into the dark interior.

'Come on,' Lita said suddenly, getting to her feet.

'What are you going to do?' asked Sheila in a worried tone.

'It must be a meeting. I'm going to find out what this is all about. Let's go and join the others,' Lita replied, as she began to walk in the direction of the big house. Sheila scrambled up and followed her. Together they went up the steps and entered the hall.

'What do we do now?' whispered Sheila, trying to see in the semi-dark.

Lita was about to reply when a voice said: 'Follow me.'

The girls started and heard the door creak shut behind them, cutting off all the noise from the fiesta.

'It's like being in a vault,' thought Sheila, and wanted to turn and rush to the door.

There was silence for a moment, then, as a torch flared, the girls managed to see the owner of the voice.

He was short and stocky, wearing a red shirt and a sombrero. Round his left wrist was a leather thong that hung down by his knees. He looked at them with coal-black eyes, his face stern and set. Slowly it slackened, and he smiled, and then began to laugh.

'Do not look so worried, señoritas,' he said, still laughing.

Sheila was about to say something, then she caught a warning glance from Lita.

'Follow me,' the Spaniard said, walking towards the stairs.

They were about halfway up when a door opened, sending a shaft of light across the hall. In the doorway a man stood silhouetted.

'Is it them, Juan?' he asked.

'It is,' replied the doorman, continuing to climb the stairs.

'Good — we are all here now.'

'What do we do?' whispered Sheila.

'I don't quite know — but we must pretend we do,' Lita answered in a low voice.

Sheila held her breath, as they reached the top of the stairs and made their way along the landing towards the open door. She clutched Lita's arm and they paused on the threshold of the lighted room.

'Come along in — we haven't much time.' A fat man behind a desk at the far end of the room spoke.

Sheila looked around and saw that there were five men in the room, all dressed the same as Juan. Behind the man at the desk stood the sallow-faced Corus Mentez.

'Close the door, Juan,' said the fat man, as the two girls came forward.

Sheila felt her heart leap as Juan closed the door and stood with his back to it. They were trapped. One false move and...

'Now, down to business,' continued the fat man, a smile coming across his podgy face. 'The raid is set for tonight and you are to take the message to our friends in Puerto. The police must not suspect anything, and the message must arrive before dawn. Is that clear?'

The girls nodded blandly.

'Good — we strike one hour after the sun sets tomorrow, and our friends must be ready at all costs!'

He paused and beckoned the girls over to the desk.

Sheila risked a quick glance at Lita, and saw that she was tight-lipped, but looking straight ahead as if nothing odd was happening.

'Here are the plans.' The fat man lifted a map and some papers out of a drawer and placed them on the desk. 'If you are stopped going to the Rambla Velazquez you have your story ready... you are simply returning from the fiesta.' He clipped the papers to the map and handed it to Lita. 'The house of Miguel Carrosa is being watched by the police, so go in the back way. Here is your payment.' He stood up and handed a pile of notes to her. 'You will receive the rest when you have completed the mission — successfully! That is all. Juan, show the señoritas out.'

In a matter of minutes, the girls were back in the square again. The fiesta was beginning to die down, but there was still a good deal of activity. The girls hurried to get away from the crowds.

'Phew! Just you tell me what was going on back there,' said Sheila, when they were clear of the square.

'I don't know for sure,' replied Lita, 'but I think we have

just been in the presence of Paco Martinez, the famous bandit, and been mistaken for his messengers.'

'Oh, no... it can't be true,' gasped Sheila. 'I was reading, about him in the papers this morning. He's a wanted man, by the account of it.'

'Yes, that's right, I saw it, too, and recognised him from the description they gave. We must catch the bus to Puerto, and instead of going to Miguel Carrosa, go to the police and warn them of the raid.'

Half an hour later, the girls climbed out of the ancient bus into the silent main square of Puerto.

'I wonder where the police station is,' Lita said.

'I don't know, but there must be a policeman somewhere around,' replied Sheila, looking about her.

Suddenly she caught Lita's arm. 'Look over by that café,' she whispered urgently. 'It's that Spaniard, Corus Mentez. He's watching us!'

'You're right,' said Lita. 'One false move now and we've had it!'

'Pretend we haven't seen him, and walk away.'

The two girls walked across the square away from the café.

'Can you see if he's following us?' whispered Sheila.

As they turned down one of the narrow little side streets, Lita glanced over her shoulder.

'We can't go to the police now he's following us. One of us had better try to give him the slip while the other goes on to Miguel Carrosa.'

The girls walked on in silence, their footsteps echoing in the narrow street between the tall houses.

'When I give the signal,' Lita said, 'you slip off and make for the police station.'

'What about you?' gasped Sheila. 'If they find...'

'Let's just hope they don't. I'll say you led the police off

'We can't go to the police now he's following us.'

on a wild goose-chase when they stopped and questioned us.'

'All right...' Sheila stopped talking and stood still.

'Listen,' she said. 'Can you hear anything?'

'Not a thing,' replied Lita. 'Why?'

'Don't you see? We can't hear the Spaniard's footsteps,' cried Sheila. 'He can't be following us any more.'

'He may have stopped when we stopped,' Lita replied cautiously.

'I'll risk a glance behind,' said Sheila. She held her breath and turned. No one was in sight.

'Phew!' she said. 'He didn't follow us after all.'

'We are probably going in the right direction for the Rambla Velazquez, and he thought we were in the clear. What a slice of luck.'

Together the girls walked on down the street to another square.

Suddenly out of one of the side streets came a policeman. Quickly the two girls ran across to him.

'Can you take us to the police station? It's urgent!' Lita said. 'We have news of Paco Martinez.'

The policeman needed no more asking, and hurriedly led them to the station.

They were ushered into the office of the inspector, and they told him the story in detail. When they had finished, Lita produced the plans and put them on his desk.

'This looks like our chance to catch him at last,' he muttered, when he had studied them. 'He obviously got two strange girls to take the message because he knows that if one of his men came here we would pick him up. What's more, they held this under cover of the fiesta because if his men came in from the hills on a normal occasion they would be easily recognised. The real messengers probably made the same mistake as yourselves and went to the wrong town. I can see the whole thing clearly now.'

Within half an hour, the whole station was a hive of activity.

In the middle of the chaos the inspector came over to the girls.

'I have a favour to ask you,' he said. 'Will you go to Miguel Carrosa and give him the plans?'

'What?' gasped the girls together.

'I know it is a lot to ask, but we must try to catch the whole band when they raid the town. This is the chance we have been waiting for, and if you go to him as if nothing has happened, they'll follow the plan and we can catch them red-handed.'

'Is it all right with you?' Lita asked, turning to Sheila.

'Yes,' replied Sheila, her heart in her mouth.

'Good! When you have done this, go straight to your hotel; they must suspect nothing. I will come and see you when it is all over.'

'Perhaps you can do something for us,' Lita said. 'Our travellers' cheques were not stamped by our bank at home, so we are stranded without any money. I wonder if you could help us?'

'I will make enquiries and let you know,' the inspector replied. 'As the English say — one good turn deserves another. Now you must be on your way.'

The inspector explained the way to the Rambla Velazquez, and let them out of the back entrance to the station.

Soon, without any more incidents, they reached the Rambla Velazquez.

'This is it!' whispered Sheila, 'I'm shaking in my shoes.'
'Well, if anything happens, just act as though you expected it.'

The girls found Miguel Carrosa's house, the largest in

the tree-lined street, walked round to the back and knocked at the door.

There was a sound of hurrying footsteps and the bar being lifted.

Then slowly the door opened and a little, rat-like Spaniard looked out.

'Who are you?' he demanded.

'We are from Paco Martinez,' Lita said, her voice steady.

'Ah,' he murmured, 'you are here at last! Come in.'

They stepped into a large hall that led to the front of the house.

'Miguel is not here. He is out at a meeting, but I was told to collect the plans and instructions. You have them?'

'Yes — here you are,' said Sheila, handing over the material.

'Good — here is your payment.' The little Spaniard handed a packet to Lita.

'Now we must leave,' said Lita, carefully placing the packet in her pocket.

'But you are to wait until Miguel returns!'

Sheila felt her heart thumping... She wanted to turn and rush to the door, but she knew their only hope was bluff.

'Paco has other work for us to do,' she said boldly. 'We must go.'

The man hesitated at the name of his leader, and Lita, seeing they had a slight advantage, pressed home the point.

'It is an order we cannot disobey, neither can you. Now we go!'

She turned, pulled open the door and stepped outside with Sheila close behind.

When they reached the hotel they hurried up to their room and threw themselves on the beds, exhausted.

The girls got up late and, not daring to go out, sat in the hotel lounge, waiting to hear from the inspector. But it was not until late in the evening that the inspector finally arrived.

He walked over to them and sat down. 'We rounded up the whole gang and have them safely under lock and key. I must thank you again for what you did!'

'We didn't have much trouble,' Lita said, and she told him all that had happened.

'Here is the remains of the money they gave us,' Sheila said, handing over the packet of notes.

'And that reminds me,' the inspector laughed, 'I have been to the bank and arranged for you to draw some money. If you go down with your passports tomorrow morning it'll be all right!'

Next day, as they were leaving the hotel for the bank, a page-boy came up with two large boxes addressed to them.

When they opened them they both gave gasps of surprise, for inside each box was a magnificent Spanish dress and a card with the words: '*With the compliments of the Police Department of Puerto, for your assistance.*'

The Secret Search

by Anne Wade

Debbie's hand was shaking with excitement as she lifted the phone. Twice she made a mistake in dialling her friend Sheila's number. Finally, when Mr Masters, Sheila's father, answered Debbie was almost dancing with impatience.

'It's Debbie Thompson, Mr Masters,' she said. 'May I speak to Sheila, please?'

'Well, she's around somewhere,' said Sheila's father. 'I'll call her.'

Debbie heard Mr Masters's voice shout for Sheila and a moment later Sheila was on the phone. 'Hello, Debbie.'

'Sheila!' cried Debbie. 'Listen. My father says we can go on a special spring holiday to Devon. The place sounds wonderful — and there's a terrific secret that I can't tell you about yet. You *must* persuade your parents to let you come...'

Sheila gave a gasp of surprise and leaned against the hall table. 'You couldn't explain all that slowly in words of one syllable, could you?' she said, laughing.

Debbie groaned. 'I can't explain it all on the phone,' she said. 'Can I come round?'

'Of course,' said Sheila. 'Come right after lunch.'

'That's fine,' said Debbie, 'but ask your father if we can both go on a holiday before we start summer term at the Secretarial College. 'Bye.'

Sheila wandered away from the phone in a puzzled daze. 'What was all that about?' Mr Masters asked her.

Sheila told him and Mr Masters looked thoughtfully at the ceiling. 'H'm!' he said. 'This certainly is the time of year one's thoughts turn to holidays — yet they still seem a long way off... anyway, we'd better hear more about it.'

Not far away, in the Thompson house in North London, Debbie had put down the phone and sunk back in the worn leather armchair.

* * *

A few days previously her father, Professor Thompson, had collapsed, exhausted through overworking in a desperate attempt to make ends meet. It had seemed certain that his old house would have to be sold at last. Old Mrs Kelly, the part-time housekeeper the Professor had employed ever since Debbie's mother died, would have to leave. The Professor would have to go to a nursing home... and Debbie? Well... as Debbie was wondering just what would happen to her, her father had called her to his room.

He was sitting up in bed peering over some old books and papers, and a recent copy of a journal read only by dealers in rare books and antiques.

He looked up, strained and tired, but with a cheerful twinkle in his eye.

Professor Thompson handed Debbie a musty old book with a broken back and tattered corners. She could just read the worn gold lettering on it: 'The History of Kingsbury Hall'.

Debbie raised her eyebrows slightly. Kingsbury Hall was in Devonshire and had once belonged to her grandfather. If it had not been for her Uncle Harry, Kingsbury Hall would still have belonged to the family. Grandfather Thompson had left the estate to Uncle Harry, trusting him to manage it and share the income with her father because he didn't want to see the estate split up.

But Uncle Harry was a waster — and Debbie's father did not see much income.

'Why are you going over all that sad old ground again?' asked Debbie.

'Sit down, Debbie,' said Professor Thompson. 'You know all about the old trouble that arose because Grandfather trusted your Uncle Harry. But, what you *don't* know is that Harry and I had trouble long before he sold up the estate. Your grandfather said, before he died, that I could take any of the old books and papers from the Hall. Harry objected violently — claiming that everything belonged to him. I put some old documents in a hiding place in the oak panelling in the library, and never thought about them again until yesterday.'

Professor Thompson picked up the journal and tapped at an open page. 'Here is an American collector advertising a high price for documents relating to a certain, little-known seventeenth century scholar — a man who was driven to flee to America because of his beliefs. He was a man years ahead of his time. He came from Kingsbury and his name was Jonathan Steele.'

'Those documents you left in the panelling!' cried Debbie. 'They weren't...'

Professor Thompson nodded. 'They were Jonathan Steele's papers. They could be worth several thousand pounds. The Hall has been made into an hotel now. I don't know what changes have been made, but there is a good chance that the documents are still there. Debbie, I'm ready to stake everything I've got to send you to that hotel for a holiday and to search for those papers!'

Debbie went round to the Masters' house, and after explaining to Sheila the real reason behind their holiday, they went together to talk to her parents. They readily agreed to the trip. Mr Masters was even a little envious.

'It sounds a grand place,' he said, flicking through the

brochure of the new Kingsbury Hall Hotel, Debbie showed him. 'A cross between a delightful old country hall, a good hotel, a super holiday camp... I see they even have their own riding stables, chalets, private beach...'

The next few days were one whirl of exciting preparations. Debbie had to get new clothes, make arrangements with Mrs Kelly to look after the house, buy tickets and wire the hotel and, finally, arrange for her father to go to Doctor Bardock's clinic for a few weeks.

She felt rather sad and wistful when the doctor called for her father on the following Friday evening. Until she had watched him struggle down the steps to the waiting car, she had never quite realised how frail and ill her father had become. But she waved cheerily as the car drew off, though her eyes were misty with tears as she turned indoors. She was only too glad that she was to spend the night at Sheila's home.

Neither of the girls slept much that night. They sat up late looking over the old history book and the Professor's notes, trying to memorise as much as they could.

'All we know is that the library was on the second floor, and that the hiding place was in the panelling in one of the side walls,' said Debbie. 'I expect they've made the library into a series of smaller guest rooms, but Daddy hopes that the end one will have retained the original panelling, and that no one will have discovered the tiny concealed cupboard.'

They talked over the matter until they could keep their eyes open no longer. But it seemed hardly five minutes before Mrs Masters was calling them down to breakfast, and then they were being rushed off to the station in Mr Masters's car.

'Now don't forget,' said Mr Masters, shouting above the noise as the train began to pull out, 'send me a wire to say you've arrived safely.'

'We will! Goodbye, Daddy,' called Sheila, and as the train gathered speed, she sank back, saying: 'Oh, Debbie! Isn't this wonderful? Off on our own on a secret mission. I'm sure I shall wake up in a minute!'

The Kingsbury Hall Hotel was all that the brochure claimed. Debbie and Sheila were very tired when they arrived that evening, but a charming young hostess, Miss Redfern, soon settled them in a pleasant room on the first floor. They had a quick impression of a magnificent old hall, completely modernised, and with deep thick-piled carpets. After supper they went to bed and made up for sleep lost the previous night.

The next morning, feeling fresh and keen to start the search, they wandered around, trying to get their bearings.

'Let's go over to the little bridge by the lake,' said Debbie, 'we can look at the Hall from there.'

* * *

From the little bridge they surveyed the scene. The hotel stood on gently rising ground, with smooth lawns sweeping up from the lake, to a broad stone terrace. It still looked old and dignified, but the ivy had been trimmed and all the paintwork was now gleaming white. On either side were woods and, beyond, a path through the trees led to the cliffs and a little sheltered bay.

'It's the inside changes that matter to us,' said Debbie. 'We must go in and find a way to wander about upstairs without attracting too much attention.'

The ground floor of the hotel was now one huge lounge. Two great fireplaces stood, one at each end, and around these were grouped armchairs and small tables.

Leading straight up to the first floor from this lounge was

a magnificent old staircase — at its head, a long gallery-like corridor ran the length of the building.

'Ah, good morning,' said the bright, pleasant voice of Miss Redfern, as Debbie and Sheila made their way across the lounge. 'Have you decided what to do on the first day of your holidays?'

'We should rather like to explore the hotel,' said Debbie promptly. 'Sheila and I are very interested in old houses!'

Miss Redfern nodded. 'It has a most interesting history,' she said. 'We have a short booklet on it. I'll let you have one!'

Miss Redfern's office was on the first floor, and Debbie and Sheila began to follow her. But, suddenly, Debbie seized Sheila's arm and whispered:

'Get the booklet and bring it to our room. I must go!'

Sheila turned in surprise — to see her friend streaking like a hare for the staircase. Debbie was out of sight along the gallery before Sheila could do so much as gasp.

Miss Redfern looked mildly surprised when she returned with the booklet. 'What's happened to Miss Thompson?' she asked.

'I think she forgot something,' Sheila stammered.

When Sheila reached their room again, she found Debbie staring anxiously out of the window.

'Debbie, what is it?' asked Sheila, but Debbie just went on staring through the window.

'I saw my Uncle Harry in the lounge,' she said, after a moment. 'I haven't seen him since I was quite small, but I've seen many photos of him.'

'Did he recognise you?'

'I didn't give him the chance,' said Debbie. 'But if he's staying here, he will notice my name and see the family likeness. But, Sheila, he must be here for the same reason we are!'

'Now what are we going to do?' wailed Sheila in despair.

Debbie suddenly pointed. 'He's going,' she cried. 'Look!'

Sheila peered through the window. Below, on the terrace, was a burly man of about fifty. His hands were thrust in the side pockets of a rough tweed jacket, as he strode round the side of the hotel.

'Sheila, we must find out if he's actually staying here,' said Debbie.

She turned from the window, her pretty face set in a frown as she thought hard for her next move. Sheila stood staring down at the terrace, and presently she cried: 'He *is* staying! He's coming back — and there's a man with his luggage!'

'That settles it!' said Debbie, dashing to the window.

Sure enough, there was Uncle Harry, striding along with a porter close behind him.

'Sheila, go and find out which room he has. Perhaps I can keep out of his sight for a day or two while we try to find the papers. Hurry!'

Sheila went out in time to see the porter take Uncle Harry's bags to the room at the opposite end of the corridor beyond the main staircase.

'Now, Sheila,' said Debbie, 'I'm going to be ill for a few days.'

'Ill?' said Sheila.

'Yes,' said Debbie firmly. 'It's the only way. You must tell Miss Redfern that I want my meals sent up.'

When Miss Redfern heard Sheila's news she came up at once. Debbie was lying on a couch with a travelling-rug over her.

'I'm very sorry,' the hostess said. 'What seems wrong? Would you like a doctor?'

Debbie's voice sounded faint, but not too gloomy, as she replied: 'I don't think so. Perhaps the journey and the change upset me. If I have some rest, I shall be all right, I'm sure.'

Debbie was a good little actress, and there was nothing so very unreasonable about the idea. Miss Redfern nodded reassuringly. 'Of course, you do that,' she said. 'Your friend can always come for me.'

'Oh,' said Debbie, when Miss Redfern had left. 'She's so sweet, I feel awful about tricking her... but I must keep out of Uncle Harry's way and try to find the papers if I possibly can.'

Sheila nodded. 'Don't worry, Debbie,' she said loyally. 'I'll help. You do the thinking and I'll do the spying!'

'Now, listen,' said Debbie. 'Take the booklet and pretend to be exploring the second floor. Find out all you can!'

When Sheila had gone, Debbie paced restlessly about the room. It was awful to be pinned down like this when her search had hardly begun. Sheila was willing and helpful — but Debbie knew it would take both of them all their time and wits.

Suddenly, there was a discreet tap at the door. Debbie jumped back on the couch and pulled the travelling-rug over herself.

The door opened and a maid came in with a glass of warm milk.

'Miss Redfern thought you might like this, miss,' the girl said, with a sympathetic smile.

'How very kind,' said Debbie. 'Thank you very much,'

'If there's anything else you want, the maids' pantry is only just along the corridor. Press number six on your house phone — that connects with the maid on duty.'

Debbie murmured her thanks again, but she was hardly able to keep up her act. The maid's entry had reminded her that all maids in the hotel wore neat, green uniform overalls and caps. Debbie had seen them hanging in the maids' pantry when some of the girls were off duty. With luck and daring, she could find an outfit her size and...

Debbie waited a few seconds, then lifted the house phone, pressing down number six button.

When the maid answered, Debbie said: 'Would you kindly go down to Miss Redfern and ask her to let me have another booklet about the hotel? I'd like to read it.'

Debbie went to the door and, through a tiny opening, watched the maid go off down the corridor. Then she moved swiftly — and when the maid returned with the booklet, Debbie was on the couch again — but, beneath the travelling-rug she had a uniform overall and cap.

When the maid had put the booklet down and tip-toed out again, Debbie jumped off the couch and tried on the overall and cap. She studied herself thoughtfully in the mirror and decided that she would pass.

Her heart was thumping when she reached the door — but she went out boldly along the corridor.

From her study of the brochure, Debbie knew that the second floor was reached by smaller flights of stairs at either end of the corridor. At one end was Uncle Harry's room — so, naturally, she chose the other end. But, when she peered round at the stair, her heart sank — two maids and a young lad were busy sorting out the laundry.

There was only one thing to do — walk the length of the corridor and round by Uncle Harry's room.

Debbie was tempted to abandon the plan until late that night, but she knew it would be useless in the dark, and so steeled herself not to break into a wild run.

Just as she reached the other end of the corridor a door opened, and a deep grating voice said, 'Hey, miss! I've been ringing for five minutes. Come in here. I want you to get me...'

With luck and daring, Debbie could find a maid's outfit her size...

Debbie didn't hear the rest of the sentence. She knew without turning, that it was her Uncle Harry. But she forced herself to realise that she was not yet trapped, and decided on a bold move. She put on a rueful look, and with drooping head she turned and spoke in a vague brogue: 'I'm sorry, sir. We've all been busy with the laundry.'

Uncle Harry lurched into his room without looking at her very closely — one maid was much like another to him.

'That's no excuse,' he grumbled.

He went to the writing table which, as Debbie noticed, was covered with sheets of hotel note-paper on which he had been making sketches and plans. He sat down heavily and growled: 'You have a booklet — a guide and history of the place?'

Debbie's heart lightened — if that was what he wanted, she could give him her own.

'I could easily get you one of those, sir,' she said.

Debbie went out, took her booklet from her overall pocket, and after a short wait, returned and laid it on the desk beside her uncle. He was too busy with his scribbling to do more than give a vague grunt. Debbie noticed with glee that he was clearly working on the idea of a search on the third floor. One paper was marked: '*John's study was here until he went to London*'. John was her father's name. So Uncle Harry was off to a false start!

Next minute Debbie was up the stairs and joining Sheila, who was wandering around the second floor.

Sheila gaped in surprise when she saw Debbie. 'What on earth... she said.

'Not so loud,' said Debbie. 'Have you found anything?'

'Yes,' said Sheila. 'The library hasn't been converted entirely into guest rooms! There are rooms at either end of the corridor here, but in the middle there is one big room.'

'Let's go and take a look at it straightaway,' said Debbie.

Midway along the corridor, they came to a huge double door. Sheila turned a massive brass handle and the girls slipped inside the room.

Debbie looked around. She was in a large, high room with a lot of objects all stacked neatly in the centre and draped with dust sheets. The wall on the far side was almost entirely taken up with windows, set in a deep bay. This wall was panelled in dark wood — and the wall behind her was panelled, too. But the side walls were just bare plaster.

'Of course,' she exclaimed, after a moment's thought, 'they chopped bits from either side of this large room to make guest rooms, as it were.'

Sheila nodded, but looked glum. 'If the panelling was on the side wall, it's probably been chopped up for firewood,' she said.

Debbie shook her head, and looked more optimistic. 'That old panelling would be too valuable. They must have planned to put the pannelling back again at some time. I bet some of that stuff in the middle of the floor *is* the panelling. Let's look!'

'It's here,' Debbie cried triumphantly. 'Look, panelling all stacked up. If the documents are anywhere they are somewhere in this pile!'

'Debbie,' exclaimed Sheila, 'it would take a week to shift all that stuff!'

'Don't be so gloomy,' laughed Debbie. 'We've been lucky so far — we may be lucky again. But, I think we should get back to our room now and wait until tonight.'

They hurried back to their room.

After a special tea, sent up by Miss Redfern, they rested until eleven o'clock.

'Come on, Sheila,' said Debbie at last. 'It's now or never.'

They crept out into the corridor and made for the second floor.

The old library looked strangely different. A bright moon shone through the high windows, casting weird beams of pale light on to the shrouded objects in the middle of the floor.

Debbie switched on her torch and a beam of light cut through the deep shadows and played around the pile of sheeted objects.

Debbie walked towards the pile. Slowly they worked their way round it, examining every object on the outside.

Suddenly Debbie bent down and made a careful study of some pieces of panelling.

'Have you found something?' asked Sheila.

'Perhaps,' said Debbie. 'Look here, Sheila. These panels aren't all alike. They have shields with various coats of arms on them, and slightly different patterns in the carving. Now, at the top of the panels that are still up on the walls there are shields and coats of arms. I noticed them this afternoon. I think I know now how we may be able to work out which panel we want!'

'But how?' asked Sheila.

Debbie was about to explain when they heard the sound of voices in the corridor.

'Put your torch out,' Sheila whispered to Debbie. For a few seconds they stood there in the darkness, while the voices grew louder, and Debbie saw a thin sliver of light as the library door opened...

She heard Miss Redfern's voice saying: 'I don't think you could have seen any lights in here, Johnson.'

'That may be, miss,' came the night porter's voice, 'but there's nothing like making sure.'

'Quick! Get under the dust sheets,' Debbie hissed to Sheila. They scrambled under the dust sheets seconds before the beams of two torches cut through the gloom, as Miss Redfern and the porter slowly circled the room.

'Nothing,' said Miss Redfern. 'However, I commend you, Johnson, and just to be on the safe side, I think we'd better lock the door when we go.'

'That's done it,' Debbie breathed in Sheila's ear.

They heard the sound of retreating footsteps, the dull click of the massive lock. Then a black, heavy silence engulfed them as they crept from beneath the dust sheets. It was getting cold now, and Sheila was shivering.

'We shan't need to pretend we're ill, if we ever get out of here,' she said dismally. 'We *shall* be!'

'There are two ways out of here,' said Debbie thoughtfully. 'The door — and that's locked. And the window!'

'They both sound impossible,' said Sheila.

But Debbie was already moving over to the high windows, studying them carefully.

'We could open this window,' said Debbie, 'and get out on to that ledge. Then it's not far to the window of the next guest room. If the guest room window is open, we could get through and into the corridor again.'

'Suppose it isn't open? Suppose somebody is in there?' said Sheila.

Debbie laughed softly. 'Well, suppose all that, and where does it leave us — still stuck in here with the door locked. So we must try it.'

She swung the window open, and clambered out on to the broad stone ledge.

The moon was shining brightly, and Debbie could see quite clearly that the guest-room window was open a few inches.

'That's it, then,' she said to Sheila. 'The ledge is broad enough and you can cling on to the ivy. The room may not be used at this time of the year. I'm going over. Can you follow me?'

'Yes,' said Sheila shakily.

'Don't look down — that's all,' said Debbie, and she edged along the ledge, clutching the thick ivy.

Sheila watched anxiously and sighed with relief as Debbie stepped across to the ledge by the guest-room window, slipped her hand inside and opened it... Next second, Sheila was out on the ledge herself, moving towards Debbie, who stood at the window, waiting...

'Is there anyone asleep in here?' Sheila whispered as Debbie helped her inside.

'Don't know,' breathed Debbie, 'and I'm not keen to find out. Let's find the door.'

In a few moments, they were back in their room again, and it was not long before Sheila was fast asleep; but Debbie could not take her mind from her problems.

They had left the library window open — would someone see it? How could they get back into the library to continue the search? How long could she keep up her pretence of illness? How soon would Uncle Harry learn of Debbie Thompson?

Debbie's mind was in a whirl, but she fell asleep at last.

At about eight o'clock, Sheila awoke to find Debbie shaking her gently.

'What now?' said Sheila, sitting up.

'Right after breakfast, you go to Miss Redfern,' said Debbie. 'Tell her I'm better, but that I've decided to stay in bed for the day. Then you must somehow persuade her to let you look round the library. Try to close the side window, but the chief thing is this — look at all the shields and coats of arms over the panelling at either end of the room. Draw a rough picture of each one, and bring your notes to me.'

Just before lunch Sheila returned, dusty but triumphant.

'I did something clever...' Sheila said, 'the sort of thing you usually think of. I didn't lock the library door again before I took the key back!'

'Good for you, Sheila,' cried Debbie.

'Well, here are the sketches,' said Sheila.

'There are eight shields on the wall where the doors are, and eight along by the windows...'

She showed Debbie her notebook. 'The first shield has crossed swords and a helmet, see? The next one has a Tudor Rose and a motto. The third...'

'But you've only drawn eight shields', said Debbie. 'What about the others?'

'I didn't bother,' said Sheila, 'not after the first one — I realised that the other eight were just the same!'

Debbie let out a whoop of joy. 'That's what I was hoping,' she cried.

'Well, just what does it mean?' asked Sheila.

'I'm sure it means that all four walls of the library had these same eight crests over each section of panelling,' said Debbie, 'and Daddy told me that the concealed cupboard was in the third or fourth section on the east wall. Now,' she added triumphantly, 'what crests are third and fourth on your list?'

'A mailed fist holding a dagger,' said Sheila, 'and a tower!'

'If only we can find the section of panelling with those crests somewhere where we can get at them! If we get discovered heaving the stuff about, the whole thing will be ruined. Yet speed is vital.'

'Couldn't we sneak up there again while everybody is at lunch?' suggested Sheila. 'If we can't find the right section easily... then we shall have to think again!'

'That's an idea,' agreed Debbie. 'We'll try that.'

Promptly at one o'clock, Sheila went out along the corridor, leaving Debbie to watch her from the door of their room. She signalled Debbie when she had made sure that the stairs were clear, and Debbie raced along to join her. There was no sign of anyone along the second floor corridor and, in less than a moment, they were in the library.

This time they searched under the dustsheets to some purpose, seeking high and low for signs of panelling bearing either the mailed fist or the tower crest. Debbie took one side and Sheila another. When they met at last on the final corner they gazed at each other with disappointed faces.

'No sign?' asked Sheila.

Debbie shook her head. 'I'm afraid not — and you don't have to tell me it was the same with you. This means our luck isn't holding, Sheila!'

They leaned against the dusty sheets at the corner of the pile and neither of them spoke for some time. All the enthusiasm and optimism in the world couldn't help them to sort through a great pile of heavy panelling, boxes and so on, as if it were a pack of cards.

At last, Sheila had an idea!

'Debbie,' she said hesitantly, 'there is just one thing we might do... we've looked each side — we can't look underneath — but we could climb on top!'

Debbie's face broke into one great grin. 'Sheila!' she cried. 'You're a genius. Of course we could. We shall get absolutely filthy and we'll have to fling all these dust sheets down...'

Sheila felt very pleased with herself, but she didn't want to court more disappointment. 'Don't let's get too hopeful, Debbie,' she said.

But Debbie was already pulling down the sheets and trying to get a foothold to climb up to the top of the pile.

The next half hour was rather like clambering over the

boxes stacked high up in the roof of a warehouse. As the search narrowed down, both girls began to feel tense and slightly pessimistic.

But suddenly Debbie gave a hopeful cry. 'Here's a mailed fist!'

'Oh, goodness!' said Sheila. 'I can't bear it! Remember, Debbie, there are two mailed fists — one to each of the old side walls — and two towers.'

Debbie was feeling with trembling fingers along the long section of panelling. Her father had said that the panel could be slid back easily. There was no spring or button — just a tiny groove near the edge into which you could grip with your fingernail.

Debbie sat back and bit her lip. 'Not a sign of...' She bent forward again suddenly. 'Of course,' she said. 'I'm an idiot. This could be the top the panel, and the concealed cupboard would be nearer the bottom.' She crawled along on the section of panelling and suddenly she gave a yell. 'I've got it!'

Sheila slid along the panelling after her, just in time to see Debbie digging away with her thumbnail. The sliding panel was stiff with dust, but it opened an inch or two at last... and, although it stuck, Debbie could then get her fingers inside the shallow cavity and pull. She dragged out a bundle of yellowed papers, tied up with faded tape.

'Oh, Debbie,' said Sheila, in an awed voice. 'It simply can't be true!'

They sat for a while unable to say a word. But, eventually, Debbie said: 'Well, the sooner we get these to Daddy, the better. Come on, Sheila. Down we go.'

They scrambled down to the floor, replacing the dust sheets as best they could.

Together they went along to the head of the stairs, dirty,

but elated, and with Debbie clutching the bundle of documents.

An hour later, a much cleaner Debbie made a startling recovery from her illness and, having made sure that Uncle Harry was in his room, went down into the lounge. She had decided on the best course of action. She and Sheila were going to the nearest post office to despatch a registered parcel to Professor Thompson.

By keeping well out of the hotel for the next day or two, and taking due care at all times while they were in it, Debbie and Sheila managed to steer clear of Uncle Harry.

At last, a telegram came from Debbie's father, cautiously acknowledging receipt of the parcel, which he followed by a jubilant letter, saying that he had cabled the American collector and received a reply saying that an agent would fly over right away.

Sheila laughed. 'Oh, Debbie, I think this has been the most exciting thing that ever did or ever could happen to me!'

'You wait,' said Debbie. 'Wait until our summer holiday. If the Thompson fortune has come through by that time, we'll all go to somewhere by plane... France, Italy, Greece... anywhere, everywhere! And we'll stay for weeks and weeks, until Daddy is well and fit and we're all as brown as berries!'

'I suppose we shall have to get this holiday over first,' Sheila said. 'And there is still one snag, Debbie. What about Uncle Harry? It would be best if he never even suspected you had been here, wouldn't it?'

'I've been thinking about that,' said Debbie. 'And I think the best thing is to invent a reason for going home. I'll say to Miss Redfern that Daddy seems to need me back again — which I'm sure is true!'

And so, next morning, while Uncle Harry was still lingering

over his breakfast, Debbie and Sheila were driven to the station in the hotel taxi.

They looked back and saw him glowering over some sheets of hotel note-paper, still looking for the documents, never dreaming that they had gone!

Rainbow Cottage

by Ida Melbourne

'THE SEA!'

As she gave that cry, Sally Carstairs bobbed up and down on the front seat of her Aunt Alicia's small, ancient car.

Breathless, with shining eyes, Sally started at the sparkling expanse of sea.

'Good gracious, girl, you've seen it before,' said Aunt Alicia, amused.

'Look at it! I'll be swimming in it,' said Sally ecstatically. 'Oh, if only you knew how I've been looking forward to this holiday with you, Aunt Alicia.'

'Keep your eyes open for Rainbow Cottage,' said Aunt Alicia. 'Tell Gyp, he knows it; he'll recognise it at once.'

Sally turned to the other passenger, her dog, Gyp.

Gyp gave Sally's hand a lick.

In fact, Gyp did recognise this place, for he had come here with Aunt Alicia when she had looked over Rainbow Cottage before renting it for the summer. She was a famous painter, and this part of the world suited her as it abounded in the type of seascape that was her favourite subject. It suited Gyp, too; plenty of runs.

He was Sally's dog, but while she was at school he was taken care of by Aunt Alicia. He got on very well with her, but Sally was his one true love.

'Not far from here,' said Aunt Alicia suddenly, as they turned a bend. 'I remember that old neglected cottage there. Beam Ends it's called, and well named, too.'

She stopped the car, and looked around uncertainly; for there was a lane to the left and she was not sure whether she had to drive up it or not. But Gyp knew. He jumped out, shook himself, then trotted on past the turning and round the bend.

'There — Gyp knows,' said Sally, as she scrambled from the car.

She shut her blazer in the door, which delayed her, and when she rounded the bend she heard Gyp yelp. Almost at once, he came backing through a gateway, snarling.

Pursuing him, waving a stick angrily, came a red-faced man; grey-haired and with a bristly, grey moustache.

Sally gave a gasp, and then started forward angrily.

'You dare hit him!' she cried. 'Stop!'

'I did not hit him. I only threatened him; but if he comes trespassing in my garden again, I certainly will hit him,' the man roared, waving the stick.

'He thought it was our cottage,' said Sally in excuse. 'The one we've rented, Rainbow Cottage.'

'Well, this is my cottage — for the summer, anyway. Beam Ends, as you can see by the name on the gate!'

'Beam Ends?' gasped Sally.

Sally looked at the cottage; charming with Wistaria growing up the front; a lovely, if small, garden — it was just the dream cottage her aunt had described.

'Rainbow Cottage,' said the man, 'is that tumbledown shack round the corner. Why anyone should want —'

He broke off. While talking to Sally, he had lowered the stick, and Gyp, who had a permanent quarrel with sticks, saw his chance. He leaped forward and seized it.

'Hey — my stick! Come back!' yelled the man furiously.

'Gyp!' cried Sally. 'Come back here — at once!'

Gyp bolted for the cliff edge, not heeding Sally's shout.

'That's a valuable stick!' shouted the man. 'What's more, if that stupid dog doesn't stop, he'll go over the cliff.'

That was enough for Sally. Heart in mouth, she went in pursuit of Gyp, calling to him in dire alarm.

Gyp was no fool though. When she found him, he was at the cliff edge looking over, the stick in his jaws.

'Gyp! Come here,' said Sally commandingly.

Gyp, looking down, as if choosing a suitable landing place for it, opened his jaws and dropped the valuable stick. Then obediently, tail down in guilt, he went to Sally.

She moved to the cliff edge and looked over. But she couldn't see the stick, which had apparently fallen between the rocks.

Suddenly she heard someone hail her. There in the sandy cove, just beyond the rocks, was a boy in shorts. He was waving to her and shouting.

'Hey! You in the red blazer,' he yelled, cupping his hands as a megaphone. 'If you want to come down there's a path...' And he swept his right arm around to signal the direction.

'Thanks... My dog dropped a walking stick on to the rocks there,' she called.

'Okay. I'll look for it.'

Sally turned to follow his directions, but Gyp loitered at the cliff edge, looking down.

'Gyp!' came a shout from the boy on the sands.

Sally wheeled, startled. Whoever, here at this remote seaside place, could know Gyp? She went back and looked over.

'Sally?' yelled the boy excitedly. 'Gosh! Can it be?'

Recognition suddenly came to Sally.

'Ted!' she cried in glee. 'Yipee! I'm coming down.'

Sally's heart leaped with joy, and her eyes sparkled as she raced away with Gyp to find the path that led to the sands. Ted Bunting — one of her best friends, whom she had not seen since the Christmas holidays — was down there.

She found the jagged cliff path and went racing down, slithering now and again but without falling, while Gyp raced ahead, and bounded through the fringe of incoming sea to where the boy was already clambering up the rocks in search of the stick.

Ted's cheery face was split in a wide grin, as he turned to pat and fondle Gyp, who leaped and barked with joy. Then Sally arrived at a run.

'This is marvellous! Terrific!' beamed Ted. 'Gosh, and I was getting really browned off with no pals.'

'Ted, it's just too good to be true,' laughed Sally. 'Are you staying here?'

'Rather. I'm staying with my Uncle William,' Ted replied.

'I'm staying with my Aunt Alicia — you know, the painter, the one I told you about.'

'Was it her stick that got dropped?'

'No.' Sally's face clouded. 'Some horrid red-faced man hit Gyp with it — and Gyp seized it, took it to the cliff top, and dropped it over.'

'He did? Good show, Gyp. That'll show him,' said Ted. 'What had Gyp done to make him mad?'

'Nothing much, you see, Gyp was here with Aunt Alicia when she looked over the cottage we are staying at, and he raced ahead to find it. Next thing I knew this awful man was driving Gyp out.'

'Shame!' said Ted. 'Which is the cottage you have taken, Sally?'

'Oh, a lovely, dream cottage, Rainbow Cottage!' she said.

Ted blinked in surprise, his jaw dropped.

'Rainbow Cottage! Why, that's the old tumbledown shack.'

Sally gave him a startled look.

'Oh, surely not! Aunt says that's called Beam Ends, although...'

'Beam Ends! Gosh, no. Our cottage is called Beam Ends... and it's a smasher; Wistaria climbing over the front... lovely garden —' He broke off as he saw Sally's horrified look. 'Why, what's wrong?'

'Ted! That's the cottage Gyp went into. That's where the awful man hit him.'

Ted's jaw dropped in dismay.

'Sally! Gosh! That man — he must be my Uncle William.'

There was a moment's painful hush.

'Oh, no!' said Sally, horrified. 'Ted, I'm terribly sorry if I...'

'Oh, that's all right, Sally,' he said with a wry smile. 'Matter of fact, Uncle is peppery. But — I say,' he ended, 'if that's his precious malacca cane with decorated silver handle Gyp took... Gosh! We'd better find it...'

They rushed to the rocks and hunted for ten minutes in vain; and then, turning suddenly, Sally saw that Gyp had found it and was settling down to gnaw it.

She rescued it, and found it little the worse for its adventure.

'We'll take it back,' said Ted, 'and I'll try to smooth things over.'

They raced to the top of the cliff and arrived within sight of the tumbledown cottage. In front of it stood Aunt Alicia and Ted's Uncle William. They were arguing angrily.

'You have had proof,' cried Aunt Alicia, 'that this, not the cottage you are occupying, is Beam Ends. This is the cottage you have rented. Very well! I demand you move your things out of that cottage where you have no right to be. It is really Rainbow Cottage. Just because I am a woman, don't think I can be fooled by your cunning tricks. You changed the name-plates by sheer fraud, to make me think this was Rainbow Cottage.'

'What! How dare you?' frothed Ted's uncle. 'I would scorn such an action. I did no such thing! I took that cottage in good faith to be Beam Ends! That was the name on the gate.'

'A man who would hit a dog would stoop to anything. I'll keep that dog well away from you... and my niece,' snapped Aunt Alicia.

'Bah! There's trickery here, madam, someone else altered those name-plates and I'll find out who! I won't be called a fraud by anyone!'

Sally tugged Ted back behind a tree, alarmed, shocked.

'Ted! They're enemies — bitter enemies. And how can we be friends if they're not? Oh, whoever could have changed those cottage name-plates?'

'Uncle didn't. I'll swear that,' frowned Ted, 'but your aunt won't be convinced without first-class proof, I can see.'

'Then we must find proof,' insisted Sally. 'Ted! If we're to have the wonderful holiday we hope for and be pals, we've got to end this feud. We've got to find out who did change those name-plates — and why!'

'Agreed,' said Ted and they shook hands on it. 'However much they quarrel, we must remain pals through it all.'

'Yes, even in secret,' nodded Sally. 'For only by working together can we end this feud.'

'Ted!' came an irate shout from Uncle William.

'Sally!' called Aunt Alicia.

Sally hurried to where Aunt Alicia stood outside pretty Rainbow Cottage.

'I've brought back the stick, Aunt,' she called, and held up the walking-stick for her aunt to see.

Ted's uncle, Major Bunting, was also outside Rainbow Cottage afire with wrath. His face was a fiery red, and he was snorting with rage.

'Oh, you got it back from the thieving dog?' he said. 'None the worse, I hope,' he added, as he studied it.

Unfortunately, there were teeth marks, and he pointed them out to Sally's aunt — and some scratches it had suffered in the fall on to the rocks when Gyp had dropped it over the cliff.

'It is unfortunate if the stick has suffered,' said Aunt Alicia coldly, 'but the dog himself would have suffered even more if the stick had hit him. Please be good enough to move all your things out of Rainbow Cottage, Major Bunting.'

Then she turned, and beckoned Sally to follow her into the pretty garden of Rainbow Cottage.

'All is well, Sally,' she smiled. 'This lovely cottage is ours after all, not that awful dump, Beam Ends. That, it turns out, is the one that Major Bunting and his nephew should be occupying; so they'll have to move their things into it. While they are doing so, we can settle down in the deck-chairs in the garden here.'

In the roadway, Sally noticed, Ted had just appeared, and his uncle was explaining the situation.

The feud was 'on'. Ted's uncle was cutting Aunt Alicia and Sally 'dead'; and they were to do the same to him and Ted. Major Bunting strode into Rainbow Cottage and brought out roughly packed suitcases, and armfuls of clothes. Ted followed him, his arms loaded.

But at last the tiresome job was done; the final journey made, and the gate of Rainbow Cottage was closed behind them.

'I suppose, Aunt,' said Sally, as they stood at the gate, 'we'll have to change the name-plates over again.'

'Let Major Bunting change them back,' said Aunt Alicia crisply. 'He obviously knows how to do it.'

She turned towards the cottage, and Sally was about to follow her when a man dressed in old flannel trousers, and a rather dirty linen jacket, came strolling up, and stood before the gate. There were paint marks on his linen coat, and his felt hat was battered. Sally, having seen some artist friends of Aunt Alicia's, guessed that he was a painter, too, which his fair goatee beard seemed to confirm.

'Ah! Pardon my staring at your gate,' he said, looking puzzled. 'But I'm sure that when I last came by here, the name was Rainbow Cottage.'

'Yes, this is Rainbow Cottage. Someone changed over the name-plates,' said Sally.

'Oh, really? Very odd thing to do,' he said, surprised. 'Why? Feeble-minded idea of a joke?'

'I've absolutely no idea,' said Sally. 'Wish I had...'

He was so friendly in manner that she told him the trouble that the change-over had caused.

'Too bad. Seems unlikely this Major Bunting you mentioned would have done it. More likely a trick by some village lout, I'd have thought,' he said. 'I'll make a few enquiries for you. I'm spending the summer here — painting, you know.'

'Painting? Oh, Aunt will be delighted,' smiled Sally. 'Do come in and meet her...'

So while Sally got the things from the car with the help of Gyp, who carried quite a few of the smaller articles, Aunt Alicia chatted with the bearded man who proved to be Mr Graham Portland, a modernist whose name was vaguely familiar to her from some of her avant-garde friends — but certainly not as familiar as she kindly pretended. However, he seemed to know her pictures and reputation so they got on quite well together.

Unfortunately, he couldn't throw much light on the change of name-plates.

'I saw the Major moving out,' he said as Sally served tea. 'And thought he might have been scared out by the ghost — like the other people were.'

'Ghost?' cried Aunt Alicia, 'Is the cottage haunted?'

'Oh, well — just village talk,' he laughed, 'Supposed to be a poltergeist. You know — the kind of ghost that throws things about; noises in the night and so on. A lot of twaddle I think. But some people are superstitious.'

'Well, I'm not,' said Aunt Alicia firmly, as she settled into the deckchair in the garden and crossed her trousered legs. 'And no ghost would drive me out of here.'

The talk turned to painting again, and Sally edged away.

'I think I'll tak Gyp down to the beach, Aunt,' she said. 'All right?'

'Yes, dear. Don't be gone for more than an hour, though. Trot on! This painting talk would bore you. Keep Gyp clear of Major Bunting,' she added more sharply.

Sally put a lead on Gyp, which rather offended him; but it was a necessary precaution as she was going past Beam Ends.

Major Bunting was not in sight, but Ted was in the garden, putting up a deck-chair.

'Come on, Gyp. Down to the cove,' called Sally, for Ted's benefit.

Down to the cove they went, and as she expected, Ted joined them less than ten minutes later.

'Gosh, it's good to see you, Sally,' he beamed, 'but I'm afraid Uncle's still snorting and gnashing his teeth about your Aunt Alicia. Talking about suing her for defamation of character if she continues to blame him for changing those name-plates.'

Sally told him of Mr Graham Portland's visit, and his promise to make enquiries.

'Might help. I know him by sight, not a bad chap. Amiable, but a bit arty — a bit too arty for Uncle William,' he added with a grin, 'although they've chatted occasionally. I say, do you think you could get off to see the pierrot show in the town tomorrow afternoon? I've heard it's pretty good.'

'I'll try hard,' nodded Sally. 'It should be fun. I do wish we could be friends openly, though. Still — as soon as we've found out who did change the name-plates, we can be. Any ideas, Ted?'

'None; but there's obviously some practical joker at work, Sally. What do you think I found in our kitchen in the real Beams Ends? A message in chalk scrawled across the wall. One or two words had been rubbed out, but one remained: "Fooled!"'

'Odd,' frowned Sally. 'But who was fooled? Your uncle? Or — or was it meant for us supposing we had gone into Beam Ends, thinking it was Rainbow Cottage?'

'Can't guess,' said Ted, 'but Uncle couldn't have written it, because I was first in. Anyway, let's forget it for a minute and go for a row, eh? That's the little boat I've hired — the one at the end.'

They soon forgot the cloud hanging over them when they were on the water. The dinghy was good fun, and Ted rowed into the next cove. They could swim from it at the right state of tide he said, and do some exploring along the coast.

When Sally returned to Rainbow Cottage, Aunt Alicia was preparing a meal, so Sally set the table on the little verandah facing the sea.

Gyp, exploring the possibilities of his new home, roamed into the garden. He was well-behaved in gardens, and helped to the extent of driving off cats — in a friendly way, of course, all bark and no bite. But there were no cats in the garden. What he did find was something really surprising — raw liver.

Raw liver! There it was, on the grass. He gobbled it up, and his keen nose led him to some more near the fence at the bottom of the back garden. Incredibly, there was another piece on the far side of the fence, so he jumped over and got it. Never before in his life had Gyp had such luck. Even when the bits of liver were quite a few yards apart, he was able to find them. And the trail did not end until he reached the garden of the real Beam Ends.

Sally did not miss Gyp until they were halfway through their meal. She called him, whistled him, and then went in search of him. Surprised, and a little alarmed, she had just returned from the garden to see if he had gone upstairs to lie on a bed — he not having been forbidden to lie on these particular beds — when the telephone bell went.

'Miss Carstairs?' raged the Major's voice.

'Oh, yes... just a minute please,' said Sally, startled, and called Aunt Alicia, who took the call.

'Oh, Major Bunting? Yes,' said Aunt Alicia coldly.

'I warned you to keep that wretched dog out of my place; yet here he is raking up the flowers! I warn you, if he comes around here he'll get a bucket of water over him! He's half killed a cat, the brute.'

'Half-killed a cat?' gasped Aunt Alicia in horror. 'Oh, I don't believe it —'

But there was no reply; the receiver at the other end had been hung up. Sally, who had heard every word, standing close to her aunt, turned pale.

'Gyp would never attack a cat. It's not true,' said Sally.

'Of course it isn't true. That man's trying to make trouble,' Aunt Alicia replied.

She turned as the telephone bell rang again, and whipped off the receiver.

'Major Bunting!' she cried in fury.

'Miss Carstairs! Kindly come and fetch your dog from my garden!' Then click went the receiver.

Sally raced from the cottage out through the back way, for she had heard Gyp bark. Down the garden she went, and through the end gate just as Gyp came along, steered by Ted, who had him by the collar.

'Ted! I'm terribly sorry,' she gasped. 'But it isn't true about his attacking a cat!'

'Attacking a cat? First I've heard of it, Sally,' he answered in surprise. 'Whoever said he had?'

'Your Uncle William when he telephoned Aunt Alicia.'

'Sally! I was standing nearby. He only said: "Kindly come and fetch your dog from my garden."'

'That was the second time. He phoned a minute before that,' Sally said.

'Uncle did? Gosh, no! We were at the table together until I heard Gyp bark; he was locked in our shed. Uncle went straight in and phoned that curt message.'

Sally stared at him astounded. Ted would not lie; yet definitely there had been two telephone calls. There seemed only one possibility — Ted was mistaken. But, hearing her aunt call, Sally could not loiter to argue the point. She hurried indoors.

'I'm going to see the Major,' called Aunt Alicia from the front door. 'Keep Gyp indoors, Sally.'

Sally shut the door and stood stock still, worried. It was baffling. Of course there had been two calls. Obviously, the first one must have been made by Uncle William without Ted's knowing.

Looking across at the telephone, Sally had a sudden idea. Seizing it, she spoke to the local exchange and asked the girl if she knew where the two calls had come from.

'I only put one call through so the other must have come from the local call box which is about half a mile from the post office.'

'Goodness, how very odd,' she said. 'Thank you so much.'

She hung up the receiver and stood perplexed. For a moment she remained there; then she fled down the garden to call on Ted. But there was no need for he was already walking towards her.

'Your aunt insists Uncle William said Gyp had half-killed a cat,' Ted said. 'But I know —'

'Ted,' Sally panted, 'that first call came from a box down the road, half a mile from the post office. Someone else telephoned from there.'

'And imitated Uncle's voice?' he cried in doubt.

'It's the only possible explanation, Ted.'

'Quick!' he snapped. 'Whoever sent that message did it to cause trouble — just as the person did who changed the name-plates.'

'The same person!' cried Sally. 'Then, my goodness, if anyone saw him phoning, we've got him.'

'Then come on, we can't waste a minute,' urged Ted. 'Your aunt and my uncle are on fighting terms now. We've got to find out who it was.'

'That must be the phone box, Ted!' Sally pointed excitedly at the public call box at the roadside.

'Yes, Sally. But there's no one about who might have seen who used it,' grunted Ted. 'Still, there might be a clue. Even the most cunning rogue can be careless.'

Sally reached the box, a little breathless from running, heaved open the door, and looked inside. Her hopes fell; there were no obvious clues left behind. It was just an ordinary phone box with phone, coin box and directory.

Gyp pushed in past her and sniffed around in an expert manner that a detective could not have bettered.

'I think he's picked up a scent,' said Sally proudly. 'He's wonderfully clever, Ted. If he gets full measure of this he may lead us to the person. Who was it, Gyp? Seek!' she commanded.

Gyp often played games of hide and seek, but he wasn't certain now what he had to seek.

'Dead end,' frowned Ted glumly, and then looked around, 'unless we can find someone who was near here at the time.'

'I say,' exclaimed Sally, after going a few steps beyond the phone box, 'there's a small general shop over the road. Someone in there might have seen whoever used this box. Shall we try?'

*　*　*

Sally pushed open the door of the little general shop and set the bell jangling. Small, but packed with groceries, confectionery and such diverse articles as swimsuits and garden implements, the little shop was generally more crowded with goods than customers. There was only one present at the moment.

'Mr Portland!' exclaimed Sally, surprised, as the customer at the counter turned. The bearded painter smiled.

'Ah, you've found the multiple store, then?'

'Yes. I — I suppose you weren't in the lane a minute ago? You didn't see someone using that telephone box?' asked Sally. 'It's rather important to know who it was. Someone phoned Aunt — and... Well, no name was given,' she added, not thinking it advisable to say too much at this stage.

The painter paid for a drawing-pad he had bought, turned and said:

'Used the telephone box? Well, I'd hardly have noticed. Not the observant type, you know, rather distrait. I'm not sure I even noticed the box, and —' he broke off sharply, and snapped his fingers. 'Yes, I did notice it. I was quite a way off, but I noticed a man ahead of me, chap with a bushy black

'Mr Portland!' exlaimed Sally, surprised...

beard and tweed cap. I was watching his rather shambling gait when he suddenly turned sideways — into that telephone box.'

'Man with a bushy black beard?' exclaimed Ted. 'Anything else you noticed about him, sir?'

'Well,' mused Mr Graham Portland, pursing his lips and arching his brows. 'A shambling gait... sailor-like, an odd swing of the shoulders. Being an artist, I notice the visual — once he got into the box I lost interest.'

Then he fondled Gyp, who welcomed him with wagging tail and uplifted paw; but he could give no further help, so handed Sally over to the shopkeeper. Unfortunately, Mrs Taggart couldn't place the man. But then, as she said, these days with so many passing motorists, and holidaymakers roaming on foot, she had so many customers that she might not recognise a description of one of them.

'Still, he must be around,' frowned Ted, as he and Sally turned from the shop. 'It's a pretty good description to work on.'

'Yes; and he'll stay around if he means to play more tricks,' said Sally slowly. 'Although I — well, honestly Ted, I just can't think how anyone could imitate your uncle's voice so marvellously that I could be deceived.'

'Well, such things happen. You've heard these mimics on the radio?' argued Ted. 'When they mimic some of the well-known people I couldn't be sure that it isn't the genuine person.'

'Y-e-es, but could an ordinary person do it — a practical joker?' asked Sally doubtfully.

Ted gave a start and an idea came to him.

'Sally! Remember I asked you to come with me to the pierrot show tomorrow afternoon — in the town? Well, I've just thought. One of the turns is 'The Man With a Hundred Voices' ...a star mimic.'

Sally stopped short in the lane and stared at him.

'Ted! You're not suggesting that man could have done it?'

'Don't know,' shrugged Ted. 'Hadn't figured it out that way, Sally. But he could do it all right — if he had a motive. And for all we know, he might have rooms out here, and live right on the spot.'

'Ted, we mustn't miss that show. We'll get the bus at two o'clock, shall we? That'll give us time.'

'Right! The sooner we get to the bottom of this the better, Sally, for all our sakes.'

They parted shortly afterwards, and while Ted took a route that led to the back of his cottage, Sally took Gyp the front way. Her Aunt was at the gate looking for her.

'Oh, Sally, I couldn't think where you'd been,' said Aunt Alicia.

As soon as they got indoors, Aunt Alicia told her story.

'Well, Sally, I went to see that awful man, Major Bunting. Can you believe it — he flatly denied saying anything about Gyp half-killing a cat. As though I don't know what I hear! And you heard it?' This was an awkward moment for Sally.

'Yes, I heard it. But was it Major Bunting? Or was it someone imitating his voice, Aunt?'

'Imitating his voice?' cried Aunt Alicia, startled. 'What utter nonsense! Whoever could imitate it so perfectly? And why, for goodness' sake? I'm surprised at you, Sally, my dear! A perfectly ludicrous, wild and impossible suggestion, even if Major Bunting says his nephew can confirm he said no such thing. Tish! I'd no more trust that lad than I'd trust his uncle.'

It was so obvious that Aunt Alicia was in no mood to listen to reason that Sally said no more about it. In a day or two, if there were no further incidents, she might be talked round — or, by then, the mystery might be solved.

When bed-time came, after a short walk in the evening air, Aunt Alicia locked up, and advised Sally to keep Gyp in her bedroom — much to the joy of both of them.

'You'll be painting tomorrow afternoon, won't you, Aunt?' Sally asked when they said goodnight. 'Would you mind if I went to the pierrot show in town? It's supposed to be good.'

'Go by all means, dear,' said Aunt Alicia.

Lights went off, and with Gyp curled up on his collapsible bed which they had brought as part of his luggage, Sally lay awake puzzling over the strange mystery. Who was the secret enemy? The man with the black beard? The mimic at the pierrot show? Or... but Sally drifted into sleep.

It was hours later when she woke up. The room was in pitch darkness, and Gyp was growling at the door. He was a restful night companion as a rule, and Sally awoke with a start and groped for the light switch. She pushed it, but no light came on.

Then Gyp whined, and Sally heard her Aunt's voice at the door.

'Sally...' The door opened and closed, and Sally, having found her electric torch, turned the rays on to Aunt Alicia, who stood in a regal dressing-gown, looking pale and alarmed.

'What is it, Aunt?' breathed Sally.

'Haven't you heard? I'm sure someone is moving about downstairs. There have been odd thumps, and strange creaking sounds.'

'Not a burglar?' breathed Sally.

Gyp was scrabbling at the door, and she opened it for him. Out he went, snarling, and raced down the stairs. In the hall, he barked excitedly and challengingly.

'It's not the supposed poltergeist?' breathed Aunt Alicia, obviously nervous. 'You remember? Mr Graham Portland mentioned it. I — I don't really believe in ghosts — but the sounds have been strange.'

Sally, with her torch, crossed to the door to follow Gyp; but Aunt Alicia held her arm and pulled her back.

'No, Sally. If it is a burglar, let him get on with it. You shan't risk being attacked; and if it is a poltergeist — My goodness!' She broke off with a gasp. 'Major Bunting!'

'Major Bunting?' echoed Sally wonderingly.

'Yes... yes! He'll have heard the story of the poltergeist. Just the thing that rascal would do to drive us out of here, so that he can come back! He's playing ghost — Gyp! Hold him!' she called downstairs. 'Don't let him escape.'

Out from the room she went, and Sally went with her. None of the lights would come on, so Sally shone the torch down the stairs. The rays fell upon Gyp, who was whining and scrabbling at the closed door of the sitting-room.

Sally reached the door first, and she opened it. Instantly, with his most ferocious burglar-scaring snarl, Gyp rushed in — and barked in disappointment.

'The window's open,' cried Sally, peeping in. 'Certainly wasn't a ghost. But, my goodness, Aunt! Just look at this room!'

They stared about them in the sitting-room. It had been ransacked in a wild, senseless manner. A vase lay smashed on the floor, pictures were swung sideways; chairs lay tipped flat on the floor; the table had been swung round; the sideboard had been moved; the carpet had been rolled back; fruit from the fruit dish lay scattered.

'B-but this is crazy. My silver hasn't been touched! None of the paintings have been stolen. The desk hasn't been burst open. It can't be the work of a burglar,' exclaimed Aunt Alicia, astounded and furious. 'It's sabotage! And only one person can be to blame — Major Bunting.'

Sally just stared about her, baffled. It really did not make sense.

'But, Aunt, why? Major Bunting wouldn't play a mere schoolboy trick.'

'No? He thinks I am just a weak, foolish woman, likely to be scared from here by a poltergeist. . . and this is how he thinks a poltergeist would behave. Very well, I'll tackle him in the morning. If he does not confess, then I'll inform the police.'

Sally's heart sank in dismay at this fearful threat. Once that happened, it would be open war.

'Aunt, I can't believe the Major did this,' protested Sally.

'Someone did it, Sally. The furniture did not move itself; and Gyp has just gone through that window after someone,' Aunt Alicia added excitedly.

Sally rushed to the window. It was a dark night, and her torch only speared it with a narrow beam; but, suddenly, as she swung the torch to and fro, she saw Gyp. He came bounding back through the garden.

He rushed to the window and put his paws on the sill, his eyes shining with pride as he held out something in his teeth.

A false black beard!

As Sally took the beard from Gyp and looked at it, her heart leaped. If Sally had been presented with a gold watch by Gyp she could not have been more excited or delighted. She petted and praised him as a good dog.

'Whatever is that?' exclaimed Aunt Alicia, amazed.

'Aunt, it's a false black beard. And Mr Graham Portland — you know who I mean — the artist who called on you this evening — he said he had seen a black-bearded man using the telephone call box in the lane about half a mile from the post ofice.'

'Well? So what, Sally?' asked Aunt Alicia, puzzled. 'Are you suggesting that that man came here — and that he disordered this room of ours, in this outrageous manner? For what possible reason?'

She swept her hand around the dark room, and then, as she moved back, stumbled over an upturned chair.

'He may have done... in fact, as he left this clue behind, he must have done,' said Sally. 'And if he did, then the Major didn't. Don't you see, Aunt? This man must have mimicked the Major's voice. It wasn't Major Bunting who spoke so insultingly to you on the telephone and accused poor Gyp of attacking a cat, but this mystery man.'

The mystery was becoming a little clearer; or anyway, Sally felt that the innocence of Ted's uncle, Major Bunting, was being made obvious — although not yet obvious to Aunt Alicia!

Aunt Alicia stood with a perplexed expression. She was a strong-minded woman, not easily robbed of her convictions, and she had quite made up her mind that Major Bunting was a rascal.

'Sally, you are talking wildly, my dear,' she said, shaking her head. 'I refuse to believe that anyone could imitate the Major's voice so perfectly that I could be deceived. And, anyway, who is this black-bearded man? Evidently, the beard is a disguise. And if that is so, how can you be sure that the Major himself did not put on the beard to use that telephone box, eh?'

'Because —' said Sally, then broke off.

She realised suddenly that she could not explain that Ted had assured her that his uncle had not left the house. As Aunt Alicia had not yet discovered that she knew Ted, Sally decided that she had better not mention him.

'Oh, Gyp,' Sally said, fondling her pet's head, 'you're really very clever; but if only you had caught him! Next time you will though, and perhaps, even now, you can track him.'

'Yes, Gyp, in the morning, perhaps you can find us the owner of this beard. And if you don't dump it at the feet of Major Bunting, I shall be surprised,' said Aunt Alicia.

Then she said they could gain nothing by further discussion. They could tidy the room and examine it more carefully in the morning. Sally, less worried than she had been, went up to bed and settled Gyp down in her room. He sank down with a kind of doggy swagger, fully aware of the good work he had done.

When Sally awoke next morning, her first thought was of Ted. He would be thrilled by the news that she had the false beard, and he could certainly assure her that it was not his uncle's.

But by the time Sally was up and dressed, Aunt Alicia had been out of doors some time. She was still out when the daily help, sent by the domestic service registry office, arrived, so Sally had to do the interviewing herself.

Mrs Bodkin was a plump, cheerful, homely woman and ready to start work right away. As she had worked for some previous tenants of Rainbow Cottage, she knew where everything was.

'If you're having breakfast on the verandah, miss,' she told Sally, 'I'll start on the sitting-room... wow!' she ended, as she opened the door and saw the confusion of furniture. 'Whatever's happened? A party?'

Her round blue eyes turned to Sally in wonder.

'Well, no, actually —' said Sally, wondering what to say.

'Ah! The lady's an artist. One of those Bohemian parties, I suppose,' nodded Mrs Bodkin, frowning. 'I hope you won't be having parties like this every night, miss.'

Sally laughed, and then decided to mention the poltergeist

which was alleged to haunt the cottage, and her own belief that the wildly disordered state of the room was the work not of a ghost, but a human intruder.

'Well, I have heard of such-like,' admitted Mrs Bodkin, shaking her head, 'and there have been rumours of this being haunted, but it ought not to be allowed. Those house agents ought to do something about it.'

Sally apologised on behalf of the poltergeist, and then set about getting breakfast, not being sure if cooking would be part of Mrs Bodkin's duties or not.

A quarter of an hour later, Aunt Alicia came back, looking a little rosier-cheeked than usual, and with eyes flashing. She was delighted that Sally had started to get breakfast, and after a peep into the sitting-room, gave approval of Mrs Bodkin. Gyp, who had carefully sniffed Mrs Bodkin's little bag, nodded agreement with a wag of his tail.

'Well, Sally, I have told Major Bunting what I think of him. I have warned him that if there is a repetition, I shall tell the police. His nephew, Ted, was there —'

'A nice boy?' asked Sally eagerly.

She knew he was nice, but she wanted Aunt Alicia to approve of her friend without prompting.

'Like his uncle, I should say,' answered Aunt Alicia. 'Naturally he confirmed every statement of his uncle's like a parrot. Looked embarrassed, though. Bad sign. You wouldn't like him,' she added with conviction. 'Not your type at all. Not that I imagine,' she concluded half apologetically, 'that you would want to know the nephew after the uncle's behaviour.'

Sally said nothing. Aunt Alicia had come as near to forbidding her to speak to Ted as was safe; and any favourable mention of him would not be approved. Certainly she dared not mention that she was meeting him after lunch to go with him to the nearby seaside town to see the pierrot show. That she was going herself, her aunt knew. If need be, they must set out separately.

After breakfast, Sally went out for a swim, with a beach wrap over her swimsuit, while Gyp trotted behind. She knew where Ted usually swam, and with joy she saw him in the water when she reached the sands.

'Gyp — guard!' she warned, putting her things down on the beach beside Ted's shoes. Then she danced into the water to hurl herself through a wave and strike out for Ted.

'This is terrific, Sally,' he called, as he lashed his way to her.

'Ted... exciting news! You know about our room — Aunt called at your cottage. But listen to this...'

She explained about the false beard, and he nodded, frowning.

'Gosh, yes, it must belong to that chap Mr Graham Portland saw,' he agreed. 'Easy disguise, that beard, especially if he took care not to let people get close.'

Both agreed that they could see no sense in the false telephone calls, nor the disordering of the room; but the effect was to turn Aunt Alicia against Uncle William, and so further their quarrel.

'But why? Why does he want them to quarrel?' puzzled Sally, as she swam lazily beside Ted. 'Oh, Ted, if only they'd be friends! I'm terrified Aunt will forbid me to speak to you.'

'Uncle William's tottering on the brink of forbidding me as well,' grinned Ted.

'Oh, Ted,' Sally said, 'we've got to find the mystery mimic. Let's hope that we can learn something at the pierrot show. Whoever is mimicking your uncle must surely be an expert. It could be that star-turn mimic with the pierrots as much as anyone else.'

'Tell you what, Sally! Let's take the beard there with us — let's call on 'The Man With a Hundred Voices,' after the show.'

Sally agreed; but there was no time for more talk as Ted's Uncle William was descending to the beach. They swam apart, and Sally watched as Aunt Alicia followed on to the sands with a deck-chair, and sited it well away from Uncle William.

Gyp was barking, being anxious about Sally staying in so long, so she returned to him. She snatched her things, and went to her aunt. Purposely, of course, she left Ted's shoes; but Gyp did not understand that. He could not see Ted, so he decided to follow Sally with at least one shoe.

After her he galloped with one of Ted's shoes. It was well meant, but unfortunate; for Major Bunting recognised the shoe and roared at Gyp.

'That infuriating dog,' he raged. 'Bring back that shoe. You, girl! Don't let him savage it. It's my nephew's. Another of your tricks... *Ted!*' he called.

Sally rescued the shoe, and Ted came to collect it. They acted as strangers, both aloof.

'Your shoe, I think,' said Sally, distantly. '*My* dog must have taken it in error.'

'Oh, thank you. Natural mistake,' replied Ted, gravely aloof.

'How could even that imbecile dog have mistaken that clodhopper for a girl's shoe?' snorted Uncle William. 'Next time, without being rude, be curter and firmer, Ted.'

Aunt Alicia had seen nothing of the incident; she was concentrating on a plan of her own to find out if the beard belonged to the Major. Presently she gave it to Gyp with instructions to find the owner, but Gyp only gave it to Sally. Then, some time later, when she saw that the Major was about to leave, Aunt Alicia decided to throw the beard down on to the sands.

'I will use my tinted glasses as a rear-view mirror, walking ahead of him and looking back,' she told Sally. 'If he picks it up and guiltily pockets it — that will be proof.'

She put her plan into action and Sally waited, amused.

'He's picking it up,' whispered Aunt Alicia, squinting into her glasses, held slightly to one side, as they walked along.

'Madam,' came a shout from the Major, 'you have dropped a hair pad.'

Aunt Alicia went crimson with wrath and turned to see the Major holding up the false beard with evident distaste. As she had golden hair, she quivered with rage. But she took back the beard, glaring.

'You may observe that my hair is blonde,' she said witheringly.

'The colour of ladies' hair is a question of fashion and personal choice,' he retorted. 'But whatever it may be, you dropped it.'

'Bluff,' said Aunt Alicia, with a toss of the head, to Sally, as they walked away. 'It's his all right.'

Sally said nothing; but she hoped against hope that she and Ted would have better luck tracking down the owner of the beard. As she turned through the gate of Rainbow Cottage for lunch, she managed to catch Ted's eye and he nodded. It was 'Okay' for the pierrot show and their interview with 'The Man With a Hundred Voices' who could imitate any voice exactly.

'Too bad I couldn't bring Gyp,' said Sally, as she settled down on the top of the two o'clock bus with Ted. 'He might have helped; but, of course, he couldn't come to the pierrot show. No dogs allowed. So Aunt's looking after him.'

'Great dog, Gyp. Wonder if he'd know the owner of that

beard?' asked Ted. 'He must have got the scent of the man who was in your house.'

The conductor came to collect the fares, and Ted paid.

'Two to the town — near as you go to the pierrot show, please,' he said.

'And how about the dog?' asked the conductor.

'Dog?' asked Ted and Sally together, startled.

They turned and gasped. There on the seat behind them, sitting up enjoying the passing scenery, was Gyp.

Sally laughed. There was nothing to do but keep him with them; for he couldn't be put off the bus alone, and they had no time to return. Fortunately, when they reached the Pavilion Theatre, the girl at the pay-desk kindly agreed to look after him.

The Pavilion was a pleasant place, even if the stage was rather small, and the show was excellent; the gay pierrots sang and fooled well. But Sally and Ted were waiting tensely for the star turn, the mimic.

Presently, dressed as a pierrot, he came on, well applauded, bowed and then in quick succession gave truly marvellous imitations of well-known politicians, comedians and other radio performers. He even mimicked other pierrots.

He was a man of average build and, like the other pierrots, wore a purple velvet mask.

'He could imitate Uncle's voice — not a shadow of doubt,' breathed Ted, 'and well enough to deceive even me, Sally.'

'Yes, he could. But why ever should he?' asked Sally, baffled.

But, equally baffling was the question: who else could do it, if not he, in this locality? Sally sat wondering, and decided to ask the mimic if he knew of anyone else locally who could imitate voices — perhaps a pupil? Perhaps someone might have asked for lessons...

Her mind was momentarily turned from the stage; but she suddenly stiffened and stared ahead when Ted grabbed her arm and gasped: 'Gosh, look!'

There was a sudden commotion in the wings of the stage; the pierrots grouping to encircle the mimic for a song, fell back in confusion, and the mimic himself turned, startled, as, bounding forward from the wings with a joyful bark, tail wagging, came Gyp.

Gyp leaped to the centre of the stage, and then, as if he had met an old friend, barked and jumped up at the mimic.

As Gyp rushed to greet the man in the centre of the stage with all the welcome a dog can give, Sally scrambled to her feet. She called to Gyp; but he did not hear. There was such a commotion all around her that even a scream would not have been heard.

Gyp had stopped the show! The other pierrots reacted as if in horror to make it seem as if this were part of the act, exaggerating fright, one jumping on to the piano, another rushing under it.

But the mimic, although he might have made a comic act of it, reacted strangely. With a savage swing of the fist, he clouted Gyp.

'No! Stop!' shouted Sally.

She scrambled out of her seat, over legs and feet, to the gangway, followed by Ted, and rushed to the stage.

'Don't hit him,' she cried.

As Sally, dodging an attendant, reached the edge of the stage, the mimic turned away as if to take Gyp by the collar. But Gyp had had enough. He snarled.

Next moment, as the man seemed likely to attack, Gyp sprang; and at the same time the curtain fell, covering the scene from Sally. She hardly saw the comedian who came before the curtain to gag and carry the show on; for she rushed with Ted to get behind the curtain and rescue Gyp.

'Gosh! Gyp knows the man,' panted Ted. 'Took him for a friend.'

'An enemy now,' gasped Sally.

An attendant barred their way; but when Sally said the dog was hers, he let her pass through the door to the corridor backstage.

Gyp was standing at a closed door, growling, and two excited men were trying to drive him away, when Sally and Ted arrived on the scene.

'The man had no right to hit him; Gyp was friendly until then,' said Sally indignantly. 'He never attacks unless he's attacked — and then it's self-defence.'

The manager did not accept that. He was livid with rage, and demanded her name and address, and threatened to report Gyp to the police.

'Are you all right, Bateson?' he called to the man behind the locked door.

'I'm all right,' came a curt reply. 'But get that dog away from here!'

Sally took charge of Gyp and soothed him, while Ted explained that they had come specially to see the mimic, and would like a word with him now.

'We'd like to apologise in person,' added Sally.

Leaving them outside, the manager went into the mimic's room; and gradually the other stage hands and attendants moved away, leaving Sally and Ted alone.

'Well, Sally, what do you make of it?' asked Ted in a low tone. 'Gyp obviously knows that mimic, although how I can't think.'

'He certainly knows him. Oh, Gyp,' said Sally, looking down at him, 'if only you could talk. Where did you meet him? Who is he?'

'Not much sense in asking him questions,' grinned Ted. 'But I think it's pretty obvious, Sally, that he's our man. Gosh — just thought of something. Whoever locked Gyp in our shed must have lured him there. That means he palled up with him.'

'Yes, of course, Ted!' said Sally eagerly. 'It's beginning to add up. There's only one man... he lured Gyp to the shed, imitated your uncle's voice, and also made riot in our sitting-room. And obviously he is...'

The manager came out of the mimic's room suddenly.

'Mr Bateson will see you after the show,' he said curtly. 'And I hope you will have full apologies ready. He has never seen the dog before in his life, he says, but thinks the dog may have been attracted by a dog-whining sound he was making.'

Ted and Sally exchanged glances, amused. Pretty feeble excuse! But as they wanted to meet the mimic face to face, they accepted that version and said they would call round after the show.

As they could not re-enter the auditorium with Gyp, they walked about outside until the show ended.

'We'll spring artful Mr Bateson a surprise,' whispered Sally. 'I've got the black beard Gyp found. If it's Mr Bateson's, Gyp will give him away when I ask him whose it is. That's his favourite trick; he gives the article straightaway to the owner.'

They heard the finale; they saw the audience throng out. Then, when everyone had gone, they went backstage to call on the mimic. Gyp pulled them to the right door, his back bristling; but even as Sally raised her hand to knock, the manager came out.

'Oh,' he said, frowning. 'It's you! Mr Bateson has gone. In any case, he has decided to overlook the matter, so you're in luck. Take my advice, and go before that dog gets into more scrapes.'

Sally looked at Ted in bitter disappointment. Defeat — for the time at least; and they were not surprised when the manager refused to tell them Mr Bateson's home address. He was dodging them!

'He's the man all right,' said Sally excitedly. 'Although how we prove it, goodness knows. I don't think I'd know him off stage if I saw him — average build, clean-shaven. That velvet purple mask hid his eyes.'

'Yes,' Ted agreed, frowning. 'He's dodging us. But, if we're right, Sally, we'll meet him again. He'll be at his tricks, and that means he'll be somewhere around our cottages.'

'Gyp, it's up to you,' Sally ended. 'Next time you see him, hold him.'

They raced for their bus, and only just managed to catch it before it drove off. As they neared their journey's end they realised that it would be as well if they separated, so they decided to get off the bus near the general store, half a mile from the village, and walk home by different routes.

'If we solve this mystery and prove that man is the culprit, we need not be friends in secret any longer, Ted,' said Sally, as they got off the bus. 'Your uncle and my aunt will be shaking hands and making it up.'

Someone was hurrying towards the bus from the village as they alighted, but, seeing them, he slowed and waved his walking-stick.

'Why, it's Mr Graham Portland,' said Sally. 'He's waving to us, Ted!'

The artist came forward, swinging his stick, and hailed them. Suddenly, Gyp leaped forward with a snarl. In alarm, Mr Portland swung his stick in front and fended Gyp off.

'Careful with the stick; don't threaten him,' begged Sally.

She grabbed Gyp's collar, and Mr Portland fingered his little goatee beard nervously.

'That's not like him,' he said. 'Could it have been the stick scared him?'

'Yes — you were waving it; and he's a bit touchy this afternoon,' smiled Sally. 'Sorry, Mr Portland; but he wouldn't have bitten you.'

'That's all right! Anyway, I was coming to bring you news,' he said. 'I was hoping to see you. Remember that man with the shambling gait and black beard? I saw him a few minutes ago as I was walking up from the village. He darted in amongst the trees not twenty yards from the telephone box. He may still be there.'

There was not a moment to lose. They thanked him briefly, and raced towards the box. Sally let Gyp go free with a cry of: 'Seek!'

Gyp was not absolutely sure what he had to seek, but he rushed amongst the trees eagerly. Then Sally produced the black beard and let him sniff it.

'Whose is it?' she asked. 'Seek!'

Gyp sniffed the beard, and looked about him, puzzled; but he went on amongst the trees, sniffing keenly.

Suddenly, he gave a growl, made for the footpath and bounded along it, barking. A man's angry cry came, and Ted stopped in his tracks.

'Uncle!' he gasped.

'Or the man — imitating him,' cried Sally. 'Come on!'

They raced on, but halted side by side when they came upon Gyp drawing back from a man who stood with his walking-stick in threatening attitude... Major Bunting.

'Uncle!' said Ted, amazed.

'Ted,' cried Major Bunting, wheeling on him, as Sally seized Gyp. 'You — walking with this girl? Am I to believe that, after all I have said, you are making friends with her — Miss Carstairs's niece? Have you gone over to the enemy?'

'Uncle — I — er — you see —' faltered Ted, uneasily.

'You had better go home, my boy — alone! I will talk to you on my return. And for you, miss, please take charge of your dog,' he ended sternly.

Then he paused to watch Ted hurry along the path. Sally, realising it would not do to go the same way as Ted, turned back, her heart heavy. At last, it had come. Their friendship was forbidden. The feud between Ted's uncle and her aunt Alicia was to divide them, too. For if Ted was forbidden to be friends with her, she could not aid and abet him in defying his uncle!

She forgot about the man with the black beard until she was once again in the lane and hurrying for home. Then, when she did remember, she halted in horror.

'Gyp! Aunt Alicia can't be right — it wasn't Major Bunting who was in our house last night?' she cried. 'You didn't mean he owns the black beard, did you?'

Sally just couldn't believe it. Nevertheless, she was not in a jaunty mood when she returned to Rainbow Cottage and saw Aunt Alicia waiting at the gate.

'I'm glad you're back, Sally. I'm calling on Major Bunting,' said Aunt Alicia.

'Oh! Has something else gone wrong, Aunt?' asked Sally dismally.

Aunt Alicia smiled.

'He is defeated,' she said. 'Perhaps I scared him about the police. Can you believe it? He telephoned me in quite a changed tone, most humble, and apologetic. He said he'd explain the whole thing...'

'He'll explain? He — he is to blame?' gasped Sally, quite shaken.

'Of course. I said so from the first. As a peace-offering, he has offered me some of his potted plants. You remember seeing them? I shan't accept, but I'm going. He shall eat humble pie.'

Sally's face fell. She knew Aunt Alicia in her moods of triumph! The stubborn artist would be quite unable to resist making the very most of this little success — and the public humiliation of the Major was about the last thing Sally wanted. Far better for her sake, and Ted's, if the whole matter could be smoothed over as gently as possible.

'Couldn't you...? Sally began — but she immediately realised that it was absolutely no use asking her aunt to adopt a more magnanimous attitude.

Sally watched in rueful silence as Aunt Alicia set out, not realising what a tremendous shock she had given Sally. Sally was too startled even to warm her aunt that Major Bunting was not at home at the moment, and might not be back for some time, even if he had only gone to the little general store shopping.

'Oh, Gyp! And to think you know whose false black beard that was! If only, if only you could speak!'

But all Gyp said quite clearly in his own way was: 'Dinner! Now! Please!'

When the telephone bell rang a few minutes later, Sally guessed it would be Aunt Alicia; but she was wrong. It was Ted's voice she heard.

'Sally! Urgent. Go to the cove; get into my boat, and row round to the little bay and wait for me outside the Bell Cave. I may be late, but if I am, wait. Bring Gyp. Important!'

Before Sally could ask any questions, he rang off as if he were in danger of being caught telephoning her — by his uncle.

There was nothing she could do, but comply.

'Gyp!' she cried, looking around for her pet. 'Come here!'

Gyp had vanished; he had gone into the garden looking for another liver trail. It was a vain hope, but he had found something more important. His excited barking could be heard from among the trees behind the cottage, so Sally raced out, calling him.

His bark was eager, sharp, and presently he came running towards her, as if summoning her, turned back, looked round to make sure she was following, then raced on again.

'Sally!' she heard Ted shout in strangely muffled tones.

The sound came from an old shack in the woods and Sally, breathless with running, reached it to see Gyp clawing at the closed door, whining fretfully.

Sally opened the door, and then fell back. Ted, arms and legs roped, was crouched in a corner, a sack pulled over his head and roped on!

She wasted no time talking. She knew there was a knife in his pocket, so she got it out and hacked at the cords until he was free.

'Ted! What happened? I've only just had your telephone call.'

He scrambled, up, patting Gyp.

'Telephone call? I haven't telephoned you, Sally!'

'You — you mean you didn't ask me to go to your boat?'

'Thought never even entered my head. Gosh!' he cried. 'The mimic! He mimicked my voice to lure you off the scene. And he must have tied me up here. Mr Graham Portland met me on the path after I left you. Told me he had seen the man with the shambling gait, but without beard, coming into this shed. The man must have been in here behind the door, because a sack was pulled over my head. I fought, but hadn't a chance. He winded me, then roped me up.'

'So you were off the scene. And — and so's Aunt Alicia.

Goodness! Was that a faked friendly message to get her out of the way — and leave Rainbow Cottage clear?' said Sally, thinking aloud. 'Ted! It can mean only one thing. That man wants Rainbow Cottage to himself, and all of us out of the way. He's there now. Come on!'

In record time they reached Rainbow Cottage, with Gyp leading, proud and praised for having heard and recognised Ted's whistling, muffled though it was, and leading Sally to it.

They went by the back way, and very cautiously crept round the side of the cottage to the front. Hearts thumping, they halted when they had a view of the sitting-room windows. The curtains were drawn. Sounds of movement, the movement of furniture being dragged about, came from within.

Warily, seeing a chink between the hurriedly drawn curtains, Sally peered in. What she saw made her catch her breath. Heads together, she and Ted peered in, while Gyp lifted his paws on the sill, and whined.

On the floor knelt a man in a hooded black cloak. His face could not be seen; nor could she clearly see what he was doing.

'He's lifted a floorboard,' breathed Ted.

'Yes, and he's taking up a box!'

They drew back, tense, thrilled. At last, they had run the culprit to earth. Here he was, caught in the act.

'Can we tackle him alone?' breathed Sally, anxiously. 'He may be tough! But if we go for help — he'll escape.'

'We've got Gyp,' said Ted confidently. 'Let's go round the back way.'

They went quietly round to the back of the house, and Sally went to the back door — only to jump back with a stab of horror as it opened slightly.

'Oh, Sally,' came Aunt Alicia's voice, a little hoarsely.

'Be a darling and go to the village shop will you? We're out of sugar. Get a two-pound packet. Hurry, dear.'

Sally stood motionless. The voice was very, very like Aunt Alicia's; the tone was dead right, and the manner, too. But, perhaps because she knew it was a fake, a cunning mimicry, she could detect a difference; it was alto rather than treble! It was a man who spoke, pitching his voice high. The mimic! Who else?

'Yes, Aunt... of course,' replied Sally, bluffing. 'Come on, Gyp!'

But Gyp was not there. Ted, as she turned, hurled himself at the door — and rebounded. It had been locked from inside.

Sally tried the windows but they were fastened.

'Round the front,' she decided.

They raced round to the front of the cottage just in time to see Gyp bound through the gateway into the lane, snarling. As they reached the gate, they heard a yell, and then his angry, threatening snarl. At the same moment, Major Bunting shouted and Aunt Alicia gave a scream.

Sally, running her hardest, rounded the bend, and then raced even faster when she saw a man sprawled on his back in the lane, and Gyp, forefeet on his chest, holding him down, daring him to move.

Major Bunting was trying to strike at Gyp with a stick, but Aunt Alicia was keeping him off.

'Sally... quick! Gyp is attacking Mr Graham Portland,' she cried.

Sally grabbed Gyp, and looked down at the white face of Gyp's victim — Mr Graham Portland. But there was something strange about his face. And in a flash she knew what that was — he had no goatee beard.

'Mr Portland? Aunt — this is the man who was in Rainbow Cottage a minute ago,' she cried.

She saw a man sprawled on his back... and Gyp, daring him to move.

'That's him all right,' cried Ted triumphantly. 'Gyp collared him when he was lifting the floorboards, taking out something.'

Mr Graham Portland struggled up.

'Utter tosh! I was walking past the cottage when. . .'

He broke off as a car pulled up suddenly, and two uniformed police officers stepped out.

'Good evening, Mr Bateson,' said one, giving Mr Portland a friendy salute.

'Mr Bateson!' cried Sally, 'Why, he's the mimic at the pierrot show.'

'Yes, miss, and a grand show, too,' said the policeman genially.

Then he turned to Aunt Alicia, who was quite bewildered by all this.

'You aren't the lady who dialled the police?' he asked. 'Shut in a room? We stopped at Beam Ends, the address she gave, but no one was there!'

This was a surprise for Sally.

'Yes, I am. I was locked in by this — this villain,' said Aunt Alicia, pointing to Major Bunting. 'But there was a telephone in the room, so I dialled 999. However, he relented and released me.'

'Madam, I tell you I did not lock you in!' fumed Major Bunting. 'And —'

A snarl from Gyp made him break off. Gyp, with a twist, freed himself from his collar, which Sally was holding, and leaped at Mr Portland-cum-Bateson, who, taking advantage of the change of interest, had suddenly moved away.

Down he went as Gyp ran between his legs.

'Hold that dog,' commanded the policeman.

'Hold that man,' added Ted, and grabbed the mimic. 'He was burgling Rainbow Cottage.'

'He locked Aunt Alicia in Beam Ends, after luring her

over there by mimicking Major Bunting's voice,' cut in Sally.

'It's a lie,' panted Mr Portland-Bateson viciously. 'Let me go!'

Gyp moved away. He was looking for something, sniffing along the roadside. He knew it had been flung away — he had seen it. Ah, there it was!

Gyp's barking took Sally's attention and she ran to him. Stooping, she dragged at it, a heavy box. The second policeman, noticing the weight, grabbed it, and took it to the group. Amidst silence, he put it down, and opened the lid.

'Gold!' he gasped. 'Gold ingots!'

While everyone stared at the gold, the first policeman took a grip of Mr Portland-Bateson; the second pulled out a folded column of faded newspaper from the box. He read it, eyes rounding in wonder.

'The remains of the Gold Bar Robbery,' he said, amazed. 'Remember the case, Jack? One of the crooks mimicked the van driver's voice — why! It was you, Mr Bateson!' he ended. 'You're the member of the gang that wasn't caught! This is a cutting from the papers, giving the story of the crime!'

Mr Portland-Bateson wriggled in vain.

'Yes, I'm your man,' he snarled. 'The chief hid it under floorboards in Rainbow Cottage where he was hiding out, the day before he was arrested!'

'So that's why you searched the house?' cried Sally.

'Yes, that's why. And if you kids hadn't been so smart... and but for that dog! He's the one that spoiled my chance,' ground out the crook, looking savagely at Gyp. 'I could fool you, but not him. He knew Graham Portland, the self-styled artist, and Bateson the mimic were one and the same.'

'And you invented the man with the black beard! Gosh, what mugs we were...' gasped Ted. 'You all the time!'

'Of course! He did it to put us off his track,' said Sally.

Gyp yawned. He had known it all along. He had done his job, though, and lost interest. But he gave a farewell bark when Mr Portland-Bateson and the box were taken away in the police car a few minutes later.

'Well,' said Aunt Alicia, quite overcome. 'So — so you were right, Sally! That awful man imitated the Major's voice!'

Major Bunting brushed out his moustache.

'Madam, I assured you I was innocent of such base conduct,' he said proudly.

Aunt Alicia was quite humble.

'Major Bunting, I apologise for my false accusations. But really — who could have guessed? It's fantastic! And did that rogue also change the name-plates?'

'It's as likely as not,' said Major Bunting. 'Evidently the scoundrel locked you in my house to have the coast clear for his searching.'

Sally looked at Ted and smiled.

'Isn't anyone going to thank us for cleaning up the mystery?' she asked.

Aunt Alicia slipped an arm about her shoulders.

'Darling, of course. That awful feud was ruining my holiday. I hate thinking ill of people.' She looked appealingly at Major Bunting.

He smiled back.

'My dear lady, I bear no ill-will,' he said. 'I quite understand you could not believe that anyone could imitate my voice so exactly.'

'Then let us forget it,' said Aunt Alicia gladly. 'I take back the horrid things I've said.'

'I apologise for any criticism of you that may have been implied in my remarks,' said the Major gallantly. 'In fact, I even forgive the dog. He behaved marvellously. The way he tackled the crook was positively wonderful!' he exclaimed.

Gyp wagged his tail, greatly pleased, and the Major patted him.

'Major, do you like lobster?' asked Aunt Alicia.

'Ah, I do indeed,' he smiled in reply.

'Then come into Rainbow Cottage and have some lobster mayonnaise — there's enough for all of us. We have so much to talk over.'

'My old friend Ted can come, too, Aunt?' asked Sally smiling.

'Your old friend?'

'Oh, well, we've known each other a long time,' said Sally. 'Eh, Ted?'

'Spent last Christmas holidays together,' nodded Ted.

'Wha-a-t?'

Aunt Alicia and Uncle William were dumbfounded.

'But you've been acting as strangers!' said Aunt Alicia.

'You didn't tell me you were friends, Ted,' exclaimed Uncle William.

'Well,' said Sally, linking arms with Ted, 'we thought you might ban it, Aunt, as there was a kind of family feud.'

'And that would have been simply awful,' added Ted. 'So we were friends in secret.'

'And worked hard to end this feud; because we want you to be friends, too, Aunt and Uncle,' said Sally, with a smile at the Major.

Aunt Alicia looked at Uncle William and they laughed.

'Sometimes the young are wiser than the old,' Uncle William said. 'Friendship is far better than feud. Come, there's plenty of holiday time left. Shall we take a lesson from the youngsters?'

He offered his arm to Aunt Alicia, who smilingly took it. So, they had a party, and Uncle William proved to be very cheery and Aunt Alicia, ashamed of having misjudged him, went out of her way to be nice.

Next day, when by arrangement they were making a joint party to go down to the cove, a police car drove up.

Statements would be required from them all a Detective Inspector explained, when he had congratulated Sally, Ted and Gyp on their good work.

'Tell me one thing, Inspector,' urged Uncle William. 'Have you found why that fellow changed the name-plates on the cottages?'

'Yes, sir. He made a full statement,' nodded the Inspector. 'His story is that he knew the chief crook had buried the gold — in a cottage he had rented. It was only after two years he found the name and location of that cottage, though.'

'And he found out that the stolen gold was hidden in Rainbow Cottage?' asked Sally. 'But why was he so long finding it?'

'Ah, he didn't know in which room, or under which board it was. And — he was having a race with a rival crook who also found out the name of the cottage at the same time. This one, Bateson-Portland-Jones, got here first. And to fool his rival, he changed the name-plates.'

Ted gave a muffled cry.

'Gosh! That's the meaning of the message in Beam Ends... "Fooled".'

'That's it,' nodded the Inspector. 'The rival went to Beam Ends, which falsely had the name Rainbow Cottage. He found a floorboard raised, and a chalked message which made him think Bateson-Portland-Jones had got there first. So — he went off, beaten. The trick worked. Portland-Jones stayed; but by then, you, sir,' he said to the Major, 'entered Rainbow Cottage, also deceived by the false name-plates into thinking it Beam Ends. And so, the trouble began.'

'And he realised it caused a quarrel, and fed the flames so the Major would be blamed,' cried Sally, 'for whatever happened at Rainbow Cottage?'

'Exactly. He had to pull up floorboards while the house was occupied, and that took some explaining away.'

'So, the poltergeist,' said Aunt Alicia, startled. 'And it was Mr Graham Portland who told me about it. The rogue! Fancy my thinking he was a painter. Well — I had my doubts,' she said with a very wry smile, 'but he did fool me.'

'Fooled a good many people, ma'am,' nodded the Inspector. 'He got a job as a mimic in the pierrot show — on his merits; and it gave him a chance to be on the spot here. The mask in the show and the goatee beard when out of it, covered him nicely.'

Gyp yawned noisily.

'Smart dog, that,' said the Inspector. 'He'd make a police dog with training.' At that, Gyp made an odd half-yawning, half-growling sound.

'Come on, Gyp... to the cove!' called Sally.

Off she went with Ted, followed by Aunt Alicia and the Major.

'Ted, if they even seem to be having cross words — we have o stop them immediately,' laughed Sally. 'Our friendship depends on theirs.'

Riverboat Rendezvous

by Frances Towers

Joy Weston stood in the booking-hall at Newnham Abbot Station in Devonshire. There was a troubled look on her pretty face, and her usually sleek brown hair was ruffled after a long and tiring journey. She had just learned from the ticket collector that there was no connection to the little town of Tonbury until next morning. Tonbury was only ten miles away, but there was no bus or taxi available either.

The ticket collector pointed to another passenger who had got off the same train. 'Mr Mitchell might take you,' he said. 'He lives at Tonbury.'

Joy looked around. A middle-aged man, with rather sharp features, and well dressed in expensive clothes, smiled at her. Then he looked down at her case, which was clearly labelled: 'Joy Weston, care of Mrs Hammond, The Ferry House, Tonbury.'

'I'd be glad to give you a lift,' he said. 'I leave my car in a garage here when I go to London on business,' he added. 'I'm going to Tonbury now, and could quite easily take you. I see you are going to Mrs Hammond's place. I don't know her personally, but I've been staying at the Tonbury Arms Hotel for some months now. My name is Mitchell.'

'It's very kind of you,' Joy said gratefully.

'I'll get the car,' he concluded, giving her a quick smile. He walked away and returned only a few moments later, driving a very slick-looking car. He heaved Joy's case into the back, and they were soon running smoothly and swiftly along the road to Tonbury.

'Don't think me inquisitive,' said Mitchell, 'but it's unusual for a young lady to visit Tonbury at this time of the year.'

'Oh,' said Joy, 'this is a late holiday, and a farewell visit to old friends. I expect you know the Ferry House. It's by the river, and the landing-stage, where the big river steamer stops.'

'Of course,' said Mitchell. 'The famous river trips are Tonbury's chief industry, one might say.'

'That's right,' said Joy. 'Well, my friend Pamela Hammond lives there. Her father and mother started the river trips.'

'Very interesting,' said the man. 'But didn't Captain Hammond die earlier this year?'

Joy nodded sadly. 'Yes, Pamela and her mother managed to carry on, but I'm afraid this has to be their last season.'

Mitchell stared at the road ahead, driving with almost automatic skill. It was a bit of luck, meeting up with this girl. He knew all about the Hammonds. Captain Hammond had 'made' Tonbury with his river trips. The place had been rapidly declining in importance, but it stood on the edge of a broad river which ran down to the sea at the big coastal resort of Tonmouth. On retiring from the sea, Captain Hammond had the brilliant idea of running a kind of showboat, making two-day pleasure cruises. The trips were something quite new in the way of an extra holiday excursion for visitors to the coast. Captain Hammond's flair for showmanship kept the big launch plying the river all summer, gay with dances, music, games and entertainment, and brought badly needed trade to Tonbury.

'I expect you've been here before, then,' said Mitchell.

'Yes,' said Joy, 'I used to go up and down the river most summer holidays when Pamela and I were at school together. It will seem sad helping them to pack up.'

'Humm!' said Mitchell thoughtfully, and a little smile of satisfaction crossed his sharp features. Then, with a deft twist of the wheel, he turned a corner and swung down the hill into Tonbury.

He halted the car outside the Tonbury Arms Hotel, which stood near the river, a few hundred yards from the Ferry House.

'Thank you very much,' Joy smiled.

'It was nothing,' said Mitchell. 'Now that we've met, do come and visit us here. I have a daughter about your age.'

Joy thanked him once again, and started to walk along the river path. Ahead she could see the Ferry House, with its balcony facing the water, its landing-stage still gay with flags and bunting. The beautiful white river steamer, *River Belle,* was moored alongside. But the house was all shuttered up. Joy crossed the landing-stage, went on the deck, and called.

Pamela Hammond came bounding up from below to seize Joy in an embrace.

'Oh, Joy, it's good to see you,' she cried. 'End of season is always a bit sad, but what with having to give up everything, well...'

'It's good to be here again, Pam,' said Joy. 'Where's your mother?'

'Down below, packing stuff in crates,' said Pam. 'But we had given you up for today. How did you get here?'

'I missed the main train and was stuck at Newnham Abbot,' explained Joy. 'If it hadn't been for Mr Mitchell, I should have been in a fix.'

'Mitchell?' said Pam, when Joy had explained more fully. 'Oh, yes, I seem to have heard of him. He's been at the hotel, with his daughter, on a long holiday. But come down below. We have so many things to do that Mother and I have been living on board.'

'It sounds fun,' said Joy, as they went below and into the

saloon lounge. Pam's mother looked up from a large crate into which she was packing crockery, and greeted Joy with an affectionate smile.

'I knew who it was the minute I heard you call, my dear,' she said. 'We are so glad to see you, but sorry things aren't quite what they used to be,' she added.

'I don't mind a bit,' said Joy. 'I'm only too glad to have a holiday at all, and a chance to help.'

It was a long time before Pamela and Joy fell asleep that night. Mrs Hammond had put them both in the little two-berth cabin they had shared many times before, and the two girls lay in their bunks talking.

'I can't see why the trips can't be carried on as usual next season,' said Joy. 'What's to prevent you and your mother running the business?'

'Well, you can't just sail a boat anywhere you like,' said Pam. 'Dad had special permission from the local authorities. But the council doesn't seem keen on giving us permission. I suppose they haven't the same confidence in Mother.'

'I don't see why not,' said Joy, rather indignantly.

'Neither do I,' sighed Pamela, 'but they talk about being responsible for passengers' safety, and so on, and I think Mother is getting weary of the struggle.'

Joy lay staring up into the darkness, listening to the slap of water against the side of the launch, and puzzling over the odd attitude of the town authorities.

Suddenly, on an impulse, Joy slipped from her bunk, thinking that perhaps a short walk on deck would help. She put on her coat and a pair of sandals, and went on deck. The moon was quite bright, and the river looked lovely.

Joy paced the deck silently, but stopped suddenly, feeling sure she had seen a shadowy figure moving about inside the wheel-house.

Joy hesitated for a moment, then tip-toed up to the wheel-house. The door was open. Joy was about to step inside, when a dark shadow rose from near the big wheel. There was a metallic clang, and then the black figure rushed towards her.

Joy shrank back and put out her hands to ward off the menacing figure. But it brushed past her, raced along the deck and down the gang-way. She ran to the rail and peered across towards the landing-stage. The figure was bounding away into the shadow of the trees beside the river path leading to the town.

Joy stood for a moment, her heart pounding. Should she wake Pam and Mrs Hammond? There seemed no point in that now. They could never catch the intruder. She gave a last look towards the river path, then turned back to the wheel-house.

Drifting clouds had hidden the moon, and it was very dark. Joy realised that, without a torch, it was useless to search the place. She groped her way out, and along the deck, back to her cabin, where Pam was still sleeping peacefully.

Joy climbed into her bunk, determined to awake early and take a look at the wheel-house in the light.

It was a bright morning when she awoke. She went over to Pam, and tapped her lightly on the cheek.

'Pam, wake up!' she whispered.

Pam stirred sleepily and sat up.

'What time is it?' she murmured.

'Never mind the time,' said Joy. 'Get dressed quickly. We had a prowler on board last night.'

Pam's eyes widened with astonishment as Joy swiftly recounted the strange incident. 'Why didn't you wake us?' she said.

'I thought it might alarm your mother,' said Joy. 'I thought we should try to find out what's going on, and spare her as much worry as we can.'

'You were right, Joy,' admitted Pam. 'Mother has enough trouble. Perhaps it was just some sneak thief, prowling around.'

Joy looked doubtful. 'I don't think an ordinary tramp would go to the wheel-house,' she said. 'The galley is more likely.'

They hurried up on deck to the wheel-house and Pam took a searching look at every familiar detail. There was absolutely nothing unusual, except for a big spanner lying on the floor near the wheel.

'Does that belong here?' asked Joy, as they stared down at the spanner. But it was obvious from Pam's face that it did not.

'It's nothing to do with the boat,' Pam said, shaking her head slowly. 'The place for a spanner would be the engine room. But everything was put away when we laid up for the winter.'

'I heard a clanging noise,' said Joy. 'There's no doubt that our mysterious visitor dropped this spanner. The question is, what was he, or she, trying to do with it?'

'There can only be one reason,' said Pam, 'someone has interfered with the steering. But why would anyone want to sabotage the boat? It isn't going to be used until next spring.'

Joy picked up the big spanner and weighed it in her hand.

'There's something behind this,' she said. 'People don't do things like this for fun. Pam, we could try to trace this spanner. I'll go to the Tonbury Arms Hotel this morning and call on Mr Mitchell. He invited me to come and see him and meet his daughter. While I'm there, I'll ask him what he can tell me about this spanner. He runs a car, and should know about such things. In the meantime, Pam, we must remember that this steering is faulty.'

The two girls left the wheel-house, and went below to find Mrs Hammond bustling about in the galley preparing breakfast.

After breakfast Pam and her mother set to work packing, but Mrs Hammond was quite keen for Joy to call on Mr Mitchell.

'We've plenty of time for packing,' she said, 'and I'd be glad for you and Pam to have some young company. Ask Mr Mitchell and his daughter to tea if you like, about four o'clock.'

So Joy set off with the big spanner under her arm, wrapped in her cardigan.

The Tonbury Arms Hotel was a pleasant old place. Joy waited in an oak-panelled lounge, while a cheery maid went off to fetch Mr Mitchell. There was a wood fire burning in the wide old-fashioned fireplace, though the day was far from cold, and Joy could hardly believe there could be a mysterious intruder in such a peaceful rural atmosphere.

Mr Mitchell came into the lounge at last, a friendly smile on his face.

'Well, it's my little lady in distress,' he said brightly. 'I'm glad you called. My daughter will be down in a moment. All your friends at the Ferry House quite well?'

'Yes, thank you,' said Joy. 'Mrs Hammond would like you both to come to tea this afternoon. But, Mr Mirchell, before anything else, I would like to ask for your help again.'

Mitchell shot Joy a shrewd glance from narrow eyes which belied his broad smile. 'Certainly, my dear,' he said.

Joy unwrapped the big spanner from her cardigan. Mitchell stared at it and frowned.

Joy laughed apologetically. 'It's an odd thing to bring when calling,' she said, 'but can you tell me anything about this?'

'What do you mean?' Mitchell asked.

'Pam and I found this on the boat,' said Joy, 'and we don't know what it's for. I thought that, as you know something about cars, you might be able to help.'

Mitchell's frown faded. 'Oh, I see,' he said. 'It may be part of the boat's gear. Let me see...' He took the big spanner, and turned it over in his hands. 'Well, there's nothing very special about a spanner,' he said. 'You use it to tighten or loosen nuts. It's the sort of thing you would have on a ship.'

'You can't tell me anything special about it?' asked Joy, rather disappointed.

Mitchell shook his head. 'It's one of thousands,' he said. What makes you think there's anything special about it?'

Joy hesitated and at this point Mr Mitchell's daughter came in.

'Ah, Sylvia,' said Mr Mitchell, 'this is the young lady I told you about. Joy, my daughter, Sylvia.'

'How do you do?' said Joy politely.

Sylvia Mitchell gave her a cold smile. Joy, who was not easily prejudiced, decided that Sylvia was a thoroughly spoiled, affected young lady.

'Joy's hostess, Mrs Hammond, has asked us to tea on the boat. I'm sure we'd like to go very much. What do you say, Sylvia?'

Sylvia glanced at her father. Joy could see that the girl did not want to accept, but Mitchell frowned and gave a sharp nod.

'I think that would be lovely,' she said.

Joy had never heard a more insincere remark in her life, but she smiled, and said: 'I must go and give Mrs Hammond a hand now, but we'll expect you this afternoon at about four o'clock.'

'We'll look forward to that,' said Mitchell, and very politely escorted Joy to the hotel entrance.

Joy remembered the spanner as she turned on to the riverpath.

'I'm an idiot!' she said aloud. 'A fine detective I would make, losing my only clue.' She promptly walked back to the hotel, but on asking for Mr Mitchell, a maid told her he was taking his car out of the garage.

Joy asked if she might look in the lounge, and there on a chair she found her cardigan, but there was no sign of the spanner.

'Here's Mr Mitchell now, bringing his car to the front of the hotel,' called the maid suddenly.

Joy ran for the entrance, and almost stumbled over Sylvia Mitchell, who was coming downstairs to join her father.

'I'm sorry,' she said, 'I forgot my cardigan.'

The girl merely gave her a bleak smile, and they left the hotel together.

'Hello,' said Mitchell. 'What brings you back, Joy?'

'I forgot my cardigan,' said Joy, 'and the spanner,' she added.

Mitchell stared at her, a fixed smile on his face. 'The spanner? Oh, yes, the spanner. But you took that with you,' he said.

'No,' protested Joy. 'I should have remembered my cardigan in that case. I wrapped the spanner in it, you see.'

Mitchell shook his head.

'You sound as forgetful as my dear Sylvia,' he said. 'You're so keen to get on with the next thing that you always forget something. I'm sure you took the spanner. I remember handing it back to you. Never mind,' he added boisterously, 'that rather neatly disposes of your little problem, doesn't it?'

By this time Sylvia had slid into the seat next to her father, and the car moved off, with Mitchell still smiling cheerfully and pretending to find the whole thing a great joke.

Joy watched the car move off, a curious little smile hovering on her lips.

'Mr Mitchell,' she murmured to herself, 'you have made a very big mistake. I may be a scatterbrain, but I'm not so silly that I can't remember when somebody hands me a great big spanner!'

She could hardly wait to get back to the boat to tell Pam that her investigations had gone better than she had ever dared to hope. There was no doubt in her mind now, that Mitchell was the prowler of last night.

'Mitchell and his snooty daughter!' exclaimed Pam, when Joy had told her all of the morning's events. 'But why on earth should he want to tamper with the boat?'

'That's something we must find out,' said Joy. 'At the moment it seems meaningless, I agree. What do you know about him, Pam?'

'Nothing, beyond the fact that they have been here some time.'

'I wonder if anyone at the hotel would be prepared to tell us anything about him,' said Joy thoughtfully.

'There's Freddy,' said Pam. 'He would help, and keep a secret.'

'Who is Freddy?' asked Joy.

'He used to work as a steward on the boat, and he loved Dad. He went to the hotel as a waiter when we closed down.'

'That's perfect,' said Joy. 'When can we see him?'

'I could go over this afternoon. What do you want to know about Mitchell?'

'Anything,' said Joy. 'As soon as we get some idea of who he really is and what he does, we may see some motive.'

'I get it,' said Pam.

'Right,' said Joy briskly. 'Now we must warn your mother that Mitchell and his daughter will be coming to tea.'

Mrs Hammond, unmindful of the strange intrigue going on around her, was delighted to think that Pam and Joy were making friends with such 'nice people'.

'Joy will help, Mother,' said Pam. 'I want to go over and ask Freddy if all the cutlery in the store room is on the ship's list, or whether some of it came from the Ferry House.'

'All right, dear,' said Mrs Hammond. Pam winked at Joy and hurried off to do her share of the investigating.

It was not until after lunch that Pam and Joy had a chance to talk alone.

'What news from your friend Freddy?' asked Joy.

'Not a lot, I'm afraid,' said Pam. 'Freddy says he will start investigating in earnest now. The Mitchells came to Tonbury three months ago. Mr Mitchell seems rich, and knows some of the local bigwigs, especially old Councillor Sims.'

'Well, it's not much to go on, is it?' said Joy. 'I suppose we must wait and see if Freddy turns up any more information.'

'Yes, and we had better change our clothes,' grinned Pam. 'It's getting on for three o'clock.'

By the time the Mitchells arrived, two very cool and poised young ladies in light cotton frocks were ready to welcome them.

'We have been over the boat before, you know, Mrs Hammond,' Mitchell said as Joy made the introductions down in Captain Hammond's private lounge. 'Sylvia and I took one of your trips down the river earlier in the year.'

'Then it's especially nice to welcome you back on board,' said Mrs Hammond sincerely. 'I'm afraid our trips this year were not what they were when Captain Hammond was alive. We could improve them in time, you know, but I don't think Councillor Sims feels like recommending a renewal of our permission to ply the river.'

The next part of the conversation was lost to Joy. She was thinking hard. Councillor Sims. So that was the man who had doubts about recommending a renewal. And one of the bigwigs that Mitchell knew was Councillor Sims. Obviously Mitchell was behind all this trouble because he wanted the river trips stopped! Joy suddenly became aware that Pam was nudging her hard.

'What is it?' she asked.

'Mr Mitchell has made a wonderful suggestion,' Pam said, smilling at her mother. 'He would like to give a grand gala-night on board.'

Mitchell nodded. 'It would be a splendid and original idea,' he said. 'And may I say that it would pay Mrs Hammond handsomely. Make a real gala-night of it, before it's really too late in the year. Invite all the prominent local people.'

Joy could only stammer: 'It sounds splendid.' But she whispered to Pam: 'I think I know what Mitchell is up to at last.'

* * *

When Mr Mitchell left the boat, at about six, he looked vastly pleased with himself. He waved cheerily from the landing-stage, and called up to Mrs Hammond. 'You work out what supplies and help you will need, and tell me the cost,' he reminded her. 'Then we'll have another meeting.'

'It seems too good an opportunity to miss,' murmured Mrs Hammond.

The time had come for Joy to speak. 'That's exactly what Mitchell is counting on, Mrs Hammond,' she said. 'But I have something very serious to tell you.'

'Goodness, Joy,' said Mrs Hammond, 'you do look solemn. What is it then?'

'Mrs Hammond,' said Joy, 'when did you first hear from Councillor Sims that it might not be possible to get permission for you to continue to run the river trips?'

'About three months ago,' said Mrs Hammond.

'I thought so,' said Joy. 'In other words, you managed to carry on, without any trouble, until Mitchell arrived. Did you know that he is very friendly with Councillor Sims? And who is Councillor Sims, anyway? Was he a friend of Captain Hammond?'

'He certainly wasn't,' Pam cut in. 'Dad didn't care for him at all. He always said Sims was an old rogue.'

'I'm not surprised,' said Joy. 'I'm quite sure now that Mitchell wants to buy up the boat, and run the trips himself.'

'What makes you say that?' demanded Mrs Hammond in surprise.

Joy swiftly recounted all that had happened, and Mrs Hammond stared in growing amazement.

'So you see,' concluded Joy, 'the steering is faulty, and Mitchell knows it, yet he wants the boat taken up the river. Why? Because the boat will run aground, and Mitchell will finally have a perfect case for saying that you can't be trusted to run the boat properly. Not everyone agrees with Councillor Sims, who has been paid to put doubts in the minds of the local authorities. But after that, they will.'

'It sounds like it,' said Mrs Hammond. 'It does indeed. But what a scheme, just to prevent me from earning a living.'

'It's more than that,' said Joy. 'Mitchell must have big plants to expand the business and perhaps that snooty daughter of his fancies herself as a showboat entertainer.'

'But what can we do?' asked Pam.

'If only we could force him to show his hand in some way,' said Joy angrily.

All three sat silently racking their brains for some plan of action until late that night but there seemed to be nothing they could do to turn the tables on Mitchell. At last they went to bed, feeling rather depressed.

Breakfast seemed likely to be a gloomy meal, but it was unexpectedly brightened by Freddy.

'Secret agent Fred Parker reporting,' he said with a cheery grin, as he peered round the saloon door.

'Freddy!' cried Pam. 'What are you doing here?'

'It's my day off,' said Freddy. 'I've got some news for you.'

'Don't keep us waiting, Freddy,' said Pam. 'What's the news?'

'Well, I was on late duty last night. About ten o'clock I had to take some tea up to one of the rooms on the first floor. I heard a great rumpus going on in Sylvia Mitchell's room. She sounded quite hysterical, and her father was getting very angry.'

'What was it all about?' asked Joy.

'I couldn't quite tell,' said Freddy. 'She kept saying something about "supposing it sinks, and we get drowned..." and getting all worked up. Mr Mitchell was saying: "Don't be so stupid. Do you think I would risk that? I tell you it will just run into the bank."'

Joy gave a whoop. 'That settles it,' she said: 'I was right! And the weak link in Mitchell's plan is Sylvia! I've got the answer now. Mrs Hammond, can you send an invitation to Mitchell and his daughter, Councillor Sims, and one or two friendly, respectable residents of Tonbury? Say that you want to discuss plans for the gala. He said there would have to be another meeting to decide the details. Then leave the rest to us.'

The idea of inviting the crooked Councillor Sims and other local businessmen to discuss plans for the gala event, seemed only natural to Mitchell. So two days later Mrs Hammond conducted a party around the boat to consider her suggestions for the arrangements. At the same time, Pam and Joy put their plans into action. Leaving Mitchell and the main party to inspect the deck, Joy drew Sylvia aside.

'Sylvia,' she whispered. 'Pam and I have and an idea about the gala night, something we three could do. I thought we might get up a little show of our own. We can use the wheel-house as a dressing-room. It's near the main deck. We can use part of that for a stage. Here, let me show you. At least you can tell me if you think it will work.'

Sylvia didn't want to spend a single moment on the boat on gala night, knowing what she did, but she allowed herself to be led away.

Pam, who was stationed near the gangway, saw Joy and Sylvia going inside the wheel-house, and watched for the agreed signal.

Inside the wheel-house, Joy continued to 'explain' to Sylvia.

'You see, there's plenty of room in here. We couldn't do anything while the boat was actually moving, of course, because it has to be steered from this big wheel here.'

Sylvia was staring at the wheel with a kind of horrified fascination.

'That's the most vital part of the boat, you see,' continued Joy earnestly. 'Give that a slight turn the wrong way, and the terrific weight of the boat, swinging against the bank would probably make a great hole in the stern, and the boat would sink in no time.'

Sylvia looked very strained. 'But it's not far to the bank, not like at sea. People could get out, couldn't they?'

Joy's imagination was really running riot now. 'They might,' said she, 'but in a very few minutes the water would probably reach the engines and the whole boat would blow up.'

'Blow up!' said Sylvia.

At this point Joy waved one arm cautiously behind her back. Pam came running over and, just as Joy was leading the conversation back to the show, burst into the wheel-house.

'I say, Joy, the boat's adrift,' said Pam excitedly. 'The mooring cable has slipped. We shall be in mid-stream drifting down the river in a minute. We must steer until we get the engines going! Here, Sylvia, you hold the wheel, and keep it exactly as it is. Joy, you watch this side, and I'll watch the other. Once we are on a straight course, we can tell the others. Perhaps the men can help start the engines.'

All this was complete rubbish, of course, and well Pam and Joy knew it. But Sylvia didn't! She began to yell as the girls pushed her towards the wheel, and put her hands on the spokes. She was still yelling at the top of her frightened voice when Mitchell, Mrs Hammond, and the rest of the party came dashing up to the wheel-house to see what it was all about.

'Stop it!' she was shouting. 'Let me get off! I can't swim... don't start the engines. Please don't start the engines.'

When Mitchell realised what was happening he tried to get to Sylvia to quieten her. But Pam and Joy were firmly holding the two side doors of the wheel-house, and the sliding glass panels were wide open, so that the whole story, gabbled

Sylvia began to yell as the girls pushed her towards the wheel.

out by the panic-stricken Sylvia, was clearly heard by at least four reliable witnesses... and Councillor Sims, who was slowly turning a pale green colour.

Soon the boat was in an uproar.

It took time to investigate the charges against Mitchell and Sims, but it was soon confirmed by a marine engineer that the steering of the boat had been sabotaged, and there was little doubt as to how and why. Mitchell tried to bluff, but Councillor Sims revealed the whole plot to ruin Mrs Hammond and buy up the river boat cheaply, so that he and Mitchell could run the very profitable business the following season.

Long before Joy went back to London she had the satisfaction of knowing she would be back again the following spring, to take up a permanent job with Pam and Mrs Hammond on the *River Belle*.

The Caravan Secret

by Peter Grey

It was almost dark when the caravan reached Netford. Tom Wayne dropped back in his seat with a sigh of relief, after bringing his car to a halt. His niece, Betty, gave him a sympathetic smile.

'Tired, Uncle Tom?'

'Not so much tired as... a bit stiff.' He groped for his pipe.

Betty spoke over her shoulder to her cousin, who was sitting in the back of the car.

'If you'll show me how to work that gas stove, I'll make some tea, Bill.'

'Right,' said Bill enthusiastically. His father made approving noises, as he drew heavily on his pipe.

Betty got out and stood for a second or two taking deep breaths of warm summer air. She gazed with wondering approval at the last rays of sunset which flamed in the sky, red, gold and orange.

'Pretty good?' said her cousin Bill.

She turned her shining eyes to him. It was more than good — it was too wonderful for words.

Bill nodded, understanding. He unlocked the caravan, and they went in.

'Look, this stove is quite straightforward, Betty... There!'

He lighted the gas-ring and flourished the spent match like a conjurer concluding a trick.

Betty smiled her thanks. Bill smiled back and began letting down the built-in table and opening folding chairs, while Betty prepared the meal.

It was a fitting end to the first day of a holiday that Betty and Cousin Bill had eagerly awaited for weeks. Uncle Tom had called one day to tell her father and mother that he had 'landed' the contract to build a government research station, down in Devonshire.

Uncle Tom never said very much about the details of his work. Betty only knew that he was some kind of an architect. But it was not the job that interested her... Uncle Tom, tired of makeshift arrangements and out-of-the-way hotels, had decided to buy the most modern caravan he could find.

Since Bill's mother had died, he said, they had no permanent home. Well, they had one now. Between terms at boarding school, Bill would come 'home' to wherever 'home' happened to be. And for the next few months it would be at Tyncombe, between moors and sea, in Devon!

Then came the surprise. What about a holiday for Betty, Uncle Tom suggested? She could drive down with them and stay until the new term started.

If he had suggested a luxury trip to the moon, Betty couldn't have been more excited. For all, or nearly all, of her thirteen years, Betty had lived in London. The idea of going off in a caravan to live fulfilled every dream of romance and freedom she had ever had.

Ready to start in about three weeks, then? Uncle Tom had asked. Ready in three minutes, more like it! But Uncle Tom had had a lot of things to arrange first. In the meantime, Bill had stayed at Betty's home, and daily he and Betty had planned all the adventures and explorations they were going to have. Together they had pored over Uncle Tom's Survey Maps, sprawled over the lawn on sunny days.

Betty had never thought that ordinary maps *could* be very interesting...

'But Dad's maps are pretty special' said Bill. 'They're not absolutely secret, but not everybody has one and certainly not everybody understands the special signs found on it.'

'Secret signs?' asked Betty hopefully.

'In a way,' said Bill.

'Show me some,' demanded Betty.

'Well...' Bill explained. 'These little groups of three lines with a line drawn across them mean that the ground there is swampy.'

'...and very dangerous?'

'Pretty dangerous,' agreed Bill.

'Gosh,' breathed Betty. 'Show me some more, Bill.'

Bill frowned. 'Over here,' he said, 'right on the Devonshire moors you see little marks like stars with old-fashioned writing underneath...'

Betty looked at some of the stars and saw these words in old-fashioned script:

'TUMULUS... TUMULI...'

'It means places where the ancient people of the moors used to bury people,' said Bill. 'They used to live up there on the moors smelting tin.'

'What a spooky place that must be,' said Betty shivering with delight. 'What else?'

'Well, you can find secret roads with this map.'

'How could you have a secret road?'

Bill moved a pencil across the map. 'Look,' he said, 'you see this road here... a red line... it joins another one, forming a triangle round the woods. The woods are in between, where the map is coloured green.'

Betty nodded.

'Running through the wood you see two lines of dots. Right next to them it says SUNKEN ROAD. Well, that road is invisible from the real road. It's like a big ditch across the wood. Trees and bushes grow over the top, so that it's like a secret tunnel.'

'Oh, let's see if there's one near where Uncle Tom's going to build the Government place!'

'I know there is,' said Bill. 'It's the first thing I looked for. Look, I'll show you...'

* * *

'What makes food taste so good in the country?' asked Bill, pushing back his plate, a while later.

'Fresh air, good appetite,' said Uncle Tom, ramming tobacco into his pipe. 'We haven't eaten much today, you know.'

The remarks reminded Betty that they had not bothered to stop for more than a sandwich and a cup of tea at a roadside café.

It had been quite an ordinary sort of place. *The Bluebird* it had been called. A converted cottage, really. There seemed no reason why it should have fixed itself in her memory. Perhaps because of that little incident of the handkerchief... Betty frowned slightly. It *was* a bit puzzling.

They had finished their sandwiches at *The Bluebird,* and gone out to the car again.

'I forgot my handkerchief,' she'd said suddenly.

Uncle Tom had grinned and made the old joke: 'You'd forget your head if it wasn't fixed on!'

She ran back to the cafe, to the table by the window. It had already been cleared. The woman who had served them was nowhere about. Betty pushed open a door that led from the café into the kitchen calling: 'Anyone there?'

The kitchen was empty. On a table she saw the tray of cups and saucers they had used. Nearby was a handkerchief. It must be hers. Uncle Tom was sounding his car horn, signalling her to hurry. She snatched up the handkerchief and ran back to the car.

It was over an hour later that she had discovered that the handkerchief was not her own. That was all. It didn't seem to matter.

'I think an early night would be a good idea,' said Uncle Tom, breaking in on her thoughts. 'You seem a bit tired, Betty, and an early start will be necessary. I want us to get to Tyncombe in good time tomorrow.'

While Betty cleared away and washed the tea things, Bill and Uncle Tom put away the chairs, and let down the bunks. The caravan had one main room, where Uncle Tom and Bill were to sleep and then, as well as a kitchen alcove, a narrow little room for Betty.

Within half an hour she was tucked up comfortably, staring up at the moon through her tiny window.

It was a glorious night. The moon shone like a silver penny lying on deep blue velvet. She seemed to lie there for hours, dreaming of the things they would do, she and Bill, when they got to Tyncombe...

Suddenly the stillness of the night was broken. Through her dreams — slowly at first — came sounds that did not seem to belong to the calm night, and her world of dreams. A muffled, metallic clank. A sense of furtive movement. A vague brushing against the sides of the caravan.

She pushed aside the bed covers, and knelt at the tiny window. It would probably turn out to be a cow or something, she told herself. But she wanted to know.

Betty peered out of the window. Everything looked strange and very different at night. But there was nothing that didn't seem right for the sort of place it was... or... was there?

Betty suddenly heard a very definite thump, and she let out a little 'Oh!' of surprise. A vague, shapeless shadow down by the car suddenly unfolded into a quickly moving figure. Before she could make another sound, the figure bounded away from the caravan, and was lost in deep shadow. As it ran, something white fluttered from it, and fell noiselessly to the ground...

It lay only a few feet from the caravan. Presently, her curiosity overcame any fears. Betty slipped from her bunk, out by the side door, and over to the white object...

As she bent to pick it up, she gave a little gasp of surprise. It was a handkerchief. And it had a smear of blood on it.

* * *

Back in her room, Betty looked at the handkerchief more closely. She could see that it had been screwed up into a rough bandage. 'They' had scratched 'their' hand, quite recently, and quickly tied the handkerchief over it. Two corners were still loosely looped together, but not properly tied into a knot. The sudden movement, the hasty flight, and... the handkerchief had slipped off.

Not only that. Betty's eyes widened. She fumbled hastily among her clothes. This handkerchief was surely... yes... exactly like the one she had picked up by mistake in the café!

She moved to the window, and in the moonlight, she compared the two... there was nothing very unusual about them, but there was no doubt but that they were exactly alike. This was no mere coincidence. It couldn't be.

'I'd better wake Uncle Tom,' she said aloud to herself.

Betty put on her dressing-gown, went to the door of the main room of the caravan and tapped loudly.

'Uncle Tom... Bill!' she called. 'Wake up!'

Betty heard Bill's sleepy voice. 'What is it?'

'Bill! It's me, Betty. I must talk to you and Uncle Tom. Bill! Are you properly awake?'

She heard Bill yawn loudly. 'Yes, I'm awake now. What's the matter? Can't you sleep?'

'It's not that,' she said. 'There's been someone outside.'

Uncle Tom's deep voice joined in. 'What's that, Betty? Are you sure? Haven't been dreaming, or anything?'

'No, Uncle Tom. Whoever it was dropped a...'

Uncle Tom and Bill struggled into dressing-gowns as she told them the story.

'I'll get a torch,' said Uncle Tom. 'Bill, you and Betty stay here while I look round.'

Bill opened the door and Betty went in. Uncle Tom, looking like a shaggy old bear, was just going out by the rear door, holding his big flashlight like a truncheon. They watched him through the window, as he scoured the field all round the caravan.

'There's no sign of anyone,' Uncle Tom said, as he came back, and stood by the door, tapping his flashlight thoughtfully on his hand. 'Come and show me just where you saw this... person, whoever it was.'

Betty led the way to the other side of the caravan.

Uncle Tom flashed his torch around and bent down by the car.

'Here?' he asked.

Betty nodded.

Suddenly Uncle Tom straightened up. Betty saw that there was a grave look on his face. The two children looked up at him, waiting for him to speak. Abruptly, as he caught sight of their puzzled, anxious faces, he forced himself to laugh.

'Oh... it's nothing...' he said. 'Nothing to bother about. Probably just some old tramp prowling about.'

He urged them gently back into the caravan.

'I don't like the idea of people prowling about trying to

steal food,' he said. 'I'd willingly give anyone a meal. But everybody doesn't take kindly to tramps. It's no wonder they try to steal. Now, you two, go back to bed and don't give it another thought.'

Betty was baffled. 'But, Uncle Tom,' she began. 'What about the handkerchief?'

'That!' said Uncle Tom. 'Well... there must be dozens of handkerchiefs like that. The tramp probably found it, or stole it. Off you go now. Have a glass of milk, and then get plenty of sleep. Early start tomorrow.'

Betty opened her mouth to say something, but Uncle Tom was busy pouring out the milk.

She took hers back to her little room, and sat for a long time on her bed. She was completely perplexed. Why should Uncle Tom look so grave, and then suddenly try to pass the whole thing off as if it had no importance whatever?

She finished her milk and knelt at the window.

She looked out... and started, nearly crying out. She thought she had seen the mysterious figure down by the car again. But this time it was Uncle Tom.

He was shading his flashlight carefully, but she could see that he had a big wrench in his hand, and that he was tugging at the coupling that hitched the caravan to the car!

Betty watched her uncle for a minute, greatly puzzled. Then, as he turned, she moved quickly back to her bunk. A faint creaking in the next room told her that he had returned to bed.

Betty was feeling sleepy herself... but she lay now, drowsy, yawning, yet unable to relax. Her mind went on asking questions she could not answer. Why had Uncle Tom changed his manner suddenly? Why was there a second handkerchief? What was he doing in the car? Questions came again and again... until, at last, she drifted off to sleep...

She awoke early. It was only five. She remembered now that before falling asleep she had thought: 'I'll get up early, and look at...'

After listening for sounds of Uncle Tom, or Bill, and hearing none, she went out quietly, and stood looking down at the coupling. Now she understood! Or did she? The coupling had been damaged. Uncle Tom had been putting it to rights. That was why he had looked grave last night.

Betty went back into the caravan. She did not want Uncle Tom to see her out there... If he wanted to keep things from her, and perhaps Bill, too, then it might be awkward for him to realise that Betty had seen through his deception. Deception! By Uncle Tom? It seemed strange.

Betty sighed, as she filled the kettle. Life had become one great mystery. She had an odd mixed feeling of doubt, concern, and... excitement.

'Betty?'

Bill's call broke into her thoughts.

'Yes, Bill! It's me. I was going to make some tea.'

'Good show! I say... you *are* early, aren't you?'

'I say, Bill...'

'Yes?'

Betty hesitated a second, then: 'Is Uncle Tom awake?'

'Not yet. He asked me to call him about six.'

'Come out here then,' said Betty, lowering her voice. 'I want to tell you something...'

They were leaning against the car, a few minutes later. Bill was saying: 'I guessed it too! I thought about it until I just couldn't keep awake. I heard Dad go out. He thought I was asleep. I don't understand it...'

'What I don't understand,' said Betty, 'is why Uncle Tom pretended it was just a tramp.'

'Because he didn't want us to feel scared, I know. That's

the funny part of it. He must think there's something to be scared of... but what?'

'Don't you think we should ask him? We could say we noticed the coupling had been damaged and then we could...'

Betty's voice trailed off. She was not sure just what they could do.

'No,' said Bill firmly. 'I know Dad. He'd feel he ought to send us back to Aunt Mary... your mother, I mean. He might do that anyway...'

'Oh, Bill!' said Betty. 'That would be awful! We've hardly started the holiday yet.'

'No,' said Bill. 'But...' He gave a big grin. 'We have started an adventure, haven't we? And with a bang! What do you say we wait and see what comes, and... how much we can work out for ourselves?'

'Of course, Bill,' said Betty.

It was an odd sort of day. All three seemed quiet... thinking, puzzling, to themselves. Betty had an anxious moment at breakfast. In spite of wanting an early start, Uncle Tom lingered over the meal. Once or twice he seemed about to speak...

Finally, to her great relief, Uncle Tom aroused himself and within half an hour they were on the road again.

Miles and hours rolled by until at last they were climbing the rolling hills of Devon.

Uncle Tom, who had spoken little all day, seemed relieved.

'Not far now,' he said. 'Tyncombe in half an hour. I've got to make a call there. Then we'll go out to the camp site.'

'Dad,' said Bill suddenly, 'wouldn't it be an idea to by-pass Tyncombe, leave us at the camp site, and then go into the village? Betty and I could be fixing things up...' Bill looked hard at Betty as he said this, and winked. She took the hint.

'Yes, Uncle Tom,' she said. 'That *would* be a good idea.'

'I could,' agreed Uncle Tom. 'All right, Bill, I'll take the left fork, then...'

'What is it, Bill?' whispered Betty.

'Tell you later,' he answered, putting his finger to his lips.

Betty stood looking across the fields, towards the sea.

Bill came running up to her. 'Dad's gone,' he said.

'Isn't this lovely.' said Betty.

'Lovely? Yes, jolly good. But we'll have to hurry. He'll be about an hour.'

'What? Oh, yes,' said Betty. 'What's this all about?'

'I want,' said Bill, urging her towards the caravan, 'a closer look at that coupling, and then... well, you'll see...'

Betty watched Bill as he examined the coupling.

'What can you see?' she asked.

'Scratches... marks... The point is, what do they mean? Now... the coupling wasn't completely smashed... nobody tried to file through it, or just loosen... I've got it! Someone forced the link apart... So... our mysterious somebody must have hoped we'd go off this morning without noticing any-thing and then after a few miles the caravan would come adrift, perhaps on a hill, where the strain would be greatest, and *crash!* And,' Bill banged his hand down on the side of the caravan, 'we could never have been sure that the link wasn't faulty in the first place!'

Betty stared at him in admiration.

'It does look like it, Bill, doesn't it? Do you think Uncle Tom knows?'

'I don't know,' said Bill. 'But come on...' and he led her towards the woods, pulling a Survey Map from his pocket.

He stopped at the edge of the wood, scanned his map, and looked up and down. Betty peered over his shoulder.

'That's... Oh, Bill! There's the secret road,' she said.

'That's right. I'm just wondering exactly where it starts. Let's set the map in line with this edge of the wood.'

Bill turned the map... 'There we are!' he said. 'The wood's on our left. Over there... the farmhouse. Now... the sunken road starts a little way from the corner of the woods.' Map in hand Bill walked quickly off, Betty bustled along beside him.

'Why are we going now, in such a hurry?' she asked. 'We ought to get the beds made up and supper ready before Uncle Tom gets back.'

'We'll have time enough if we don't dawdle,' said Bill. 'But we mustn't let Dad know we suspect anything until we've solved the mystery. One of the things we must have is a secret hide-out where we can talk in absolute secrecy. The sunken road will be ideal... Another thing, the sunken road curves out at one point and almost touches the other side of the wood. From somewhere along it we can watch the camp site, the caravan, the whole country for miles around. Here we are!'

'I don't see any road...' began Betty.

The woods where they had stopped looked so tangled that even a rabbit might find it hard to get through.

'Well, it won't exactly look like a High Street,' said Bill laughing.

'We'll have to push our way through. But let's try not to leave traces.'

'Wait a minute, Bill...' Betty had been looking around and an idea struck her. 'It would be easier to climb that big tree, and drop down, wouldn't it?'

Bill looked at the tree. 'Betty,' he said, 'that's a very bright idea. I'll go first and just make sure there's a safe spot to land on.'

The tree was an easy climb.

'This is fine,' he called. 'As good as a ladder.' He dropped a few feet to a thick carpet of leaf-mould.

Betty followed him. 'There it is now!'

* * *

They were now in a little clearing which sloped rapidly down towards an opening in the woods. Just as Bill had said... the sunken road! Like a deep ditch completely overgrown with trees and creepers. Then together they walked towards the opening, speaking in whispers.

'It curves to the right,' said Bill. 'We're getting nearer the other edge.'

It grew suddenly lighter. The trees above them were less tangled, and Betty could see that to the right only a thin screen of trees separated them from the fields. Bill climbed the side of the road, and peered through.

'This is fine,' he said. 'Look, we can see everything from here.'

He reached a hand for Betty. She took it, and felt about for a foothold. Near the top of the ditch, Bill let go of her hand, thinking she was safely up. But she had not had time to get her proper balance. She leaned backwards, wavered wildly for a second, then slipped and rolled down into the ditch.

She was not hurt, just startled. She gave a little shout as she fell, and clutched out blindly. There was a mass of creeper growing from the top of the ditch, hanging down into it like a waterfall of leaves. She grabbed out at it, but it snapped off like thin cotton in her hands.

Now she was lying on her back on the thick mass of dry leaves.

Bill called to her in alarm: 'Betty! Are you all right?'

She nodded ruefully. 'Yes. All right. You let go before I'd got my balance.'

She glanced over at the creeper. Her eyes widened.

'Bill,' she called, excitedly. 'There's a sort of tunnel. Come down here.'

'What?' Bill lowered himself into the road.

Betty had uncovered a small opening, dug in the side of the bank. It was narrow, but big enough to admit a grown man. 'It is a tunnel,' said Bill.

He pushed aside the creeper, and went in. The tunnel was very short, and sloped upwards. A few steps brought him to a small cave-like room. There were boxes lying about, and piles of sacks. Light came through a small window-like opening which, as he discovered, looked out over the camp site. It was a perfect look-out post.

He went back down the tunnel and called Betty.

'This place wasn't made last week, or last month either,' he was saying, half to himself. 'See the earth has been properly bolstered up with wooden beams and this window place, that's built up with sandbags! They've rotted away in places, but that's what they are. This must be an old Army dug-out left from the days when the Germans were expected to invade. What luck, Betty. We couldn't have found a better place.'

'You're right, Bill, some of these boxes have the letters WD marked on them. That means War Department, doesn't it? That's it, for sure. I say, Bill, there's another opening here! Behind these boxes.'

Betty was tugging at a pile of boxes stacked against one side of the earth wall. The boxes were light and quite empty. Bill cleared them aside to reveal another opening, lower and broader than the entrance to the look-out post. He knelt down and peered inside. It was quite dark.

Bill struck a match and held it as he crawled through the opening. He found himself in a small dug-out hardly bigger than a large cupboard. Before the match flickered out he saw something that made him start in surprise. He turned to Betty.

'Somebody else is using this place, Betty,' he said.

'How do you know?'

'Wait,' Bill struck another match. On a box inside the smaller room was a candle, some tin mugs and a magazine. 'Look,' he said, squeezing aside so that Betty could see. 'Those things haven't been here long. They're not even dusty.' He leaned forward, and picked up one of the cups. There were dregs of tea in it.

'Still wet!' he whispered. He picked up the magazine, and added: 'Last week's!'

Bill dropped the match and backed out.

'This gets more and more mysterious. . .' he began.

But Betty darted her hand out suddenly and grabbed his arm.

'Listen, Bill.'

They crouched there like two frozen rabbits. Two voices in gruff conversation could be heard coming up the sunken road.

The voices were nearer now. They could catch the words:
'*I told you always to drape the creeper over the opening.*'

'*Aw, nobody ever comes up here.*'

'*You'll do as I say, you careless fool!*'

'They're coming in,' Bill said. He looked around desperately. Then: 'Get in,' he said. 'It's our only chance.' He pushed Betty into the inner dug-out and replaced the boxes over the opening as well as he could from the inside.

A second later two men came into the look-out post.

Bill leaned against the wall, hardly daring to breathe. He

heard a scuffling as the men dragged up boxes and sat down. They began to speak: 'Well? What have you got to report?'

This was the man with the harsh voice. He seemed to have authority over the other man.

'Here,' the man with a slight whine in his voice spoke. 'I did this yesterday. It was quite a job, I tell you. But it should be very useful.'

The other man snorted. 'What's it supposed to be?'

'Can't you see? It's a plan of the place. I sat here for hours drawing in all the trenches they've dug for the foundations.'

'That's no good. You wasted your time. We've got all that from above. Photographs. Dozens of them, bah!'

Bill heard a sound, as if the man had thrown a sheet of paper down.

'If you were smart enough,' said the man with the harsh voice, 'to think for yourself, but you're not. That's why you'll do what you're told. Understand?'

'You didn't say...' began the other.

'I say now,' shouted the harsh voice. 'And mark my words, or you'll find yourself in trouble. You've wasted a whole day. You get started right away. And don't come near the top place again, ever.'

'I don't see the good of it,' began the man with the whining voice.

The other turned on him, shouting, 'You don't see? Who ever expected *you* to see?'

Bill crawled the few inches that separated him from the boxes. He raised himself and tried to squint through into the main dug-out.

He could just see a large sheet of paper, on which was drawn a rough plan. Beyond it was a pair of dusty boots with about three inches of blue overall trousers showing above them.

To the right was a brown shoe, a red sock, an inch of dark grey slacks.

Dare he try to move the boxes? Widen the crack? It was too risky. The boxes were too lightly balanced. The only thing to do was to listen, and hope... He felt a gentle tug at his foot. He edged himself back. Betty put her lips close to his ear, and whispered:

'Oh, Bill! Uncle Tom will be back...'

'Ssshh!' Bill was listening again to the two men.

'...now, get on with it...I'm going back to the top place... and I want to see something worth having when I come tomorrow or...'

There was the sound of movement as the men got up...

'You don't expect...' the whining voice was speaking now, '...me to *sleep* here again?'

'Yes', said the other promptly. 'You'll never be here on time otherwise. Besides, somebody might see you arriving. It's all right, isn't it?'

'Take a look,' said the whining voice. 'How would you like...?'

Bill's heart thumped so loudly he thought it must sound like a steam hammer. A few quick steps, and a thin ray of light filtered into the opening... They were taking away the boxes! He shrank as far back as he could, dragging Betty with him...They flattened themselves against the earth wall... and waited.

Outside...in the woods...not far from the dug-out...a bird fluttered up excitedly. The slight figure in the black siren suit and black beret had lain motionless for over half an hour watching the road, and the entrance to the dug-out. Now it moved, brushing leaves and branches aside, startling the keen-eared thrush with the faintest crackle of sound.

The figure rose carefully to its feet, moved quickly and

silently towards the dug-out...passed on a few yards. Above, on the bank, was a hollow tree. The figure slipped into the tree and lowered itself into a gaping hole inside. Then it lifted a small trap in the side of the well-like hole...and looked in on...Betty and Bill.

Betty and Bill, huddled together, were staring at the opening, tense and drawn.

They had no eyes for the slim, dark figure kneeling at the trapdoor, slipping a black silk scarf over its face. The harsh voice was saying '...I know it's not the best place in the world, but...'

Betty and Bill heard no more. The black figure reached out... clapped firm hands over their mouths, pulled them towards the trapdoor, whispering fiercely: '*Keep quiet, and I'll get you out of this. Do you understand?*'

Before they had grasped what was happening, they were both on the other side, the dark figure pressing them against the side of the hole beneath the hollow tree. They could still hear the voices of the two men...muffled, quarrelling. Presently the voices died away. The black figure spoke: 'Listen to me... When I go...wait a minute, then follow. You'll find yourself in a hollow tree, a few yards from the dug-out. You understand?'

Bill nodded.

'Get out of the wood, and stay out!' said the figure. 'Never come here again. You won't be lucky another time.'

The voice was angry, even though it spoke in a soft, urgent whisper. Bill could see its dark eyes glinting above the scarf which covered its face. The figure turned, scrambled up, and vanished.

'Come on,' said Bill, and his voice was shaky. 'Let's go!' He climbed up, helped Betty after him, then peered cautiously out. It took him a few seconds to realise where they were. He drew back quickly as he heard the voice of the harsh man below him...leaving the dug-out. When he looked again he saw a burly figure in grey slacks and a lumber jacket, walking quickly along the sunken road. A bird fluttered again on the other side of the wood, but Bill did not notice the black figure gliding off into the woods.

Breathless, they arrived back only a few minutes before Tom Wayne. He grinned at them as he climbed out of his car. 'I didn't think you'd get much done,' he said. 'Been exploring?'

Betty nodded. 'We rather lost our way.'

'Hoped you'd be too hungry to go exploring,' he said. 'How do you like the place?'

'It's wonderful, Uncle Tom,' said Betty. 'We love it, don't we, Bill?'

'Rather,' said Bill.

Uncle Tom grinned again. 'You two been up to some mischief?' he asked amiably, then turned away without waiting for an answer.

'Do you think we ought to tell?' Betty asked Bill. He shook his head. 'Wait...' he said.

For the next hour or so they were all three busy getting supper, and preparing the caravan for the night. Betty and Bill got no chance to talk again except for a brief moment when Uncle Tom went out to put a tarpaulin over his car.

'Gosh, Bill! What a day!' said Betty, coming back.

'What a day indeed,' said Bill. 'Hush now. Dad's coming back. We will talk about it all when we can get a moment to ourselves in the morning.'

Tom Wayne returned to the caravan to find them both deep in their books. He sat for a bit looking over his papers. Presently he suggested bed and soon they were all fast asleep. Night settled over the caravan like a black velvet cloak.

Even with a bright moon it would have been hard to see the slim black figure that still watched and waited, not far away.

* * *

'Goodness!' Betty blinked in surprise.

Uncle Tom took his pipe out of his mouth: 'Looks different, eh?'

They were standing looking over the fields towards the camp site. The fields now were swarming with people; cars and trailers were pouring in with supplies; bulldozers were at work; concrete-mixers churned away and several large huts were already half-erected.

A tall, sun-tanned man, in overalls, came up to Uncle Tom.

'We'll have your office ready by midday, Mr Wayne,' he said. 'The young lady is already down there.'

'Thanks, George. George, this is Betty, my niece, and Bill, my son...This is Mr Brent, our foreman,' he added to Betty and Bill.

'Hello, Betty, and Bill.' Mr Brent waved a big hand cheerily. 'Want a ride on a bulldozer?'

Bill grinned. 'Love one, wouldn't we, Betty?' he said. 'But not this morning. We want to explore a bit more first. Only got here yesterday afternoon.'

'Off you go and explore then,' said Uncle Tom. 'I've got to work. You can say "hello" to Miss Simpson, though. We shall see a lot of her. She's going to be my assistant in the office, taking care of plans, correspondence, and so on.' She was sent down from town a couple of days ago, so we haven't been working together very long. She seems a nice girl, though, very competent at her work and good fun!'

* * *

He led the way down the field to where a gang of men were putting up a pre-fabricated office. A pretty girl of about twenty-three was standing watching.

As they came up she smiled.

'Good morning, Mr Wayne...Mr Brent. You two must be Betty and Bill. I've heard about you from your uncle,' she said.

'Hello, Miss Simpson,' said Betty.

'You can call me Peggy,' said Miss Simpson. Turning to Uncle Tom, Miss Simpson said: 'Is there anything I could be doing, Mr Wayne?'

'Well, you might get the plans of 'A' Block separated from the others.'

Uncle Tom and Peggy Simpson began to talk business. Bill nudged Betty, and they crept off quietly. When they were clear of the main field, Bill sat down under a hedge.

'Are you game for some more investigating?' he said.

'Of course,' said Betty. 'But are you going to the look-out post again?'

'No, and not because of what 'it' said either. But because what I want to know is *where is the top place*? You heard that man say: "We've got all that from above. Photographs..." when the other chap gave him his plan?'

'I don't know, Bill,' said Betty, puzzled. 'I was so scared I couldn't take anything in. What's it all about?'

'It's obvious,' said Bill, 'that old Army look-out post has been used to watch what goes on at the camp. The man in boots and overalls had made a rough plan of the work done so far. But his boss hadn't wanted a plan; he'd already got dozens of photographs of the work *from the top place*. That's the real key to the mystery, Betty.'

'Maybe,' said Betty. 'But how are we ever going to find it?'
But Bill had already bent over his map.

'Imagine yourself standing in the middle of that field,' he said, 'just about where the concrete-mixer is working. That's about *here* on the map. Now, somewhere beyond the woods, and roughly on a line with the centre, must be this top place.'

Beyond the woods the ground sloped upwards. Bill's finger traced a route through the woods, to a main road behind them, across it, and on to a series of hills. 'There. You see that, Betty? I can't be sure, but from one or other of those three hills I should think you could see the camp site perfectly. It's a bit of a walk, but what we've got to do is go to each of those hills, and look for some signs of *the top place.*'

It was more than an hour before they had circled the wood, crossed the main road, and reached the foot of the first hill.

'I doubt if it can be the middle hill,' he said. 'I can see now that the other two are much higher. Hey! Here's something! I thought this mark on the top of the first hill was meant to represent a clump of trees but it's really trees and a church. That's funny.'

He showed Betty the map. Inside a small patch of green she could see a tiny black square, with a circle, and cross on top. Bill checked the sign with the reference list at the bottom of the map. 'It's the sign for a church, all right,' he said. 'Let's take a look.'

They climbed the hill and, on reaching the top, they saw a clump of low trees and in the centre a small building that looked like a cross between a church and a house. In front was a small tower, with a Gothic door, and high windows. But the rest of the building was like an ordinary Devon farmhouse.

'I get it,' said Bill. 'It's a very old church converted into a house. This would be ideal for *the top place*. I wonder.'

Bill started forward. Betty hesitated.

'If there's somebody inside,' she began.

'Then they've already seen us,' said Bill. 'Let's go on up, and ask for some milk or the way to Tyncombe or something.'

They went to the back of the house, and knocked boldly on the door. They knocked several times, but there was no answer. Bill tried the door, but it was locked. They walked slowly round, looking in at the windows. There was no sign of anyone. When they reached the tower Bill turned the great iron ring on the tower door. The door swung slowly open, noiselessly, as though its hinges were very well oiled. Bill looked inside. A door ahead led into the rest of the house. To the left a stone spiral staircase wound upwards.

'I'm going up,' said Bill.

The steps ended in a small stone landing near the top of the tower. A wooden ladder led on through a square opening cut in the floor of a room high above. Bill went up and peered into the room. Set near the window was a table. It held papers, a telephone, a powerful telescope on a small stand.

'This is it!' he whispered to Betty, who stood a few feet below him.

He was about to clamber into the room when they heard a low whistle... Three times it went, seeming to come from below. They stood still, listening... The whistle was repeated. Then a voice from the bottom of the tower steps called: '*It's me...I must come up...It's urgent.*'

It was the man with the whining voice.

Bill stood clutching the ladder, and did nothing. There was nothing to do. There was nowhere to hide...so if the man came up, they would have to bluff...If he wouldn't be bluffed they could try and make a dash for it. They waited...

Bill tried the door, but it was locked.

five…ten…maybe twenty seconds before the man called again. They heard his footsteps on the bottom steps. Then, with a vague muttering he turned away, convinced that the tower was empty.

Bill's instinct was to creep down, and get out of the tower as soon as possible. But his reason told him they must give the man time to get clear. They must know, if possible, what his movements were.

'Wait there,' he whispered to Betty, then climbed up into the room.

As he suspected, the window commanded a fine view right over the woods, the camp, and beyond…over the sea itself. But Bill was not interested in the view. He looked down, hoping to get a sight of the door of the tower. This was impossible, without actually leaning from the window.

There was no sign of the man with the whining voice.

Bill started to count three hundred, trying to think of a clock ticking off the seconds. At two hundred and one, a man in blue overalls and a cloth cap came into sight, and walked off through the trees. Bill came down the ladder.

'Down you go, Betty,' he said quietly. 'He's going, and it's time we were going too.'

The man was out of sight by the time they left the tower. But to be on the safe side Bill led through the trees and down the other slope of the hill in a wide detour, reaching the main road again about half an hour later.

* * *

They arrived back at the caravan about lunch-time. Uncle Tom and Miss Simpson were seated at the table. They had sandwiches and coffee before them, as well as a mass of plans, files and papers.

'Hello,' said Uncle Tom, looking up. 'And goodbye, too, for that matter.' He took a final swig of coffee, swept up some of the papers and plans, and started off.

'I'm pretty busy,' he said. 'We've struck one or two snags this morning. I shall have to go over to the material contractor's depot and, Miss Simpson, you'll go into Tyncombe when you've finished your lunch. You might like to take Bill and Betty in for the ride. If they want to go, that is. Don't hurry. There's nothing more we can do until we get this matter straightened out, I'm afraid.' He waved to them, and went out.

'Uncle Tom seems in a bit of a flap,' said Betty. Miss Simpson nodded.

'I'm afraid some of the material that's been delivered is the wrong sort for the job,' she said.

'Will that hold things up?' asked Bill.

'It will, but it's just as well. If Mr Wayne hadn't noticed, well, the results might have been serious.'

'Faulty material?' said Bill.

'Well, unsuitable,' said Miss Simpson. Bill got the impression suddenly that she did not want to pursue the subject. It was so faint an impression that he thought he might have been mistaken.

Bill was about to ask another question. Instead he eyed the sandwiches, and remembered he was hungry. Miss Simpson smiled.

'You must both be starving,' she said brightly. 'Would you like me to make some more sandwiches?'

'I'll make some,' said Betty. 'You can finish yours.'

Betty went into the kitchen.

'What are you going to do in Tyncombe?' asked Bill, sitting down in Uncle Tom's place, glancing over the plans and files.

'Nothing very much,' said Miss Simpson. 'I have to leave some papers with someone there. What would you like to do? I could take you both in the car. We could have tea there.'

'That sounds great,' said Bill. 'Do you understand all these plans and figures, Miss Simpson?'

'Call me Peggy. Miss Simpson sounds awfully unfriendly.' She gave Bill a frank smile.

'Okay, Peggy,' he said. He paused. She had not answered his question. Instead of repeating it he went on looking over a large sheet, covered with figures and headed: 'Specifications for Materials. List 46.' Miss Simpson was silent for a bit, then: 'I can't help feeling pleased, in one way... it's such a lovely afternoon.' She seemed to be talking to herself as much as to Bill.

Betty came in at that moment with some fresh sandwiches, fruit and milk.

'You don't come from Devon, Peggy,' said Betty, by way of starting a conversation.

'No. I live in London. They sent me down from the Government Office in charge of this work your uncle is doing,' she said.

'Have you got a caravan?'

'No. I'm billeted at the farmhouse.'

Peggy Simpson began to gather up the plans and files, putting them into a large portfolio.

'Mr Wayne went in on the truck with George Brent,' she explained. 'He left me his car keys. Bill, would you put this portfolio in the back of the car for me?' She handed him the plans and the car keys.

Walking over to the car Miss Simpson pointed across to the farmhouse. 'Look,' she said to Betty, 'I can see my window from here. It's that one, right by the end gable. I never saw such an odd shape. It slopes down to the floor at one side.'

Tyncombe wasn't a very large town. Most of the shops and offices were in the main street. Peggy Simpson drove straight to the town and left Betty and Bill in the car while she called in at an office, in a tiny building wedged in between a shop and a café. Bill noted that there was a small brass plate on the door that said: 'VALLEY DEVELOPMENT & TRUST'.

'Peggy is very nice, isn't she, Bill?' said Betty. 'Or don't you think so? You seem very quiet this afternoon. Didn't you want to come here?'

'Huh?' said Bill, evidently deep in thought. 'Oh, yes. I wanted to come. But I keep going over this thing again and again. There's something very odd going on; and that's a masterly understatement if ever I made one. About Peggy Simpson. I don't know what to think. She certainly seems very nice, but I don't know, she gives me the idea she's not quite fair and above board.'

'Oh, Bill,' said Betty. 'You can't go around suspecting everybody! I was almost hoping...'

'What?'

'That we might sort of ask her what she thinks about all that's going on.'

'No. Don't do that, Betty. We don't know who might be at the bottom of this. You see what's happening now, things going wrong with the material. I'd like to know just *what* was wrong, by the way, and I'm going to ask Dad tonight. *Shush!* Here comes Peggy Simpson now. Don't say a thing, mind, until we're sure we can trust her.'

'Well, that's the easiest afternoon's work I'll ever do, I bet,' said Peggy Simpson, getting into the car again. 'Now, we shan't want tea for an hour or so, shall we? Let's go for a nice run. What would you like, moors or sea?'

It had been an uneventful afternoon, Bill was thinking. He was sitting with Betty in the caravan, waiting for his father to get back from the material contractor's depot. Peggy Simpson had brought them back a few minutes before, then gone over to the farmhouse.

'What's the matter, Bill?' Betty asked him. 'You do look glum.'

'Glum? Not exactly. But if only we could really get to grips with this thing.'

'I think we ought to tell Uncle Tom,' said Betty. 'I don't see what else we can do.'

They sat silent for a while. Bill kept running over the events of the past day or so . . . First the mysterious attempt to damage the caravan . . . the handkerchief that Betty had picked up . . . the discovery of the dug-out . . . and their release by the strange figure in black . . . the tower . . . and . . . he could not help adding Peggy Simpson's evasion of his question . . . and this business of faulty material.

Of course! There was the link. What did all of this amount to but clues to a plot to sabotage his father's work? He had realised that this was an important contract but, until he had seen some of the plans and papers he had not thought of it as a military matter. All those plans had been marked MOST SECRET. The list of specifications had quoted WAR OFFICE Serial Numbers 1785674 . . . and so on . . . He was about to say something when they heard someone approaching the caravan.

The caravan door opened and Peggy Simpson looked in.

'Bill . . . Betty,' she said, 'I've just had a telegram from Mr Wayne. He won't be back until the morning. He wants to stay on and get this matter of the materials settled. He suggests either that you come over to the farmhouse, or that I stay here.'

Bill saw an opportunity.

'I don't think we ought to leave the caravan unattended,' he said. 'While we were on our way here, some tramp tried to break in.'

Peggy Simpson looked at him. 'Really?' she said.

Betty nodded. 'I saw him run off.'

'I'll stay here,' said Bill firmly. 'You and Betty can have this room, and I'll take Betty's bunk for tonight.'

Peggy Simpson hesitated ... then, slowly, she said: 'I don't see any reason to worry. There are watchmen about to look after the materials ... If you'd rather stay here, why not? It might be awkward to put us all up at the farm. Unless you want me to stay, I'll stay on at the farm. I have work to do there, and all my papers are in my room.'

'We shall be all right,' said Bill. He was secretly pleased at this quite unexpected opportunity of a whole night free for some real investigating. In fact, he was thrilled to bits, but he tried to show nothing of what he was feeling.

Miss Simpson didn't seem keen on the idea of making any changes either.

'I'm sure you will. I'll tell the watchmen to keep a look out for any stray tramps.' She seemed slightly amused, as she said: 'Goodnight, then. Don't stay up too late!'

When she had gone, Bill turned to Betty:

'Now here's our chance. How sleepy do you feel, Betty?'

'Not very. But, Bill, we can't go wandering all the way to that tower in the dark. What are you going to do?'

'To tell you the truth,' said Bill, 'I'm not sure. But what do you say to another visit to the dug-out once we're sure Peggy Simpson's out of the way?'

Betty looked perplexed and doubtful. 'Bill,' she said, 'you know I'll do anything you say, but are we doing any good going on like this?' She caught sight of Bill's face. 'Oh, all right,' she said, 'I'm game.'

It was past eleven. A warm night, but scarcely a sign of the moon. Betty and Bill sat outside the caravan, waiting and watching Peggy Simpson's window.

They could see the farmhouse outlined dimly against the sky. Two of the windows glowed faintly, pale yellow squares of light cut out of the inky blackness. By eleven-fifteen, one light had snapped off, leaving only Peggy Simpson's window cutting into the dark silhouette. Five minutes later this too disappeared abruptly and only the tall chimneys and sharp angles of the gabled roof stood against the faint background of the sky.

'Looks as if she's gone to bed,' said Bill. 'We should be okay now. Here's the plan.' He started to outline his plan to follow the line of the woods until they came abreast of the dug-out from the outside, but he broke off before he had said more than a few words. 'Look,' he whispered.

In the darkness Betty had no idea where he was pointing, but with her eyes still on the farmhouse she could see Miss Simpson's window suddenly light up again...Only for a second...then again...three times quickly...three times slowly...

'She's signalling!' said Bill. 'Never mind the dug-out. We're going over to the farm.' They started off across the fields towards the farmhouse.

Once more, as they approached, Peggy Simpson's window flashed its signal.

The way to the farmhouse led through a wide cart-track with barns and outhouses on either side. Under the cover of the outhouses, Bill and Betty went almost to the house itself but stood waiting, before crossing the farm-yard, listening to the faint rustling of stabled horses, the rattle of chains as a dog turned restlessly in his kennel.

Presently the farmhouse door opened slightly, and Peggy

Simpson slipped out of the door, a few feet in front of them.

Bill let her get a few yards ahead, then, taking Betty's hand, he followed stealthily. Miss Simpson was making for the woods.

Wispy clouds kept drifting across the pale moon from time to time, obscuring even what faint light there was and it was difficult to keep Peggy Simpson in sight. Bill and Betty did not dare to hurry, for fear of getting too close to her, but they pressed on towards the woods.

Nearing their own camp, they caught a quick glimpse of Peggy Simpson as she hesitated for a few seconds and stood outlined against the white background of their caravan.

'I hope she's not going to look in to see if we are asleep,' Betty whispered.

Bill nodded. He was watching Peggy Simpson closely. She seemed merely to be listening and, perhaps, checking her bearings for suddenly she started off again. She walked to the end of the woods, and was soon lost to sight against the dark background of tangled trees. Bill edged cautiously along, but when he too reached the end of the woods, there was no sign of her. She must have slipped into the woods near the sunken road, he thought.

Bill and Betty crouched down in the grass, and held a whispered conference.

'She's making for the dug-out,' said Bill. 'She must be. Where else could she go?'

'She couldn't have gone across to the building site?' queried Betty.

Bill peered across towards the field. 'Doubt it,' he said. 'Can't think she had time. No. I think the dug-out is most likely. What could she want over at the site that she couldn't do much more easily during the day? I think if we stick to our original plan, and go along the edge of the wood, we'll kill two birds with one stone.'

'Do you think we shall be able to find the place in the dark?' said Betty.

'Should be able to,' said Bill. 'She's bound to be meeting somebody there, and they'll be talking. Then we can creep up close to that window place and listen in.'

They crept along the wood and turned left at the corner. Bill counted his paces softly to himself. He reckoned that the dug-out was about a hundred yards along the sunken road. So, allowing for the curve in the road, it should be between fifty and a hundred yards going by the almost straight edge of the wood. Say a hundred of his long strides.

After taking one hundred strides, Bill sank down on the grass again and peered around. It seemed darker than ever. The trees to their left loomed up like the impenetrable wall of some sinister stockade. Ahead, they could distinguish nothing. Away to their right, the field sloped gradually down towards the building site. Bill realised that their plan was now very nearly at a standstill. True, he could go forward, or find his way back — but if he missed the dug-out... It couldn't be far away, but in that sea of darkness a miss was as good, or as bad, as a mile. For the moment he felt baffled.

'What is it, Bill?' Betty's uncertain little whisper broke in on his thoughts.

'Just checking up,' he breathed.

Without realising it, Bill had done about the best thing possible. When the eye cannot see, the ear can strain to catch the slightest sound, and does so — automatically.

Bill became aware of the faintest crackling somewhere beyond the trees to his left. It was no more than a furtive movement in the woods, but he swung his head to the left.

A second passed... and then there was the briefest flicker of light... as if someone flashed a shaded torch. That told Bill all he wanted to know.

Someone, only a few yards from them, in the woods, was walking along the sunken road just where it curved in towards the dug-out. So his estimate of distance had been nearly correct! The dug-out was not more than a few yards ahead. He felt a thrill of satisfaction and, tugging at Betty's hand, signalled her to follow him, as he crept slowly forward.

The opening was well-concealed, even by daylight, but Bill felt a slight but tell-tale rise in the ground, caught the subdued murmur of voices... muffled, and sounding so strange coming from somewhere beneath the earth. He wriggled as near to the opening as he could, and tried to see into the dug-out. He could see only a faint light from a shaded torch, or candle, set somewhere on the opposite side. It took him a few seconds to attune his ear to the low-pitched conversation.

Men's voices, seemed to come and go, fading in and out of earshot, like a far-off radio station. Sometimes he thought there were three men. Certainly, he felt sure he detected the whining tone of the man who wore blue overalls, and the other, or one of the others, was harsh and commanding. Or was that merely guesswork? He couldn't decide. He listened again, carefully.

'... take months, perhaps, to build up the information, yet ... complete information ... not a mile away...'

'... mustn't act too soon ... besides ... Wayne...'

'... can't remember all of it. Anyway ... truth about Wayne ... come out soon...'

'Not necessarily.' The harsh voice? No. Definitely a third voice — one Bill had never heard before.

'Wayne could return. He knows nothing about us ... Or, he could talk ... will talk in time. What we must decide now is...'

Bill got the impression that the speaker had broken off in the middle of the sentence. There was a silence for a bit, then:

260

'I say, let *him* make a direct job of it, *now.* If he doesn't find it we're no worse off. If he does, so much the better.'

'Agreed.'

There was a shuffle of feet. Someone must have moved in front of the light, for the dug-out grew dark, then glowed with faint light again. Bill moved back quickly.

The conference seemed on the point of breaking up. He heard a crunching of heavy boots, and one or two sharp words, almost like commands.

When he peered cautiously into the dug-out once more, it was like putting his face against a cold, black curtain. The faint light was gone.

Bill rolled over on to his back, and lay staring up into the starless sky. What did all *that* mean? he asked himself blankly.

That was what Betty wanted to know, too.

'What did you hear?' she asked.

'I *heard* something all right,' Bill answered. 'But I don't know what to make of it. There were definitely three men in there. They were talking about Dad . . . and about getting hold of some information.'

'Was Peggy Simpson there?'

'No.' Bill chewed thoughtfully on a blade of grass. 'I don't think she was; if she was, she didn't say a word, I'm sure. I heard only men's voices.'

'Then . . .' Betty sounded very mystified, 'where did she go, Bill?'

'That's another poser. I haven't the faintest idea. I feel sure she couldn't have gone down to the building site. Why should she? Yet where else would she go? Not to the tower. That's miles away, and not in this direction. But we'd better get back. We aren't doing any good here now. All we could do would be to follow those men, but it's hopeless to try that now.'

They made their way back along the woods to the caravan.

As they turned the corner, Bill stopped and watched carefully. They were approaching the point where the sunken road led to what they regarded as 'their' edge of the woods. He listened and watched for some sign of the three men, but everything seemed still and quiet. The men had plenty of time to get clear, but it was as well to be sure.

Betty stifled a yawn as Bill turned to her and said sympathetically: 'I feel tired, too. Come on, Bet, I think we can go back now and get some sleep.'

Betty sighed, and looked affectionately towards the caravan, its gleaming paintwork showing as a smudge of friendly white against the almost unrelieved darkness of the night. She took Bill's hand . . . he felt her fingers clasp his own lightly, and then tighten into a frightened, tense grip.

'Bill! Look!'

But Bill needed no telling. He too had seen the sudden light at the caravan window and heard the sound of clumsy movement within.

'Wait here, Betty,' said Bill.

'Bill, you're not going over? *You mustn't!*'

'I must,' said Bill urgently. 'I've an idea. If I'm right, there's no danger and we shall have solved the biggest part of the mystery.' He pushed her restraining arm gently aside and ran towards the caravan.

The light was still flashing on and off at the caravan windows. Betty couldn't quite understand at first what was happening. Then she realised that someone was moving quickly about inside, flashing a torch, as they searched about. As Bill ran towards the main door at the rear of the caravan she saw that the torchlight was now flickering from the window of her own tiny room. She watched it, picturing the intruder by her bunk, searching and probing. Then her eyes switched to Bill, now a vague, shadowy figure, shown up against the caravan wall.

He seemed to crouch near the door, opening it to peep inside.

She held her breath. Bill, suddenly bold or impatient — she couldn't tell which — had opened the door and slipped inside. There was a momentary flash of light near the door at the front of the caravan. In that split second she realised that the intruder was leaving, even as Bill was entering.

Instinctively, and with no particular plan in mind, Betty began to run towards the caravan. As she did so, the lights in the main room blazed on. They threw broad beams of light into the darkness, ending in little squares of yellow on the grass. The rear door opened and Bill stood framed in the doorway.

'Too late!' he said, as she came panting up to him.

'I was too late. She got away.'

'She?' asked Betty.

'I don't know.' Bill sounded very dejected. 'I thought it was Peggy Simpson. I still think so. But — it's no good if I can't prove it.'

'Somebody went out by the front ... Bill!' Betty broke off, and looked in horror at the caravan. It was in a state of complete confusion. There seemed to be nothing that hadn't been examined, and then thrown hastily aside. The place had been ransacked from top to bottom. A cyclone could hardly have left greater chaos.

Bill closed the door behind them, and slumped down on an ungainly heap of cushions.

'We're in a fine mess now,' he said. 'I think she put one over on me, all right. I think she must have known we were following, and deliberately put us off the scent so that...'

Betty could hardly drag her mind away from thoughts of the terrible confusion in the caravan, of how they were going to put it right, of what Uncle Tom would think when they had to explain.

'What's that you say, Bill?' she said.

Bill slowly repeated his remarks in a patient sort of voice.

Betty, who usually let Bill do the thinking, protested. 'That's not very likely, Bill, now is it? She might have signalled to those men to let them know...but...Oh, it's too complicated! You said yourself that she could get into the building site more easily by day. So she could have searched around *here* more easily too. After all, why should she go to this trouble when she could have made us stay at the farmhouse, for instance ... Or could have taken us out, as she did today, and told someone to search the caravan in peace. And what were they looking for anyway?'

'Oh, stop,' said Bill. 'My head's spinning.' He jerked himself unwillingly to his feet. 'Let's get started. We must put some order into all this.'

Betty looked around, hardly knowing where to begin. 'I think we shall have to tell Uncle Tom tomorrow,' she said sadly.

They moved rather wearily about the caravan for five minutes or so, picking things up, sorting and tidying. Fortunately, nothing much seemed to be broken. Bill was almost beginning to hope that they might keep the worst from his father.

'Perhaps we could...'

Betty shook her head firmly, when he broached the subject. 'We must tell him everything,' she said. 'He'll have to go to the police, and they'll want to know about everything, exactly as it happened.'

'*I'll say they will!*' said Bill suddenly, in an alarmed voice. 'This explains a lot.'

He was bending over a small drawer, let into one side of the caravan. It was not exactly a secret drawer, but it was not a very obvious one either. Neither Bill nor Betty recalled having noticed it before. Now they could hardly help noticing it. It had been wrenched open, and a long sliver of wood had been splintered away from it. Inside the drawer Bill had found a stiff cardboard folder. He was holding the folder up. It was empty. But it wasn't hard to realise that it had, until recently, been full of documents of some sort. These had been torn out, leaving pieces of paper still caught in the wire clips. The cover was marked: MOST SECRET. WAR OFFICE EXPERIMEN-TAL PROJECT K. Underneath this ran the words:

Under no circumstances must the contents of this file be seen by unauthorised persons.

'That's what she ... they ... were after,' said Bill.

He dropped the file cover back into the drawer. 'Well! All we can do now is to tidy the place up, and wait for Dad to get back,' he said. 'I suppose I've been an awful chump trying to do things my own way.'

Betty didn't know what to say. Bill had done his best. 'Don't feel too badly about it, Bill,' she said. 'We both tried to do what we thought would help. After all, there's a lot we can tell the police that will help. Things they would not know, but for us.'

'*I don't think you'd better tell the police.*'

Bill and Betty spun round at the sound of a soft, angry voice behind them. Standing in the doorway was the black figure from the woods. It held a roll of papers in one gloved hand. Its other hand was pressed lightly against the door. Its eyes glittered coldly above the black, silk scarf that covered its face.

'Sit down, and don't get alarmed,' said the black figure.

Bill's lips set in a determined line. He moved away from Betty and would have tried to tackle the masked figure, but the figure saw what was in his mind and dragged a chair between them, saying:

'Don't do anything silly. Just listen to me for a moment. Last night those men you saw in the dug-out kidnapped your father.'

Bill started. 'How do you know?'

The black figure waved its arm impatiently. 'Never mind. I do know. They wanted information about this work your father is doing for the government. They didn't get it, firstly because Wayne wouldn't give it and, secondly, because he couldn't have remembered all the details anyway. What the men wanted was this.'

The figure waved the roll of papers in the air. Bill's eyes darted to the drawer. The figure nodded.

'I see you realise what happened. These papers are the contents of your father's secret file. I recovered them, after they had been stolen from this caravan. Here...'

The figure threw the bundle of papers on to the table.

'What about Uncle Tom?' said Betty anxiously.

'If you do as I suggest,' said the figure, 'you can help him. But the one thing you must not do is to go to the police, or let anyone else know. Tomorrow morning you will probably get another telegram. It will be a fake. It will say that your father is still delayed ... something like that. You must pretend to believe this, then go into 'Tyncombe and' phone this number.'

The figure fumbled in a pocket of its siren suit and brought out a card.

'Ask for Mr Peter Dean. When you get through to Mr Dean himself, say that you are Tom Wayne's son and that you want to see him right away about Project K, S.O. Understand? Project K, S.O. Then he'll give you instructions to meet him. When you do, tell him everything that's happened and give him those papers to keep.'

The figure turned to go.

'How do I know any of this is true?' asked Bill. 'For all I know...'

The figure paused.

'You don't know,' it said. 'You'll have to believe me. I've helped you twice — that should be some proof — but you must

266

make up your own mind. However, I give you warning that if you go to the police you'll scare these men into some drastic action and — that may not be too good for your father.'

With that the figure went out, leaving them staring down at the bundle of papers, and a small white card.

*　*　*

In spite of the fact that he had slept for only four hours, Bill woke early. He knocked on Betty's door.

'I'm awake, Bill,' she said. 'Shan't be a moment.'

Betty was soon up and preparing breakfast. They sat over their meal, trying to decide what to do.

'I think we should do as "it" said,' was Betty's opinion.

'I wish I could be sure,' answered Bill. 'But we must get help to Dad.'

Bill stared down at his cup for a moment, then: 'We'll do as the figure in black said,' he decided. 'If we go straight to the police, there *is* the risk that some harm may come to Dad.'

'Let's hope someone will be going into Tyncombe this morning,' Betty said. 'And that they'll give us a lift in and leave us there.'

'Otherwise we'll try and hitch-hike. Now, Betty, we'll need those handkerchiefs as clues.'

'They're in my case,' said Betty. 'I'll get them right away.'

She went into her room and brought back the handkerchiefs. Bill put them on the table with the secret papers.

A little after seven Peggy Simpson walked in.

'Good morning,' she said cheerfully. 'I'm on my way to the site. Thought I'd look in and see how you were.'

'Hello, Peggy,' said Betty. 'We're fine, thank you.'

Peggy nodded. 'Good,' she said. 'What are you going to do today?'

'We thought we'd like to go into Tyncombe,' said Bill. 'I suppose you don't know whether there's a lorry going down this morning?'

'I should think there's bound to be. Why not come down in about an hour, and ask the foreman?'

'Right you are, Peggy,' said Bill, assuming a friendliness that he certainly did not feel. Peggy smiled. As she went out, she swept past the table and knocked one of the handkerchiefs to the ground. She turned back, bent down, and picked it up. She looked at it quickly and said, quite casually: 'Oh, it's mine. I don't remember using ...' She shrugged lightly, put the handkerchief in the pocket of her jacket, and went out.

'What did I tell you?' said Bill. 'I'm glad she didn't notice the other one!'

Betty's feelings were a mixture of amazement and indignation. 'She's a crook!' she said angrily. 'But, Bill, she's supposed to be from the Government department!'

'If she really *is* Peggy Simpson,' said Bill. 'After all, we don't know *who* she is; they could have kidnapped the real Government person, too. Listen, Betty, the sooner we get some action the better. We must get to Peter Dean and give him this Project K ... S.O. routine as soon as we can. I wonder why that figure said Tyncombe. Isn't there a phone nearer than that?'

'I don't know of one,' Betty said. 'There must have been some reason. We'd better do exactly as "it" said.'

Bill nodded agreement. 'S.O.', he said. 'I wonder what that means, and why it seems familiar?' He picked up the papers from the file, fitted them roughly into the cover he had found in the drawer and flicked through them. 'There's no mention of S.O. anywhere here,' he said, musing aloud. 'Every reference is simply to experimental Project K.'

'It's obviously some kind of code signal,' said Betty. 'It could mean anything, I guess. Bill, who could that black figure be? It seems to be on our side against those men, at any rate...yet...'

'It could be playing a game of its own too,' said Bill. 'That's what bothers me a bit. But why would it give us back the papers and warn us that Dad had been kidnapped? But this is no time for wondering. We must get over to Tyncombe as soon as we can.'

They found Peggy Simpson talking to the foreman. She had a telegram in her hand.

'I was just wondering if you were on your way down,' she said. 'I've had another wire from your father, Bill. He won't be back until later today. He's going on with his enquiry into the faulty materials. But that needn't affect your plans. There's a truck going through to Tyncombe in a few minutes. I've spoken to the driver. He'll be glad to drop you. I shall be going over myself this afternoon and I can bring you back. If you've got money for your lunch, you can get it at that café we went to the other day, and I'll see you there again for tea and bring you back.'

'That's fine,' said Bill.

'Have a good time!' called Peggy as they walked off.

Half an hour later they were in Tyncombe Post Office, dialling Peter Dean's number.

'Dean speaking.' Bill heard a deep voice at the other end of the line. He hesitated a second, then pressed button A, and said:

'Mr Dean? This is Bill Wayne. I'm Tom Wayne's son. I want to see you right away about Project K ... S.O.'

He heard what sounded like a sharp grunt at the other end. 'Project K ... S.O. Where are you now?' asked the voice quickly.

'At Tyncombe Post Office.'

'Stay there,' said the voice. 'I'll pick you up in ten minutes. My car is a black Rover. When you see it, get in as quickly as possible.'

There was a click and then the line went dead. Bill put the receiver down and left the phone box.

'We are to wait for a black Rover,' he told Betty.

They left the post office and stood pretending to look into a shop window next door.

The ten minutes seemed more like ten hours. But at last the car drew up, right opposite the post office. The man at the wheel reached out and opened the rear door.

'In you get,' he said. 'Keep down on the floor.'

Bill and Betty bundled into the car and crouched on the floor. The door slammed behind them and the car moved off.

'You can sit up now,' said the man at the wheel after they had raced along for some time. Bill and Betty scrambled up to the seat. They were well clear of Tyncombe now and driving along the main road.

Bill looked at the driver. He was a pleasant-looking man, neither old nor yet young, dressed in a sports jacket and an open-neck shirt. He was very fair and had amiable blue eyes.

'Well, Mr Dean,' began Bill. But Dean shook his head.

'Wait a bit,' he said. 'You can tell me all about yourselves when we get well out of sight. I should never have picked you up if you hadn't given me the distress signal. Where did you learn it, anyway?'

'That's all part of the story,' said Bill.

Dean nodded as if he understood. He was turning off the main road now and into a narrow gravel road that might once have been the approach to a large estate. A few hundred yards along the road they stopped next to a lodge.

Dean switched off the engine and got out.

'Let's get inside,' he said, 'and you can tell me the whole yarn from start to finish.'

The lodge was poorly furnished. There were a few hard chairs, a ramshackle table, a box or two. Everything was dusty.

The windows were barred over and had not been cleaned in months.

Dean leaned against the wall, near a window, and started to fill a pipe. 'Fire away,' he said to Bill. Bill looked around doubtfully, then plunged into his story.

Dean listened carefully, without saying a word. Betty watched him, as Bill talked. But his face gave no clue to his thoughts. He remained leaning against the wall, puffing at his pipe and glancing through the bars of the window, as if watching the road. Even when Bill had stumbled to a halting finish, Dean still made no comment. They stood there in silence, all three of them, for several minutes. Then Dean removed his pipe and said to Bill:

'Do you think that your father has been taken to that place with a tower you were telling me about?'

'I don't know,' said Bill. 'That would be the first place I should look.'

Dean tapped his pipe and slipped it back into his pocket.

'Here's what you must do,' he said. 'Wait here while I go and make some investigations. Your black figure was quite right when it said that this gang of men must not be alarmed. If you or the police go anywhere near the tower they'll know something is up. Nobody connects me with this business. I'll go and see whether your father is actually at the tower. If he is, then we can do something about it. If he is not, then I must get you back to your camp as if nothing had happened. Then you'll have to act as my agents and report to me whatever developments there may be. It's all we can do at the moment without showing our hand and thus perhaps risking your father's safety.'

'I see all that,' said Bill, 'but who *are* you, Mr Dean, and who is that figure in black? How did it know that distress signal of yours? There's a lot of things you should tell us.'

Dean smiled. 'I agree,' he said. 'I appreciate all that. But I can't give you any explanations at the moment. Just wait here. It's not very comfortable, but perhaps you can amuse yourselves for a while.'

Dean went outside and backed his car down the road. Bill and Betty watched him from the window. When he was out of sight, Bill turned to Betty and shaking his head said: 'I don't know if we should trust him but, as he said, what else can we do?'

'I don't know, Bill.'

They sat down on the dusty chairs, and gave themselves up to their own puzzled thoughts.

The three men were after details of the secret project. That was clear now. But where did the black figure and Peter Dean come in? And Peggy Simpson? She must be in league with the gang. It was her handkerchief Betty had found both at the café and later, beside the caravan, that first night. She too had signalled to the men. Bill saw again in his mind's eye the farmhouse windows lighting up in the night, three short flashes, three long ones.

Three short and three long! Bill jumped up suddenly, with something like a groan. 'What a prize idiot I am!' he said.

'What is it, Bill?'

'We've been tricked,' he cried. 'Swizzled! Bamboozled! It's just dawned on me why S.O. seems familiar. *That was the signal that Peggy simpson flashed from her window. It was in Morse Code. Three dots, three dashes. That's S.O.* I don't know what they are playing at but it's obvious that they are all in this together. It couldn't be a coincidence *using the same signal!* We've got to get away from here and go straight to the police.'

He ran over to the door. But it would not open. It was locked.

'So much for our Mr Dean,' he said in a furious voice.

He looked swiftly about the room. Those barred windows looked a hopeless proposition, unless he could find a substantial screw-driver, which wasn't very likely. There was a door at the end of the room which looked less solid than the one in the front. But it was almost certain to be locked. He ran across to it. Yes. It was locked too.

'However,' he said, as if Betty had guessed his thoughts, 'it seems the weakest point, so we must try.'

Bill studied the lock. It was a simple one. It had two bolts, or tongues, of brass. One, operated by an oval-shaped handle, moved back and forth easily. The other, operated by a key, held firmly against the side of a box-like fixture screwed to the door frame.

'Here's one bit of luck, anyway,' said Bill. 'We are on the inside. If I can unscrew that thing, I can pull the door open.'

He took his jack-knife from his pocket and looked at it thoughtfully. The screws holding the fixture had been painted over. It would take a strong turn of a good screwdriver to loosen them. He doubted whether his knife would stand the strain.

'It's all I can do,' he thought, and started to scrape away the paint, prising and loosening the screws as much as he could.

It seemed a pretty hopeless job.

Fifteen minutes later, Bill had made little progress and his first attempt to turn the screws resulted in a snapped blade.

Bill tried to turn this mishap to good account. The broken blade was more like a screw-driver, but it was impossible to put any pressure on it without the knife snapping shut and nearly cutting his fingers.

'Isn't there anything here we could use?' said Bill, looking about impatiently.

Betty wandered around, searching everywhere...but there was nothing that by any stretch of imagination could serve as a screw-driver.

Suddenly, Betty had a bright idea.

'Suppose you tie the knife to a piece of wood, along the side of the blade, with just a bit of the knife jutting over the top. That would stop the blade from closing up, wouldn't it, Bill?'

'It's an idea,' said Bill, with renewed enthusiasm. 'Find a piece of wood, then.'

'Break a bit from one of these boxes and cut it,' suggested Betty, 'and tie it with the cord from your knife.'

'That's it!' cried Bill. He pounded at one of the boxes with his heel, until he broke off a piece of wood about the size of a foot ruler. He trimmed it roughly, then bound it along the side of the blade. It was a clumsy looking object when he had finished, but it enabled him to tackle the top screw with some hopes of shifting it. It was a hard struggle. Many times the cord gave, and the knife slipped sideways and had to be bound on again and again. But Bill seemed to get the knack of things eventually and at last the screw began to turn. Once loose, it turned freely and in another minute Bill could turn it with his fingers. 'It's out,' he cried. 'Now for the bottom one!'

'There's no need,' said Betty excitedly. 'Can't you just push that thing sideways, or wrench it off?'

'Brains!' said Bill admiringly. It was true. Inserting his improvised screwdriver between the door frame and the fixture he prised the latter forward. There was now nothing to hold the brass tongue firm and with a good pull the door swung open.

The next room, much smaller than the main one, was a surprising contrast. It was comparatively clean and tidy, furnished like an office, with a desk, files. . . and a high-powered wireless set!

'This is some sort of headquarters for Dean, and maybe the masked figure,' said Bill, as they tip-toed into the room.

'Looks like it,' said Betty.

Bill nodded. 'But let's get out,' he said. There was a small back door, with the key in the lock this time. Bill turned it with relief. 'No more screwdrivers,' he said. When they were outisde the lodge Bill locked the door and put the key in his pocket.

'Now for Tyncombe and the police,' he said, and started off down the gravel road.

On reaching the main road Bill paused. He had been thinking hard as they came down the road from the lodge and realised that he was being forced into a decision he did not want to make.

'What are we waiting for, Bill?' asked Betty.

'I think,' said Bill slowly, 'I think we ought to split up, Betty. The most important thing is to get to Dad and try to free him. I should go to the tower and see what I can do. Meanwhile, you get to Tyncombe and bring the police.'

'Bill. . .' began Betty hesitantly, then she nodded agreement. 'Be careful, Bill,' she said.

'I will.' Bill squeezed her arm affectionately. 'Off you go. It's a straight road into Tyncombe. If you can get a lift, do so, but watch out for Dean's car!' Betty smiled, and turned off towards Tyncombe.

* * *

As he made his way along the road, Bill began to recognise the countryside and realised that he was nearer the tower than Betty was to Tyncombe. It was about four miles along the main road from the tower to Tyncombe. He judged that he had about a mile to go, whereas Betty had three. This meant that, unless Betty got a lift, he would be at the tower in fifteen minutes, while she would take up to an hour before she could get back with the police. An hour, then, was all he had.

Bill heard the sound of a car, suddenly, and ducked quickly into the bushes by the side of the road. As it flashed past he could see that it was not Dean's car.

'I hope Betty manages to hitch that one,' he thought, returning to the road again. But if she should, then his time was running short. He quickened his pace. He reached the first of the three hills in under ten minutes. As he heard the sound of a second car he realised that it would probably be safer now to leave the road altogether and strike out across country. It would be harder going, with the hills to cross, but he didn't want to be spotted before he had time to find out just where his father was kept prisoner.

He left the road again and watched the car speed past. It was Dean's car! He bit his lip and hoped earnestly that Betty had caught the first car. But there was nothing he could do to help now.

He came up the last few yards of the hillside bent low and using every dip and fold in the ground as cover. Then lying flat just below the crest, Bill scanned the thin screen of trees at the rear of the converted church. It seemed all right. He topped the hill and made the cover of the trees in one short rush, then edged forward slowly towards the building.

The house looked as deserted as on the day he and Betty first visited it. Bill lay in the shelter of the trees and tried to reason out a sound course of action. If any of the men were inside, where would they be? Up in the tower? There seemed no point in that now. Dean had the precious file and that would tell them all they wanted to know. No doubt he had driven straight to them, given them the papers, then left to deal with Betty and himself, expecting to find them still locked in his hide-out. No, they would hardly be up in the tower.

Where then? With the papers in their possession surely they now had all they wanted? The logical thing for them to do now was to clear out. But...what had the masked figure said? They had tried to get his father to talk, but even he could not remember all the details without the secret file. Maybe, thought Bill, at this moment they are trying to get Dad to explain the file to them. After all, it might not mean very much to them.

What if his father refused? And he would refuse, of course. Bill clenched his fist at the thought that some bunch of roughs might be forcing his father to reveal vital government secrets. This was no time for being over cautious.

Bill left the covering trees and ran to the house.

The house was not large and consisted of one storey only. There was a small square window near the door at the rear and, as Bill recalled, two large windows at one side. He had passed these on his previous visit. That meant two rooms, most probably, on that side — perhaps only two rooms in all. How safe would it be to edge his way round to the side and take a look in? Flattened against the wall, near the back door, Bill took a second to consider the point. His eye fell on a refuse bin, with its tin lid only half-covering an accumulation of tins, papers, potato peelings. That gave him a better idea. He lifted the lid of the bin and threw it down with a great clatter on the stone flags outside the back door. Then he dashed to the other side of the house and hid himself just round the corner. Surely somebody would hear that and come out to take a look? If they did, he thought, there was a chance they would blame a breeze, or a scavenging cat. If they did not...

Bill waited one or two minutes. Nobody came. He went back to the bin and gave it a hearty kick. If fell with a clatter and rolled against the back door with a loud thump. Bill dashed to his corner again and waited. Not a sign; not a sound. Bill felt hopeful, yet definitely puzzled. *Was there anybody in the house at all?*

'There's no one in the back room, that's a certainty,' he thought, returning and looking down at the scattered refuse piled against the door. He tried the latch. As he expected, the door was locked. He looked in through the window on to an ordinary, rather untidy, cottage kitchen. It was small, and beyond a cluttered table he could see a further door that led into the house. It was half-open. Almost on an impulse, Bill dragged the refuse bin to the window, set it upside down and stood on it. Then he methodically kicked the glass out of the window and stepped carefully through it, into a large stone sink.

Betty had looked back once or twice after parting from Bill and seeing his brisk, purposeful pace, had quickened her own. She had no idea just how far away Tyncombe was, but progress seemed very slow. After what seemed a long time she could still see the spot where they had parted. At this rate she would never get to Tyncombe for hours, she thought. *If only she could get a lift!*

Betty hurried on. A lift? She stopped suddenly. She could hear the sound of a car now. Thank goodness. It was quite a long way off, but in the still quiet afternoon the slightest sound carried. The sooner she moved to the middle of the road and started to wave the better. She was about to start hailing the car when something stopped her. Instinctively she leaped for the shelter of the bushes.

In a few moments the car flashed past. Betty stamped her foot in disappointment. It was not Dean's car. Nothing like it. She clambered through the bushes to the road again, feeling flustered and annoyed. This was a silly, and impossible, position to be in. She couldn't think why she hadn't realised it before. How could she ever get a lift, *after* she had hidden herself away and checked on the colour and model of the car?

It was difficult to decide. If she met Dean, that would ruin the whole plan. If she was too long delayed in getting help, then what might happen to Uncle Tom and Bill, and the whole plans for the secret Project K? Secretly, she rather hoped that she would never have to decide, hoped that no more cars would come along, or that something like a lorry would come. Something that was very obviously not Dean's car, anyway.

But even as she turned these thoughts over in her mind, she heard the distant purr of an engine. She stopped again and looked back anxiously. Her look confirmed what she already suspected. It *was* an ordinary car, and a black one at that. What should she do?

The car came nearer and nearer...braked sharply as the driver caught sight of her hot, flustered figure, frantically waving a grubby handkerchief...screeched to a halt only a few yards from her.

Betty's hand dropped like a stone to her side. Her eyes widened in alarm. It was Dean.

For a second she stood there, staring at him. He looked at her curiously, then gave an odd, satisfied smile, and opened the door.

Betty turned and ran for the bushes, scrambled through and raced across the field.

She heard Dean shout; heard the soft, steady thump of his feet on the rough grass.

He was shouting after her. She paid no heed to what he was saying. She had no idea where she was going, or what she hoped to do. She just ran for all she was worth, her chest heaving, her blood pounding in her ears.

* * *

Bill jumped down and walked boldly into the next room. The table was littered with photographs — obviously enlargements of the building site taken from the tower with a special camera. Bill pictured the men sitting there, trying to learn the secret of Project K. Had Dean now handed over the file? And if so, had they now abandoned the house, taking his father with them?

He passed on to the next room. This was smaller and more like a hall. Three doors led from it: one to the tower, one to a bedroom containing three untidy camp-beds, and a third led to a room roughly fitted up as a darkroom. On a narrow trestle-table was an array of developing equipment and the one small window had been screened by a square of black cloth. Bill reached up and tore it down. The room looked cold and drab in the faint light that filtered through.

Bill's heart suddenly missed a beat. He stood rigid, every nerve alert. From somewhere close at hand came a muffled *thump! thump!* It seemed to be in the room and yet... He looked round. There was nothing but the table and two large boxes.

Thump! Thump! There was no mistaking it now. It came from the corner of the room... *Below* the floor! Bill crossed over. Three strong hinges and a large iron ring, not visible from where he had been standing, told their own story. This was a trapdoor into a cellar. One box was drawn across the trap making it impossible for anyone below to get out. *Of course!* Someone was trying to get out and who would it be but his father?

'Dad!' he shouted, dragging at the box. The thumping ceased. In half a minute Bill had moved the box and lifted the trap.

Standing on some wooden steps was Tom Wayne, looking anxiously upwards.

'Bill! he said. 'It *is* you! I couldn't believe my ears.'

Tom Wayne climbed into the room.

'How long have they kept you down there?' said Bill indignantly.

'Not long. Only from time to time when they had to go out. But we must get away, Bill.'

'It's all right, Dad,' said Bill. 'I think they've gone. The police should be here soon. This is what's happened...'

Bill poured out his story, but when he explained his belief that Dean had handed over the file, his father disagreed.

'He can't have done that, Bill,' he said. 'They would certainly have asked me to explain it to them. Until half an hour ago I was with them and nobody came near the place. But, *listen!*' Tom Wayne started in alarm. 'They're coming back!'

Bill listened. There was a sound of angry voices. They had discovered the broken window.

'We've got one thing we can try,' said Bill. 'Shut the trapdoor, Dad, quick!'

Bill hastily covered the window, while his father closed the trap and replaced the box.

'Behind the door, Dad!' whispered Bill urgently. 'I'm going behind that other box. I hope they all look for you in the cellar. If there's a chance to push them down, I'll yell — *Rush.* If there isn't, when I yell — *Go,* let's try and dash out.'

Bill darted behind the box and Tom Wayne flattened

himself behind the door a split second before the men came tramping in.

They made straight for the trapdoor.

'He can't have escaped,' said one. 'The box hasn't been moved.'

'Then what about that outside window?'

'Never mind the arguments. Take a look. Is he down there, or isn't he?'

They moved the box aside and flung the trapdoor back against the wall.

'Come up, Wayne.'

No answer.

'Anybody got a torch?' said the man with the whining voice.

'Why would I carry a torch in the daytime, idiot? Go down! Perhaps he's fainted — it gets pretty stuffy down there.'

The man climbed down. Bill peered round his box. One man in the cellar; one kneeling, looking over the edge; one standing. It was now or never!

'Rush!' yelled Bill. 'Take the tall one, Dad!'

Tom Wayne shot from behind the door, hurling his full weight against the standing man. Bill darted to the wall and brought the trap down on the head of the kneeling man.

The tall man dropped like a stone into the cellar; the other lay stunned, pinned by the trap. Bill lifted the trap slightly. They bundled the dazed man down and dragged both boxes across.

'I don't think they'll shift that,' Tom Wayne said grimly. 'Let's go, Bill.'

Betty raced on, feeling that soon her lungs must surely burst. She could still hear Dean shouting after her, but even as she fought for breath she realised that she had gambled and lost. Where could she go? What could she do? There was no sign of a house. Even if she could outrun Dean, it would take hours to get to Tyncombe across country. *And I can't run forever*, she thought. Her head began to swim; stupid images flicked through her brain. *Can't run forever... run forever...* She saw herself running round the world with Dean in pursuit. Then, abruptly, everything exploded in a shower of bright lights and she fell into a great, black void...

When she came to, a moment later, she was lying on the grass, a sharp pain in her ankle. Dean was bending over her, smiling.

'I'm sorry you fell,' he said, 'but I'm glad you stopped somehow. What's happened to your cousin?'

'I shan't tell you,' said Betty defiantly.

Dean shook his head. 'Listen! You've got to believe that I'm on your side. Your uncle is in the tower and we must release him. I am a Government Security Officer — see for yourself.'

He held out a card. It carried his photo and certified him as a Security Officer attached to the War Office.

Betty regarded it suspiciously. 'How do I know it's genuine? she said. 'Why did you lock us in?'

Dean sighed. 'I had to. I was afraid you'd do just what you have done: rush off and give the show away. I can't blame you, but we must have disciplined action. Now, then, where exactly is your cousin?'

'At the police station in Tyncombe,' said Betty.

'Why aren't you with him?'

'We thought it better to split up.'

Dean frowned. 'Then I must get to the tower at once. You don't seem to realise that those men will never leave your uncle free to give evidence. Not only that, they'll bargain their freedom against his life. We may even have to let them leave the country, with all they know, rather than have harm come to him.'

Dean replaced his card. 'I'm going,' he said. 'You had better stay on the road and stop the police car. Tell them to avoid rushing in *at all costs*. Tell them...'

Betty struggled to her feet. 'You are going to let me wait for the police?'

Dean nodded.

'In that case,' she said, 'I'm convinced. I was bluffing you. Bill went straight to the tower.'

'Good grief!' said Dean. 'That does it! Down to the car, quickly! The only thing to do now is wade in and hope!'

He started off towards the car with Betty limping along behind.

'Here!' he said kindly, looking back, 'grab my arm and hop.'

'We'd better make for the camp, Bill,' said Tom Wayne as they reached the main road.

'Shouldn't we wait for the police?' said Bill.

'Perhaps you're right. Hello! There's a car coming.'

Dean's car came racing towards them. Betty was waving out of the window.

'It's Dean!' cried Bill. 'And he's got Betty!'

'It's all right, Bill,' called Betty. 'He is a Security Officer. Oh, Uncle Tom, I'm so glad to see you! How did you get out?'

Betty leaped from the car and rushed to her uncle. Dean followed.

'Mr Wayne,' he said. 'I'm Dean of Security Branch. I was assigned secretly to this area. I work under cover from the Valley Development and Trust offices in Tyncombe. What's been happening here?'

Tom Wayne glanced at the card Dean offered, with an understanding nod.

'Well,' he said, 'it's been Bill's show so far.' He gave Dean a quick explanation. Dean grinned admiringly.

'Good show, Bill!' he said. 'Come up with me and show me this cellar. Mr Wayne, you stay with Betty. If anything should go wrong take my car and go to the police. But I don't think it will!' He tapped his hip significantly and, beckoning to Bill, led the way to the tower.

Dean drew his automatic and pushed open the tower door.

'Through there,' whispered Bill, 'and the darkroom is on the right.'

Dean nodded. 'Stay this side of the door until I call.'

As the inner door closed behind Dean, Bill heard a soft pattering on the stone steps of the tower. The thought flashed into his mind that the men had escaped and lain in wait in the tower. He turned and saw the masked figure in black leap lightly down the last three steps!

Bill didn't think. He just acted. He met the figure head on, with an ungainly but effective flying tackle. The pair crashed to the ground, Bill hanging on like grim death and yelling for Dean.

But the figure made no move. It lay with Bill gripping its ankles and gasped for breath.

Dean, who had seen that the boxes were still in position and heard the men thumping vainly at the trap, dashed back to the tower.

He lowered his gun. 'All right, Bill,' he said. 'You can let go.'

The figure sat up and took the scarf from its face.

'Whew!' it said. 'I thought I'd never breathe again.'

It was Peggy Simpson.

Dean grinned. 'Bill is a remarkable young fellow,' he said.

Bill met the figure head on...

'He never gives anybody much time for explanations. Bill, meet my assistant, Junior Security Officer Simpson! It's about time she showed up.'

'We've met,' said Peggy ruefully. 'Head on!'

'Your assistant!' Bill gasped.

'Let's get those characters from the cellar,' said Dean, 'and then I'll tell you all about it.'

Betty, Bill, Uncle Tom, Peggy and Peter Dean sat round a table in the offices of the Valley Development and Trust in Tyncombe. The few remains of a superb high tea from the café were still before them. Uncle Tom and Dean were filling pipes.

'I suppose it seems pretty baffling when you know only one side of things,' Dean mused. 'But the explanation is simple...

'The government decided to build an experimental station to test a new form of aerial defence. My job was to watch over the whole project. Well, to make it brief, we got a hint of a plot brewing. Headquarters let the plot develop in the hope of getting the ring-leaders of a wide espionage system.

'Now,' he continued, 'the men we caught today were prepared to spy for weeks, months, if necessary. But they also knew that the secret of Project K was summed up in the brain of Mr Wayne and in his secret file. So we assigned Peggy, here, to the double job of assistant and investigator. Peggy secretly watched over you all the time — or rather, she watched over the gang. You can tell them your part, Peggy.'

Peggy pushed her cup aside. 'The main points concern the roadside café and your first halt at Netford,' she said. 'I was at the back of the café, by arrangement with the owner, when you all came in. The men had been in and had left only a short time before. It's a usual stopping place and I was quite prepared for them to make some trouble there. However, they didn't!

'When Betty came dashing back, I was nearly caught. I never gave my handkerchief a thought, of course.

'But it was at Netford,' she went on, 'that the gang made the first move. They damaged your caravan, hoping to find you stranded on the road. They would have taken the papers, set fire to the wreckage, perhaps, so that the whole thing would seem like an accident, and the War Office would assume the plans destroyed.

'I watched them damage the coupling that night. When they went away, I examined it and guessed what they were planning. I tried to right the coupling, and cut my hand doing so. At this point Betty came into the story. Again I had to leave in a hurry, for it was essential to keep my identity secret. Unfortunately, I dropped the second handkerchief. I never realised what clues I had left! But there wasn't much I could have done about them if I had.'

'Did *you* guess what had happened, Uncle Tom?' asked Betty.

'Yes and no,' answered her uncle. 'I had been told by the War Office to be surprised at nothing and to push on at all costs. My orders were: "Yours not to reason why".'

'Well,' resumed Peggy, 'you reached Tyncombe safely. I turned up ready to appear as Mr Wayne's assistant and to carry on investigating. Then, the real complications came.'

Peggy turned to Bill and smiled. 'You were a real problem, Bill. I had planned to use the escape hatch to that old dugout to spy on the men. But I had to get you out of trouble in case the whole scheme was compromised. I tried to scare you off, but you weren't to be scared. When the incident of the faulty materials took your Uncle away, I admit that I didn't suspect anything at first, but when your uncle failed to return I knew something was wrong. The telegram that reached me didn't seem quite genuine, so I put your minds at rest, or so I thought, and left myself free to contact Peter Dean with our emergency signal — S. O. for Security Operations. We were not supposed to meet by daylight... You can carry on, Peter!'

Dean removed his pipe. 'I agree with Peggy,' he said, 'that the gang had obviously decided to make a bid for getting their information quickly. This was what we wanted, but we didn't want Mr Wayne to be endangered. I told Peggy to carry on and go to the dug-out, while I tried to locate Mr Wayne.

'As you know, the men were at the dug-out planning the raid on your caravan, having found that Mr Wayne wouldn't talk and wouldn't be able to help them anyway without his file. Peggy planned to get in ahead of the man sent to ransack the caravan. But, finding you two absent she was alarmed. She went over to the farm to see if perhaps you had gone there, then she returned to the caravan just as the intruder ran out and you two both returned.

'She next had a very ticklish job and her success in doing it really saved the day. She had to trail the man who had taken the file, sneak into the tower before the others returned and change the file for some unimportant papers. She couldn't let the gang keep the file, but if she had simply taken it they would have been warned. *It was essential to let them think they had taken the wrong papers!*

'I think the rest is clear. The gang knew that soon your uncle's disappearance would bring trouble, so they strove desperately to complete their mission in a day or so. We, for our part, were as desperately afraid to show our hand before we had released your uncle. So you see,' he added, 'Betty and Bill started out by being a mighty complication. But I must admit that you turned the situation for us at the crucial moment. I think perhaps we should have joined forces from the start!'

'I think I'd rather have them with me than against me,' said Peggy Simpson.

'I think we'd make jolly good Security Officers,' said Betty. 'And... I'm almost sorry it's over! But it *is* about time we had a *holiday* sort of holiday. Don't you agree, Bill?'

* * *

Bill wasn't listening. He was staring out of the window with an intense frown on his face.

'What is it, Bill?' asked Dean.

'It's a funny thing,' said Bill seriously, 'but a man left his car outside that shop and a few minutes later a completely different man came out and drove it away!'

Dean threw back his head and roared. 'Oh no, Bill!' he said. Not another mystery before we've finished this one!'

'Come on, kids,' said Uncle Tom. 'Let's get back. I've a lot to do tomorrow.'

'Well,' said Bill, 'I suppose so, but you never know!' he added darkly.

Peggy and Dean watched from the window as the three piled into Tom Wayne's car.

'I used to think,' said Dean slowly, 'that we were working to protect nice people like that. But, you know, they are quite capable of protecting themselves!'

Dean clipped some papers into a folder marked Project K. 'That's for Headquarters, Peggy,' he said. 'See that it goes off tonight.'

Peggy sealed it in a large envelope and addressed it to the War Office.

The adventure and mystery of the Caravan Secret was ended.

The Castle Secret

by Jane Davis

Loch Ferris sparkled a deep blue in the early morning sunlight. The sun caught Judy's cropped blonde hair, making it gleam gold as she ran down the wide old oak staircase to the main hall of Ferris Castle.

When Judy's old school-friend, Fiona Carrick, had asked her to come and spend several weeks at her home in Scotland, Judy had accepted gladly. Spring had not yet penetrated foggy London, and Judy had been eager to get into the fresh country air once more before she started her first job in some stifling office. Her delight had been doubled when, on her arrival at Ferris, she found that Fiona lived in a four-hundred year-old castle — a bit tumbledown, it was true, but still a castle!

But Judy had not been at Ferris very long before she discovered what made the Carricks look so troubled.

'It's not an easy business maintaining a castle,' Jem, Fiona's older brother, had explained to her one morning. 'It takes a lot of money. Besides the interior of the castle, there are the grounds to be kept in order — orchards, woods...'

'And now,' Fiona had broken in bitterly, 'it's not a matter of keeping things in perfect order — it's a matter of keeping the wolf from licking the peeling paint off the gates!'

'I didn't know things were that desperate,' Judy had said, shocked to see her friends' unhappy faces. 'It's so beautiful here, and your family has been at Ferris for generations. What's going to happen?'

'It looks very much as if father's going to sell it,' Jem had

Judy discovered Fiona lived in a four-hundred-year-old castle!

answered, looking soberly round the old gun-room where they were sitting. 'That agent, Temsley, is round most days — I suppose he'll find a buyer for it. Like as not they'll turn Ferris into some terrible phoney tourist hotel?'

'You mean that horrid little man, who always seems to be snooping about the place, is actually an agent?' Judy exclaimed indignantly, stroking Bengy, the Carricks' rather soulful red-setter, who had leaned his head on her lap and was looking hopefully at a large box of chocolates. 'Why, I thought he was an arch-criminal or a poacher — he always looks as if he's up to no good.'

Fiona and Jem let out a shout of laughter at their guest's description.

'Aye,' Jem agreed, 'he's always crawling all over the castle. Yesterday I went up to one of the attics to fetch something, and there he was going through everything just as if he owned the place — I can't think what he's looking for. I was a bit sharp with him and he went and told father that I already fancied myself as Laird of Ferris!'

Judy saw that Jem was beginning to get rather heated and tactfully suggested that they went out fishing as they had planned. The Carricks agreed eagerly, and no more was said about the fate of Ferris.

'It seems such a waste!' Judy thought for the umpteenth time as she reached the big hall, and gazed with delight at the heavy carved walls hung with great oil paintings of past Carricks.

Fiona and Jem had almost finished their breakfast.

'I'm sorry,' Jem apologised, getting up and smiling down from his great height at Judy. 'Father had to go to Edinburgh on business for a few days and we got up early to see him off. He sent you his regards and hoped you'd excuse him. We didn't see the point of waking you so early as you're on holiday.'

Judy liked Mr Carrick almost as much as her own father, but couldn't help thinking that it would be fun to have the castle to themselves for a few days!

* * *

Judy sat down at the table and smiled her thanks to Morag, the Carricks' old cook, as she put a plate of porridge before her. Morag had been Jem's and Fiona's nurse. She didn't live at Ferris any more, but now came over from her brother's cottage each morning.

'Well, now I suppose you two are in charge of Ferris?' Judy said, sprinkling sugar liberally on the porridge.

'For the last time, I'm afraid,' Fiona answered quietly, and looked away from the table through the window at the misty mountains. 'Father's fixing up to sell Ferris. We'll probably go to live in some poky flat in a town, far from all this!'

Judy felt terribly sorry for the Carricks. She wished very much that she could help them, but there was nothing she could do or say. They had almost forgotten Judy's presence and were engrossed in discussing their past life at Ferris.

'But what's the use of talking?' Fiona said miserably. 'Ferris will soon be in the hands of that dreadful Temsley and we'll see it no more, unless...'

Judy looked up. Fiona had broken off quickly. Jem was looking at his sister angrily. 'Fiona, be your age!' he said shortly. 'That old story! You surely don't still believe it?'

Judy's curiosity got the better of her. 'What old story?' she asked.

'Och, it's just a silly old tale,' Jem answered, helping

himself to toast. 'Our great-great-grandfather was a keen collector of old pictures and beautiful antiques. Most of these had to be sold. But one, so the story goes, was never sold and it was hidden somewhere at Ferris. It was the most valuable and most beautiful. A da Vinci painting of the Nativity. But it's nowhere in the castle, I'm sure — so it couldn't possibly help us now.'

'But, Jem, be reasonable,' Fiona pleaded earnestly. 'It's never been traced, so it must be still at Ferris, and therefore it belongs to us. I bet that Temsley knows this and will buy the castle for a song and then get the painting. If only you and father weren't so obstinate!'

'Well, why don't we look for it?' yelled Judy, her face flushed with excitement as she jumped up from the table. 'Look, we've got until your father comes back to find it, and when we do you won't have to sell Ferris, and...' Her voice trailed off as she saw that neither of the Carricks was very impressed.

'It's no good, Judy,' Jem explained gently. 'Two generations of Carricks have ransacked this castle and found nothing. If it's here, it's keeping awful quiet!'

'Well, that oughtn't to make you give up. It must be somewhere. I think Fiona's right, too. I bet that agent knows all about it and that's what he's always snooping about for... He looks like a beetle!' Judy added inconsequentially.

Her last remark relieved the tension between brother and sister, and made them all laugh. Both Fiona's and Jem's tempers matched their flaming red hair, and once they started quarrelling there was little that could stop them.

'Searching for the picture would help take our minds off leaving Ferris,' Fiona said, shooting a pleading glance at her brother.

'O.K., you two girls win,' he growled. 'Only we're not

going to spend the whole of a glorious day indoors. We'll take a picnic lunch and go fishing in the loch, and later this afternoon we'll come back and start on this mad search.'

The sun was just beginning to slip behind the jagged purple peak of Ben Mor when they trudged back to Ferris. They had not caught much, but, as Fiona pointed out, there was enough for supper. Fiona took the fish to the kitchen and Judy hovered between there and the gun-room, where Jem was drying the lines. But when she found that she was getting in the way, she went upstairs to see the sunset from one of the attics.

Judy was happy! It was tremendously exciting being almost alone in an old castle, and she could imagine knights on gleaming horses, fair ladies in sweeping gowns, wild borderers in their bright and colourful plaids.

Twilight was rapidly approaching, and Judy found herself looking rather nervously round the big, old attic. It was all very well to have an imagination, but the attic was definitely eerie in the blue half-light, and Judy decided that fancies were for midday!

She was just going to turn away from the window when she had the odd feeling that she was not alone. Judy stood stock still. Her heart thumped furiously. Then she became aware of something else — a sweetish, almost sickly smell, and it was familiar! At first she had thought she was either imagining things or that one of the Carricks was playing a trick on her. But Fiona never wore perfume and, of course, neither did Jem.

In a flash, she remembered where she had smelt the scent before. Mr Carrick had once invited Temsley, the agent, to lunch, and Temsley had brought with him a fat man in a loud check suit. He had a soft, sneering voice, and was interested in buying a castle. Judy shuddered. There had been something about the man that had scared her! He had pudgy hands, and he had been scathing in his remarks about the younger generation. He had seemed to take special joy in making Jem angry, too. He had been wearing a strongly scented brilliantine or shaving lotion — and now this scent was filling the darkening attic! Judy dreaded turning round. Would she find that sinister, smiling figure, and what could he possibly be doing in the attics of Ferris Castle?

Judy tensed herself, and turned round towards the door. To her astonishment, there was no one else in the dark, eerie attic. But the sweetish smell still lingered!

'Judy, supper!' called Fiona and Jem suddenly, and they came racing breathlessly up the stairs to the attic.

'What on earth's the matter?' asked Fiona, as she saw Judy's anxious face.

Judy grabbed her arm urgently. 'Fiona, do you remember that awful man — what was his name — Blundon? Well, *sniff!*'

Fiona and Jem gazed at Judy as if she were crazy. Suddenly, Fiona let out a gasp. 'Judy, that scent he was wearing — hair cream or shaving lotion or something — I can smell it! Is *that* what you mean?'

Judy nodded. Jem struck a match and held it up, but its flickering light showed only dark dancing shadows on the walls. The only people in the attic were themselves! Jem dropped the match as it burned his fingers. 'Well,' he said, more briskly than he felt, 'those books in the corner have been disarranged, but there's no one here now. Let's go and eat, and then, while we're searching for that mysterious picture, maybe we'll find a clue as to why that awful man was here.'

Ferris Castle was no easy place to search — some parts of it were almost in ruins — but directly after supper they collected torches, some string and chocolate, and began a systematic search. When they had finished with the Great

Hall, all the ground-floor rooms and all the bedrooms, they hadn't found so much as an old paint brush, let alone a painting.

'Well, that's that!' said Jem, definitely. 'What isn't down must be up. Come on!' And he led the way up the narrow, twisting stairway to the turrets and attics.

Judy and Fiona searched feverishly, and were soon covered in dust and cobwebs. But Jem still couldn't help regarding the missing picture as a joke. It wasn't until they got to the attic where Judy had been that evening that anything was said about the intruder.

'I vote we really have a good old search here,' Jem said, resting his torch on a pile of dusty boxes. 'And not just for the painting either — we must try to discover what that awful Blundon was doing here.'

'I don't know about you two,' sighed Fiona, wiping a damp strand of hair from her forehead, 'but I'm jolly tired. Let's have a break and eat the chocolate we brought with us.'

'You're just not used to work!' Jem told his sister — but he and Judy stopped searching readily enough!

Fiona was brooding on Jem's remark, when Judy suddenly burst out laughing and said: 'Do you play the bagpipes, Jem? I've found some in the corner and I'd love to see someone playing them.'

Fiona groaned aloud. The trouble was that Jem was only too willing to demonstrate his so-called skill on the bagpipes. He wasn't a bit of good, and soon the attic was full of a sound like a dozen sick cows moaning with pain. But soon he began to splutter and choke, and he dropped the pipes hastily while he fished out his handkerchief. The bag and tangle of pipes thudded against the wall and let out a final ghastly squeal. Jem recovered his breath and surveyed the two girls gloomily.

'I'm just out of practice,' he declared, 'and I'd forgotten they would be full of dust!'

The bagpipes had thumped down to lie against some decorated panelling, low down in the old stone wall.

Judy was staring down at the floor, looking at the discoloured bagpipes, when her eyes caught something near Jem's foot — a dark crack, about two inches wide, had appeared in the wall.

'Jem, Fiona — look!' Judy said, pointing excitedly at it. 'There's a crack in the wall — you couldn't possibly have made it by dropping the bagpipes, but...'

Jem let out a wild yell. 'This must be the entrance to the secret passage described in that old book about the history of Ferris,' he said. He went down on his hands and knees and tried to lever the crack open. But it wouldn't budge so much as an inch.

'Jem,' Fiona said, going over to him, 'I don't think it works like that!'

'Of course it doesn't,' returned her brother a trifle angrily, 'but how *does* it open? Just tell me that!'

Judy went over to the wall and very carefully moved the bagpipes. 'Look,' she cried, 'the pipes must've touched a secret spring in the wall.'

Eagerly they ran their hands over the carved panelling. At first nothing happened. Then Judy's hand touched a small carved rose, and suddenly the whole section slid silently away, leaving a black, gaping hole with large uneven steps going down into inky darkness.

'This must be what the book called "Ferris Passage"!' Jem shouted excitedly.

'This, so the book says,' Fiona explained to Judy, 'goes right down to the Great Hall.'

'We must go down and explore,' Judy said immediately.

'Jem, Fiona — look!' Judy said... 'there's a crack in the wall...'

'Well,' Fiona said rather doubtfully, 'I suppose we *could* go down, we've got torches — but say we can't get out through the Great Hall? And we might not be able to open this from the inside.' She pointed to the panel.

'Surely the answer is,' Judy said firmly, '*not* to shut the panel behind us — it can't possibly shut by itself, it's too heavy.'

'Do let's,' Jem said to his sister, gathering his string and torches together. 'This is too exciting to leave — wait till we tell Father! I'll go first.'

He started to descend the roughly cut steps, his torch making a pool of light in the inky blackness. The smell of damp, cold air rose to Judy's nostrils, and, as Jem took her hand to help her down, she could hardly suppress a thrill of fear.

Suddenly, Judy stopped in her tracks. 'I've got it!' she shouted. Her friends stared at her in amazement. 'Poor girl!' Fiona said, grinning. 'The excitement's been too much for her...'

'No, don't you see?' Judy said. 'This is where he must have gone — that's why we could smell that scent in the attic and not find him.'

'Gosh! You mean Blundon?' Jem said, flashing his torch into the darkness.

'I wonder how he knew all about the passage?' Judy said thoughtfully.

'He was awfully interested in the history of Ferris when he came to lunch that day!' Fiona exclaimed. 'He spent about an hour in the library with Temsley, browsing through all the old books on Ferris.'

Suddenly, Judy realised why Blundon had been in the attic. 'If he read the books on Ferris, he must have known about the missing painting,' she gasped. 'That's what he must be after!'

Jem let out a low whistle.

'He must have hidden in the passage until we went out of

the Hall after supper,' Judy went on, 'and then made his escape through the Great Hall and out of Ferris!' She began to follow Jem quickly down the old stone steps, with Fiona close on her heels.

The passage was cold and damp — very narrow at first with a ceiling high enough to let even Jem stand up with ease.

Finally the passage widened into almost a room — and ended in a blank wall. Judy looked anxiously at the Carricks. 'Now what?' she asked.

Jem found a small knob in the wall, turned it, and, with a great deal of creaking, a door opened. They went through.

'It's funny...' Fiona said loudly. Judy clutched at her arm in surprise as an echo repeated Fiona's remark in a hollow, ghostly whisper.

'Don't worry, Judy,' Jem said. 'This must be what the book called the Whispering Gallery — it probably served to frighten off pursuers in the old days. We're almost at the Great Hall now.' He turned to his sister. 'What's funny, anyway?'

'There's no sign of Blundon — not even his scent,' she answered.

'Gosh,' Jem exclaimed, 'I'd practically forgotten him. Perhaps the scent was from something else, and Judy just imagined there was someone in the attic!'

Before Judy had a chance to protest, Jem continued: 'Here we are — this panelling must lead to the Hall.' He ran his hand over it. Nothing happened. He tried again. 'The mechanism must be jammed,' he said cheerfully.

'Wh-what shall we do?' Fiona asked, trying to sound casual and unafraid.

'You great idiot,' returned her brother, in his usual charming manner. 'We get out by the panel in the attic — we left it open for that.'

Quickly, they retraced their steps.

'But this hasn't solved the mystery of the painting...' Judy began. Then she broke off. The opening through which they had originally come was nowhere in sight! The panel had been closed.

A cry of astonishment died on her lips as Fiona gripped her arm. There were voices on the other side of the panel.

'Well,' came a soft, menacing voice, which Judy identified as Blundon's, 'that's got rid of those children.'

The voice that answered him was unmistakably Temsley's. 'Good, now we can start on a proper search for that picture...' The voices faded and, no doubt, the men had begun to search. It was obvious, too, that they didn't know they were being overheard.

The Carricks' faces went white with rage. 'Those crooks!' Jem spluttered. 'They know the painting is somewhere in the castle, and that's why they want to buy Ferris. We've simply *got* to find it first. Just wait till Father comes home...'

He broke off. Judy said in a trembling voice: 'We may never be able to find the picture *or* tell Mr Carrick and stop those two miserable crooks searching. Do you realise — *we're trapped?*'

Jem and Fiona stared at Judy in dismay as what she had said dawned on them. They were just like three people cast up on a little desert island of light in a great, inky sea of blackness. One of the torch batteries flickered out and now they had only two torches left between them.

'The best thing we can do,' said Judy, surprised at how calm she felt suddenly, 'is to go back to the part of the passage that is like a room, just before the Whispering Gallery. We won't be so cramped there!'

They had been at what they termed 'headquarters' for over an hour. Neither Judy nor the Carricks had said much.

Judy sat chewing her lip in concentration, thinking alternately of how to get out and where the missing painting might be hidden.

'I'm jolly hungry,' Jem complained for the twentieth time, as he paced the floor. Their only food was one small bar of chocolate. Light came from only one torch, as they had decided to economise and save the other for an emergency.

Suddenly, Jem bounded to his feet. 'We're absolute prize idiots!' he exclaimed. 'In the morning Morag will obviously notice we're missing, and if we bang loudly enough on the hall panel she's sure to find a way to let us out.'

'Of course!' the girls breathed, sighing with relief.

'Until then,' Jem said firmly, 'I vote we try to get some sleep.'

Judy felt sure that she would never shut her eyes, lying curled up on that stone floor, but at last a troubled, dream-filled sleep overcame her. She was woken by Fiona shaking her arm.

'It's morning,' Fiona said urgently.

'We've got to go and bang on the panel...' She trailed off into uncontrollable giggles. 'Jem is already roaring his head off — listen.'

Judy also laughed as she heard Jem yelling hoarsely: '*Let us out! Let us out!*'

Morag's sharp eyes and shrewd brain soon found the hidden spring which opened the panel and, finally, with much scolding, she let them out.

'Och, what troublesome bairns,' she declared, with a twinkle in her eye. 'Fancy getting shut in all night!'

They said nothing to her about Blundon and Temsley, but just that in the excitement of finding the passage the panel had been shut in error.

After hot baths and an enormous breakfast they felt like

new people. Ferris was exceedingly untidy, and it was obvious that Blundon and Co. had been making an extremely careful search.

'The trouble is,' Jem said to Fiona and Judy, 'we just don't know whether they found the picture or not.'

The sky was grey and sodden until 12 o'clock, when a watery sun appeared. There was no hope of going fishing — the burns and lochs would be too full of water. Jem and Fiona, because of their practically sleepless night, decided to rest until lunch, and Judy thought that she would, too.

She lay fully-dressed on her bed, but couldn't sleep. Soon, putting on a large black oilskin and gumboots, she slipped out of the castle and walked down to the loch. Everything was soaking, but the rain had left the grass and trees clean and sweet-smelling. There was a small disused crofter's cottage on the other side of the loch. It was very picturesque from a distance, but quite derelict when you got close. Idly, Judy made her way towards it. She was deep in thought, wondering if Blundon had found the picture and, if not, where it could possibly be hidden. She was just coming out of a small copse near the cottage when she heard voices. She backed hastily into the copse and hid in some uncomfortably wet bushes.

The voices came nearer — and they were familiar! Then she saw Temsley and Blundon, who had obviously just come out of the little croft. Both were wearing oilskins, and Judy couldn't help thinking that Blundon looked rather like a large, black, shiny elephant in his.

'I can't understand it,' he was saying in an angry voice. 'Absolutely no sign of it in the cottage or in the castle.' Judy couldn't hear Temsley's answer, but then Blundon spoke again. 'You don't think those wretched children have found it and got it safe somewhere?' He laughed at something

Temsley said, and continued in a menacing tone: 'We can soon get it back from them with a little *persuasion* if they have got it!'

Although Judy shivered at his tone, she couldn't help feeling light-hearted when she realised that the two villains hadn't found the painting yet.

She waited until they had gone, then made her way towards the castle.

It was not until after lunch, when Morag had gone down to the village to shop, that Judy had a chance to tell the Carricks what she had overheard. They were overjoyed that the painting hadn't been found, and Jem even wanted to celebrate by playing the bagpipes!

It had started to rain again and there was no point in going out, so they sat on the floor in front of the huge log fire, reading and drowsing.

Suddenly, almost as if someone had come and whispered in her ear, Judy had a brainwave.

'I've got it,' she cried, her eyes shining with excitement. Fiona merely yawned, and Jem said, laughing: 'She's started again, Fiona. Do you think she's caught something or...' He wasn't allowed to finish, as Judy came and stood over him, brandishing a cushion.

'All right,' Jem said hurriedly, 'I was only teasing. What have you got?'

'I know where the painting is!' Judy said calmly. She didn't have to repeat this!

'Holy smoke!' yelled Jem. 'Why didn't you say so before?'

Judy refrained from pointing out that he wouldn't let her, and simply said: 'I saw a film about hiding paintings ages ago — it's really a very simple idea.'

Fiona was almost hopping up and down with impatience. 'Judy,' she begged, her face flushed and serious, 'please tell us quickly — it'll save Castle Ferris from those awful men!'

Judy smiled and looked mysterious. 'Which is the portrait of your great-great-grandfather — the one that bought the picture originally?'

Puzzled, Jem pointed silently to a gloomy oil-painting of an old man wearing a kilt and bearing a splendid sword.

'Can you lift it down?' Judy asked Jem, who immediately reached up and carefully carried the picture over to the table and laid it down. The sun had come out again, and bright sunlight shone in through the windows, on the three heads bent over the old portrait. Slowly, Judy ran her fingers under the corners of the frame and gently levered out the portrait of the old man. There beneath it, in its calm, serene beauty, lay the wonderful old masterpiece. They said nothing, but simply gazed spellbound at its beautiful rich colouring and fine brush-work.

Fiona was the first to break the spell. 'Judy, thank you,' she said very solemnly. 'You've saved Ferris — we'll never be able to thank you enough...'

Her quiet little speech was cut short by the voice of Blundon.

'Yes, thank you, my dear young lady,' his voice sneered at Judy. 'You have saved us an awful lot of work — and money, too. We don't have to buy the castle now, we'll just take the painting.'

Judy gave a horrified gasp and backed towards the painting. Jem's face blazed with anger.

'You're not going to lay a finger on that,' he said tensely. 'It belongs to the Carricks...'

The only reply he got was Blundon's laughter as he walked calmly over towards the painting — but he hadn't reckoned with Jem, who stepped forward and gave the fat man a neat clip on the jaw. Blundon reeled to the floor!

Temsley had just been standing there, and at first hadn't

realised what was happening. He stepped forward now, his face ugly with greed — and Jem gave him precisely the same treatment.

Jem produced some string from his pockets and expertly tied up the two scoundrels. 'You see,' he said triumphantly to the two girls, who had always laughed at the amount of string Jem carried around with him. 'I told you that string always comes in useful!'

Judy was spared telephoning the local police-station by the arrival of Mr Carrick, who saw to, as Jem put it, all that legal stuff!

It was only after supper that evening that Mr Carrick heard the full story. He smiled at Judy warmly.

'You have done a wonderful thing in finding this,' he said in his soft Scottish voice. 'Through this beautiful painting we will now be able to restore the glory of Ferris Castle.'

Judy had an odd little lump in her throat. Her happiness lay not just in the thanks of her wonderful friends, but in the fact that she had made it possible for the beauty of the painting to be seen by all.

A Cruise for Chris

by Anne Wade

The young man seated at the huge glass-topped desk smiled as Christine came in. 'You're persistent, aren't you?' he said.

Christine did not know whether to return the smile or not.

'I'm very keen, sir,' she said pleasantly, and left it at that.

The young man, Harry York, who was in charge of engaging all staff, other than seafaring men, for the *Far Eastern Navigation Company*, glanced through the file which his secretary had put before him.

'Miss Scott, isn't it?' he said, and gave a faint sigh of sympathy and regret. 'We've had your application for some time now. I'm afraid there still isn't anything I can offer you.'

Christine had been trying for over a year now to get a job in one of the *Far Eastern* liners, either as Purser's Assistant, or even as Stewardess. There was practically nothing she didn't know about liners, the *Far Eastern* ships especially.

Her mother had died when Chris was only three, and she had been brought up largely by her father who had been a sailor. Christine had longed for a chance to travel ever since she could remember.

Often she wished she had been a boy. She could have signed on with any ship then — even a tramp steamer. Christine wouldn't have minded what kind of an old tub it was. Or so she thought!

Harry York was about to say something when his phone rang. 'Hold on a moment,' he said, picking up the phone. Chris waited while Harry York held a brief conversation. When he put the phone down he had a thoughtful look. He stared hard at Christine.

'I'm sorry,' he said suddenly, 'I'm afraid I must seem rather rude. But I've been trying to make up my mind about you.'

'About me?'

'Yes...I've been wondering...'

The young man shrugged, then said: 'This has nothing to do with the *Far Eastern*. A friend asked me to meet him for lunch. In ten minutes' time at that quick lunch bar in Haymarket. If you happened to drop in...'

He nodded significantly and touched the buzzer on his desk. Christine concluded that the interview was over.

She wandered out into Trafalgar Square and automatically turned towards Haymarket. She was still puzzling over this unusual conclusion to the interview.

Every two months for over a year now she had called at the offices. She had not always seen Mr York, but the interviews had all ended with a sympathetic 'wait and see'. At least this was different!

She reached the quick lunch bar and ordered the cheapest sandwich and a cup of coffee.

In a few minutes Harry York came in. He greeted a man of about his own age who was already at the counter. Then he made a faint pretence of greeting Chris as if surprised to see her.

'Well, come and join us,' he said, giving her a solemn wink. 'This is David Andrews. David — Miss Christine Scott.'

David Andrews was a tall, well-built young man with dark curly hair. He looked very bronzed and fit. He smiled at Christine and shook her hand. 'Glad to know you, Miss Scott. Are you in the shipping business with Harry?'

'She is not,' interrupted Harry, 'but she should be. David, I am now going to do you a very big favour.'

'This,' said David grinning, 'is liable to cost me money. What's the favour, Harry?'

Harry swung himself on to a stool and leaned against the polished counter.

'My company could use Miss Scott as an Assistant Purser. But we haven't been able to fit her in yet. I know you need someone for your next trip. And, well, here she is. It's as simple as that.'

Christine felt that her mouth was gaping in surprise. She had thought Mr York was merely intending to soften her disappointment by being sociable.

David Andrews seemed very interested. He turned a friendly but critical professional gaze on her. 'You may have something there,' he said thoughtfully.

Harry York turned to Christine. 'Let me explain,' he said. 'David works for a new company that runs two very super luxury liners, the *New Age* and the *New World*. They only make luxury cruises. He is Entertainments Officer in the *New Age*, and needs a lady assistant. On his last trip he realised that something was lacking on the social side: the woman's touch. I think he'd be an idiot not to take you on for the next trip.'

'Thanks for running my business for me,' said David dryly. 'But for once you may be right. Don't let's get too many rosy ideas into Miss Scott's head, but...' He smiled encouragingly at Christine. 'Suppose you tell me about yourself, Miss Scott.'

Christine never did remember how she managed to stammer out her story. She was so overcome by the possibilities that had so suddenly opened up that she could hardly put one word after another. But she left the lunch bar an hour later, having arranged to see David Andrews, and some of the men he called his 'higher-ups', the very next day.

Within a few weeks, after some agonising days of waiting for the results of interviews and enquiries, she had definitely signed on to act as assistant to the Entertainments Officer on the forthcoming scheduled cruise of the liner *New Age*.

The ship was to sail to Cherbourg, New York, pick up passengers there and then cruise to Colombo and Singapore.

'I can't believe it,' she told her father. 'Even now I can't believe it!'

Her father, an old Merchant Navy Captain, crinkled his leathery face in a smile.

'That's the way things do happen, Chris,' he said. 'You know the saying: "Stranger things happen at sea?" There is no calling like ours for strange unexpected things happening.'

Chris felt very proud and happy to hear her father speak of their 'calling'.

A few days later she was on her way to join the *New Age*, berthed at Pier 12, sailing next day on the noon tide.

Chris, for all her knowledge of ships, had not fully imagined how big the *New Age* would be. It looked enormous — like a floating hotel! She saw as she approached the gangplank that there were still several decks below pier level.

This was to be her home! Her greatest ambition was realised — she was going to sea!

David Andrews was waiting for her at the head of the gangplank. 'I thought you would arrive on that train,' he said. 'Your kit has arrived and is in your cabin. Come and look over the part of the ship that will concern us most.'

He led Chris through to an enormous hall, then up a double flight of stairs. At the top of the wide stairs were offices — and even shops. It was hard to imagine that one was in a ship. It was so exactly like the lobby of a huge hotel.

'This is the main dining room,' David said, after whisking her along corridors and up flights of stairs.

Chris looked in on a huge, luxuriously appointed room that seemed like several fashionable London restaurants put together. She was hardly able to conceal her excitement.

'There's another on the top deck, and then there's a sort of sun lounge café. Most of our dances and concerts will be held here.'

He led Chris out again, along more corridors, pointing out various offices, wireless rooms and so on.

'I don't expect you to remember all this,' he said, laughing. 'You'll have plenty of time to get familiar with the ship between here and New York. Most of the passengers come aboard there.'

He stopped suddenly and showed Chris into a beautifully furnished suite of offices. 'This is our home, when working,' he said.

Chris looked around at the magnificent fittings and furniture. It was all very modern, especially designed for the *New Age*, and illuminated by concealed neon lights.

'I don't think I shall do anything here but sit back and dream,' she said laughing.

'You'd soon get tired of that,' David said. 'I don't think you'd like to be a passenger on this ship any more than I would.'

'Why ever not?' asked Chris. 'You don't make a very good advertisement!'

'I mean, I'd rather have a job of work to do any day.'

Chris nodded. 'I agree,' she said, 'and I have to do something to prove to my father that I'm not just a fair weather sailor!'

David smiled. 'Oh, we shall get some problems, don't you worry! But I'll take you to your cabin now. By the time you've settled in, it will be time for dinner. We'll meet and talk over plans for the voyage.'

David rattled away cheerfully as he led Chris down to E Deck, to her cabin.

'Here's your cabin,' he said, and Chris felt a thrill of excitement.

It looked wonderfully comfortable and her luggage was waiting for her.

'This ship was built for luxury cruising,' David explained, 'and there's only one class travel: first and best. You'll find the stewards will give you all the service you want, except that the passengers have priority, of course. But it's in our interest to keep passengers happy. I don't need to give you a long lecture, I'm sure, but remember that we must do anything at any time for the passengers. We must make them feel that our ship is the last word in service and efficiency.'

Chris thought perhaps she should say: 'Aye aye, sir,' and salute. But she said: 'I understand, Mr Andrews.'

'Don't call me Mr Andrews unless you need to sound impressive,' grinned David. 'The obvious sort of discipline and formality can be dispensed with between us. We don't want the passengers to feel that our idea of efficiency is to go about saluting each other. They're on holiday and not in the Navy, you know!'

With that David left Chris alone in her cabin. For a few minutes she could do nothing but sit and look at her trunks, her cabin, and all the details and gadgets which told her that her dearest wish had come true. Even now she felt like pinching herself to make certain it wasn't just a wonderful dream!

Then she said to herself: 'Christine Scott, you came here to do a job...and what was it that David said: anything at any time for the passengers.'

Chris sang as she began to unpack her trunks, warbling brightly when she came to her gleaming white tropical outfit.

She felt like dancing too, but even the luxury cabins of the *New Age* weren't exactly built for high steppers! Chris knew she would bounce about ten feet into the air if she took one joyous step!

Anything at any time for the passengers, she thought happily, and pictured herself doing everything from rescuing old ladies from drowning to climbing the wireless mast to amuse the children.

Chris finished unpacking, then made her way back to David's office.

David was sitting at his desk as she came in.

'I was just thinking about you,' he said. 'I wondered whether you would find your way back. You seem to know the ropes though. And that's the first thing a sailor has to learn, I guess.'

'I'm not exactly a stranger to ships,' Chris told him. 'Before my father retired, I went over a good many. Not as big as this, of course.'

David nodded. 'I've been looking over the passenger list,' he said. 'Jack and Lois Bridges are joining us at New York. You've heard of them?'

'The musical comedy team?' said Chris. 'Yes. They made a film a little while ago, didn't they?'

'Yes,' said David. 'They're brother and sister. A very versatile couple, but for some reason they don't seem to be a really howling success. The film wasn't too good. But they'll be fine for us. I want you to make a special point of getting to know them, Chris. Do your best to persuade them to perform at ship's concerts. If you handle them well we shall have a couple of star performers.'

'Don't worry,' Chris assured him, 'I'll handle them like visiting royalty.'

'That's the spirit. I admit I muffed my chances over something like this on the last trip. That's why Harry was so right about my needing someone like you aboard.'

'Why?' asked Chris, looking rather doubtful. 'Was it so difficult?'

Chris had plenty of self-confidence, but she wasn't the type to be cocksure.

She looked on David as the expert and wondered how she would be able to succeed where he had failed.

'Well,' David said, 'we had a big-time magician on our last voyage. I barged right in as soon as he got aboard, loaded him with flattery and asked him to perform. He got very angry and practically ordered me out of his cabin.'

Chris laughed. 'Well, what did you expect?' she said. 'How would you feel if you came aboard expecting a nice luxurious holiday, and were greeted by a live-wire Entertainments Officer who wanted to sign you up for a series of concerts?'

David gave a smile of satisfaction. 'You've seen the point,' he said. 'I *thought* I'd got the right girl! Well, Chris, I'll leave the Bridges entirely to you.'

'I shan't say a word about performing until we're well out to sea and they feel very pleased with life,' said Chris firmly.

'That's the idea. Come on now, I'm hungry. Let's go down to the staff-room and see what's for supper,' suggested David.

The staff dining-room was much smaller than the huge restaurant on the top deck, but Chris liked it all the better for that. There was absolutely no difference in the food, service, or comfort, and a really friendly spirit prevailed. There were a number of people already waiting for supper.

David greeted most of them as old shipmates and introduced Chris.

'Jack's in the Purser's office. . . Fred mucks up all the wireless messages. . .' So David went on, and ducked as Fred pretended to throw an ashtray at him. 'Johnny here. . . well, nobody ever did find out what use he was. . . Then there's Sally, who just sells stamps, and warns passengers when to take salt tablets, and looks after children as far as I can make out...'

Chris was happily aware of a long line of cheerful smiles, friendly greetings and some pleasant banter.

'I shall never remember your names,' she said. 'Not for a day or so. But you won't mind that, will you?'

Nobody seemed to mind.

'Now come on,' called David, 'enough of this. Let's eat. Oh, Chris...here's somebody special...'

David was steering her towards a table where a dark, pretty girl of about her own age was already seated and smiling towards them.

'This is Molly,' said David. 'Molly, this is Chris. Molly is our guardian angel, Chris. She'll be in the office with us, and will do all the really clever things like typing lists, remembering faces, reminding us about dates and times, and forgetting to have her own meals.'

Molly made a little face at David and pretended to look offended.

She smiled at Chris and, in a sweet voice, with a trace of Irish in it, she said: 'I've heard all about you, Chris. I'm sure we'll get along fine. Pay no attention to him. If you want anything, come to me.'

Less than a week later, Molly and Chris were sitting in their offices, every available space covered with papers, lists, folders, menus, diaries and so on, as busy as bees. Early the previous morning they had stood by the rails and watched the Statue of Liberty and the huge skyscrapers of New York looming out of the dawn.

'Take a good look,' Molly had said. 'This is about all we shall see of it this trip anyway. Here's where we really start to work.' The passengers had come aboard and here they were with only half an hour to sailing time, checking, planning and recording.

David Andrews dashed in and out again every so often.

On many occasions, but for Chris's quick brain, there might have been trouble or delay. For although it was not the Entertainments Officers' business to arrange passenger accommodation and services, it was essential for David and Chris to take an active interest in passengers' welfare, and be ready to step in quickly with help and information, wherever they found a puzzled face, as David put it.

But the busy day came to an end at last and by supper time the ship was well out to sea, and Molly, Chris and David relaxed gratefully in the staff-room.

'Not a hitch anywhere,' said David. 'I knew there wouldn't be but . . . it makes life very hectic for a day. For us anyway. We can take things a bit easier tomorrow.'

'I can't,' said Chris. 'I haven't done any more than meet the Bridges and see that they were really comfortably settled.'

'How did they seem?' asked David.

'Very nice,' Chris said. 'But I was rather surprised. Nobody came to see them off. They had no flowers, telegrams or last-minute visits from friends. They seemed to want to sneak on board and shut themselves in their cabins as soon as possible.'

David stifled a yawn. 'I dare say they have just finished one of those long tours of American theatres. They travel a great deal, you know, and must be tired . . . and I don't suppose they find travelling any novelty now. If that's the way they feel it's a good job I didn't grab them and start talking about concerts.'

'It certainly is. But I shall make a tactful approach tomorrow,' said Chris.

'You might make a tactful approach to a Mr van Rheiner too,' said David. 'But his case is rather different. He's an old man travelling for his health, and he wants a quiet, peaceful trip. You have to do your stuff in reverse where he's concerned, Chris. I want you to make sure that he's never bothered, and that at all costs he doesn't get the impression that we're trying to get him to join in the fun.'

'What a life!' said Molly. 'Some of 'em wants fuss and fun, and some of 'em wants peace and quiet. If it was me, I'd give them all a badge. On one side it'd say: "Fuss and Fun," and on the other: "Rest and Quiet." And I'd call over the loud-speakers every morning: If you wants "Fuss and Fun" will ye please turn your badges the right way round.'

Chris and David laughed.

'You lock this crazy Irishwoman in the office every morning,' David ordered Chris. 'I can see her pushing awkward old gentlemen into the sea before very long!'

* * *

Molly and Chris were up early next morning and had managed to do a good two hour's work before most passengers had had breakfast.

Chris wanted the morning free so that she could get to know some of the passengers, especially Jack and Lois Bridges and Mr van Rheiner.

She left Molly to carry on with the spade work, as they called it, and began a tour of the ship. There were quite a few passengers already in the lounges and reading rooms, and one or two couples had settled themselves in the sun lounge.

Chris could see no sign of Jack and Lois Bridges, nor Mr van Rheiner. It was not surprising that old Mr van Rheiner preferred his cabin. But she was surprised that a young and vigorous couple like Jack Bridges and his sister were not taking a turn around the decks.

Chris went down a deck and asked a steward: 'Morning, Tom. Are the Bridges up?'

'Yes, they're up, Chris. But they seem to be waiting for the sun, I think. Miss Bridges joined her brother in their sitting room.'

Jack and Lois each had a magnificent cabin on B deck, with another large room in between, making a small suite. There was no reason at all why they should not spend their time there, but Chris thought it slightly odd.

'Perhaps so,' she said to the steward. 'I want to get to know them but I don't want to give the impression of bothering them. Perhaps they'll emerge about lunchtime.'

She went along almost to the far end of B deck and enquired of the steward there: 'Mr van Rheiner?'

Old van Rheiner wasn't even out of bed yet, she learned.

So the rest of the day is my own, thought Chris. *It's a shame to take the money!*

She had no intention of taking the day off, of course, but there didn't seem any point in going back to the office right away.

I'll go up into the lounge, she thought, *and if any of the passengers look as though they might welcome a bit of organisation after lunch ... well, we might think up something.*

Chris was turning over a few entertainment ideas in her mind as she went down to E deck, intending to call in at her cabin to fetch a list of suggestions she had made out the previous evening before going to sleep.

Her own cabin was in a small corridor that led from the main way to the side of the ship. It was rather like a small blind alley, with three cabins either side. Her cabin was on the right at the far end. As she entered the corridor, she felt sure she heard her own cabin door shut with a bang ... and the sound of muffled voices within ...

She paused outside her door, her hand hesitating over the knob. *It must be someone tidying up,* she thought.

But stewards usually left the doors open and banged about

briskly. They didn't slam doors and talk to themselves. Chris frowned. She was puzzled rather than suspicious. Then she pushed open the door.

Jack Bridges and his sister Lois were standing in the middle of her cabin, looking confused and flustered — rather like a couple of children caught in the act of raiding the larder.

* * *

Christine stood awkwardly at the door of her cabin and couldn't think what to say. Both Jack and Lois Bridges seemed tongue-tied too. Jack was a slim, wiry man, with smooth black hair — a typical dancer. When he smiled he looked very charming, but in repose his face had a rather strained, worried look.

Lois was not as dark as her brother. Her hair was a dark brown, and she was slim and attractive.

Chris found her tongue at last. 'Excuse me!' she said. 'I was so surprised! But you should have sent for me, or phoned the Entertainments Officer for any information.'

The tension relaxed. Jack Bridges' face creased into a smile of obvious relief. Lois beamed at Chris, but behind her broad smile Chris detected a very sharp enquiring look. Chris had saved the situation — did any of them believe her explanation?

'Well,' said Jack, 'Lois said: "Why don't we look up the entertainments people?"'

'I'm glad you did,' Chris assured them. 'But why don't we go to one of the lounges and talk?'

Chris led the way from the cabin.

'I hope you won't be sorry you decided to look me up,' she said, 'because I'm going to sign you up for a few of the ship's concerts.'

'Oh, that's okay,' said Jack, who seemed to have control of

Christine stood awkwardly at the door of her cabin...

himself again. 'We expected as much, didn't we, my dear?'

'Yes, indeed,' said Lois, 'but we don't mind. Can't afford to get stale in our business. As a matter of fact ... we wanted to ask you if there's some place we could practise...'

'Why, of course,' said Chris. 'There's a gymnasium, you know. I'll speak to Mr Andrews — that's my boss,' she explained.

They sat in the sun lounge for about half an hour. Jack promised Chris that they would not only appear in concerts, but help plan and arrange them.

'Well, I must go back now,' Chris said at last. 'I can't tell you how grateful I am for your co-operation.'

'It's nothing,' Jack said, flashing his professional smile.

Chris smiled back. But as she turned to go she couldn't help noticing that the smile fell from his face in an instant.

'That's a funny couple,' she said, as she breezed into the office, to find Molly chewing thoughtfully on the end of her pencil.

'Meaning who?' asked Molly.

'Jack and Lois Bridges,' said Chris.

'All actors are crazy,' declared Molly firmly. 'Won't they do their tricks at the concerts then?'

'Oh, yes. But they just seem a bit odd, that's all. I suppose one only thinks of such people as they appear on the screen, or in the fan magazines.'

'I dare say,' said Molly. 'But what's the matter with 'em?'

Chris told Molly how she had found them in her cabin, and how she couldn't avoid the impression that they had later been playing a part to cover their embarrassment.

'Ah, you'll get used to this sort of thing in time,' said Molly roguishly. 'You meet the funniest people at sea.'

'Listen to the wise old woman,' said Chris. 'Anyway, David should be pleased.'

'He should that,' said Molly. 'And so shall I when I've had me morning coffee. How about it?'

'All right,' said Chris.

It was not until well after three that Chris gave another thought to old Mr van Rheiner, her other special passenger. At lunch, David had said: 'Put on your most attractive evening dress tonight, Chris. You and I must act as host and hostess at a party. We'll let passengers know we're ready to organise anything they want in the way of entertainments.'

'That's a lot better than just planning things from the office and then making announcements,' said Chris enthusiastically.

'Exactly,' said David. 'I find that people don't want to feel organised, and yet some planning is essential. We must both get to know the guests and get an idea of their wishes, then pool ideas and plan something for everybody. Relax until about six, then join me in the staff-room looking good enough to eat!'

'That's a tall order,' said Chris, very thrilled at the prospect.

David looked at her almost affectionately. 'You'll manage it,' he said quietly.

So here she was on the deck outside the staff-room, snuggled deep in the most comfortable deck-chair she had ever seen — with the fresh salt smell of the ocean breeze in her face, when she remembered Mr van Rheiner.

I'd better not ignore him, she thought, as she slipped from the deck-chair and made her way to his cabin.

Chris knocked on the door of van Rheiner's sitting-room.

'Good afternoon, Mr van Rheiner,' she said.

Mr van Rheiner grunted. He was propped up in an armchair. He wore a heavy dressing-gown, and looked very old. His hair was a grizzled grey, rapidly turning to dirty white, and it looked dusty. His face had a yellow tinge. He wore dark glasses although the light was not strong.

'Sit down, miss,' he said in a quavering voice.

'Oh, I don't want to disturb you,' said Chris. 'I only wanted to see if there was anything we could do to make your voyage really helpful ... to your health, I mean.'

'Can't do anything to help that,' the old man snapped. 'I'll never be well.'

'At least we can see that you have some comfort, and that...'

Chris had an impression of small beady eyes looking at her from behind the dark lenses. She couldn't say why.

There was something sharp and alert about the old man despite his appearance.

Perhaps he's one of these rich people who can afford to make the most of their ailments, thought Chris, and decided then and there that she didn't much like Mr van Rheiner.

'What sort of things do you do?' demanded van Rheiner sharply.

'Well, we arrange anything that passengers want. I could get you some library books. Or maybe you like to play quiet games? Chess, for example? I could find one or two passengers who might like a quiet game in your cabin.'

'Could you now?' said van Rheiner, and gave a curious little grating laugh.

Chris nodded. There didn't seem any reason to be amused, she thought.

'Would you come and play chess with me?' demanded van Rheiner suddenly.

'If Mr Andrews approved, I guess I could. I don't play chess very well,' she said, 'but I can play draughts or card games.'

Van Rheiner seemed to find all this very amusing.

He creaked away, laughing like a rusty gate swinging in the breeze.

'Okay,' said van Rheiner, 'suppose you come here at six o'clock and play draughts with me.'

'I'd be glad to,' said Chris, 'but I can't play this evening.'

'All right, some other time then,' he said wearily, and waved his hand as if to say: 'Go now'. Chris wasn't sorry to leave.

She went back to the office.

'I thought you were decking yourself in glorious technicolor for the fandango,' said Molly as she came in.

'Glorious as I may look,' said Chris languidly, 'it won't take me all afternoon.'

Molly threw a scribbling pad at her and made a very inelegant face.

'You want to learn to take your time off when you can get it,' she said, as Chris retrieved the scribbling pad. 'It's not like being ashore, you know. When you're finished there you can go home. On board it's ... Sullivan just do this, and Sullivan just do that...'

'Anybody would think that you were a galley slave, instead of a privileged member of the staff of a superb luxury liner.'

'Ah, will ye get away with them romantic notions, now,' said Molly. 'Work's work wherever ye do it.'

'You love it,' said Chris. 'And so do I. Now I *will* go and change. It must be past five already.'

'Goodbye, Cinderella,' said Molly. 'I'll send the ship's pumpkin for ye at six o'clock sharp.'

Chris went down to her cabin and made a leisurely change into her evening clothes.

She was about to go up to the staff-room when she thought suddenly of old Mr van Rheiner and how dreary it must be to sit alone all day in the cabin.

I could easily slip along and talk to him for a little... she thought.

So instead of going along to the staff-room she turned down to van Rheiner's state room. She was halfway along the corridor when a man with a thin, sharp face came hurrying along and cannoned into her.

'Sorry,' he grunted in a rasping voice. His face was lean and leathery, and he looked as if he hadn't shaved for a couple of days. He had a cap pulled down over his eyes and he wore a dark jacket with a high collar. He was gone before she could get a word out.

She stared after him for a second. She could only assume he was one of the engine-room crew, but it was odd to find him wandering around the passengers' quarters.

She dismissed the matter from her mind, and went along to van Rheiner's sitting-room and tapped on the door. There was no answer. She pushed open the door.

'Mr van Rheiner?' she called.

It was obvious that the cabin was empty.

Chris went back along the corridor.

'Hello there, Miss Scott,' said a little cockney steward as she passed his galley. 'You're looking a treat. But what's happened to your flowers?'

Chris glanced down at the spray of artificial roses she had put at the shoulder of her dress. They were torn and draggled.

'Oh, somebody almost knocked me over,' she said. 'He must have torn my flowers. I'll have to fix them. Has Mr van Rheiner gone to bed?'

'Not that I know of,' said the steward. 'He usually calls me before he goes. He's not in his sitting-room?'

'No. But it doesn't matter, thanks.'

Chris looked down at her torn flowers and muttered: 'That's what comes of trying to do a good deed for the day. Now I shall have to go back and find a pin or something.'

She caught up her dress and ran quickly down to her cabin. There was very little light coming through the single porthole, and as she entered she stretched out her hand to switch on the light.

Long arms reached out of the gloom behind the door, and strong, cruel fingers closed over her eyes and mouth, stifling the cry that rose to her lips. Intense pressure was applied behind her ears, her head swam, and suddenly she fell into an inky blackness, the blood pounding in her ears.

When Chris recovered consciousness she was lying on the floor of her cabin. Her head was swimming. She dragged herself over to the mirror above the wash-basin. Two red spots showed beneath her ears and her neck felt bruised and sore.

She splashed her face with cold water, then sank on to her bed.

This was crazy! Without rhyme or reason.

Chris picked up a comb and arranged her hair. It was a tense, thoughtful face that looked out from the mirror. She was no simpleton. Her father had told her many tales of crimes at sea. She knew only too well that robbery was committed for very little gain.

But a quick glance round the cabin told her that nothing had been disturbed. What was there worth taking anyway? Her clothes, a few trifles of little value and no actual cash at all. All the money she had was in the Purser's safe.

And on a ship like this where every passenger had paid a small fortune for the trip, who could be bothered to steal from one of the ship's staff?

Chris's fingers trembled slightly as she adjusted the torn flowers on her shoulder. She hardly knew what to do, or say, about the whole episode.

But in a few minutes she must join David and play her part in the social evening. Until that duty was over and she had time to think, she decided to say nothing to anyone.

During the evening, Chris moved among the passengers gathered in the sun lounge, talking now with one group, now another. Yet, all the time, her mind was turning over the events of that afternoon.

What did it all mean? What should she do about it?

Strong, cruel fingers closed over her eyes and mouth...

'You're doing wonders, Chris,' David whispered in her ear as he passed. 'I've been following you round. Hardly anybody failed to tell me how charming and sociable you were, and how much they appreciate the idea of a lady hostess.'

Chris gave him a quick, grateful smile and, as he moved on, she wondered why she did not confide in him completely. It would seem so easy to talk to him after the social, and yet...

Chris watched him move from group to group, bringing people together, introducing the shy ones, tactfully restraining a few big businessmen who seemed to think they had bought the whole ship.

I know why I don't tell him, she thought. *He has too much on his mind already and ... well ... I just don't want him thinking me a fanciful scatterbrain ... because, after all, the whole thing is unbelievable!*

Chris stood for a moment before a huge plate-glass panel that formed part of the wall of the lounge. Behind her were the bright lights, the laughter and happy chatter of the passengers; beyond, a few feet of deck and then the vast expanse of dark, blue-black ocean stretching out, out... it seemed almost to the world's end.

The ship's lights shone out over the water for a little way, far enough to pick out clearly the great dark waves, fringed with frothy foam, that sped past them as they cut their way through the Atlantic. Above, in a velvet-black sky, a few stars twinkled coldly.

It was a strange, impressive contrast. She felt poised between two worlds...one comfortable and happy, the other...empty, cold, threatening.

'I think we might leave them now.'

David's voice broke in on her thoughts. Chris turned to find him standing right behind her, smiling.

'They'll drift off to read, play cards or anything else that takes their fancy. We don't want them to think that we are pestering them. We'll compare notes in the morning and get out some kind of programme. I don't suppose you will be sorry to turn in. Thanks for putting up a grand show, Chris.'

Chris couldn't find any words. She just smiled. David offered her his arm and escorted her from the lounge.

'I have to go down to the office,' he said, 'but you needn't bother. Goodnight, Chris. Sweet dreams!'

'Goodnight, David.'

As he walked away she wanted to call after him. But she checked her impulse.

'It could have been a fainting fit...' she told herself, as she too turned away. But her hand stole up to her neck as she walked back to her cabin. 'Yes...' she imagined her own voice saying to her, 'but just what kind of fainting fit grabs you from behind and leaves red marks on your neck?'

It was almost in fear and trembling that Chris pushed open her cabin door, hastily switched on the light and gave a quick glance around.

'Christine, you're getting jumpy and you are not being your father's daughter,' she told herself severely.

She made an effort to put morbid thoughts out of her mind. It might be a good idea to read something light for a while, she thought. She slipped on her housecoat and had just settled in her chair with a book when there was a loud banging on the door which made her swing round, all her anxious fears returning in a flash.

A second later Molly O'Sullivan pushed open the door. Chris gave a little gasp of relief. 'It's you, Molly!'

'And who else would it be?' demanded Molly. 'You were not expecting the Captain himself to come and pin a medal on you for behaving like a grand lady at the party, I suppose?'

Chris laughed. 'Oh, I'm so glad you dropped in,' she said.

Molly advanced into the cabin and pretended to look very annoyed.

'Glad are you, me fine madam? Then what's the idea of moping down here all by yourself, with never so much as kissin' your hand to your shipmates, and never a word to meself?'

'Oh, Molly!' Chris's hand flew to her mouth. 'I suppose it does seem thoughtless of me, but...'

Molly came over and sat on the bed beside Chris.

'Ah, I was only foolin'. The truth is that you're down here moping by yourself because you've had something on your mind all evening. You can't fool the Irish, for they've fooled far too many themselves in their time! Come on, now! What's the trouble?'

Chris didn't answer for a while. She sat staring down at the cabin floor, wondering whether it would be wise to say anything at all.

'I know,' said Molly. 'The great man of tact entirely forgot to make a fuss of you for doing so well tonight. You feel a bit unappreciated. That's it, for sure!'

Chris shook her head and smiled. 'No, it's not that. David was very nice, and anyway he would be quite entitled to take my work for granted. It's...' She hesitated, then: 'Molly, do you think there could possibly be a stowaway on this ship?'

'A stowaway?' repeated Molly in amazement. 'Whatever in the wide world put that notion into your head? Not a chance in a lifetime, I'd say.'

'I suppose not,' said Chris. 'But it seemed the only answer.'

Molly looked hard at Chris. 'You'd better tell me what's on your mind,' she said.

'You'll promise not to say a word to anyone...without my permission?'

Molly was entirely serious now. This was so unlike Chris! 'If it will help you, Chris darlin', I'll promise you the moon itself, so I will!'

So Chris told her everything. Molly's big round eyes grew bigger still as she listened.

When Chris had finished Molly drew a deep breath. 'Goodness!' she said loudly. 'If it was anybody but yourself, I'd be thinking you'd read too many thrillers in bed at night.'

'That is exactly what anybody would think,' said Chris quietly, 'and I could hardly blame them.'

'It ought to be reported,' said Molly.

Chris shook her head. 'No, Molly. I've made up my mind. I don't want David thinking I'm a nervous idiot...over imaginative, or whatever you call it.'

'Then,' said Molly firmly, 'we've got to see into this together...at least until we've enough clear proof to go to the Captain.'

'Thanks, Molly,' said Chris. 'I knew you would understand.'

'I don't think I understand,' said Molly solemnly, 'but I see what you mean.'

Chris laughed. 'That's Irish, if you like!'

Molly and Chris sat talking earnestly for a long time. Who was the strange man Chris had seen on her way to old Mr van Rheiner's cabin? Could he have been making for Chris's cabin for any reason? If not, who else had any reason to attack Chris?

And why had Jack and Lois Bridges seemed so embarrassed when Chris found them in her cabin? And why had they not called at the Entertainment Office, like anybody else?

'Sure, me head's going round like a top,' said Molly at last. 'We can sit here all night asking questions, but we'll get no answers. I'll tell you what we'll do Chris. There's a practice fire-drill for all staff and crew twice a week from now on. We must get a good look at all the hands when they assemble and see if you can pick out the strange-looking man.'

'But we shall have to take our own places. We can't be on all decks at once,' objected Chris.

'I know,' said Molly, 'but maybe you could persuade David that you want to get a complete idea of the whole fire-drill. At least we could check up on the engine-room. From your description I'd say this man's an engine-room hand.'

'Well,' said Chris, 'we can but try.'

'And we'll keep our eyes on Jack and Lois Bridges too,' said Molly. 'Now, Chris, lock the door when I go, then turn in and get some sleep.'

'Goodnight, Molly. Thanks a lot.'

'It's nothin',' said Molly as she left. 'Mind you lock this door now!'

Chris locked the door, undressed, and climbed into bed. It was a long time before she got to sleep. The slightest creak made her tense and stiff. When she finally drifted off from sheer fatigue, her dreams were troubled full of shadowy menaces that kept her twisting and turning on her pillow.

Meanwhile the ship ploughed its deep furrow in the fathomless dark waters of the Atlantic. Miles spun behind the foaming white wake of the huge floating hotel.

Chris was mercifully unaware of the dark figure that crept under cover of every shadow right to her cabin door, turned the handle stealthily, gave an exclamation of annoyance on finding the cabin locked, and then crept back into the shadows.

'Chris! Chris! Wake up. It's me — Molly!'

Chris raised herself with an effort, gathered her fuddled wits and stumbled to the cabin door.

'It can't be morning, 'she said as Molly O'Sullivan came in.

'I'm afraid it is,' said Molly. 'I thought you'd need a call this morning. I left it as late as I dared.'

Chris sat down and her head dropped. 'I never felt so witless in my life,' she murmured drowsily.

'Get along to the shower with ye,' said Molly. 'Then get a good sniff of that sea breeze. I'll have a gallon of the strongest coffee cook can brew and...why, you'll be ready to swim the rest of the trip!'

Molly was off again in no time. Chris put on a dressing-gown and went to the showers.

She was certainly ready for the coffee which Molly, true to her word, had ready on the table in the staff-room when she arrived.

'I think I'm with you again, Molly,' she said. 'Thanks for everything. It would have looked bad if I'd overslept. It took me ages to get settled last night after you left.'

'I did my share of puzzlin' too,' admitted Molly. 'It's no good, Chris. When there's something on your mind you just can't forget it. Do you know what I did this morning?'

Chris shook her head.

'I got up at four o'clock and did a bit of wandering.'

'You did?' said Chris. 'I wish you'd called for me.'

'Ah, I thought you needed some sleep, even if 'twas only an hour or so. You had a bit of a shock yesterday, you know. More than you think — and then there was the strain of that social evening affair. Anyway, I had the idea to go down to the Duty Officer in the engine-room, sort of pretending I couldn't sleep or somethin'!'

'I bet he gave you a suspicious look and told you to go right back to your cabin,' said Chris. 'He doesn't approve of anybody taking an interest in his world of mystery!'

'Aye,' said Molly, 'but I never got to the engine-room. I thought, do you see, that I might recognise somebody down there answering your description of that strange man you saw.'

'Yes, yes,' said Chris excitedly, for she guessed by this time that Molly had something important to tell her.

'"Twas sort of an instinct made me go round to your cabin first.'

At that moment David Andrews came in and, seeing the two girls already at breakfast, naturally came over and joined them.

'I'll tell ye later,' whispered Molly.

The three of them had a busy morning and round about twelve o'clock David said: 'This list is about ready to discuss with the Captain now. Why don't you break until two?'

'You mean, why don't we break *in* two,' said Molly, 'or have we done that already? I wouldn't know. Tell me, Mister Andrews, were you ever on a slave galley?'

David grinned and went out to see the Captain.

'Come out on deck,' said Molly. 'I can't stand the sight of programmes, maps, times, dates and the like any longer!'

The two girls found a couple of deckchairs in a sheltered spot.

'I've been bursting to tell you this all morning...' Molly began.

'I know,' said Chris. 'Come on, what is it?'

'I found this down by your cabin door early this morning.'

Molly held out her hand. Resting in the palm was a fragment of silver chain to which was attached a tiny silver shield. Engraved on one side was the word *Seattle*, followed by a date: *April 1964*.

'How did you find this?' asked Chris.

'It was a bit of a fluke,' said Molly. 'I came up to your door and tried the handle. I heard a tinkle and I looked down and there it was, caught in the beams of one of those little lights they leave burning all night.'

Chris looked down at the little shield. 'How do you suppose it got there?' she mused.

'It might have been wrenched off in the scuffle when you got half-strangled, you poor darlin'. But I don't think so. It would have been *in* the cabin in that case, wouldn't it?'

Chris nodded. 'And we might have seen it before this too. But if it wasn't...' Chris suddenly felt a shiver go down her back. *'You think somebody came back last night and tried my door?'*

'I do,' said Molly solemnly. 'Because there was a Captain's inspection at eight o'clock this morning, and I think the steward would have been sweeping and polishing all last evening so as not to have much to do this morning. If that thing had been there early last night, it wouldn't have been left there.'

Chris sat staring out to sea for a moment. Then she reached out her hand.

'Let me have another look at that,' she said. Her hand shook slightly as she took the little silver shield.

'Do you think maybe we should report the whole thing to David?' asked Molly.

'Seattle...that's in America, isn't it?'

'It is that,' said Molly.

'Passenger list!' said Chris. 'Who comes from Seattle?'

'I don't think it's going to be as easy as that,' sighed Molly. 'But we'll try it.'

But there was nobody on the passenger list recorded as coming from Seattle. They had just finished checking this after lunch when David came back.

'All settled,' he said cheerfully, 'much to Molly's relief, no doubt.'

'It is that,' said Molly with feeling.

'There's just one thing,' said David. 'The Captain thinks

we should stage a concert before we get to any port. That means tomorrow night, in effect, as we're due at Algiers the day after. We don't want the passengers to feel that we are simply taking them to ports and leaving them to find their own entertainment. Get it?'

'I get it,' said Chris: 'And I also get the point that your eager assistant had better get busy!'

'I think you might get some definite action on our various promises. We need Jack and Lois Bridges to do their stuff.'

And so the afternoon's work started.

At about three o'clock Chris left the ofice and wandered around the top deck. There was no sign of Jack Bridges or his sister Lois.

They must be in their suite, thought Chris.

When she reached the Bridges' sitting-room, Jack and Lois seemed to be having a violent argument.

Chris hesitated. Perhaps she should go away? On the other hand, time was short and some diversion might prevent the argument developing into a quarrel.

'*Look,*' Lois was saying in no uncertain manner, '*this is getting crazy. That's what I think. It's going beyond anything either of us counted on. And I don't think there's any point in trying to be too smart.*'

'*Ah, don't keep on!*'

Jack Bridges' nasal tones cut in sharply. Normally Bridges spoke in a pleasant enought American voice, but when he forgot himself it was harsh and coarse.

It was all part of his odd personality. Like that smile of his, that seemed so charming. But the moment his face relaxed you noticed that it was thin, with hard little eyes like points of steel.

'...all right, so maybe we rushed things a little. I was too eager, that's all. We'll play it cool from now on.'

Chris made up her mind suddenly. She tapped on the door and Jack's rasping voice stopped dead.

Then Lois Bridges called: 'Who is it?'

'Christine Scott, Miss Bridges. From the Entertainments Office.'

Lois opened the door. 'Well, come on in!' she said with a broad professional smile.

Her eyes didn't match her smiling lips. Chris could almost see Lois setting her features into a mask of amiability before opening the door.

'I hope I'm not disturbing you,' said Chris, 'but it's about the concert. We'd very much like to put on a show tomorrow night. I hope that's not too short notice for you.'

Jack Bridges had his back turned. He was obviously making an effort to control himself and assume his best professional poise too. He swung round and gave Lois a sharp look. His sister had been about to say something. And Chris had a shrewd idea that it had been on the tip of Lois Bridges' tongue to make excuses; refuse to do a show at such short notice.

'Sure,' said Bridges heartily. 'We'd be glad to help! It might be a little rough in places...not exactly a Broadway production, but...we'll start 'em smiling and leave 'em laughing, eh, Lois?'

Lois took the cue from her brother. But Chris noticed a split second's hesitation. Then Lois beamed and said: 'We'd love to help, honey. You just name the time and place...'

'Thanks very much,' said Chris. 'The Entertainments Officer will be delighted to hear this. Could I say that you'd come along and discuss details with him in a couple of hours?'

'Why wait?' said Jack. 'What's the matter with right now?'

'Nothing at all,' Chris said, 'if you're sure that's convenient.'

Jack came across to Chris and put his arm around her

shoulders in a big friendly, 'I'm-everybody's-big-brother' way.

'Nothing's ever convenient for show people,' he said, 'but we take life as it comes.' He put his other arm around Lois and led them from the suite.

Chris was very conscious of Jack's arm about her shoulders. Deep down in her brain something was prompting her to take notice, to remember...

It wasn't until they had met David and all four gone down to the gymnasium that she realised what that curious feeling was.

There had been something about Jack's arm — something that didn't seem right.

'We could open with that old routine we did in the Follies show,' Jack was saying. He stripped off his jacket, and stood in his sports shirt, a brilliant orange silk affair with short sleeves. 'You remember, Lois. Open with a few bars of *Anytime you're in Virginia...*'

Jack began to hum and beat out a rhythm which Lois picked up quickly, falling into position beside him.

But Chris had no eyes for the dance. Her gaze was rivetted on the tinkling silver chain around Jack's wrist, from which hung several tiny shields exactly like the one Molly had picked up outside her cabin door at four o'clock that same morning!

Chris couldn't give much thought to concert plans that afternoon. Her mind was fixed on the bracelet she could see fastened to Jack Bridges's wrist.

'Did you make a note of that?' she heard David say suddenly. She was startled into realising that Jack, Lois Bridges and David were staring at her. She hadn't taken in a word for the last ten minutes!

'I'm sorry,' she stammered.

David gave her a stern look. He didn't like this show of

slackness before passengers. 'I thought you were making notes,' he said. 'We shall have to go over that again.'

Chris made some confused notes and the planning continued. When they finally walked back to the office David said sharply: 'I hope you got all those points. We can't expect passengers to do the work, you know.'

Chris was feeling the full effects of her restless, strained night by this time. She bit her lip in an effort to control herself, but it was no use. In a second she was crying openly.

David looked irritated. Was she a girl with no staying power, after all? A stupid little thing who burst into tears the moment anything went wrong?

'Look here,' he said, 'I'm bound to maintain discipline, Miss Scott. You were very slack this afternoon, and you won't help matters by bursting into tears.'

Chris wouldn't wait to hear any more. She thrust the notes at him and fled to her cabin.

In less than five minutes Molly came down.

'David told me you were having hysterics,' she said. 'I'm supposed to calm you down. What on earth's the matter?'

'It was stupid of me,' said Chris miserably. 'I could kick myself overboard.'

Between sniffs, she told Molly everything.

'I'm going right back and tell him everything, so I am,' said Molly angrily.

'It's too late now,' said Chris, making an effort to control her feelings. 'I must find out what this is all about, and prove my story. Whatever I say now will sound like a crazy attempt to justify myself. . .'

'What about the lucky charm from Bridges's bracelet, or whatever it is?' asked Molly indignantly.

'That could be coincidence,' said Chris wearily. 'It might have been lost anywhere. Anyway it isn't positive proof.

How can I accuse them of anything simply because we found that little shield?'

Molly nodded gloomily. 'I guess you're right, Chris,' she admitted. 'Fix your face. David wants to see you.'

When Chris returned to the office David was pacing up and down, looking sternly official.

'I'm sorry,' said Chris, 'there isn't anything I can say except that I was very tired.'

'I'm sorry too,' he said, 'but that isn't my business really, is it? Slackness and temperaments can't be ignored, you know. I don't want anything like this again.'

Chris saw there was nothing for it but to accept the reproof for the moment. Her cheeks were burning as she strode from the office.

Relations were rather strained all round the next day, but by the middle of the afternoon arrangements for the concert were completed.

'You will both have a very full evening,' David said, 'so perhaps you'd better take a rest.'

He looked hard at Chris as he said this. She flushed but said nothing. David looked away hastily.

'Report to me in the cinema, not here,' he continued.

The ship's cinema had a stage large enough for quite an elaborate show.

'I want you, Miss Scott,' David went on, 'to make the opening announcement. I'm arranging a surprise effect with Bridges. I have your speech here. You just read it over the mike when the curtain goes up.'

Chris nodded. She took the sheet of paper with her speech, and went off to her cabin without another word.

At about six o'clock one of the stewards called at her cabin with a note from Molly.

Dear Chris: We all forgot about old van Rheiner. He sent up a message asking why we didn't arrange for him to go to the show. If he can't walk to the cinema, you are to arrange with the junior officer of the watch to send two hands to take him on a stretcher or something. If you can manage to drop him into the hold somehow he'll be quiet for the rest of the trip maybe. Molly.

Chris grinned, and hurried along to van Rheiner's sitting room.

'Huh! What do you want, young woman?' he snorted.

Chris explained politely. Van Rheiner questioned her about the concert as if she were a guilty person in a witness box. Finally he snapped: 'Have everything ready and call for me at seven-fifty. I'll let you know then.'

'Old codger!' muttered Chris. 'He put us to this trouble because he's peeved. When we get there he'll say he doesn't want to come after all!'

Chris arranged for two men to be ready to come down to fetch van Rheiner. 'But I'm sure he won't really come,' she told the junior officer of the watch. 'I'll just look in at seven-fifty, and if he insists I'll phone you.'

'Okay, Chris,' said the young officer. 'If you don't phone by five to eight, I'll the send men along to the cinema. They need all hands tonight.'

When Chris went down to van Rheiner's cabin that evening the door was open but there was no sign of the old man.

'Mr van Rheiner?' she called, looking towards the door that led into the bedroom. There was no answer.

Chris looked anxiously at her watch. She was due on stage at eight sharp. David would never forgive another mistake.

'I'm sorry about you, Mr van Rheiner,' she muttered, 'but I'm not waiting here.'

As she crossed to the cabin door, it swung shut! One quick tug at the handle told her that it was locked!

Chris ran to the bedroom door. That was locked too! It

was three minutes to eight. She ran back and began to pound on the other door in the forlorn hope of attracting attention. But she knew that every available person was on duty at the cinema, or in the lounge adjoining it. They were all up there waiting for her to walk on stage and open the show!

Chris pounded desperately on the door until her watch said one minute past eight. Then she realised she was beaten.

What had happened? The door must have been locked deliberately, and so must the connecting door to the bedroom, which stopped her using the bedside telephone.

Someone must have locked the connecting door, slipped out from the main bedroom door, and then locked the sitting-room door from the corridor. But surely that must mean that van Rheiner himself was party to the plot? But why?

Chris felt that she must surely be going mad. Or was van Rheiner crazy? Was he a stupid, malicious old man playing a practical joke?

Chris might have believed this if it had not been for all the other mysterious happenings. And but for that tiny silver shield from Jack's bracelet, she might have believed she was the victim of delusions. Yet, where did Jack and Lois Bridges fit in now?

But the immediate question was: how long would she be left shut up here? It was now twenty past eight. Surely someone must come soon?

She turned again to the cabin door. It seemed pointless to keep thumping at it, but it was all she could do. She banged at the door and rattled the lock. Suddenly the well-oiled catch slipped back and the door swung open. It was difficult to convince herself that it had ever been locked!

Chris ran out, her one thought to get to David and explain. But even as she ran she knew in her heart that, once again, she would never be able to prove a thing!

David was backstage looking very harassed. He gave Chris one piercing glance, and beckoned her to follow him into the lounge.

'David, please listen to me,' Chris pleaded, determined to tell him everything.

'I haven't time to listen to excuses,' he snapped. 'You simply can't make excuses on a ship. What would you think if the navigating officer ran us on the rocks and then offered excuses?'

'I understand that,' began Chris.

David ignored the interruption. 'Not only did you muff the opening, but you've infuriated old van Rheiner. Why on earth didn't you do something about him?'

'What?' exclaimed Chris. 'I've just come from his cabin. That was the whole trouble.'

'Look,' said David, 'I haven't time to waste. Van Rheiner just sent up a furious message to say that he's been waiting in his suite for half-an-hour. He says you promised to make arrangements to fetch him for the concert.'

'But he was not in his suite!' insisted Chris. 'I've been down there since...'

David cut her short. 'No purpose is served by this,' he said. 'Go down to van Rheiner and apologise, and try to calm him down. Please don't make things worse than they are by a lot of evasions. Van Rheiner wouldn't kick up this fuss for nothing. That's an order, Miss Scott,' he added.

Christine nodded in a dazed way and went back to van Rheiner's cabin.

Van Rheiner was sitting in his chair, dressed in an old-fashioned evening suit. He had a plaid shawl round his shoulders and a silver-knobbed stick in his hand.

'It's too late now!' he screeched at Chris. 'What's the idea of foolin' me around like this?'

Chris stared at him. 'You must know the answer to that question,' she said.

'No impertinence now!' snapped the old man. 'You forgot all about me.'

Chris's shoulders drooped souddenly. There was only one thing to say and she said it, in a low trembling voice: 'I'm very sorry, Mr van Rheiner. I don't know how it happened. I hope you'll overlook it.'

It's for David, she thought. *I can't blame him, and it's the least I can do.*

'Talking's cheap!' snarled the old man. 'Get out!'

Chris stumbled back to her cabin. She had never felt so desperately alone, baffled and miserable in her whole life.

Late the following evening the ship docked at Algiers. Molly and Chris should have been looking forward to a trip ashore the next day. But David had felt bound to refuse to grant Chris shore-leave. So the two girls were having a miserable argument down in Chris's cabin.

'I'll not go without you,' said Molly.

'That won't do any good,' said Chris. 'Please go, Molly, and then you can bring back some souvenirs. I shall have to take something home to Dad.'

'Come and have a look at the place, anyway,' said Molly. 'Let's go up and look at the lights.'

They went up to the top deck and gazed out over the city.

'It looks just like a lot of other places at night,' admitted Molly. 'Lights twinkling; docks; natives swarming all over the place.'

Chris leaned over the rail and peered into the night. 'This is simply tormenting myself to no good purpose,' she said suddenly. 'I'm going to bed. Goodnight, Molly. See you in the morning.'

Molly sighed. 'Goodnight, Chris. We'll see Colombo, or

some other place together. It's not the end of the world.'

Chris walked the length of the deck, lost in her own thoughts. It scarcely mattered now whether she went ashore at any port or not. Everything was spoiled. She stood by one of the huge ventilator shafts, and stared up into the heavy tropical night. *What was it all about?*

Suddenly a voice called out of the darkness, somewhere behind her: 'That you, Bridges?'

Chris slipped behind the shaft, and held her breath. It was van Rheiner's voice. What was he doing up here... an old, crotchety invalid who never left his cabin unaided? That's what they'd all thought until that evening of the concert when he insisted he'd never left his cabin, although Chris had been locked in alone.

'Over here!' came a hissing whisper.

'No tricks now!' snapped van Rheiner's voice.

This time there was no doubt about it. It *was* van Rheiner. Chris strained her eyes. She could see nothing. But from somewhere behind her, in the shadow of one of the lifeboats, she could hear van Rheiner and Jack Bridges holding a converstion in fierce whispers.

'I suggest we come to terms,' van Rheiner was saying. 'We can't discuss it here — it's too risky. Meet me in Algiers.'

'I don't trust you,' snapped Bridges.

'I don't trust you either,' snarled van Rheiner, 'but we've got to make a deal or we all lose money. I'll be at the *Crescent Moon* café. Upstairs. From noon tomorrow. If you've any sense you'll be there. Ask Lois. She'll agree with me.'

The rest of the conversation was lost to Chris. A sudden breeze carried the words of the two men in the opposite direction. Chris peered intently towards the lifeboat, and soon she saw Jack Bridges move quickly and hurry away. Not long afterwards, van Rheiner followed him.

But not the crotchety van Rheiner that Chris knew.

It was the thin dark man who had almost knocked her over the first time she had gone to van Rheiner's cabin!

So he was van Rheiner! Suddenly part of the mystery became as clear as daylight! Van Rheiner, or whatever his real name was, was playing a dual rôle.

Chris hurried down to Molly's cabin. 'Molly,' she said excitedly, 'I've solved part of the mystery!'

'Well now, it's about time somebody did,' said Molly. 'But how?'

'I heard van Rheiner and Jack Bridges talking on the upper deck. They had obviously arranged a secret meeting. They know each other but don't want to admit it,' said Chris. 'And what is more, van Rheiner isn't van Rheiner at all. He's the man who nearly knocked me over... the man we thought might be an engine-room hand. Now I know why van Rheiner always poses as an invalid. Why he never goes out. Why he wears those dark glasses and a dressing-gown all the time. He's not an old man at all. He's a Jekyll and Hyde!'

'Wait a minute,' said Molly. 'Are you sure it was van Rheiner?'

'I'd know his voice anywhere,' said Chris. 'It was the voice I recognised, long before I saw either Bridges or van Rheiner, minus his glasses and dressing-gown, etc.'

'But why all these Jekyll and Hyde goings-on, at all?' asked Molly.

'That I don't know,' said Chris, 'but we can find out. If Jack and Lois go ashore tomorrow you bet it will be to meet van Rheiner. Molly, I've got to find out what goes on at that café tomorrow.'

'But, Chris, even if you break the rules and go ashore without permission, you can't visit Algiers alone!'

'I'm going to find out what happens, somehow,' said Chris, grimly determined. 'I've had a bit of luck, and I'm not going to fail to use it.'

'Oh, glory!' said Molly. 'Why don't you tell David? He'll surely not refuse you a chance to clear yourself. It's not safe for you to try tracking this thing down on your own.'

'The old ramrod!' said Chris. 'If he refuses, then where shall I be?'

'At least you'll be in one piece,' said Molly. 'Think it over, Chris, and we'll talk to David in the morning.'

Chris suddenly stopped arguing. 'All right, Molly. We'll see what tomorrow brings.'

She went towards her own cabin with her mind firmly made up. She could see Molly's point, but she was determined to present David with an unanswerable case. She would go ashore tomorrow by hook or by crook!

Instead of going to her own cabin, Chris went to the office, calmly wrote herself a pass, stamped it with the ship's stamp, and signed it herself. Nobody was going to look at it very closely. In her uniform and with ship's papers it would be taken for granted that she was likely to go ashore. Nobody would miss her at breakfast.

As soon as it was light, Chris slipped down the gangplank, near one of the unloading hatches. Sleepy dock officials seemed surprised to see her, but her papers seemed to be quite in order and it was no business of theirs.

Within a few minutes, Chris was alone in Algiers.

To get quickly away from the ship and find the *Crescent Moon* café was the only clear plan Chris had. These were desperate measures, and there was no time and no point in trying to think too far ahead. She saw there were two or three rather ramshackle cars with native drivers outside the dock area. Chris didn't know it, but they were waiting there on the off-chance of picking up passengers who often left ships early in order to drive round the city, and some way into the interior.

Chris approached one and asked him: '*Crescent Moon* café?'

He looked a bit annoyed and called out something to the other drivers. They laughed. Finally he shrugged and motioned her to get in. He had hoped for a longer booking. But when she had settled herself in the rear seat he began to race along like a crazy fire-engine, determined to deliver her at the café and race back to the docks again as soon as possible.

Chris was bumped and swayed around in the car like a pea in a pod. Its springs were none too good, and when at last the vehicle came to a sudden, sickening halt, she was almost flung through the window.

Thank goodness that's over! Chris thought, as she climbed out, feeling dazed and shaken.

It took her a second or so to sort herself out. When she did so, she suddenly had the most awful sensation! It was like falling down a great well. For she remembered that she had absolutely no money of any kind. Every penny she owned, and all her accumulated pay, was simply a few entries in the Purser's accounts. She had completely forgotten all about the need to draw some money.

The driver was quick to spot the trouble when he realised she was hesitating. The little English he knew soon gave out.

In no time at all he was gabbling furiously at her in an unknown tongue, shaking his fist, and dancing up and down on the pavement like a dervish, calling on the police, his relatives, and a great variety of Eastern gods, to witness how he, a poor struggling driver with thousands of starving children had been robbed and tricked.

Chris tried to explain, tried desperately to think of something to offer him... if only she had a ring, or a brooch! But it would have been quite useless in any case. He had already given himself over to his furious grief and clamour, and was determined to raise half Algiers to see the indignity he had suffered!

It didn't take long for a policeman to appear. He roughly silenced the driver and then turned to Chris, speaking in broken English.

'Why you not pay?' he asked.

Chris explained.

'From big ship and not got money?' said the policeman incredulously. He was very familiar with the idea of sailors not having money when going back to their ship after leave, but...

Chris realised that she would probably have to go back to the ship, if the policeman would allow it, accept defeat again, and ask David to pay the driver and settle matters with the police.

She bit her lip in exasperation. Across the road she could see the *Crescent Moon* café. It was rather flashy and cheap — the native owner's idea of looking 'western'.

If she could only get the lay of the land before twelve... there might be some way she could listen in on van Rheiner and Bridges...

Chris was not going to be defeated again so near her goal. She had probably burned her boats as far as her job was concerned anyway. Almost without stopping to calculate the consequences, she suddenly brushed the policeman aside, and dashed across the road and darted off down a side alley.

A babble of unintelligible chatter broke out behind her.

Chris ran the length of the narrow alley, then turned blindly into a wide street. But she had not gone more than a few hundred yards when a car drew up behind her with a screeching of brakes. She heard a shout, a pounding of feet... and a voice called: 'Chris, you little idiot — stop!'

It was David Andrews.

Chris stopped and turned to him. 'You can't blame me for trying,' she said in a breathless but sadly resigned tone.

'Whew!' gasped David. 'Don't worry — you've made your point! Molly told me everything. She suddenly realised what you intended to do. You only got away from the ship by about fifteen minutes. I followed as fast as I could. One of the other drivers heard you ask for the *Crescent Moon* café. But wait while I settle this with the policeman.'

Molly saw now that David had been followed by the irate driver and the policeman. David gave both his and Chris's driver a large tip and scowls changed like magic to oily smiles. Then he steered Chris into a café and ordered iced drinks.

'Chris, why on earth didn't you come to me?' he asked plaintively.

Chris sighed. 'I suppose my pride made me want to justify myself. You weren't very encouraging anyway. Not that I can blame you.'

David bit his lip. 'I suppose I was a bit harsh,' he admitted, 'but tell me all that has happened.'

So Chris told him everything, hardly pausing for breath.

'...I see now what happened the night of the concert,' Chris explained. 'Van Rheiner took off his glasses and dressing-gown, slipped into the corridor and locked me in his cabin. I don't know *why* he did, but he must have returned twenty minutes later, unlocked the door and left me to find my own way out.'

'And he and Bridges need to come to terms, yet they don't trust each other and have pretended not to know each other,' mused David. 'Well, one thing stands out clearly — all this centres on _your_ cabin. What can there be about your cabin to account for it?'

He sat tapping his fingers restlessly on the table.

'What is it?' asked Chris.

'I was thinking,' said David. 'We must find a spot opposite the café and keep watch.'

They left the café and walked back into the street where the _Crescent Moon_ was located. David looked about and finally saw a small native curio shop.

'That's not ideal,' he said, 'but if we sit in the upper room we'll be able to see anybody who arrives at the café.'

They went over to the shop and, after a good deal of bargaining, the native owner led them up a flight of stairs and into a small room overlooking the street. Chris perched on a stool and stared out of the latticed window.

Minutes went slowly by... The native owner brought them sweet, scented coffee in tiny cups and strips of what Chris could only think of as solidified jam!

They sipped and nibbled doubtfully. Suddenly Chris cried: 'That's van Rheiner as he really is! The man I saw talking to Bridges!'

'That's good enough,' said David grimly. 'Back to the ship, Chris. We'll be waiting for him!'

'And look! There are Jack and Lois,' cried Chris, pointing to another car just drawing up. But David was already on his way and Chris hurried after him.

'It's thankful I am to see ye in one piece,' said Molly as they appeared in the office some time later. 'What happened?'

'Quite a lot,' said David. 'The wires are buzzing!'

'We've seen the Captain,' said Chris, 'and sent radio messages checking on both van Rheiner and the Bridges.'

'Right now we must search Chris's cabin,' said David. 'We must find what van Rheiner couldn't. Come on, Chris.'

'Do you think I could come too?' asked Molly, sheepishly.

'Why not?' said David. 'It's your day off!' and in a few moments three puzzled people were standing in Chris's cabin.

'It's pretty clear now,' said David, 'that van Rheiner and the Bridges were both independently looking for something in this cabin. That silver shield Molly found obviously means that Jack tried to get in — and van Rheiner made two attempts at least. He called Chris to his cabin the night of our party to make sure she was out of his way. But Chris returned to fix her flowers. I think he attacked you then, Chris.'

Chris nodded. 'That sounds right.'

David continued: 'Next time he made quite sure by locking you in his cabin. He still didn't find what he wanted so he decided to make a deal with Bridges. But what are they looking for? It must surely be wealth in a small, portable form.'

'Like jewels?' suggested Chris.

'That's the most likely thing,' said David. 'Where would you hide jewels here?'

Chris thought for a bit. 'This cabin was cleared after the last trip and nobody used it until I came. Right?'

'Absolutely right,' said David. 'All passengers went ashore the day we docked and the ship's company went on leave a few days later.'

'So this must be something left over from the *last* trip,' said Chris. 'If you were forced to leave jewels behind on a ship you would have to hide them in the woodwork, or some of the fittings, and come back again later, wouldn't you?'

'Wait!' cried David. 'You've got it, Chris! On the last trip there was an awful row because a rich American woman said she had been robbed of her jewels. We could do nothing because she hadn't left them with the Purser, and there was really no proof that she had ever brought them aboard. The thieves must have been too scared to take them ashore and hidden them here!'

'But where?' said Molly. 'It's like an oven down here and I'll be baked before we solve the mystery, so I will!'

David laughed. 'It *is* pretty warm! You'd better sit down under the blower and cool off!'

Like most ships the *New Age* was fitted in every cabin with adjustable pipes that blew streams of cool air from various angles. There were two such 'blowers' in Chris's cabin.

'You had best sit on the bed then,' said Chris, 'because the blower over there doesn't work.'

The words were no sooner out of her mouth than the same thought struck all three of them.

'*The blower!*' cried Chris.

'It doesn't work!' said Molly.

'And I hope I know why!' yelled David. 'Molly — get a screw-driver, get a chisel, get anything...'

'A bulldozer if need be!' said Molly.

It took ten minutes to get the tools and take the faulty blower to pieces and another ten seconds to find a small leather bag wedged just in the turn of the pipe. They looked in wonder at the fabulous jewellery which Chris drew from the bag.

The rest of the trip was a triumphant tour for Chris. Her adventures received world-wide publicity and the value of this to herself — and the shipping company — was enormous. The insurance company's reward for the recovery of the jewels she divided between the ship's company, but fees for her own story in magazines and newspapers made a modest fortune for her old father and herself. She had many offers of jobs, but she decided to stay with the *New Age*, David and Molly.

'The only sad part,' she said afterwards, 'was about Lois.'

For Lois was really Jack's wife, not his sister. On their return to the ship, the Bridges and van Rheiner were arrested. Lois broke down and confessed and her evidence, together with information received in answer to radio messages, made it clear what had happened.

On the previous trip, van Rheiner and two other crooks had stolen the jewels, agreeing to hide them until the publicity had died down. But they quarrelled because the man who had hidden them kept the exact place a secret, to protect himself. They quarrelled also over dividing the spoils and arranging to recover them.

Van Rheiner killed one man and the other, called Burke, had fled. Jack and Lois Bridges met Burke while touring the American theatres and Jack, realising that he and Lois were on the down-grade, had been tempted to put their savings into a trip to recover the jewels. Like van Rheiner, Jack only knew from Burke that the jewels had been hidden somewhere in the cabin allotted to Chris.

They soon realised that they were working against van Rheiner, who had then offered to pool resources... but only until he had his hands on the loot.

'I told Jack to give up the idea,' Lois sobbed. 'Van Rheiner would have killed us. But you don't know what it's like to get so near the top only to start going down again. In a year we should have been a couple of "has-beens". I know how Jack felt. I used to give him one of those little shields every time we scored a hit in a new show. There hadn't been a new shield for a long time and...'

Here Lois broke down completely, but she had said enough. All three were put ashore to await deportation. Van Rheiner stood trial for murder and Jack got a heavy term of imprisonment, but Lois's confession — and the fact that she was married to Jack — got her a light sentence. But their careers, unfortunately, were over.

For Chris, however, her career was only just beginning.

'And what a beginnin'! said Molly O'Sullivan in her Irish brogue.

Acknowledgements

The publishers wish to express their thanks to IPC Magazines Limited for permission to include the following stories in this collection: HOLIDAY RIVALS by James Stagg, MINE OF MYSTERY (formerly entitled Gina's Caravan Adventure) by J. A. Storrie, CLARE AND THE ARAB PRINCESS by Arthur Catherall, UNWELCOME GUESTS (formerly entitled Trouble at Highridge) by Clare Robinson, THE FIESTA INTRIGUE (formerly entitled Stranded in Spain) by Neil Rogers, THE SECRET SEARCH (formerly entitled Debbie's Spring Holiday) by Anne Wade, RAINBOW COTTAGE (formerly entitled Mystery at Rainbow Cottage) by Ida Melbourne, RIVERBOAT RENDEZVOUS (formerly entitled Joy's Riverboat Adventure) by Frances Towers, THE CARAVAN SECRET by Peter Grey and A CRUISE FOR CHRIS by Anne Wade.